VALHELLIONS

D1239340

BOOKS by TIM AKERS

Knight Watch
Knight Watch
Valhellions

The Horns of Ruin

The Burn Cycle
Heart of Veridon
Dead of Veridon

The Hallowed War
The Pagan Night
The Iron Hound
The Winter Vow

To purchase Baen titles in e-book form, please go to www.baen.com.

VALHELLIONS

TIM AKERS

VALHELLIONS

This is a work of fiction. All the characters and events portrayed in this book are fictional, and any resemblance to real people or incidents is purely coincidental.

Copyright © 2022 by Tim Akers

All rights reserved, including the right to reproduce this book or portions thereof in any form.

A Baen Books Original

Baen Publishing Enterprises
P.O. Box 1403
Riverdale, NY 10471
www.baen.com

ISBN: 978-1-9821-2595-0

Cover art by Todd Lockwood

First printing, March 2022

Distributed by Simon & Schuster
1230 Avenue of the Americas
New York, NY 10020

Library of Congress Cataloging-in-Publication Data

Names: Akers, Tim, 1972- author.
Title: Valhellions / by Tim Akers.
Description: Riverdale, NY : Baen Publishing Enterprises, [2022] | "A Baen Books Original"—Title page verso.
Identifiers: LCCN 2021057133 | ISBN 9781982125950 (trade paperback) | ISBN
9781625798565 (ebook)
Classification: LCC PS3601.K48 V35 2022 | DDC 813/.6—dc23
LC record available at https://lccn.loc.gov/2021057133

Printed in the United States of America

10 9 8 7 6 5 4 3 2 1

DEDICATION

This book is dedicated to Sir Jesse Cornwell
The nicest human to ever beat me
at a game of toy soldiers
Rest in Pizza

VALHELLIONS

CHAPTER ONE

My strange times have become very normal. I mean, my normal times are consistently strange, and that's very normal. Very *not* normal, that is. For me. It's normal for me. Which is strange.

Let me go back.

I used to be a very normal person, but a lot of people thought I was strange. I had strange hobbies. I wanted to be a knight, for example. I used to dress up in faux-armor and a tabard that my mom stitched for me by hand, and go to public parks with a bunch of other people who also wanted to be knights, and maidens (gender-inclusive), and bards (mostly drunk), and pirates (rarely sober), and puppeteers (verdict out on sobriety, but the puppets were *always* plastered) and other interesting people. And together, we would pretend to be those things, and it was a lot of fun. But none of it was real.

And then, one day, it got about as real as it gets. I found out the mundane world was just the shiny wrapper meant for public consumption, and underneath that wrapper was an Unreal world of dragons, demons, knights, and wizards. It was pretty swell, right up until my best friend, Eric, almost killed me, and my ex-girlfriend Chesa Lozaro turned into an elven ranger-princess, and I . . . well, I almost became a knight. I met a whole team of people who really were the things I dreamed about being: the heroic swordsman, the enigmatic mage, the stealthy assassin, the blissed-out cleric. They called themselves Knight Watch, and they were in the hero business, protecting the mundane world from the Unreal, and vice versa. And now (after a bit of a rough interview period that involved driving my mom's car through a dragon's brainpan) I'm in the hero business, too.

It's still a lot of fun. But it's also dangerous, and sometimes you find yourself in some very strange situations. Which is perfectly normal.

But today was getting weird.

"John! Sir John Rast! Earth to John!" Chesa bellowed at the top of her very pretty little lungs. She was standing just inside the doors to the Mickleville Community Center and Water Park, just past the bored as hell ticket agent, blocking the flow of traffic in and out of the convention. Tembo's smooth black head was barely visible above the crowds of wizard hats and spaceman helmets. The new guy, who had replaced our swordsman Clarence when he retired to a life of draconic ease, was already gone, carried away by the river of enthusiastic con-goers. Saint Matthew, our super-chill healer with eyes like diamonds, was nowhere to be seen. For the saint, though, that was because he was back at HQ, lounging in his domain with the angels. Something about medium-high holidays, and the Mayan calendar, and a long overdue vacation. We each have a domain, a metaphysical home where we recharge our magical powers. Without them, we're just posers in expensive costumes, so it's important for the healer to stay topped up, in case something bad happens. Which it often did.

It's just that I hated it when the healer didn't show up for a mission. Bad things always happened. Usually to me.

"John!" Chesa repeated. "What the hell are you doing?"

"They misspelled Renaissance," I said, pointing at the banner that hung over the door. "Ren-Yay-Ssaince. Doesn't even make sense."

"These guys aren't exactly Guild-certified," Chesa said. "Now stop gawking like an idiot and get your butt inside."

"Ren-yay-ssaince," I muttered under my breath as I strolled toward the double doors of the Mickleville CC&WP. "I swear, these people have no respect for the language."

"From the smell of the place, they don't have a lot of respect for deodorant, either," Chesa said. She was dressed in her low-fantasy elf get-up today, not the high-Tolkien starsilver armor with matching crown and elderwood longbow that was her usual outfit. This was a simple leather jerkin and breeches, stained the color of deep forest shadows, with a cloak that shifted color and pattern as the light played across it, and boots that could have walked from Mordor to Tar Valon, with a quick stop in Arborlon for good measure. She wore a crescent-shaped blade at her hip, and a brace of throwing daggers close to her vest, all as real and as sharp as her tongue. Chesa's eyes were the color of uncut emeralds, and the tips of her tan ears poked out of the complicated braids of her hair. Professional cosplayers would have been really impressed with how realistic both the eyes and ears looked, but only because Chesa was cheating. Those were her actual features, now that she'd assumed the role of Forest Queen of the Everealm. Hardly seemed fair.

Standing next to Chesa, I felt like a pauper. My clothes were simple and comfortable, the plain tunic and tabard displaying a golden dragon rampant against a quartered field of red and black, with breeches the color of spilled wine and leather pauldrons that were more for show than they were for turning a blade. If it came to a fight, I would depend on the clever shield strapped to my back, and the sword swinging from my belt. Both were already peace-knotted, but our friendly assassin Bethany had done the knotting. The ropes would slip off at the proper touch, a trick she had taught me by tying me up and then laughing as I hopped around, trying to work my way free. A proper comedian, our Bethany, not at all concerned with being funny or making other people laugh. As long as she was amused, that was joke enough for her.

The guard at the door barely glanced at my weapons as I passed. I wasn't sure if that was the work of the knots or simply the fact that members of Knight Watch were so Unreal as to seem mundane. We usually flew around in a Viking longship made out of toenail clippings, and that hardly drew a second glance. Reality worked overtime trying to convince normal people that we weren't there at all, just a figment of the imagination. Really helpful when you're walking through a convention center in full medieval battle rattle.

"Alright," I said as I joined Chesa, "what are we looking for in here? Hidden djinn? A coven of harpies? Undercover goblins operating a gold-laundering scheme?" I planted my fists firmly on my hips and peered around suspiciously. "Presbyterians?"

"The Anomaly Actuator couldn't really get a fix," Chesa said, doing her best to act like we weren't together, even though we were walking side by side and, theoretically at least, holding a conversation. Ex-girlfriends are like that sometimes. "There's too much interference in this place. But something's out of place."

"Makes sense. There's an awful lot going on, isn't there?" I asked as I took in the sights. The Ren-yay-ssaince convention was an unsubtle blending of fandoms and lifestyle choices, from the traditional medieval reenactors, to grimdark science fiction cosplayers, to fully immersed book nerds, and everything in between. There were booths stuffed with uncomfortable-looking corsets for men and women, stacks upon stacks of new and used books that smelled like mildew and imagination, enough jewelry to choke a rust monster, and at least three chandlers hawking dice-scented candles. About half the people crowding the aisles were dressed like some character from the far reaches of the imaginary world, while the rest wore sweatpants and clever black T-shirts that said things like MY OTHER BODY IS CHARISMA 20 and COLD SCREAMING VOID FOR PRESIDENT. I would have fit right in before my induction into Knight Watch. Hell, I fit in now.

The problem with all this cleverness was that it made it difficult for the Anomaly Actuator to get a bead. Knight Watch has a machine back at HQ, left over from World War II, that can detect Unreal intrusions into the mundane world. Whenever a selkie decides to screw around with fishing lanes in the North Sea, or a vampire discards their mortal disguise and starts feeding on isolated goths in some small midwestern town, the Actuator lights up like a Christmas tree, and Knight Watch rolls out to set things right. And at the moment, the Actuator was signalling a major incursion here at the Mickleville Community Center, but there was so much interference from the various fandoms at play, it was impossible to know what we were looking for. That meant getting hand-stitched leather boots on the ground and keeping an eye peeled for anything unusual.

"I joined Knight Watch to get away from this kind of scene," Chesa grumbled at my side. "It's supposed to be all elven villages and demonic lairs. Not . . ." She gestured broadly at the fluorescent lights buzzing overhead, the visible funk of body odor shimmering in the air, and the hordes of anachronistic costuming. "Not this nonsense."

"'Tis a perilous job, my lady," I said. "One that requires nerves of steel and razor-sharp reflexes. Sometimes we face dragons"—I killed a dragon once, and make a point to mention it at every opportunity—"sometimes we descend into the depths of shadowy darkness, to shine the light of—"

"You're starting to sound like Eric," Chesa said dismissively. Eric, my friend who used to be a villain until we put him back in his right mind, was also a writer. Mostly a writer of adjectives. Long, complicated, sussurating adjectives. I blushed.

I was just about to continue when a young man dressed in a black cloak muscled his way between us. He wore a semi-military-looking uniform under the cloak, and his face was covered by a cheap white mask made to look like a cracked human skull. He stepped on my toe as he passed, and elbowed Chesa quite solidly in the boob.

"Hey, asshole!" she snapped, grabbing his shoulder and spinning him around. "Watch where you're going!"

The guy stared at us, his pale blue eyes blinking quickly behind the mask.

"Yeah, you really should apologize," I said. He looked over at me, then back to Chesa.

"Sorry," he whispered. "That you're such losers."

"Oh, no you didn't," Chesa said. Her hand went to the crescent-shaped blade, one finger flicking the peace knot onto the floor. "Try that again, before I open you up and feed you your own liver."

"Ches, we're here to stop an anomaly, not start one," I said under my breath. The dude's eyes had gone wide, and he was grinning crookedly beneath the mask. He swept his cloak back, revealing a sword that looked like a cross between gothic architecture and a costume piece from a German propaganda poster from the Second World War. I cleared my throat and stepped between Chesa and the guy she was about to kill. "Just clear off, you pathetic man-child."

He snorted, then swept dramatically around and bullied his way through the crowd. Chesa shook me off.

"I think that guy might have been an actual Nazi," she said.

"There has been an uptick of that stuff recently," I answered. "Anyway. What was I saying? Oh, right. The point is the job sometimes calls for heroic stuff in distant castles. And sometimes it calls for not beating up some guy at a convention just because he doesn't know how to make friends."

"I don't beat you up," she said. "And you clearly don't know how to make friends."

"I have friends," I protested. "Just . . . not real ones. It's fine. Whatever."

"Whatever," she agreed.

"If the two of you are finished with your lovers' quarrel, we have work to do." The voice was clear and sterling, the kind of voice you'd expect from the male lead of a romance novel. I sighed. Chesa sighed. Our sighs were completely different.

Gregory Chastain de Beuregard d'Haute slipped into view, his armor polished to a mirror shine, his oiled locks spilling down his shoulders like a cascade of fine silk. He smiled, and the small crowd of girls who had been following him giggled. Gregory struck an appreciative pose, bowed to the nearest girl, and swept her hand briefly to his lips. She melted.

This was the new guy. We were not real friends.

"Dearest Chesa," he said, turning to us and completely forgetting about the chorus of girls in his wake. "I was so worried that I had lost track of you. It would not do for us to be separated by circumstance or peril. Come, I will escort you to the food court, and stand watch while you refresh yourself before our mission continues."

"The mission doesn't call for a food court, or refreshing," I said. "This is serious stuff, Greg—"

"Sir Gregory d'Haute," he said to me, without ever taking his pale blue eyes off Chesa. "If you don't mind. John." He managed to say *John* the same way most people said *septic backup*. I bristled. Chesa put a hand on my wrist, which I suddenly realized was already on my sword.

"We're here to stop an anomaly, John," she reminded me. "Not start one."

"Yes, yes. Hero stuff," Gregory d'Whatever said. He offered Chesa his arm. "The food court, my lady?"

"I suppose the food court needs patrolling just as much as the rest of this place," Chesa said, lightly placing her hand on Greg's steely forearm. "John, see if you can find anything among the board games."

"I just—" But they were already off. The chorus of girls gave me half a look, then wheeled around and followed Greg. I sighed again, just for good measure, and headed toward the gaming tables.

The sound of Chesa's laughter carried over the crowds. Just to be clear, I joined Knight Watch to get away from the real world of popular kids and awkward silences. The real world just seemed determined to follow me around.

CHAPTER TWO

The clatter of dice and shuffling of cards and general cacophony of the gaming tables did little to salve my wounded pride. There was a time when I was able to find solace in the tumble of polyhedrons and the sweet smell of plastic tokens, when I could pretend to be something completely different from what I was—stronger, or more charismatic, or clever (the number of times I fell back on "I say something clever to the barmaid" *rolls dice*), or even brave, simply because there was nothing to lose. Times had changed. I was braver than I had been. Cowards don't kill dragons, after all. But I was still John Rast—lanky, gawking, awkward, quiet, and frequently alone.

Even in the company of Knight Watch, I was something of an outsider. After all, it had been my best friend who nearly destroyed the organization, barely six months ago. Eric used me as a battering ram to sneak into the Unreal, pulling me and Chesa along with him. While the team seemed to accept Chesa well enough, I was still having trouble acclimating, even after a lifetime of hoping for this kind of chance. Yet here I was, wandering the gaming tables of some small-town nerd convention, while my ex swooned over the new guy.

"You are looking glum, Sir John of Rast." Tembo's smooth voice rose over the exultations of a crowded table of Interstellar Soldiers hooting heresy. The bald mage ambled up beside me. Dark blue robes, custom tailored and exquisite, slid quietly across the floor, while the luminescent tattoo that surrounded his right eye shimmered weakly under the fluorescent lighting of the convention center. He walked with his hands clasped behind his back. I had seen this man hurl fireballs, and summon shimmering shields of light, and transform into a hulking elephant creature, as majestic and as powerful as any Ken Burns documentary. But under those fluorescent lights, Tembo looked like a cheap parlor trickster, a deck of marked cards in his pocket and silver highlighter smeared across his cheek. The mundane has a way of degrading us. I made a mental note to avoid any mirrors. If Tembo looked this bad, I must look truly pathetic.

"Nope! Everything's great, Tem. Just doing the patrol thing," I said. "Checking out these game tables, just in case one of them is a portal to another dimension. There was a lot of that going on back in the eighties, I'm told. Lotta"—I waggled my fingers, as though casting a spell—"demon summoning. Dice and an active imagination are a very effective tool for calling forth hell-beasts."

"That was a story, told mostly by demons, it turns out. A publicity stunt," Tembo said. He looked around casually, then leaned in close. "You do not like the new guy."

"What? No, don't be ridiculous! Gregory Hosenlinger Von Froo Froo is my favorite guy!" I insisted. "If you asked me to line up the guys I like best, why, old Froo Froo would be top of the list."

"I am glad to hear that, Sir John. Because we are a team. Each member of the team is very important." Tembo's tone reminded me of a schoolmaster in a Victorian drama. "We are a single body: the healer, the warrior, the mage, the warden." He nodded to me when naming my role. I never wanted to be a warden, but the myths chose that role for me, so here I was. All shield, no glory. "Each part of the body must function correctly. And it must trust the other parts. A warrior cannot heal. The mage cannot ward. And the healer—"

"The healer isn't even here," I said. "So let's not act like we're some kind of superhero squad. You can't expect me to like a guy like Gregory. But I can work with him. He fights, he gets the girls, and I get smacked in the face so he can act heroic. I get it. You don't have to rub it in."

"You are important, Sir John. We value you."

"Thanks, Counselor Rick. Now if you don't mind, there's an anomaly around here somewhere. Be best if we spread out," I said.

"It would be best if we stuck together," Tembo answered. "But I see you are not interested in that. If I am attacked, I will start screaming like a butchered calf."

"Butchered calf. Got it. If I don't hear a calf being butchered, I'll just mind my own—"

Somewhere, not so far away, someone started butchering a calf.

"Sweet hell, Tem! That's a neat trick. You scared half the life out of me!" I said.

"That is not me," Tembo answered. He flicked his hand, and a long staff of silver-bound wood appeared out of nowhere, bouncing off the floor to smack meatily into his palm. He made another gesture with his left hand, and the runes engraved on the staff flashed to life, followed closely by the tattoo surrounding his eye. "We have found our monster."

"Or the monster has found us," I said, reaching for my sword. The peace knot kept me from getting more than an inch of steel out of the scabbard. Swearing, I did the little trick Bethany had taught me, flicking at the knot with thumb and forefinger before drawing the sword again. This time I got less than an inch of steel, and somehow managed to get my pinky tangled in the knot itself. The rope pulled tight, cutting off circulation to the digit. "Damn it! I just . . ." Hooking my thumb around the knot and tugging only managed to trap the entire hand. "Bee, you bitch! What'd you do to my sword?"

"Pull and flick, Sir John. We don't have time to screw around," Tembo said.

"I know, I know." A long strand of rope uncoiled from the knot, giving me the false impression of progress. "There it is!" I grabbed the rope with my other hand and gave it a pull. Something tightened around my belt, and then the blood traveling to my right leg was cut off. I yelped and dropped the rope, but somehow the fraying ends had woven themselves around my wrist, and when I tried to reach down to the loop around my leg, I instead cinched my arm firmly against my waist. I stumbled forward, but found that all I could do was hop on one leg, as my other was already numb and tingling. "Bethany!"

"Good grok, Rast, you're a mess," Bethany said. She appeared from the same nowhere as Tembo's staff, bouncing excitedly in front of me, like a puppy who needs to pee. She wore her usual black braids, only today she had them curled tightly against her head, pinned in place with a crown of tiny silver daggers. The rest of her outfit was nondescript; maudlin leather, a belt of pouches, and a thin cloak that I knew hid more knives than could ever possibly be necessary. She eyed me up and down, her green eyes laughing as she took in my predicament. "You even found a way to break my rope trick! You're something else."

"What I am is going to kick your ass when I get out of these ropes!" I shouted.

"So maybe I just leave you in them, then," she said. "Besides, you're kinda cute when you're tied up. You and Ches ever get into that kind of thing?"

"I . . . what . . . ? That's none . . ." I sputtered.

"My dear Bethany, we are needed quite urgently in the direction of the screaming, so if you would be so kind as to free our warden," Tembo said anxiously.

"Sure, sure. Just having some fun," she said, her eyes twinkling. Bethany drew a hefty dagger and pointed it at my belly button. Her eyes darted at the various knots and entanglements holding me in place. "Okay, Rast. Don't. Move. A muscle."

"I hardly think—" I started. Then Bethany moved in a blur of dark hair and cold steel. My breath caught in my throat. I could feel the razor-sharp blade pass between my skin and rope, at wrists, at elbow, somehow against my thigh and between my fingers. It was over in a heartbeat. The ropes fell to the ground.

"There now. All better," she said, sheathing the dagger. She winked at me. "But let me know if you change your mind about that rope thing." Then she was gone, another blur in the crowd.

Tembo growled and rushed into the crowd, staff in the lead. Free and blushing like a sunburned Irish bride, I drew my sword and swung the clever shield down from my shoulder. The shield was the embodiment of my mythic self, the very essential thing that made me a warden. It was magic, able to change shape and size to meet the needs of the moment, incredibly strong, even capable of entombing me in an impervious shell for brief moments. Nothing could hurt me while I wielded it, as long as I knew the threat was coming and could keep my wits about me.

Nothing except a cute girl's wit, apparently. And a difficult knot.

The crowd that surrounded us seemed generally nonplussed by the screaming, or Tembo's glowing face, or even Bethany's knife tricks. That's the way it was with the mundane, when the Unreal broke the surface of the world. The world would carry on, acting as if everything was perfectly normal, right up until the point it wasn't. And by then it was usually too late.

Passing Tembo, I lowered my shield and bulldozed my way through the closely packed crowd. Shoving through the steaming mass of body odor and cheap costumes drew a lot of angry words and the occasional threat, but I didn't care. These people were mundanes, and I was the hero, making my entrance, here to save the day. I reached the edge of the crowd and burst into the open.

My leather boots squeaked as I slid across the linoleum floor, finally coming to a stop in the middle of a small clearing in the murmuring crowd. I was in full action pose: crouched forward with my heater shield covering me from throat to thigh, longsword at a guard position in my other hand. Tembo followed close behind. The lanky mage towered over me, his staff held aloft in one arm, magical bracelets rattling as he formed runes in the air with his casting hand. Silver light crawled across his tattoo, matched by the scintillating light of the staff. Bethany darted into the clearing, appearing and disappearing in a quick drumbeat of shadowsteps, each time leaving a cloud of curling smoke behind. She finally settled just to my left, displaying a collection of wicked daggers that would have made a Scotsman blush. Bethany's cloak hovered in midair, as though she were still flying through the air.

Three people, two men and a woman, stood in the middle of the clearing. They wore a cross between fool's motley and punk garb, mixed jeans and wallet chains across patchwork vests and pirate shirts that were three sizes too large. The woman had collapsed into the arms of one of the men, caught mid-swoon by our interruption. A dagger protruded from between swelling breasts held in place by a highly structured corset that barely seemed up to the task. Several red streamers coursed down from the dagger, fake blood in the form of linen.

Bloody actors. We had interrupted some kind of impromptu play.

All three of the actors stared at us with open mouths. The woman was still screaming, only much more quietly and with less curdling of blood. The man holding her slowly lost his grip, and didn't recover until she hit the convention center floor with a thump of gathered skirts and jiggling flesh. Then both men rushed to her aid, which she firmly refused with sharp elbows and sharper tongue. Everyone was still staring at us.

"Tembo," I said as quietly as I could manage, though the silence around us was so absolute that I might as well have been shouting. "Cut the light show."

"Hm?" the mage muttered, then realized he was still manifesting his mythic self. "Oh, yes. Sorry. Show's over, folks!" He straightened, letting the glowing runes that hung midair around him dissipate, his tattoo fading back into silver highlighter, and the laser show that crawled across his staff disappeared with a sizzle. Bethany followed suit. Her cloak dropped to the ground and her daggers disappeared, as though they had never even existed. I sheathed my sword and tried to stand normally. I've never been good at standing normally, even when I was normal. There's nothing harder than doing something "normal." Especially when everyone is staring at you.

There was a smattering of applause from the audience. The mundane world taking over, convincing them that we were part of the show. The three actors took the cue, bowing extravagantly, hands clasped together. The commotion must have drawn Gregory, or maybe it was the applause, because he and Chesa burst into the circle seconds later. The paladin's arms were bare and bulging, the ridiculously large zweihander sword held vertical and gleaming. Chesa danced over the tops of the crowd, landing to my right with her own brace of crescent-shaped swords drawn. There was another round of awkward silence, then the crowd went wild. Gregory took it in stride, bowing majestically, all smiles. Chesa looked at me and rolled her eyes.

"Can't keep from making a fool of yourself, Rast?" she asked.

"It's not my fault this time! She was screaming. Like, really screaming."

"Whatever. Just try to not drag the rest of us into it next time." Chesa slid the two crescent blades together, locking them into a single short scythe, then magicked them away under her cloak. "We have enough trouble with the mundanes, without you making it worse."

"Don't be so hard on the boy, Chesa," Gregory said, somehow without moving his gleaming smile. "He's doing the best he can."

"I'm not just some 'boy,' pretty man," I snapped. "I've been part of this team longer than you. Let's not forget that."

"And yet you still keep screwing up," he answered. "But I imagine it's hard to find a good warden. Such thankless, drab work, isn't it? So little glory. Why, it's hardly heroic at all."

"Alright, Smiles, that's it." I snapped my left wrist, triggering the magic in my shield and transforming the heater into a Viking-style round. I ran my sword along the steel rim of the shield, drawing sparks from the blade and applause from the audience. Gregory just watched me, one eyebrow cocked at a jaunty angle. "Let's settle this!"

"John, you're being an idiot," Chesa whispered quietly.

"Let him be an idiot," Bethany said. She stepped back, arms folded across her chest. "Let the boys fight. Take off your shirts! No shirts!"

"That is not helping the situation," Tembo chided. "Please, if everyone would just calm down."

A woman stepped out of the crowd, clapping slow and loud. She was dressed in leather armor and Viking bling, with a batwing tiara that didn't really contain the complicated braids of golden hair, and thick eye black that ran a stripe across her face. Her features were so Nordic as to appear alien. And she was hot as hell, which of course had nothing to do with the fact that I just stood there, staring at her in dumb fascination, rather than stepping up smacking the obvious villain in the face. She didn't appear to be armed, but something about her dress and manner marked her as different from the rest of the crowd. Her armor looked ancient and functional. Her boots were flat and heavily scarred, not the wedge heels that cosplayers often subjected themselves to. She cut across the clearing to stand next to the gawping actors.

"Bravo, bravo. A well-rehearsed exchange. A maiden in distress, and now the heroes have arrived. The audience recognizes them clearly enough. So brave, and handsome, and foolish." She smiled at me when she said that, and I felt a shiver run down my bones. Something about the woman looked familiar, as though I had seen her before. "But enough with the introduction. It is time for the villain to make their appearance."

"I know a villain when I see one," Bethany said. She had wrapped herself in her mythic presence again, all cloak and dagger, with a side of shadow. "It's always the creep in the black armor who's talking too much."

"Oh, but I'm not the villain in this story, child," the woman said, her smile as sharp and as cold as an iceberg. "At least, not yet. No, I am merely the chorus. This"—she gestured to the crowd—"is your villain. But I will allow him his own introductions."

And, of course, the mask-wearing edgelord with the propaganda sword stepped into the clearing. His mask looked more substantial, the paper replaced with pale metal, the simple grimace now a full-on death's howl. His uniform still felt oddly out of place, not as medieval as it should be. Yet when he drew that sword, there was no question it contained magic. Oily smoke dripped from its fuller, gathering in puddles of sick shadow at his feet. The hilt was all skulls and gravestones and cloaked figures, and the ornaments on his armor followed the theme.

Honestly, he looked like a castoff from a goth metal band, the kind of guy who might have been cut from the lineup for trying too hard. I had to laugh. That didn't sit well with King Edgelord.

"I am the Totenschreck! Terror of the Dead! Master of the Veil! Lord of—"

"Sure you are, kiddo," I said. "And I'm the Tatertot King. Playtime's over."

Knight Watch fell in behind me, weapons glowing and mythic spells powering up. The high keening sound of Tembo's fireball shrieked through the enclosed space of the convention center. Even Gregory stood at my side, his smirk for once directed at someone else. My shield unfolded into a full tower, the face emblazoned with my golden dragon. I raised my sword overhead and charged forward, screaming at the top of my lungs. The rest of Knight Watch flowed in behind me.

Edgelord Prime cackled, then slammed his sword tip-first into the tiles of the convention floor. The ground erupted into a spiderweb of pale green light, fracturing like an eggshell, and stopping us dead in our tracks. Tendrils of thick mist uncoiled from the earth, instantly obscuring the area.

Hands crawled out of the broken earth. Skeletons, their bones translucent, their eyes glowing with ghostly light, dragged themselves out of ruptured graves. They surrounded the cloaked figure of the edgelord.

The crowd, which had up until now been watching with keen interest, finally decided that something was badly wrong with this show. Screaming, they ran in all directions, lost in the mists and driven by pure animal terror. The skeletons fell on them, tearing at stained black shirts and mismatched cosplay, cutting into flesh with blunt teeth and bony fingers. The screams grew desperate. The mists rose, turning the convention center into a hellscape. Half-obscured shapes stumbled through the darkness, their screams mingling with the dirge-like moans of the risen dead. The only thing I could see clearly was the cloaked figure and his grim sword.

I put my head down and charged.

CHAPTER THREE

I collected the first skeleton against the broad face of my shield, bashing it aside before chopping down with my sword once, twice, the third blow shattering whatever magic held it together. It fell to the ground in a jumble of broken bones. I slid through the detritus of its corpse, scattering the bones with my boot like dice, and met the shambling wave behind it with a broad sweep of my sword. Skulls clattered against steel as they clawed at my shield with gaunt fingers. I let the momentum of my swing carry me forward, deeper into the horde, closer to the jerk in the cloak.

"John, you bastard, don't leave us here like this!" Chesa's voice was laced through with panic. I pummeled another skeleton, kicked its (once again) lifeless body away, then turned around.

The team was in a bad way. Gregory d'Jerkface stood a little apart from the others, surrounded by a slowly growing pile of bones. Bolts of fire arced down from the ceiling, guided by Tembo's hand, keeping the space around him clear, though the lanky mage sported a rash of cuts across his face, and his robes were torn and in disarray. Chesa stood at his side. The silver blades of her crescent swords whirled through the air, but they were better suited to cutting flesh than bone. The shambling tide of skeletons was getting closer and closer to the three of them. There was no sign of Bethany. That wasn't unusual, she usually disappeared into the shadows in situations like this. The only concerning thing was that between the mists and the press of undead, there really wasn't anywhere to hide. I put her out of my mind. Bethany could take care of herself.

The team, on the other hand, needed my help.

I flicked my wrist, reconfiguring the magical shield to one of its Doomsday Modes. It formed into a brass disc, resembling the hoplon of Grecian fame. I rolled it like a bowling ball, releasing everything but the hand strap. The shield hit the ground next to Chesa and then spun, unfolding into a miniature wall about six feet high, made of brass discs that linked together with leather straps. The unfolding wall traveled around Chesa and Tembo, circling around until it reached Gregory, then finally returning to me. The skeletons unfortunate enough to be in its path were cut down like chaff, and those trapped inside quickly fell to Gregory's blade and Tembo's flames. We stood inside the brass ring, catching our breath and listening to the skeletons try to claw their way through my barricade. Tembo took a deep breath, then turned on me.

"You should not run off like that, Sir John. It is your duty to protect the rest of us," he said. "Not charge blindly into the night."

"First rule of killing necromancers," I said. "The skeletons are just chaff. You've got to get to the summoner."

"You've killed a lot of necromancers?" Chesa asked sharply.

"Yes, of course," I answered. *With dice and clever dialogue*, I left unsaid. "We can kill as many of these bastards as we like. This isn't going to end until we put that creepy bastard down."

"They'll run out of bones eventually," Gregory said. He kicked at the pile of bones at his feet. "I thought it was going pretty well."

"Maybe if we had a healer," I snapped. "But we don't. We're going to bleed a lot more than these guys. So if we move, we need to move as a team."

"You're the one who ran off, fella," Gregory answered. "Leaving me to defend the fair lady on my own."

"The lady did not need defending, thank you," Chesa said.

"What makes you think I was talking about you?" Gregory motioned behind him, where the members of the acting troupe cowered on the ground. "We have mundanes to think about."

Chesa rolled her eyes and was about to answer when Tembo stepped between them.

"Sir John is correct," he said. "We need to stop the summoner before he turns this whole place into a mortuary. And now that we have our warden, we can proceed." He tipped his head in my direction. "Sir John? If you would lead the way?"

"If you guys can keep up this time," I said, adjusting my helmet. "There are a lot of them out there. Hopefully most of the mundanes have cleared out, but watch where you put your sword." Gregory rolled his eyes, but Chesa gave me a sharp nod. "And that ice bitch is out there somewhere, too. Gonna guess she's more than just a hype man for the goth lord, so keep your eyes—"

"Just bloody *GO!*" Gregory shouted. I grimaced at him, then strapped my hand into one of the loops holding the wall together.

"Ready?" I asked. The team sounded off, so I pulled the wall down. The bronze discs collapsed together, piling up and disappearing, until I held a single round shield in my hand. The seething horde of skeletons shambled past. They seemed to be ignoring us for the moment.

We went at them like a wedge. I took point, shield up and sword in a low support. Gregory and Chesa flanked me, with Tembo trailing a little behind. I crashed into the wall of skeletons, scattering them like dry leaves. Gregory cut through the shambling legion in a blur of shining steel and singing blade. The skeletons offered little resistance. Chesa fought a quieter battle. Her crescent blades flashed against weathered bone. The occasional flash of burning fire let me know that Tembo was still with us, though his magic was little needed against our quiet foe.

Gregory's sword whirred through a lumbering revenant, severing the beast at ankle, shoulder, and wrist. He ended by plunging his sword into the rattling rib cage. It would have been a mortal blow to a more mundane opponent. The skeleton just dragged itself down the length of the blade, clawing ineffectually at Gregory's face. The paladin spat in disgust, then punched the creature in its leering grin until it collapsed into component parts. He kicked the bones away and prepared for the next wave.

I heard a strangled gasp and turned around just in time to see Tembo hit the ground. The shadow of a cloaked figure flickered just out of sight.

"He came out of nowhere!" Chesa shouted. Crescent blades shattered the trio of skeletons that faced her, then she went to one knee at Tembo's side, running her hands over him. "I don't see a wound . . . wait. Maybe a scratch on his cheek? He's still breathing."

"Bastard!" Gregory howled. "Stand and fight like a man, will you!"

"Men fall. Men struggle. Men die." The wheezy voice came from all around us, and I realized it was the skeletons, speaking in chorus. "I am meant for greater things!"

"You're a coward!" Gregory answered. Chesa and I were back-to-back, guarding Tembo's fallen body, but Gregory pushed to the edge of our defensive circle. "Fight me!"

"Gladly." This time the voice was close. Dark shapes whirled out between the nearest skeletons. The cloaked man formed out of mist, rushing past Gregory, sword down to one side. Gregory saw him and brought his zweihander up. Steel skated across steel, gathering sparks, and then the cloaked figure was past. He disappeared between the shambling ranks and was gone.

"That was hardly a fight. Hardly a fight at all," Gregory d'Dickhead said. He looked down at his palm. A line of bright blood beaded across the skin. "Barely a scratch."

He fell in a clatter of armor and glistening hair. Chesa stepped toward him, but I grabbed her shoulder and pulled her back.

"We can't get separated. He could be anywhere. We have to keep our eyes—"

I was staring at Chesa when the black cloak appeared behind her. He simply laid the flat of his sword against the naked flesh of her neck. I saw the cut. I saw the blood. She gave a startled gasp, then fell into my arms.

"Ches! Chesa!" I shouted. She tried to say something, but then I felt her skin go cold. Thin laughter rose from the mists. I laid her down as gently as I could. "You're going to die, you bastard!"

"I thought you were the tatertot king?" He appeared on a slight rise in the distance. The world was changing around him. The ceiling of the convention center was sprinkled with stars, and the distant shapes of trees rose from the displays and along the walls. Even the air tasted different; less sweaty convention, more decrepit mausoleum. "Come, Sir Kartoffel. Meet your heroic end."

Skeletal arms grabbed at my legs and clattered against the broad face of my tower shield. I plowed through them, breaking bones and cracking skulls, driving toward the shadowy figure of the man in the mask. Bony fingers closed around the wrist of my sword arm, yanking me around. I tried to turn to face my attacker, but dozens of ghostly hands held my shield in place. I bashed the shield forward, flicking my wrist to change the shield's configuration. The tower folded down to a heater, severing skeletal fingers as its metal panels scissored shut. Free, I whirled on the creature holding my wrist.

A big brute of a man stared at me with dead eyes. Skin hung in tatters from the fingers of his right hand, and a slick of fresh blood from a gash in his throat spilled across a black T-shirt. He was dead, and he was about to beat the living shit out of me. Dumbstruck, I just stood there as he reared back with his other fist and punched me hard in the jaw.

The shock of impact shook me out of my stupor. I punched him once with the rim of my shield, then again when that didn't seem to faze him at all. He tried to grab at my shield, the blood-slick tatters of his ruined hand sliding off the metal and wood. He was clumsy and slow. I sent a prayer up to George Romero and I brought the shield down again and again on his face. Finally something cracked, and he slumped to the linoleum tiles. I had to peel his fingers away from my wrist. His skin was cold as clay, and the blood that slipped out of his throat was black and stank of the grave.

A zombified gamer girl in a YES, THEY'RE NATURAL 20S shirt stumbled into me, gnawing at my leather pauldron with teeth that were yellow with decay. I shoved her back into the crowd of skeletons, trying not to hurt her any worse than she was already hurt (which was dead and reanimated, so I'm not sure what good I was doing), and started to fight my way toward the cloaked figure. Ghostly hands, mixed with the fetid flesh of newly minted zombies, grabbed at me from a press of bodies on all sides. It was hard to differentiate between summoned skeletons and the freshly undead. Try as I might to preserve the con-goers, by the end I was hacking at anything that moved, leaving severed arms and broken bones in my wake.

Suddenly I was on him. The skeletons thinned out, and the man in the cloak stood before me. He had changed with the world. Mists seethed beneath his cloak, and the mask glowed with unholy light. The only thing about him that seemed substantial was the sword. It looked heavy, almost unnaturally massive, as though the world bent toward it. Despite that, the man lifted it with one thin arm.

"Your armor will do you no good, fool. Death cuts deeper than steel, deeper than flesh, deeper than—"

"So we play for points. I get it," I said, and charged forward.

Edgelord swept his sword up in a blow that would have nicked my arm if not for the shield. Fortunately there was no force behind the swing, so the massive sword just skated across steel. I pressed, blinding him with my shield while I swung low at his ankle. My blade cut into leather, and he gave a very un-edgelord yelp and whimper, then pulled back. My next blow sliced a bit of cloak free. He was backpedaling, off-balance. The eyes behind his mask were wide, his mouth set in a desperate snarl. I got cocky. It almost cost me my life.

The valkyrie's spear pierced shield and sabaton, slicing into my skin. The spear's barbed head snagged against the enarme straps of my heater, wrenching the shield from my grasp. She rose over me on black wings.

Well, at least I knew why she seemed familiar. The smirking smile that valkyrie had given me still burned in my heart. And my loins. Very much my loins.

"No! This is my fight!" Edgelord yelled. He pushed the valkyrie aside, putting himself between us. She fluttered awkwardly through the air, the weight of my shield upsetting her balance. The shield slid free, clattering to the ground. "You promised!"

"You are not ready—" the valkyrie started. I didn't let her finish. One step forward and I brought my sword down on the edgelord's petty little skull.

He collapsed. Well, the cloak collapsed, falling to the floor like a banner from the wall. Inside were nothing but bones. A shiny skull bounced free of the cloak, to roll to the valkyrie's feet. She looked down at it sadly, then gestured with her free hand.

The cloaked figure reformed in her grasp. She clasped him to her breast like a child. He was wrapped around the gothic sword.

"Not ready, it would seem. Mortals rarely are," she said, glaring down at the sleeping figure. "Perhaps next time. As for you . . ." She looked up at me. "Be grateful he is so weak. Next time, you shall not be half as lucky."

She swept into the sky on black wings, spear dangling behind her. Mists swirled in the wake of her flight. I watched her climb higher and higher, until she was just a glimmer of light among the stars.

Then the fluorescents flickered back on, and I was blinded.

CHAPTER FOUR

I stood in the middle of the convention floor, blinking rapidly. Murky shapes moved at the edge of my vision. Hunkering behind my shield, I turned in a slow circle, preparing for an attack that never came. Ghostly moans reached my ears. My feet shuffled through the fallen bones of my assailants, but for now, it didn't seem like anyone else was going to take a try at biting my face off. Slowly, my eyes adjusted to the harsh fluorescent lighting.

The first thing I noticed was the lack of dead people. Con-goers stood around numbly staring at the destruction. A couple of them were hurt, especially the ones I had . . . ahem . . . interacted with. The big guy in the clever T-shirt had a bloody nose, but there was no sign of the gash in his neck or the ruination of his hand. Natural 20s sat on the floor nearby, spitting bits of leather out of her mouth. Everytime I took a step or turned around, there was a plastic clattering sound at my feet. A pile of plastic skeleton bones covered the floor, wrapped up in a cheap acetate cloak that was frayed at the edges. I went to one knee to stir through Edgelord's faux remains. The stitching on the cloak was poorly done. The skull was just a volleyball with a cheap child's Halloween mask stapled to it. I picked it up and stared at the hollow eye sockets, and wondered what had become of my enemy.

"John? Are you alright?" Chesa was just standing up. There was a silvery mark on her neck, kind of like frostbite, but she seemed otherwise unharmed. She looked around with a slack look on her face. "What the hell happened?"

"Wish I knew. Captain Tatertot turned into a pile of bones, then the valkyrie flew away with him . . ." I turned to her and pointed at the ceiling. "A *VALKYRIE*, by the way! I thought we were supposed to have some kind of treaty with the valkyries!"

"Totenschreck," Tembo said, getting stiffly to his feet. He was staring at his hand, opening and closing his fist. "Terror of the dead, I think. Esther will know." He took a deep breath, letting it out in a slow whistle. "I saw the end, my friends. I saw what stands beyond the gates of Gravehome."

"What? You died?"

"I walked the final path, yes," Tembo said. "I suspect we all did. And yet here we are. Puzzling."

"Where'd that bastard go?" Gregory d'Hernia kicked up to his feet, the maneuver ruined by the piles of plastic bones that littered the floor. He slid gracelessly back and forth for several heartbeats, then sidestepped into a display table of novelty dice-shaped candles. Gregory planted his fist into a dodecahedron of beeswax and started swearing.

"He's gone, hero-man," I said. "Everything's back to normal."

"No, it's not," Chesa said. "These people are going to need debriefing, and someone's going to have to file a lot of paperwork. But I think we're done here. We need to get back to MA"—Mundane Actual, our headquarters—"and talk to Esther. She'll know what to do."

"What? We drove off the weird cloaked figure with the skeleton-making sword," I said. "That feels like a win to me."

"It feels like we stopped something terrible, yes. But I don't think it's over. Not by a long shot."

"I agree with Chesa," Tembo said. "A blade that kills with a touch, and skeletons, and zombified mundanes. Our morbid assailant was trying to enter the Unreal, just like your friend Eric. We stopped him for now, but that will not be the end of it. He will try again."

"So we watch the Actuator. When he makes a run for the gates of reality again, we show up and put him down," I said. "Straightforward."

"Hey, we need to talk." It was the guard from the door, pudgy hands on pudgy hips and a very cross look on his face. "I don't know how you got fog machines and several hundred plastic skeletons past our rigorous security, but someone's going to have to pay for all this damage. And those swords need peace knots!"

"I'm sure this will cover the damages," Bethany said, stepping out of the crowd. She handed the guard a wrinkled stack of dollar bills. "We're part of an . . . Internet . . . influencer? Consortium?"

"Well, I . . . I think . . ." He stared down at the cash in his hand with confusion. "This is a lot of money."

"Yes! Very real money, too," Bethany said with the brightest, fakest smile I had ever seen. She turned to us. "And now I think we really must be going."

Bethany looped an arm around me and Chesa, then hurried toward the exit. People were definitely staring at us. I leaned down to Bethany's ear.

"Not real money?"

"No, no, it is. It's just the money from the till. And maybe his wallet. And a few other wallets from the crowd. Folks were distracted," she answered. "So we really should hurry."

"We were fighting skeletons and zombies, and you were looting the bodies?" Gregory asked sharply.

"Rogues gonna rogue," she said sweetly. "Come on, paladin-boy. A little hop in your step. That pretty smile isn't going to fool anyone for long."

I was getting used to the smell of foot cheese. It's a necessary emotional callus to develop when your main mode of transportation is a flying Viking longboat made of toenail clippings. On hot days, the deck of the Naglfr smelled like a foot-slapping contest. And that's a contest no one wins. No one.

We were flying high above the endless cornfields that surround Mundane Actual. The boss discovered a long time ago that everywhere in America was within five minutes of a cornfield, at least metaphorically, and actual proximity to the husky starch helped the Actuator tap into the country's mythical gestalt. It also meant random folks were less likely to stumble across the threshold and contaminate the sensitive anachronisms that ran the operation. But it also meant we lived in a cornfield.

The mood in the boat was sour. We had been properly beaten back at the Mickleville Community Center and Swim Park. Even if our healer had been there, it wouldn't have mattered. This weird Totenschreck character had beaten us all with little more than a touch, then escaped on the wings of a valkyrie who had otherwise stayed out of the fight. There was a lot to be sour about.

We arrived home with our foul mood firmly in place. Mundane Actual, our center of operations as well as the portal into our various mythical domains, is housed beneath a lake in the middle of nowhere. My theory is that it used to be a missile silo, but Esther won't let me wander around unattended. Mostly because I break technology just by being close to it, and there's a *lot* of technology in the silo. Heck, I even have to take the stairs, for fear of plummeting to my death when the elevator stops . . . elevating, I guess? The point is that I'd already had a long day, and there were about a thousand steps between me and anything that vaguely resembled a comfortable bed.

I was saved from this fate by Esther MacRae. The Naglfr descended through the waters of the lake (a process akin to gargling rotten cottage cheese) and settled into the underground dock that housed all the magical vessels at the disposal of Knight Watch. Esther was waiting for us on the pier. She had a clipboard in one hand and a revolver-style grenade launcher in the other. The grenade launcher didn't bother me. Fondling the safety mechanism on a grenade launcher is how Esther let you know she cared enough to provide suppressive fire at the drop of a hat. It was the clipboard that gave me pause. Nothing quite as dangerous as the boss with a checklist to fill out. As the gangway rattled against the pier, Esther slung the launcher over her shoulder and produced a pencil.

A very sharp pencil. I swallowed the bile that instantly bubbled up into the back of my throat and started down the plank.

"You can hold it right there, Rast," Esther said. She peered at me with cold green eyes. "New protocol for Ren faires. Gotta make sure we don't have another disaster like that business with Kracek." The dragon I killed. Have I mentioned that? I killed a dragon. "I'm still filling out the paperwork for that one. Did you know his wife has filed ten wrongful slay claims against you?" She scratched a note in the corner of her clipboard. "Need to put some kind of language in the boilerplate that limits our exposure on any heroic action taken before induction into Knight Watch. These lawyers are costing us a fortune."

"Lawyers? You guys use lawyers for this stuff?"

"What else would we use? Courts don't recognize the Danelaw anymore, especially in the US, and demons are a bitch to work with. Always putting tricky business in the fine print. Okay, let's go over the checklist." She looked up at me, pencil at the ready. "Kill anything?"

"Yes. But—"

"No buts." She ticked a box on her sheet. "Mundane or mythic?"

"Not really sure," I said.

"You think you'd have the hang of this by now. Did it glow, emit tentacles, utter dark vows, consume inanimate objects, speak in high chant . . . ?" She scanned the rest of her sheet and looked back at me. "This is kind of a long list, Rast. Am I getting warm?"

"I want to amend my previous statement. I did not kill anything."

"No?"

"Nope," I said. "Except for this creepy edgelord-looking guy."

"So yes?"

"Yes. Except he didn't die. He disappeared, and then the valkyrie flew off with him."

"A valkyrie flew off with a noble of the edge realms?" Esther asked.

"A what? No, an edgelord. You know, like . . ." I made a brooding face and pulled my tabard over my head so it looked like a hood. "They brood a lot. Get real mean on the Internet. An edgelord!"

"Well, whatever you say about this guy dying or not, the Actuator picked up a lot of mythic deaths in the area, and considering I've got a full head count of elites standing in front of me—"

"No, no, that was us," Chesa said. "We died. All of us but John."

"You . . . died?"

"Yes, Captain MacRae," Tembo said solemnly. "We have walked the final path and come back again. It was harrowing."

"Did the Saint show up or something? None of you look dead."

"Super observant," I said. "But no, Matthew never showed up. But when I knocked the creepy dude's teeth in, they . . . un-died?" I described the fight as quickly and clearly as I could, ignoring Gregory's dismissive snort at my depiction of his utter and humiliating defeat, ending with the valkyrie gathering the man-child in his arms and flying away. "So that's what happened," I finished.

"Okay, so . . . guy with gothic sword manifests necromantic

powers, kills most of the team with a single touch of aforementioned gothic sword, raises a bunch of skeletons and then, when defeated, escapes in the arms of a valkyrie," Esther said. "Do I have that right?"

"Correct," I said.

"Very well." She scanned her sheet, turned the page, then made a single check mark. "Now if you'd just sign and verify for the record."

"You had a single checkbox for all that?" I asked.

"More or less." Esther turned the clipboard around and handed it to me, along with the pencil of +2 sharpness. There was a place for me to sign and date at the bottom. I scanned the page. The only mark was next to a single word:

Ragnarok.

CHAPTER FIVE

The end of the world had a checklist. Everything in Knight Watch had a checklist of some nature, accounting for every possible situation and eventuality, from invasion by djinn to anthropomorphization of cutlery in the break room, and everything in between. One time, when Clarence's companion dragon, Kyle, had gotten a bad case of indigestion from eating all the urinal cakes in the men's room, I had personally watched as Esther filled out a step-by-step guide to extinguishing dragon flame, taking the time to read each step out loud before executing on the procedure. Needless to say we lost the bathroom, but Esther had her list. So it shouldn't have surprised me that Ragnarok was just another jot on a countdown, filed away for the inevitable.

"Step one!" Esther shouted at the top of her lungs. There was no one else in the harbor, just the tired members of Knight Watch and our boss, waving a pencil like it was Excalibur. "Establish a safe perimeter and secure against immediate incursion!"

"We're inside Mundane Actual," I said. "How much more secure could it get?"

"We could be in our domains," Bethany said, almost but not quite under her breath. "Taking a nap. For example."

"Agreed, Rast. Perimeter nominal. Incursion chance nominal."

"Thank the gods we've established that. Now if we can just—"

"Step TWO!"

"How many steps can there be to the end of the world?" Chesa asked.

"Fifteen, unless we get stuck in an Armageddon loop, and then we have to go through the eschatological subroutines," Esther said. "Step Two! Secure Fenrir and apply the Mark XXIII muzzle. That's a problem. We never did develop the Mark XXIII. Or determine the location of Fenrir. Hopefully it'll be awhile before he shows up. Guess we should skip ahead to..." She flipped a page, squinted. "Well, everything else involves that dog, so I suppose we're out of steps. Really should have updated this thing."

"Esther, may we get off the boat?" Tembo asked. "I am tired, and my feet hurt. I would like to get back to the herd and refill the cistern of my soul."

"Gravehome will have to wait, Tem," Esther said. She slapped her sheaf of checklists closed, then shoved her pencil in the tight iron gray bun of her hair. "We will need to speak to the valkyries. Everyone back on the boat."

"Oh, gods, Esther, I'm seriously tapped out," Bethany said. "I just need ten minutes. Three days tops. I'll be in and out before you know it."

"If what you say is true, then we honestly don't have time," Esther said. "We need to get this ship turned around and flying to Valhalla in ten minutes. Someone go get the Saint."

"Valhalla?" I asked as nonchalantly as possible. My mind went back to the valkyrie I had briefly met months ago, during my introduction to Knight Watch. She had a smile like a sunburst, and an ass like... well, I'm not good with ass metaphors. She looked good. I wanted to go there. "Where the valkyries are, right? Like... all the valkyries?"

"Ladies and gentleman, Sherlock Bones, the finest mind this side of a spatula," Bethany said. "Yes, Rast, where all the valkyries are."

"Well, I mean, if Esther thinks it's important, then I say we go. I'll go. Like, right now. Let's go."

"Rast, you understand that they're immortal beings charged with collecting the war dead of generations of Viking warriors?" Bethany asked. "Like, real Viking warriors. Before men had to do CrossFit to feel good about themselves. They've been around real men longer than you've known how to hold a spoon properly."

"Well, maybe they're tired of 'real men,'" I said. I tried to be offended by this, but of course she had a point. I was Sir John of Rast, champion of suburbia and the kind of guy who somehow made walking look awkward. "Maybe they've developed a taste for the quiet, sensitive type."

"Sure," Bethany said. "Lotta women prefer the quiet, sensitive type when they're surrounded by half-god body builders for eternity."

"Not only that," Chesa said, "but Gregory will be there."

"Yeah, yeah, okay, I get it," I said. I turned around and stomped up the gangway. "Let's just get this over with."

"I will retrieve the Saint," Tembo said. "Perhaps he will have a balm you can rub on your pride, Sir John."

"Gonna take a lot of balm," Chesa whispered to Beth, just loud enough that everyone could hear it.

I sat at the back of the bus and waited for the holy man to make an appearance.

Saint Matthew isn't the kind of holy man who's good at reading the room. He was dressed in his casual robes, the heavy cream vestments swooshing loudly against the deck as he crossed the harbor. His lanky black hair hung to his shoulders, and his face was split open in a grin as bright as a fluorescent bulb connected directly to a sunbeam. I mean that literally. His teeth were glowing with holy energy. Usually he wore some kind of mask to keep the light of divinity from blinding us, but today he just had on a pair of Ray-Bans and a heavy layer of what might have been sunscreen. How he got away with these anachronisms was a bit of a mystery to me. Matthew's mythic identity hovered somewhere between medieval monk and stoned-out poet, and he rarely bothered to differentiate between them.

He strolled casually up the gangplank, walked to the back of the aisle, and sat down heavily next to me. The plank seat (also made of toenails, along with everything else on this horrorship) creaked under him as he threw an arm over my shoulders and hugged me close.

"You smell nice, John," he said. "Like citrus. You change your hair care routine?"

"I have to eat a lot of oranges to keep from getting scurvy," I mumbled.

"Oh, right. Diseases. Man, that would suck. You got something that needs healing, big guy?" He waggled his fingers inches away from my blinking eyes. "I've got a lot of juice today. Angels were in a good mood."

"I don't want to know about it," I said. He shrugged and leaned back, his arm still around me, dragging me into an uncomfortable slouch.

"Going to be a good day, man. I've got a great feeling about it."

"It's already been the worst of all possible days," I answered. "Haven't you heard? The world is ending."

"Magnificent!" he declared, then leaned against me and fell asleep.

"I should have been a healer," I said, giving Matthew the side eye.

"They are rarely like this," Esther said. "Healers, that is. Usually a lot of flagellation and reading. Matthew seems to be the exception to the rule."

"You've been through a lot of healers?" Chesa asked.

"Smart monsters kill the healer first," Esther answered. "Okay, everyone strap in. We're going to make this a fast one."

"The horrific toenail ship doesn't have seat belts," I said.

"Figure of speech!" Esther shouted, then pounded her fist against the fuzzy gray length of the main mast. "Valhalla, big guy! Make it snappy!"

Naglfr was apparently anxious to be home, because it roared across the harbor and through the underwater tunnel that led out of Mundane Actual, shooting like a cannonball into the sky. I would have been screaming, but my mouth was full of foot-scented bath water, and my body was simultaneously trying to vomit and choke and scream and eject my lungs through my mouth. I made a sound that approximated these actions. Matthew slept through it.

Once we were safely in the air and headed north—I could not have pointed to Valhalla on a map, and neither could you, but it's safe to say you can get there by heading toward the coldest place you can find—I tapped Tembo on the shoulder.

"So what are we hoping to find in Valhalla?" I asked, trying to recover my dignity with curiosity. I had learned that in Knight Watch, if you're asking questions no one can laugh at you for saying something stupid.

"We have a treaty with the valkyries. It governs their activity in the mundane world, as well as our activity in the affairs of Valhalla.

Mythic beings like to handle their affairs privately, and rarely want Knight Watch barging in. The feeling is mutual."

"Ah. So if one of them is violating this treaty, we need to investigate."

"At a minimum, Esther must serve Runa Hellesdottir notice of the violation. Which should be an interesting interaction," Tembo said, with the kind of smile that said he was not interested in this interaction. "They have history."

"What sort of history? Girl history?"

"Runa was Freya's top officer in the war."

"Oh, so they worked together?"

"No. They did not," Tembo said, then turned around and wouldn't answer any more questions.

I settled into my seat, trying to ignore the clouds screaming past us, and the fact that the air temperature had dropped by about a thousand degrees, and also the way the sun and moon were moving across the sky, like they had come loose in their orbits and were dancing drunkenly among the stars. Esther sat up front, going through paperwork. She had left her grenade launcher at home, I noticed. That was worrying. But other than that, she didn't give any indication that she cared about the upcoming meeting one bit.

Considering we were going to heaven to talk to some valkyries about the end of the world, that was even more worrying.

My reverie was broken by the arrival of a fighter jet escort. Or at least, that's what I thought it was at first. A blur of light flashed off the portside bow, the roar of its passage battering us and stealing the breath from my lungs. The shape tore past us and then turned in a long sweeping arc. Sunlight glinted off steel wings as it came about for another pass. I stood up, grabbing the mast for stability.

"That's definitely going to break some mundane brains," I said. "Tower, this is Maverick. I've got a Viking longship flying over Toledo. Please advise."

"They'll just think we're a spaceship. They always think we're a spaceship," Bethany said. She was the only one of us to not stand up when the jet flew past. "Odds are their cameras will fritz out. Nothing to worry about."

"Long as they don't get too close," Chesa said. "Wouldn't want Rast's antitech bubble to knock out their engines."

"It's not a jet," Esther said quietly. She stood at the bow, arms crossed, frowning at the shape swooping toward us. "It's our escort."

The blur slowed down, wings dipping to bring it level with our flight path. A trail of water vapor curled out from the tips of its wings, rainbows dancing in the contrails, and that's when I noticed that Esther was right. It wasn't a jet. It was a woman. A woman dressed in unrealistically skin-tight metal armor, with a steel visor that didn't appear to have eye slits, but that only covered the top half of her face. The helm was polished to a mirror shine that caught the sun and threw it back at us like a laser beam. At first glance, her wings looked like they were metal, too, but then I saw that they were simply moving so fast that they glowed. What I had mistaken for the roar of a jet engine was in fact the endless thunder of displaced air, propelling her through the air. Her arms were outstretched like . . . well, like Superman, and she carried a winged sword at her waist.

She pulled level with us, her flightpath wavering slightly side to side as she looked over our ship. Then she saw Esther, and her face twisted into the kind of frown that sinks ships and starts wars. With a jerk of her head, she drew the sword and pointed it at Esther. For a long moment neither of them moved, Esther's arms crossed defiantly across her chest, the valkyrie's sword tracing a line that would have passed straight through Esther's heart. Then the valkyrie banked away, dropping into the cloud deck like a bomb.

"Good to see you, too," Esther said. Then she turned away, strolling to the back of the ship to sit next to Tembo. The two of them fell into a hushed conversation.

Greg's heavy hand came down on my shoulder, and he leaned against me, bringing his cinnamon-scented mouth close to my ear.

"Well, that was certainly the finest piece of aeronautical technology I've ever seen," he said, his voice dripping. "Looks like Valhalla might be my kind of place."

"Don't be a creep," I said.

"Or a hypocrite," he answered. "Your jaw is still on the floor, Sir Rast. You are going to catch your daily allowance of bugs before we arrive."

I clapped my mouth shut and turned angrily away. Behind me,

he gave a little amused snort. I had something clever to say, I really did. I just . . . hadn't thought of it yet.

The Naglfr banked smoothly, following the valkyrie into the clouds, and beyond.

CHAPTER SIX

The clouds cleared, and Valhalla opened up before us. A green field swept up out of the cloudbanks, like an island of emerald earth set among the storms, bounded by snow-peaked crags that disappeared into the surrounding cumulus clouds. A long building sprouted out of the grassy hills, its roof thatched with golden hay and woven through with battle-scarred shields, bristling with chimneys that belched thick, black smoke. Two wide doors led into the hall, carved with intricate scenes of warriors and dragons and giants, all doing battle. A tree as tall as the sky loomed over the hall. Its leaves were golden red, and its bark was the color of fresh snowfall.

It was a breathtaking scene, and one completely ruined by the fact that Valhalla seemed to have been vandalized by a squad of disgruntled toddlers with a very poor understanding of color theory.

Swatches of colored fabric hung from every branch and twig of the majestic tree, a mismatched harvest of greens and yellows and bright reds that clashed with the subtle beauty of the foliage. Strands of rope hung with bone ornaments looped their way over the front of the beer hall, cluttering the simple architecture with a clattering, gruesome display. And music filled the air. Loud music. Music that sounded like it was being produced by banging together two halves of a broken piano.

It looked like they were having a festival. Or a riot. Or had been burgled.

Naglfr settled onto the grassy plain with a groan of toenail clippings. Our escort did a final pass overhead, then zoomed down next to us, landing like an artillery shell. A plume of hot air washed over our longship. The valkyrie straightened up, but did not sheathe her sword, or stop frowning, or anything else that might have made us feel welcome.

"Bloody show-off," Esther muttered. "Should have never let them rent *Top Gun* that one time in Topeka. Flying around like complete knobs ever since." She stood at the front of the boat and addressed us like a general overseeing a landing party. "Keep in mind why we're here. We need to find that sword, and learn what we can about Valhalla's involvement in the attack. This can be a pretty distracting place. Stay on target, all of you." She pointed at me and scowled. "Especially you, John."

"Hey, what'd I do?" I asked.

"Nothing. Yet." Esther answered. Then she threw the rope ladder overboard—I want to emphasize that this rope ladder was, somehow, still made of toenail clippings. This was a persistently unpleasant ship—and clambered down onto the field. I followed close behind. This place wasn't that different from the soccer field where I'd first met Knight Watch. Ren faires often had a lot of random pennants and a discordant backdrop of music and drunkenness. Fewer valkyries. A real pity, that.

"Esther MacRae!" the valkyrie boomed. "In accordance with the Compact of 1947, the Greater Danelaw Alliance, and the prophecies of the elder crow, I am required to welcome you into Valhalla." She strode forward, sword held to one side, as though she meant to sweep its shimmering blade through our party at the slightest provocation. "Enter, and find peace."

"Hardly a glowing welcome," I said to Chesa, who was standing a little closer to me than was her usual manner. I found it comforting. Perhaps there was some hope between us after all. I glanced in her direction to try to make eye contact and saw that she was only close to me because I had ceased to exist in her mind as anything other than an obstacle. Her attention was elsewhere.

Specifically, her attention was on the doorman. As was Bethany's attention, and Esther's, and maybe even Greg's. This man stood with fists planted firmly on hips, legs spread confidently, head thrown back and flowing locks of hair dancing on a breeze that seemed to blow only for him. A luxurious beard of golden curls descended from a jaw that could have broken boulders, and his eyes twinkled as clear and blue as the finest topaz. He smiled like a god of drunken joy.

Oh, and he was naked. Naked, and bulging with improbable musculature, and *glistening* like a waterfall of jelly. The only thing even close to clothing was a brightly colored sash that ran from left shoulder to right thigh, and read MR VALHALLA in golden runic script. The lower end of the sash barely, technically, might have covered his pendulous manhood. All things considered, I would have preferred a larger sash. Or a smaller man. Preferably both.

"Oh, Lord, what is happening?" I muttered.

"Why have we not been to Valhalla before?" Bethany asked breathlessly. "How is this not a regular occurrence?" She turned to Esther. "I have many questions."

"I only have one," Chesa said, shouldering past me. "Does he have a name?"

"He doesn't need a name, sister," Bethany said. "Look at those abs!"

"Alright, alright, I think we've had enough of the lurid meat show," I said. "It's hardly appropriate for two ladies of the Knight Watch to conduct themselves like skittish fangirls."

"You can just shut right up!" Bethany said without looking at me. "You were heels-on-fire to get here, back when you thought it was full of Nordic battle witches and their impossible cheekbones. Well, here we are. Now be quiet and let the ladies enjoy the grand tour."

Esther was ignoring all of this. After giving Mr. Valhalla a brief perusal (and blushing, to her credit) she had turned back to the attendant valkyrie. Esther was mirroring our escort's stance, though rather than holding a sword with which to strike, our fearless leader had a clipboard and a pencil.

"Inge. I thought we would never meet again."

"The gods willing," Inge answered. "Though in this case, they have left us disappointed, and questioning their wisdom. What brings you to Valhalla, Captain MacRae?"

"I need to speak to Runa. A matter has come to my attention that requires her counsel." She marched up to the valkyrie, stopping within striking distance, and presented the clipboard. The valkyrie didn't move for the longest time. Then, slowly, she raised her hand and slid the visor of her helmet up, revealing her face. The whole helmet folded into her collar like a magician's trick.

She was wearing a pair of mirrored aviator sunglasses, and her white-blond hair was braided into a complicated knot that clung close to her scalp. Inge glanced down at the clipboard and sniffed.

"Wow, they really went whole-hog on the *Top Gun* thing, didn't they?" I whispered. Tembo, his voice low and rumbling, answered carefully.

"Yes. Several of their number were exiled to Kansas for a period of months in the eighties, as part of an incident involving three magical scarecrows and a great deal of cocaine. Their hotel had a VCR player." He let out a long, steady sigh. "Esther has regretted that decision ever since."

"You always did have a prodigious amount of paperwork," Inge said. Her voice was sharp and slightly dissonant, as though it was being played on a musical instrument that was out of key. "You will find that such things mean little to us, here in Valhalla."

"They meant enough when you were signing the Accords, valkyrie," Esther said. "Our world runs on magical contracts and the spells they bind. Without them, we would both be in a lot of trouble. Now, are you going to honor our agreements, or do I need to get the djinn involved?"

"Okay, that sounds serious." I glanced nervously at Tembo. "Are you sure we're allowed to be here?"

"Allowed? Yes. Welcome?" He shrugged bony shoulders. "They are still working things out. Do not worry. Esther has a form. She always has a form."

"My papers grant emergency access to Valhalla, and to your leader. So unless Runa Hellesdottir is currently locked in a fishing competition with Njorth, I need to speak with her." She pushed the clipboard into Inge's glimmering breastplate. "Immediately."

Inge scowled at Esther for a long, long time. Then she sheathed her sword and pushed the clipboard back.

"Don't be ridiculous," Inge said. "The fishing competition isn't until Freyday."

She turned and strode up the grassy slope to the door leading into the beer hall proper. This meant walking past the glistening man-mountain, a prospect that I viewed with increasing unease the closer we got. As we approached, he glanced in our direction, and I swear I could feel the smoldering heat of his gaze washing over me. He ignored the ladies, but his eyes lingered on Gregory, Tembo, and eventually me. Then he snorted and returned to staring heroically at the distant horizon, as though daring the sky to fall on his majestic head.

"You will need to sponsor greater champions than that, Inge," he said. His voice was like molten copper, warm and rich and capable of melting your face off if you get too close. "None of them stand a chance."

"These are guests of Runa Hellesdottir," Inge said derisively. "Certainly not champions."

"I killed a dragon," I said, though my voice came out as a barely audible squeak. It was still enough to draw the attention of Mr. Valhalla. He scanned me quickly, then turned to Inge and laughed.

"They aren't making dragons like they used to, eh, Inge? What is the world coming to?" He shook his head, then threw his arms wide and shouted. "Bring me your champions, children of Valhalla! I will pick my teeth with their bones, and wear their entrails as a crown! Bring them to me, that I might grind their brains into paste, and crush their hearts in my teeth!"

"A pleasant fellow," I said to Tembo as we passed by. I glanced back, inadvertently confirming that Mr. Valhalla wore nothing under his sash. "Does he greet all the glorious dead this way, or are we a special case?"

"You have come at an inconvenient time," Inge said. "We are in the middle of the Mr. Valhalla competition. If you are fortunate, no one will think enough of you to offer a challenge."

"And if we're unfortunate?" I asked.

"How do you look in a sash?"

"I, uh . . . I've never . . . I don't think I would . . ." I fell silent, bracketed by laughter from the girls, and Tembo's demure chuckle.

"I think we've come at the most convenient of times, actually," Chesa said. "Might be a chance for you boys to work out some of those latent aggressive tendencies."

I didn't answer, and we passed through the doors to the beer hall. Inside we found an impossibly large space, lined with benches and tables, and lit by flickering torches that cast everything in a bright, golden light. The thatch roof stretched overhead, so high that at its peak it disappeared into a silver haze. Birds flew between the massive pillars that supported the thatched sky. The floor was hard-packed dirt, sometimes overlaid with thick carpets, while elsewhere lines of white-painted stones marked off pits of loose sand that served as wrestling rings and sparring circles. Small groups of scantily clad competitors battered one another on the blood-soaked sand, roaring as they flung themselves into battle armed with nothing more than drunken confidence and their fists. Crowds of fellow competitors and onlookers in full battle armor cheered them on, or mocked them in equal measure. Sometimes one of the competitors would tumble into the crowd, and the overly enthusiastic fans would join the fight, spilling off their benches to tumble onto the sand.

I was surprised to see a fair number of the competitors were women. One more misconception to toss in the garbage pail of history, I suppose.

We had come to a stop just inside the door and looked around. There had to be thousands of long benches, some arranged in neat rows, others dragged together in loose circles around the wrestling pits, or to form small cliques of similarly dressed champions. Most of the worthy dead who filled the hall looked like traditional Vikings, some in fur and leather, others wearing battered ring mail, a few in the silk of nobility. The air was filled with the sweet scent of woodfire and seared meat, along with the boisterous cheering of the host, and the clamor of combat.

"Somehow, this isn't what I was expecting of Valhalla," Gregory said. "This looks like a college frat party more than the glorious halls of heaven."

"Pagans," Matthew said. "Always having a party."

"Seems okay to me," Bethany answered. "Are those . . . volleyball courts?"

We looked in the direction she was pointing. A line of fishing nets, hung with skulls and strung between spears thrust into the ground, served as volleyball nets for pairs of sweating, screaming competitors. The ball flying through the air appeared to be wearing a helmet and smiling. When one of the players spiked it into the sandy court, the ball gave out a little scream that drew a round of laughter and applause from the audience. I swallowed the bile in my throat and turned away.

"It isn't usually like this," Esther said. "That time in Topeka, again. There was a pageant at the Holiday Inn across the parking lot, and they kept wandering over and taking notes. They've thrown a Mr. Valhalla competition ever since."

"Please tell me there's a swimsuit competition!" Bethany squeaked.

"There is not," Inge answered. "Foolish child. Vikings wear armor, not swimming suits."

"Well that's a relief," I said, looking around. "Good to see they've covered the gender gap, at least. All's fair in love and war, right?"

"Sounds like a great opportunity for you, John," Bethany said. "You might meet someone."

"Eh, yeah. Ha. Pity no one's available at the moment."

"Yes, I am available," someone said. Before I could turn around, they grabbed my wrist and dragged me bodily away from the rest of the team.

She was a little shorter than me, but built like a main battle tank with braids. Glistening chain mail and banded leather shone under a shawl of fox pelts, and her hair was woven through with charms. The hand wrapped around my wrist was thick but soft. She carried half a roast chicken in her other hand, the grease dripping down her bronze bracer. She turned to look at me. Her cheeks were rosy, and her eyes glassy with drink and cheer, and when she smiled she could have been any maiden in any grand epic.

"Where have they been hiding you, then?" she asked. "Or are you one of the recent inductees? You dress like one of Rollo's boys—pretty hair, and such fine fingernails. You are bound to find a place on Naglfr with cuticles like that." She jerked me forward to examine my fingers, all while dragging me through the crowd. "Such delicate fingers. A bard, perhaps? Even bards die in battle, I suppose. Though most of the bards I knew just drank and hit on the servants. Are you listening?"

"Yes . . . yes, I'm sorry. Where are we going?"

"What a funny accent you have!" she said with a laugh. "Oh, gods, you aren't one of those Christians, are you?" She somehow managed to put five syllables into the word "Christian." "How would a Christian get into Valhalla?"

"We had . . . paperwork . . . ?" I sputtered.

"That sounds right," she said. "I am Solveig the Bashful. I think it is meant as a joke, but I have never laughed at it. So, here we are."

A line of painted stones marked off a blood-spattered pit of sand. Solveig pulled me across the line, then dropped my hand and crossed to the other side of the pit. I stood dumbfounded while she took another bite of the chicken, then tossed it aside and wiped greasy fingers across her tunic. Chewing noisily, she did a quick set of calisthenics, then drew a short sword and sliced at the air a couple times. Apparently satisfied, Solveig turned to me and raised her weapon.

"I would prefer no shield. The whole shieldmaiden thing gets old, you know? But if you insist, I will allow you this advantage."

"What is happening?" I asked.

"You asked if there were any women willing to fight. And yes." She held her arms out, as though announcing the grand-prize winner at the lottery. "I am willing to fight!"

"But I don't think—"

She lunged at me.

CHAPTER SEVEN

Solveig came at me like a thunderstorm. I clutched my shield in both hands as she rained down on it, blow after blow, steel ringing off steel until the sound became a constant ringing in my ears. Each strike sent shivers down my arms and through my spine. My muscles shook so hard that I thought they were going to turn to jelly under the assault.

And then it stopped.

"You know, the whole Mr. Valhalla thing gets old after the first decade or so," Solveig said, almost casually. I peeked out from behind my shield. She was dancing back and forth, feinting at the empty air. "It sometimes feels like we're just going through the motions, you know? I hardly care who wears the crown of entrails anymore."

"Crown of entrails?" I croaked.

"Yes, of course." Solveig shuffled forward and laid her sword across my shield, wrenching my shoulder to one side. "Say, do you even have a sword back there?"

"Sure, sure, hang on." I thumbed my shield into a lighter configuration—her initial attack had triggered some kind of panic response in me, and I had unfolded the shield into a full tower—then drew my sword. Clearing my head, I fell into a basic defense, sword and shield supporting each other, arms close together like the prow of a ship.

"Much better! I was starting to feel like I was doing all the work in this relationship," Solveig said. She circled around me, watching my footwork, weighing her attack. "Good to see you're willing to put in a little effort."

"I just think there's been some kind of—" I shut up as she drifted forward, swinging and then immediately reversing her grip to stab down at my head. The force of the downward strike banged the shield into my forehead. I stepped back just as she swept the blade through the air that used to contain my midsection.

"You can block with the sword too, if that's all you're going to do," Solveig said. To demonstrate, she danced her blade up and down the length of my sword, from forte to tip, clanging the steel like a bell. "Block block block block BLOCK! Maybe you should just carry two shields. You can hit back, yes?"

"My father always taught me to never hit a girl," I said, though in truth I had no trouble hitting girls, especially girls who were actively hitting me, double especially girls with swords. Unfortunately my ability to act on this willingness was deterred by the fact that I was fully engaged in not getting my brains splattered all over the ground by this psychopathic Viking lady.

"That is a good idea. I like that. I wish more men would follow your father's advice," she said, then dove to one side, drawing the attention of my shield just long enough to plant her pommel in my kneecap. I yelped and limped away. "Would make my job so much easier."

I backed away, folding my shield into a more manageable shape, shrinking it until it was a simple disc of beaten bronze, not much larger than my fist. Solveig's brows shot up.

"So is that a magic shield of some kind?"

"What? Oh, yeah. I can change its size and shape at will." I took a step back as she lunged forward, then made a counterstroke that she took off the forte of her blade. Sparks flew over our heads.

"That's a pretty good trick. When it is bigger, it is heavier, yes?" She didn't wait for an answer, but tested my reactions with a series of slashes. "You have kind of small arms. Lot of shield for such a little man."

"I do alright," I said, though my arms were getting tired. She had really hammered me in the opening moments of our match. "Is that why you don't carry a shield? Girl arms?"

"Oh, ho! He has a mouth on him!" Solveig hooted. "Better do the shield trick, hero. You're going to need something to hide behind!"

She charged in, laying her blade across my knuckles just as I folded the shield larger. I whipped the enarme straps around my neck, releasing the shield and taking my sword in both hands. While she battered the shield I slid around its edge and took a nick out of her thigh. Solveig hissed with appreciation, then kicked me in my already lame knee, followed up with a hip check into my collapsing leg, then thrust her boot into my chest. I hit the ground like a sack of potatoes. I tried to bring the shield around, but she kicked it aside, then slapped my sword out of my hand and rested the tip of her sword at the base of my throat.

"'Girl arms,' eh?" she said, breathing heavily. "We will see about that."

"Wait!" I shouted, just as she leaned down on the blade. I felt the tip press against my skin, and the first trickle of blood pooling.

A second blade flashed out of nowhere, stabbing Solveig's weapon in the fuller, sending the tip skating across my throat to land heavily in the sand next to me. The pain was immense but not, as I expected, fatal. I scrambled back, grabbing at the trickle of hot blood pouring down my neck.

Inge had joined us in the pit. Her glittering blade crossed Solveig's, both of them smeared with the bright red of my blood. She had saved my life.

"This one is mortal, Bashful," Inge said. "You would have killed him."

"Mortal?" Solveig said, mortified. She looked at me in horror. "But what is he doing in Valhalla?"

"Making a nuisance of himself," Inge said.

"Excuse me, I think I might still be dying," I said. There was a lot of blood spurting from between my fingers, and I was starting to feel light-headed. Solveig took a step toward me, a look of concern on her face, but Inge pushed her back.

"Do not get involved, shieldmaiden," she said. Fortunately, Saint Matthew shouldered his way through the crowd. He walked across the sand, ignoring the gritty blood staining his cream-colored robes, then knelt beside me.

"Looking rough, warden," he said quietly. I tried to answer, but my mouth was filling up with blood. Matthew smiled and pressed his hand against my throat. "It's alright, buddy. It's going to be okay. Everything's going to super chill."

Brilliance ran down his hand into my throat. I felt blood harden under my fingers, then the skin knit itself back together. My head cleared, and the pain in my throat melted like frost in the sun. I coughed, then spat a chewy slug of rapidly coagulating blood onto the sand.

"Better?" he asked.

"Super chill," I said.

"That's the spirit," he said, slapping me on the shoulder. Then he rose and helped me to my feet. "Come on. We've got to talk to this valkyrie queen lady. Apparently it's important."

Inge led us out of the sandpit, leaving Solveig standing alone. The crowd in our immediate vicinity had grown very quiet, so I was able to hear my sparring partner.

"Sorry, mortal man," Solveig said. I turned around and waved.

"I'll be fine," I said.

"Yes, I suppose. But look at it this way: When you die, you might still earn your way into Valhalla," she said. "And maybe by then you'll have learned how to have a conversation with a real woman."

"Yeah, maybe I will," I said. Then Matthew pulled me through the crowd, and I lost sight of my almost-murderess.

The rest of the team waited in a tiny knot. Inge passed through them. Gregory clapped me on the shoulder as I approached.

"Little man, doing big work!" he said. "We'll make a swordsman of you yet."

"I killed a dragon," I muttered.

"Yes, yes. And someday you will prove that was more than a fluke," he said.

"Hold that thought," Esther said. "Inge, we really need to see Runa. Where is she?"

"On her throne, watching the world fall apart," Inge answered. "This way."

We wound our way through the hall, avoiding kegs of spilled beer and the occasional spatter of blood from the surrounding fighting pits. The gathered host ignored us. I spotted a scattering of valkyries watching the proceedings, apparently serving as judges and arbitrators in the various competitions, though a few seemed to simply be sitting back and enjoying the spectacle, drinking horns in hand. The valkyries watched us very closely. One, a tall, black-haired warrior with severe features and a scar across her lips, turned to follow our progress before lifting into the air on raven wings and gliding smoothly to the back of the hall. Judging by the hall's size, it felt like we should be walking for hours, but it took mere minutes to arrive at the wooden throne of Valhalla.

The throne was broad, carved from a single trunk lying on its side, the far edges still rough with bark and tangled roots. Three seats made up the throne, the center one elevated and crowned with a carving of a tree and two ravens, while the flanking two seats were more diminutive, though still grand. The whole triumvirate was worked with engravings of various mythological animals, from scaled dragons to sharp-eyed foxes, and a stag whose rack grew into a flowering tree. The wall behind the throne was made of piled logs, and bristled with every manner of weapon the Norse mind could imagine, each one buried deep into the wood. A wide firepit stretched in front of the throne, straddled by a half dozen cooking spits, laden with roasting pigs. Sizzling fat dripped onto the hot coals of the fire. Tembo saw me scanning the wall of weapons.

"The weapons of the dead," he whispered into my ear. "Every soul here died in battle. And these are the blades that killed them."

"Cheery," I said.

"They're Vikings," Tembo said with a shrug. "They do cheer differently."

Two winged figures lounged beside the throne, while a rather regular-looking man in leather armor lingered to one side. One of them was the raven-winged valkyrie I had noticed earlier. She stood next to the smallest seat, one hand resting on the carved horn of a wyrm, the other cradling a silver goblet. She was speaking to the other valkyrie, a plainly dressed woman seated on the left-most seat, whose wings rustled against the back of the throne. Her hair was the color of gold shot through with veins of copper and steel, and she wore a black bar of paint across her face, turning her eyes into pools of bright green in a field of shadow. As we approached, she waved the other valkyrie away and stood up. The man watched us closely, but made no move to join the conversation.

"Esther. I never thought I'd see you again," the golden-haired valkyrie said.

"Runa," Esther said. Her voice was unusually tense, even for her. "I'm sure the feeling was mutual."

"And yet here you are," Runa said, smiling tightly. "Come to offer an apology?"

"No. But I do have a warning." Esther hesitated, then looked to the man beside the throne. "Who is this?"

"Aelwulf," Runa said. The man nodded. He had deeply set eyes, and dark hair that hung in braids around his face, with eyes of startling blue. A single scar ran from his left eye down his cheek, but it did little to blemish his rugged handsomeness. The ladies had certainly noticed him. Runa continued. "My personal attendant, and onetime skald. Whatever you must say to me can be said to him."

"He will only wheedle it out of her later," the dark-feathered valkyrie said. Aelwulf glared at her, but then smiled and nodded to us.

"If you would be more comfortable in my absence, I am happy to oblige."

"Don't be ridiculous," Runa said. "The crone of Knight Watch will have no secrets from you. Speak, Esther, that we might get back to our celebration."

"The world is coming to an end," Esther said simply. Aelwulf's brows shot up, but Runa simply snorted.

"The world is always coming to an end," she said. "That is the nature of the world. That is why we are here, preparing for the war that will follow."

"Well, you might want to kick those preparations into high gear," Esther said. She produced her clipboard and thrust it in Runa's direction. The two valkyries exchanged a look, then Runa stood and took the board.

"What is this?"

"After-Anomaly Report," Esther said. "My team had to attend to a creep in a Halloween mask raising the dead with a magical sword. The guy had a valkyrie for a girlfriend. Sound familiar?"

"Sounds like the cover art from a heavy metal band," Runa said. I laughed, but shut up when she looked at me. She was absolutely serious.

"Do you know where all your girls are, Runa?" Esther asked.

"There are no time cards in Valhalla," she answered. "The cadres come and they go. I do not keep track of them."

"Well, maybe you should," Esther said. "Because it sounds like you've got a rogue valkyrie trying to rush Ragnarok to the brink."

Runa Hellesdottir reviewed the paperwork for a long moment. The black-haired valkyrie drifted closer, reading over Runa's shoulder. Aelwulf just stared at us coldly. Eventually the other valkyrie grimaced and muttered something into her goblet of wine.

"We don't know that," Runa answered. She looked up at the team. "Is the agent here?"

"Solveig the Basher just about killed him," Esther said, gesturing to me. Runa looked me over again, this time with curiosity. Aelwulf's gaze was less forgiving. I started blushing.

"Bashful. Her name is Bashful," Runa said absently, her eyes still scanning the document. Then she looked up, fixing me in her icy gaze. "This is true? The dark knight with a thirsty blade, and a valkyrie at his side?"

"Uh, yeah. Yeah, that's what happened. Though the term 'thirsty' has changed meaning a little since—"

"We will talk," Runa said. "Inge, you and Revna see to the proceedings. The volleyball competition has gone on too long. They are simply taunting that poor head. Make sure that Hrapp gets his skull back. Aelwulf, prepare a table for our guests. They will be hungry after their long journey."

"Yes, my lady," the two valkyries said in unison. Aelwulf simply nodded and turned away, disappearing behind the throne. Runa gestured back to us. "Let's find some privacy. There's no reason to interrupt the festivities for this."

CHAPTER EIGHT

Runa led us outside by a side door. The clamor of drunken brawling and shouting crowds was immediately replaced with a chorus of birdsong. The air, which inside smelled like dried blood and spilled mead and sweat, was filled with the scent of fresh rain and untrammeled sod. A cold breeze blew down from the surrounding peaks. I took a deep breath and released it in a contented sigh.

"It really is very pleasant here," Tembo said.

"Don't get used to it," Esther answered. "All this is turning into wolf-chow the second Ragnarok starts."

"Hopefully I'll have something to say about that," Runa said. "Our gathered dead have been training for centuries."

"Somehow, I don't think the end of the world is going to be settled with a volleyball match," Chesa said. Runa laughed and shook her head.

"Every contest is a battle, no matter how harmless it seems." She looked over to where Mr. Valhalla was greeting another contingent of contestants, escorted by three or four valkyries. The enormous man was shouting, "You're a failure!" into their faces at the top of his lungs. "And they like the competition!"

"I'm sure they do," Esther said. "So are we going to sneak behind the dumpsters to smoke, or are we going to talk about our little problem?"

"Not here. We will be seen, and the honored dead will worry," Runa said. "Come, this way."

The valkyrie turned and headed up the path. Gregory followed eagerly, but Esther hesitated.

"She's hiding something from us," Bethany said quietly.

"Yeah," Esther answered. "The question is what. And why."

"Want me to stay behind and watch the hall?" Bethany asked. She was already disappearing, the edges of her form wisping into mist. Esther shook her head.

"I don't want to arouse suspicion," she said. "Stay with us for now. But be ready to move on a moment's notice. All of you."

Runa led us to a rocky platform that overlooked the grassy field in front of the hall. The golden boughs of the tree hid the entrance, but I could still hear the mead-soaked revelry. I wasn't sure what phase of the competition had begun, but it seemed to involve singing and the rhythmic clashing of shields. The sun was beginning to set, and the tree threw long shadows across the plain.

The tall valkyrie stood at the edge of the precipice, staring down on her domain. In the harsh shadows of the late evening, she looked like a statue commemorating grief.

"What's going on, Runa?" Esther asked quietly. "What are you hiding?"

She didn't answer for a long time. We shifted uncomfortably on our seats, but Runa didn't move an inch. Finally she let out a sigh worthy of an immortal being tasked with training the rowdy dead for a fight that might never come. She turned to face us.

"Valhalla is a delicate place, Captain," she said. "We drink our mead and we sing our songs, but in the end, we are all just dead warriors. We have already lost everything there is to lose, everything but the battle in front of us, and the battle to come. I would protect them from losing that, as well."

"What are you talking about?" Esther said.

"Yeah, this seems like a pretty peachy deal, to me," Bethany said. "Do you need more gorgeous men? I'm sure we could find some volunteers in the real world. I think your marketing just needs a quick polish."

"They grow restless," Runa answered. "The dead, yes, but especially the valkyries. We were promised a final battle at the end of an age. But our numbers have stagnated, and those few recruits we get are more interested in the party than the training."

"Be glad your ranks aren't needed. Ragnarok seems like a pretty bad deal for everyone involved," Esther said.

"To you, perhaps. To us . . . it is our destiny. And there are those who would rush that destiny, before it is meant to arrive."

"You have people in there trying to kickstart the end of the world?" Chesa asked. "That's insane!"

"I don't know," Matthew said. "We have a few of those in the ranks of the saints. Depends on your point of view, and what you expect to get out of it."

"Runa, if there are elements within Valhalla working to start Ragnarok, then that's something we need to know about. Something we need to prevent."

"They don't mean to start Ragnarok. But they're tired of hiding in the Unreal." Runa sat on the ledge and folded one knee over the other, pulling her battle skirt up to her thigh. There was a lot of leg there to admire, and I quickly looked somewhere else. "Dragons and the fae may be content lurking in the shadows of cubicles and doing yoga, but that is not for the valkyries. We are not soccer moms, and never will be."

"You read the report. It looks familiar to me. That sword sounds a lot like the Totenschreck," Esther said. The word tickled my head. Something about potatoes. Runa was nodding sadly.

"Yes, it does. But it could not be," she said. "The sword is safe. As is the vessel."

"What are you guys talking about?" I asked. "The dude in the mask said something about tatertots, or something. Total shriek?"

"Totenschreck," Tembo said quietly. "Terror of the dead. It was a sword that harnessed certain necromantic powers usually reserved to the servants of Valhalla. A weapon the Germans deployed during the war, if my memory of history serves."

"A nasty weapon, too. Anyone killed by it would return to serve the bearer in death. And each time they died, the sword would bring them back," Esther said. "Forged in Valhalla, and powered by the tears of one of their missing goddesses. Freya, wasn't it?"

"The Tears of Freya have restorative properties," Runa said sadly. "And the sword bound them together. Life and death in one weapon. Not our proudest moment. It is why I turned my coat, Captain. You know this."

"But not before you took some of my best men," Esther said. Her voice was fragile. In the failing light, I thought I could see tears glisten in the boss's eyes. "And made me kill them, over and over again."

"The past is the past," Runa said. "That is the purpose of the Accords. To make peace between us. Let it go."

Esther didn't answer immediately. Instead, she rubbed her face and cleared her throat. When she spoke again, her voice was back to the steel I remembered.

"Those Accords put that sword back into your care, along with the Tears," Esther said. "To safeguard against mortal meddling."

"Which is how I know it could not be the same sword. The Totenschreck is safe."

"And the Tears?"

"I don't know. We designed it that way," Runa said. "Two of our sisters foreswore their powers and cut themselves off from Valhalla, to keep anyone from being able to trace them. I have no way of finding them. And neither do you."

"Wait. Why did you trust the very people who created the sword in the first place to protect it?" I asked. "If it was used by valkyries to kill mortals, shouldn't it be in mortal hands? Or destroyed?"

"Both the Tears and the sword are elements of our domain. They could not be destroyed without threatening the stability of Valhalla," Runa said gruffly. "We would never have allowed it."

"As for the sword being in valkyrie hands," Esther said, stepping in, "the valkyries can't wield it. Part of the ritual requires it be wielded by someone born of mortal blood."

"I have absolute control over all who enter Valhalla. No one gets in here without my knowledge," Runa said. "Which is how I know you must be mistaken. The sword is safe."

"We saw what we saw," Chesa said. "And what we saw sounds an awful lot like what you're describing. Especially the Nazi bits."

"It could be someone searching out the mythic nature of the blade. A mortal, guided by a valkyrie, could approximate the sword without actually having the weapon," Tembo said. "Though it wouldn't have the same amount of power."

"Explains the weird plastic skeletons," Esther said. "Replicating as much of the power as possible. They could be training the next bearer."

"Possibly. But you have nothing to worry about. The sword is safe, here in Valhalla. I control all entrances, and know all who come and go. This pretender will never get close to the blade," Runa said. "Not until Ragnarok."

"Well, let's hope it doesn't come to that," Esther said. "I'd like to set a watch on the sword, Runa. A few of my elites, and maybe some agents from Mundane Actual. At least until we get to the bottom of what happened at the convention center."

"I volunteer!" Bethany squeaked.

"Impossible. Mortals who tarry too long in Valhalla lose themselves to the mead, and the melee. They are driven mad by the glory."

"I absolutely volunteer!" Bethany said.

"I think the elites can handle it. After all, they're already in touch with their mythic identities," Esther said. That was a fancy way of saying that we'd already lost ourselves to the Unreal, or maybe found ourselves in it. We were already the heroes we imagined ourselves to be. "Worst that could happen is that they pick up a taste for bloodshed."

"I'm sorry, Esther, but it's not going to happen. The Accords are very clear on this. You handle the mundane world, and keep it safe," Runa said, hooking a thumb in her scabbard. "Valhalla is my responsibility."

"If one of your girls goes rogue and kicks off Ragnarok, I'm going to have trouble holding up my end of the deal," Esther said.

"That's not going to happen. And even if it does, we'll be ready." Runa clapped her hands together. "Now, if I'm not mistaken, they are starting the shield-breaking contest, and after that we have the armor competition. Aelwulf will see to your needs. Mix with the crowd, enjoy the contests. Maybe one or two of your members could participate."

"We wouldn't want to embarrass you, Runa," Esther said. "Doesn't look good for the title of Mr. Valhalla to go to a former phys ed teacher from Dubuque."

"And if that happens, then maybe it really *is* the end of the world," Runa said. She smiled one more time, then headed down the path. Esther watched her go.

"Still think she's hiding something?" Chesa asked.

"Nope," Esther answered. "Now I'm sure of it."

"So what do we do?" Tembo asked. "She won't let us guard the sword. We don't even know where it is."

"Don't worry," Esther said. "I have a plan. John, you, Gregory, and Tembo are going to enter the Mr. Valhalla competition."

"I don't think that's a good idea," I said. "For starters—"

"I think it's a *GREAT* idea," Bethany interrupted. "Rast is going to look ridiculous in a sash. I can't wait!"

"To what purpose, Ms. MacRae?" Gregory asked. "Don't get me wrong. I'm happy to prove my worth against these barbarians, but this hardly feels like the time for games."

"You heard Inge. The fishing competition isn't until Friday. By entering, you'll be granted access to Valhalla for the next three days," Esther said. "Play a couple games, get beat, then we'll limp away with our collective tail between our legs. But before we go, we drop the three of you off right back here. Runa's magic would alert her to intruders, but not to legal competitors. Then you just need to sneak down here tonight while everyone else is asleep and find that sword."

"So you're going to strand us in Valhalla?" I asked. "This is genius. And when they find us and figure out what we're doing, how are we supposed to escape?"

"You're clever lads. I'm sure you'll figure something out." Esther started down the path, then paused and looked back at us. "One last thing: Try not to get killed."

"Cool. Don't get killed playing volleyball," I grumbled. "Great."

CHAPTER NINE

The mood in the beer hall was reaching a fever pitch. The interruption of the volleyball tournament had led to a kind of shirtless diaspora, and now a bunch of disgruntled Vikings with pecs like boulders were wandering the crowds, looking for some way to vent their frustration.

"It feels like we're on the verge of a riot," I said.

"That might well be the next event," Matthew said. "Disorganized melee, followed by a round of slowly bleeding to death. Last man to death rattle wins."

"That's a pretty sharp escalation from volleyball," I said.

"They *were* playing with a human head," Chesa said.

"Point taken."

Aelwulf appeared at our side, as though summoned by magic.

"Esther tells me you would like to participate in some of our games?" he asked. "I must warn you, the boys can be rambunctious. The sagas are littered with tales of mortals trying to earn a place in Valhalla through the games. They rarely do well. Or survive."

"Not a worry," Gregory said, flashing his million-dollar smile. "We've got a healer."

"I hope he is very good," Aelwulf said, glancing at Saint Matthew, who had become fascinated by the flames in a nearby brazier.

"He's the best," Greg said. "Now. What sort of contests are we talking about? Bear wrestling? Stone throwing? Sword fighting?"

"Can you swim?" Aelwulf asked.

"Of course!"

"In armor?"

"Of... Maybe? I've never tried. Why would I?"

"I'm glad you mentioned a bear. I think that would be a nice addition to this year's festivities." He clapped Greg on the shoulder. "Come with me, my friend."

We stood on the muddy bank of a pool that had apparently been dug directly into the floor of the beer hall expressly for the purpose of drowning otherwise healthy men. There were already a number of bodies floating peacefully in its depths, along with several large logs. Between the churned-up mud and a fair amount of blood, it was impossible to judge the depth of the pool. Certainly deep enough to drown, though.

Gregory d'Having-Second-Thoughts stood on one end of the pool, staring desolately at his opponent across the way. The other man was packing four hundred pounds of muscle into a two-hundred-pound body, and wasn't shy about his skin. He still wore armor, but only on his shoulders and around his waist, kind of like a poodle that had been bred with an armored personnel carrier. His hair was bound in a long braid that hung all the way down his back. He sneered at Greg, then spit into the pool and drew a battle-ax from his belt. The dark-feathered valkyrie, Revna, had joined us. Aelwulf observed from a distance, hovering like a butler but also an assassin. I kept glancing at him. The man smiled every time, and the way his face wrinkled around that scar made me a little uncomfortable.

"This should be interesting," Chesa said.

"Aren't you supposed to be poking around? Trying to figure out what Runa's hiding?" I asked.

"Sure. And right now I'm poking around here," she said. "You think this guy's going to kill Gregory?"

"I think it's a distinct possibility."

"That would be a pity," Chesa said.

"I'm not sure I understand the rules of the contest," Greg said. "First in the water, is that it?"

"First to drown," Revna said. She was sitting in a lifeguard's chair on the other bank. She even had a whistle around her neck, though I wasn't counting on her saving any lives, or even getting close to the water. "Death by any other method is strictly barred."

"Wait? *DEATH?* What kind of—"

"I said that mortals didn't do very well in these contests," Revna said. "Horeth, are you ready?"

"I will fill this coward's lungs with his own stomach acid!" Horeth, the poodle-shaped opponent, shouted.

"I'm not a coward!" Greg yelled back.

"He's right. That's more *my* thing," I answered, but Revna ignored me.

"Does that mean you are ready, mortal?" Revna asked.

"Is the saint around?" Greg asked.

"I'm here, buddy," Matthew answered. Behind his mask, his face was glowing like candlelight. "Just say the word."

"If I'm drowning I can't say much," Greg answered.

"Yeah, that makes sense. I'll just improvise," Matthew said.

"Saint!"

"Be cool, be cool. Panicking is John's thing."

"I already pointed that out," I said. "Kind of goes with the 'coward' thing."

Revna blew the whistle, and the contest began.

Horeth leapt from the bank onto the first of the logs. The log rolled under his feet, but he danced across it, getting closer and closer to where Greg was standing. Greg finally stepped gingerly onto a different log, balancing carefully as he edged his way across the pool. Horeth bellowed and charged, leaping from log to log.

The two combatants met in the center. Horeth struck a mighty pose, ax poised to strike, his muscles rippling powerfully under his scant armor. Gregory, not to be outdone in the pose-striking department, brought his zweihander to bear. The steel blade flashed in the torchlight.

"Prepare to die, little man!" Horeth boomed.

"I will fight for the honor of Knight Watch, and the glory of my name! To the breach! To the walls! For *GLORY!*" Gregory d'Monologue shouted.

"Oh, I almost forgot the bear," Revna said. She blew her whistle again, and the crowd behind her parted to reveal a bear rumbling toward the combatants. It was the size of a VW bug, and each step of its rolling gait sent shivers through the ground and kicked up waves in the pool. Both Horeth and Gregory froze in place, their mouths hanging open.

"When did they add a bear?" Horeth asked quietly.

The bear reached the edge of the pool and, roaring like a thousand angry bullhorns, launched itself into the air, paws extended, slavering mouth flapping open, muscular body extended. It hit the water at a thousand miles an hour, right on top of Gregory and Horeth. They disappeared in a plume of water and splintered logs.

"Going in," Matthew said as he shouldered past us, stripping off his robe and sunglasses, until all that was left was complicated underwear and shining, golden skin. He slipped into the churning, bloody water of the pool like a sunbeam. Chesa and I stared in horror and the tumult.

"The bear is a nice touch," one of the other onlookers said happily.

"Well, that was more satisfying than I expected," I said as we strolled casually through the crowds. Bethany had joined Chesa and me, while Matthew was still attending to Gregory. Aelwulf trailed behind us, like a bad scent. Apparently the bear had won the contest, to the delight of everyone not directly involved in being drowned by an angry bear. But at least I had gotten to hear Greg scream like a frightened girl. It gave me hope for the rest of the day.

"It felt a little one-sided," Chesa said, "even without the bear. How is someone like Gregory supposed to win against an immortal Viking?"

"My understanding is that they *can* die. They just come back in the morning," Bethany said. "Just like the sun."

"Or a rash," I grumbled.

"A particularly well-muscled rash," Chesa said. A group of drunk Vikings barged through our group, brushing me aside on their way to more mead. The girls watched them go with very inappropriate and lingering gazes. I cleared my throat.

"The two of you are supposed to be figuring out what Runa's up to," I said. "And it feels like you're not really doing that."

"Well, you can't say that we're not keeping our eyes open," Chesa said.

"Or paying attention to our surroundings," Bethany continued.

"I think you might be missing the forest for the abs," I said.

"This looks interesting." Bethany nodded in the direction of a platform raised above the crowd. Two firepits had been set up, each with a pyramid of logs arranged in the center. As we approached, a pair of valkyries were dousing the logs in a clear liquid.

"Kerosene, probably," Bethany said. "That's going to make one hell of a boom."

"Actually, I think it's water." Matthew slipped up behind us. His robe hung loose over his shoulders, and his hair hung in damp curls down his face. His skin had lost most of its pearlescent glow, but his eyes were still piercing orbs of light behind his sunglasses. "They stole this one from us. Might be some copyright violations going on. I'll have to check."

"Your priest is correct. The contest is to see who can burn the offering. The water is meant to replicate the Tears of Freya, shed because she misses her husband," Aelwulf said, glancing at Matthew. "Which is a completely Nordic tradition and has nothing to do with any previous event."

"Whatever," Matthew said, rolling his eyes.

"How's Gregory?" Chesa asked.

"Recovering. I was able to fix everything except his pride. Cost a lot of Brilliance, though."

A bell rang, and out of the crowd emerged our mage. Tembo climbed onto the platform. He was joined by a pale, crooked-looking man in patchwork leather robes. He leaned on a bent staff that was hung with fetishes and burned bark. At first I thought the man wore the same black makeup as Runa, but it turned out that he was blind, and his face was simply smeared with ash. One of the valkyries helped him up onto the platform, where he stood working his mouth, pale tongue flicking out between yellow teeth, as though he was scenting the air.

"Now that's a creepy dude," I said.

"Be respectful of our rites," Aelwulf said. "At least we don't go around baptizing each other."

"He's a priest of some sort, or a skald," Matthew said. "Looks like Tembo's gotten himself into a *burning things* competition."

"Tem's going to win the hell out of that," Bethany said. "I've seen him light up most of a city block with that staff."

"Yeah, well, Greg said he knew how to swim, and look where that got him," I said.

Truthfully, Tembo looked pretty confident up on the platform. He examined the pyre, testing the depth of the water that pooled at its base and the quality of the timber. Meanwhile his opponent continued to open and close his mouth like a giant, fleshy flytrap.

"What are the conditions of victory?" Tembo asked.

"Biggest flame," the attending valkyrie answered. "It should be pretty obvious, but the crowd will determine close results by applause."

"Hardly scientific," Tembo said with a sniff.

"We're talking about starting fires with pagan rituals and thaumaturgy wrestled from the land of the dead with profane vows and blood magic," the valkyrie said. "Science doesn't have a lot to do with it."

Tembo and the blind priest moved to opposite ends of the platform, with the two unlit pyres between them, and the valkyrie at the exact center. She signalled to Tembo to begin. Our friendly mage rolled up the sleeves of his robe and gestured lightly toward the closer pyre. The damp logs started to hiss and steam, and then a tongue of flame licked across the rough bark of one of the logs before disappearing in a flash of steam. Tembo curled his fingers into a fist. A bolt of scintillating light jumped from his hands to the pyre. The pyramid of stacked wood erupted in a ball of flame. The crowd let out an appreciative *Oooooooo*, and then the flames subsided into a heartwarming crackle.

"Get it, my man!" I shouted, then let out a long whistle. "Tem! BO! Tem! BO! Tem—!"

With an almost dismissive gesture, the blind skald flicked his hand toward the other pyre. The logs exploded in flame, showering the crowd with sparks and sending a plume of bright cinders curling into the air. The valkyrie smirked, and looked back to Tembo.

Tembo stared numbly at the priest's inferno. Then he cracked his knuckles and summoned his staff of white ashwood. The staff appeared in a flash of amber light, echoed in the glowing runes around Tembo's left eye, and the silver bracelets on his wrists. Gripping the staff in both hands, the mage turned to the flickering flames of his pyre and spoke, his voice a low, even growl.

"I have faced many problems in my journeys, and overcome many foes. But there is no enemy that I have faced that could not be laid low by a ball of fire," he said. Tembo swung the staff over his head. Flames gathered on the whirling tip, roaring to life as he spun the staff around and around, growing larger and larger until a ball of coruscating fire the size of a wolfhound clung to the tip of the staff. "Behold the fire of my rage!"

Tembo slammed the staff to the ground, hurling the ball of fire into the stacked logs. With a thunderclap they burst into white-hot flame, the black outlines of the logs washed out by the bright light of the fire, quickly disappearing into ash and swirling cinders. The pyre burned like a magnesium flare, a constant, even, roaring flame that consumed the wood, drank the water, and cracked the stones of the firepit. Heat pressed the crowd back.

The blind priest smiled. It was a horrific sight. His mouth bristled with spit-slick yellow teeth, set in blackened gums. A burning cinder landed on his pale, snake-like tongue, sizzling against the flesh. The priest tasted the cinder, chewing noisily and with apparent relish. Then he cast his patchwork robes aside and strode, naked and knobbly, into the flames of his pyre.

"This is full-on crazy, right?" I asked.

"Or heavy, heavy magic," Matthew answered. "Probably a little of both."

Flames caressed the bony length of the priest's legs. He kicked aside the stacked logs to stand in the middle of the pyre, oblivious to the glowing coals underfoot or the ashes that clung to his skin. He lifted his hands to the sky and began to speak dark, broken words.

The sound of his voice rolled out across the audience. They made my skin crawl, and the hair stand up on the back of my neck. Bile rose in the back of my throat as the flames burned the priest's skin. The smell of burning meat filled the room, and thick black smoke wafted off his flesh. The priest lifted a dagger of sharpened bone over his head, then plunged it into his chest. Dark blood splashed off the blackened stones, feeding the flames.

A tornado of flames whipped out around the blind priest, joining his voice with its own roaring fury. The inferno obliterated the priest, the pyre, the stones, and half the platform in a whirlwind of screaming flame and cutting wind. I threw my arm across my face, but I could still see the white-hot fire through my eyelids, their fury burned into my brain like a brand. When I opened my eyes, there was a crater where the priest's half of the platform had been. The edge of the crater looked like it had been cut with a blowtorch.

Nothing was left of the priest other than charred bones and a skull, still smiling with those crooked, yellow teeth.

The valkyrie turned to Tembo and raised her brows.

"Elephant man?" she asked.

Tembo shrugged.

"Nice trick," I said. "Too bad you can only do it once."

"Nonsense," Bethany answered. "He can do it all over again tomorrow. Immortal, remember?"

"Yeah," I said. The crowd was dispersing. We watched as Tembo descended from the platform, his shoulders slumped. "Really not fair."

"No one said it was going to be fair," Chesa said. "Now. Let's go find this armor competition. I've heard good things."

CHAPTER TEN

I sat nervously in the front row of a boisterous crowd of valkyries, shoulder to winged shoulder. Chesa had wandered off to look for Esther and report on our limited findings, which at the moment consisted of Tembo's loss and Gregory's recent drowning and resurrection. We hadn't seen anything more unusual than . . . well, everything we had seen. But nothing suspicious. Aelwulf was keeping a tight rein on us, though, so it was hard to say if we were being steered away from anything important. Even now, he stood to one side, arms folded and impassive face locked on the stage.

"What are we supposed to be looking for anyway?" I asked Tembo as we settled into our seats. "Aren't the valkyries supposed to be on our side? Why doesn't Esther trust them?"

"Because they don't trust Esther, either, and Knight Watch by extension," Tembo said. "Meet a valkyrie in a dark alley and she's just as likely to try to kill you as she is to welcome you with open arms."

"Hell of a friendship," I said.

"Our alliance with Valhalla is complicated. They were forced to sacrifice some of their powers to give Knight Watch its foundation. The magic that runs our domains and gives us some measure of authority over the mundane world stems from Valhalla," Tembo said. "Have you noticed anything unusual about this place?"

I looked around at the crowds of sweating, wrestling warriors, most of them still bearing the wounds that sent them to the afterlife in the first place. My eyes lingered on the volleyball game that had apparently resumed, and the leather-wrapped skull that bounced over the net, complaining loudly the entire time. The valkyries gathered in clusters, apparently drawn from every culture in the world, all breathtakingly beautiful and harsh in equal measure. We had apparently caused quite a stir with our presence. Every time I looked at one of the gatherings of winged supermodels, they were staring in our direction and whispering among themselves. It made me nervous. Everything about this place made me nervous. The hall itself was larger than any structure I had ever seen in my life, and yet seemed close and intimate, like a friendly pub. The size of the place reminded me of the tree outside, as tall as a skyscraper. I looked back to Tembo.

"Not particularly," I said. "Why?"

"Valhalla is the home of the Norse gods, where they gather their worthy dead and prepare for the end of the world with constant fighting and bloodshed and strife," Tembo answered. He held up his index finger. "First, no gods. Faded away as the world fell into modernity. Only the servants remain, those who interacted with the real world on a regular basis. This is true of most mythologies, and the reason Matthew deals directly with angels, and nothing else. But these servants were orphaned, and have had to make do ever since. For Valhalla, that means valkyries and other lesser creatures."

"Explains why I haven't seen Thor," I said. "But what does that have to do with the alliance?"

"Our own magic depends on the existence of these lesser creations," Tembo said. "The magic that we draw into our domains, the powers that we express through our mythic selves . . . Knight Watch's very existence depends on Valhalla. That was part of the Accords Esther and Runa keep talking about. Without Valhalla, we're screwed."

"So we have to trust Runa?"

"Runa, or whoever sits on that throne," Tembo said, nodding in the direction of the massive structure where we'd first met Runa. "Runa Hellesdottir leads the valkyries by default. It is a position that she usurped from another, a sister who had led Valhalla truly astray. The war settled that, when Runa betrayed her leader because of a promise Esther made. A promise that they would be spared, should they surrender."

"And what happened?" I asked, afraid that I already knew.

"Esther lied," Tembo said. "One-third of the valkyries were

destroyed in the fighting that followed. The rest are imprisoned here, as part of the Accords. We depend on them, but they depend on us, as well. It was not a bright chapter in our history."

I sat back and thought about that. Runa betrayed her sisters during the war. When I was first introduced to Knight Watch, I assumed the war they kept talking about was the Second World War. I've since learned that, though concurrent, the struggle Esther fought in was unrelated and, in some ways, more widespread than the one I had learned about in school and through video games. There had been battles across cosmologies and mythologies, with warzones that stretched from the Americas to the Arctic Circle. The more I learned about it, the less I understood. But if Runa and Esther had been enemies during that war, and then briefly allies, only to have it undone by Esther's lies, it would certainly explain our current situation.

Hooded attendants had set up a stage, framed by massive curtains that reminded me of *The Muppet Show*. I half expected a puppet to stride onto the boards. Instead it was Mr. Valhalla. Thankfully, he was wearing clothes this time around. Blackened leather armor etched with runic ravens covered his massive chest, while more traditional iron greaves and chain mail struggled to contain his arms and legs. He even wore an iron cap with an eyeguard of shining gold, though his beard still flowed luxuriously down his chest. The crowd roared when he appeared. Waving and smiling, he stomped to the center of the stage and waited for the cheering to stop.

"Ladies!" he boomed, immediately prompting another tinnitus-inducing round of cheering and the slamming of drinking horns against shields. He motioned for silence, which only brought more cheering. Finally, the catcalls and hooting subsided. "And gentlemen! Welcome to the armor competition. We all know why we're here! So let's get started with the competitors!"

The muscle-mountain lumbered off the stage, and the crowd grew hushed. There was a shuffling sound from stage right. A pillar of stacked armor appeared that, after a few seconds, I recognized as a human being. The competitor wore at least three chain shirts, an oversized hauberk, and a cuirass of beaten brass that was completely out of place in the golden halls of Valhalla. I could just make out his eyes under two different helms, each one offset to limit the exposure of his face, and what might have been a pair of children's fuzzy earmuffs. The man's hands looked like cartoon sausages under the layers of chain mitten and lobster plate. There was a shield strapped to each of his forearms, hanging loosely from the enarme straps, while three more shields hung around his neck, forming a pendulous necklace of steel that should have toppled him. In fact, I have no idea how this man was moving at all. The tasse, meant only to cover the hips, was so long that its edges scraped against the floor. The stage creaked under the weight of his ponderous advance. Clattering like a stack of mismatched plates, he tottered to the center of the stage.

"That doesn't look practical," I said.

"You'll see," Tembo said.

"But, I don't understand how he's supposed to—"

"You'll see," he repeated.

The man cleared his throat and, from the depths of oiled steel and tightly bound leather, spoke.

"Hildr Knotte, for your consideration."

The crowd roared their appreciation and stood as one, drawing spears out of thin air. The valkyrie nearest me hefted a spear at least ten feet long, with a haft of light-colored ash that was at least as thick as my wrist. The iron head that tipped the spear was as black as ink and several feet long. It looked like the kind of weapon you would throw at a god, while swearing an oath of eternal rebellion. I looked around. Everyone had a spear, even Runa and Revna, and the aviator-bespectacled Inge.

"What the hell is going on?" Gregory asked.

"Did I miss anything?" Solveig asked as she pushed herself onto the bench beside me. She had a quiver of short spears with heavy broadleaf heads of forged iron. "Oh, good! I would hate to miss this!"

"Begin!" Mr. Valhalla shouted, and they did. Enthusiastically.

A cloud of iron-tipped spears sailed through the air, blotting out the thatched sky and turning the stage as dark as night. I heard Hildr Knotte make a quiet squeaking sound just as the hail of projectiles fell on him. It sounded like an iron trellis bridge collapsing under the weight of ten thousand steel bells and falling into a canyon stacked to the brim with pottery.

When I looked up, poor Hildr Knotte stood naked on the stage. Well, nearly naked. He wore a codpiece of burnished brass, and a single gauntlet that had somehow migrated to his left ear, as well as three bronze torques that pressed tightly into the flesh of his forehead. He staggered slowly back and forth, eyes half-closed, emitting a low, whimpering moan. Other than that, he was untouched.

"Very good, very good," Mr. Valhalla said. "That looks like two pieces left, and the tiniest shred of decency, to boot! Well done, Hildr!" Hildr smiled, though in parting his lips he gave four broken teeth the chance to slip free from his mouth and dribble bloodily down his chest.

"Well that's a satisfactory result," Bethany said. She looked around. "Are there really no more spears? Not even one? I could have a throw."

Turns out that there was one more spear, hurled from the back with great force. It arced slowly over the crowd, then descended like a thunderbolt. It struck Hildr squarely in the chest, piercing flesh and bone and whatever organs his death in glorious battle had left him. It seemed he still had a heart, though, because when the spear ran him through, Hildr cried out and collapsed to the ground, as dead as a doornail.

"Who threw that?" Mr. Valhalla shouted. "Hertha Grunsdottir, was that you?" He stomped to the center of the stage, looming over Hildr's dead body and casting his gaze back and forth across the audience. "You know the rules, Hertha! No killing the competitors. Gods almighty, now we will have to delay the rest of the competition until poor Hildr can rejoin us in the morning. Such a bloody inconvenience!"

"Perhaps it is for the best," Revna said, standing up. "Our friends from Knight Watch have joined us, and one of them has entered the armor competition. It is a rare privilege. We don't often allow mortals to take part. Come, Sir John of Rast. Three hundred spears, thrown by the strongest arms in all of Valhalla. We will see how you fare."

"You are going to do great!" Solveig said, patting me on the knee enthusiastically. "I can *not* wait to see how you perform."

"Wait, *this* is my contest? I thought I could at least . . . wrestle? Or maybe demonstrate some clever poetry skills? Aren't there poets in attendance?" I looked hopelessly around the crowd. They did not seem the poetic type. Bethany pulled me to my feet.

"What's the matter, John? Performance anxiety?"

"But . . . I'm not wearing a codpiece . . ."

"Yay!" Bethany and Solveig crowed in unison.

Under the gleaming eye of Mr. Valhalla, I crossed the stage and stood on the spot where just a short time earlier the unfortunate Hildr Knotte had met his end. There was a fresh bloodstain to help me find my mark. In fact, looking around, the stage was mottled with bloodstains of various size and quality. I swallowed hard, then looked up at the audience. Aelwulf watched from the wings, arms still crossed, but the look on his face was almost anxious. At least he understood how much danger I was in. Solveig waved at me from the front row as she lay half a dozen spears across her muscular thighs. Bethany was weighing a spear in her hands and asking Solveig a series of questions.

I'm not sure if you've ever stared down a couple hundred valkyries eager to throw spears at you. It's not the sort of thing that comes up in everyday life. But if you have, I'm sure you'll understand my predicament. Rows and rows of battle-hardened shieldmaidens loosening their shoulders and testing the tips of their iron spears, discussing with one another the best points of impact for maximum disrobement. Add in the simple fact that I wasn't really wearing that much armor, certainly not in the way that Hildr had been, and I was really beginning to feel like I had reached the top mast of a sinking ship, and was quickly running out of places to go.

"Quite an interesting strategy on this one," Mr. Valhalla bellowed. He pinched the top of my head and turned me back and forth for review. "Perhaps he hopes to make it difficult to hit the armor at all?"

"Or that no one wants to see him naked!" a voice called from the crowd. That met with a round of jeers. I swallowed nervously for, by my count, the millionth time that day.

"They're not all going to throw at once, are they?" I asked.

"Probably not," Mr. Valhalla said. "They will want to knock your armor off one piece at a time. You've so little of it on that they might accidentally kill you otherwise. Kind of defeats the purpose of the competition."

"Oh, well, that's a relief," I said. "I really thought this was going to be dangerous."

"Oh for you it is very dangerous! But look on the positive side," He leaned close and winked. "If you do very well you might prove yourself worthy of Valhalla, and then we can play this game together for the rest of eternity."

"Ah . . . shit," I turned back to the crowd and set my feet. The valkyries were still talking among themselves. I hitched my shield against my shoulder, keeping it in its traditional heater configuration, then drew my sword and prepared to face the onslaught.

"Look, he has a sword! He is going to cut your spears, like a true champion!"

"Don't be ridicu—" I started.

"BEGIN!" Mr. Valhalla boomed.

Fortunately, the valkyries didn't really seem to know what to do with me. For the Hildr Knottes of the world, all they had to do was throw three hundred spears and see what was left when they were done. But I was in just a steel cuirass with interlocking pauldrons over a chain shirt. I wasn't even wearing the lower half of my usual battle kit because . . . well, frankly, because it was uncomfortable to sit in it for a long period of time, and the benches on the Naglfr are notoriously hard. It's almost as if toenail clippings weren't the best material for ergonomic seating. I was regretting that decision.

A few desultory spears arced in from the back of the crowd. Two I was able to simply sidestep, which drew biting jeers from the crowd, and the last I took on my shield. The valkyries started to mutter, and then there was a quick outpouring of spears, at least a dozen, that came from all directions, all thrown with sharp precision and the kind of velocity you'd expect from a ballista. One slammed into my shoulder, piercing the steel and peeling the armor there back like a can opener. I staggered under the impact, huddling behind my shield as iron points dimpled the surface. I felt steel sting the top of my head, and the heavy shaft of a spear rattled against my skull from a near miss.

This seemed to get their blood up. With a roar, a new wave of spears came at me. There had to be at least a hundred this time. I lost sight of the crowd, and the thatched sky, and even the flickering torches that lined the pillars surrounding the stage. All I saw was a swarm of angry spear points bending down toward me like a black-toothed storm wall.

"Ho-ho, here it comes!" Mr. Valhalla hooted.

"You're doing great!" Bethany shouted.

"Screw you guys," I said, then pulled the rip cord on my shield.

Not a literal rip cord. Just the big cooldown, the emergency release, the break in case of fire . . . basically, my best trick. I started by flicking the shield into its tower formation. The steel rim of the shield slammed against the stage. The first spears were already reaching me, glancing off the heavy face of the shield to bury themselves in the wooden planks of the stage. Lumber splintered, and steel dimpled, torquing against the straps and threatening to wrench the shield from my hands. The weight of the falling spears was enough to flatten me if I didn't act soon. I strained against the impetus of their assault, then continued the transformation.

Panels folded out of the side of the shield. One sliced a spear in half as it flew past, sending the shaft clattering across the stage and into Mr. Valhalla's voluminous chest. He was looking at me with growing concern. The blossoming shield hid him and his majestic smile from my view, as it wrapped around me, quickly enveloping me in a cocoon of solid steel. It even sealed at the top, until I was thoroughly protected from the valkyries' attack.

The sound of spears shattering against my shield continued for a few moments. I slumped against the inside of my bulwark until the deadly rain subsided, breathing heavily, thankful for the rest.

"Egress in five seconds," the shield whispered. It never spoke to me at any other time. I had to wonder why it bothered now. I nodded and grabbed the enarme straps that hung from the middle of my steel tomb. "Four . . . three . . . two . . ."

I closed my eyes and braced for impact. On "One!" the panels of the shield blew outward, sending the remnants of the cloud of spears into the crowd and showering the valkyries with the splinters of their own failure. It also only left me with a single panel, a shield slightly smaller than my usual heater and completely drained of its magical power. It was the kind of thing I had to recharge back in my domain, like Matthew's Brilliance, or Tembo's flames, or Gregory's . . . hair care products, I guess?

The crowd sat in stunned silence, staring at me. Splinters and bits of broken spear stuck out of their finely braided hair, and poked through their armor. The panels of the shield had blown far and wide, burying themselves into pillars or the ground. The rest of the Knight Watch team slowly got off the ground. They must have dived for cover when I castled up, familiar as they were with the final form of that transformation. There was a Mr. Valhalla–shaped gap in the debris cloud, and the man himself stood to one side, shaking splinters out of his beard. For the first time since I had met the man, he was not smiling. I laughed.

"Ha! How you like that? Huh? Whatcha think of me now, kids? Not what you were expecting, was it? Was it!" I shouted. From the wings, Aelwulf pinched the bridge of his nose and shook his head sadly.

Because it is never wise to taunt valkyries. Especially when they still have around a hundred spears to throw at you, and your magic shield is out of juice.

Let me repeat: one hundred spears. They only needed the first twenty. The rest were for the fun of it.

CHAPTER ELEVEN

Aelwulf stood over me, his face creased in concern. Not, I suspected, concern for me, but rather concern at the inconvenience of having to mop another pool of blood off his precious stage. Matthew knelt beside him, shoving things back into me and tutting quietly to himself. Finally, he flared a cloud of Brilliance. I felt my bones knit back together.

"There we go, big guy," Saint Matthew said gently. "Good as new."

He helped me into a sitting position, then grabbed me as I toppled over in the other direction, then braced me again as I simply collapsed in place. He poured another draught of Brilliance into my skin to finish his work. But it did nothing for my pride, or my decency. I was wearing half a sock, which was just enough to preserve my privacy, though that ship had sailed long ago. Happily, the valkyries had not tried to kill me. They had simply humiliated me, then left Knight Watch to clean up the mess.

"You look well enough to walk," Aelwulf said. "Come. They must continue the competition."

"So I didn't win?"

"Most certainly not. Quickly now."

He led us to a small tent behind the stage, apparently where the competitors prepared their armor before the contest. As soon as we got there, I sat in the middle of the floor, while the rest of Knight Watch paced around or lounged on uncomfortable stools. *Maybe Vikings don't understand comfort?* I wondered. Esther sat across from me, her arms folded and a distant look in her eye. Aelwulf stood in the entrance of the tent.

"Is there anything else you will need at the moment?" he asked.

"Because I have shield-breaking to arrange, and someone is going to have to slaughter the evening's boar . . ."

"You're free to go," Esther said. "We'll let you know if we need anything."

Aelwulf disappeared, letting the tent flap fall shut. Esther let out a long sigh.

"Sorry, boss," I said. "I did my best."

"Given the circumstances, you performed admirably. Just, in the future . . ."

"Yeah, leave the taunting to things that aren't divine beings, especially ones that are famous for holding a grudge. Got it," I said. "Between Greg's drowning and Tembo getting his ash kicked, it doesn't seem like we did a good job."

"You weren't supposed to win. All you needed to do was enter and not die," Esther said. "So one out of two ain't bad. It was also a good opportunity for the ladies and me to take a look around. Speaking of which . . ." She looked at Chesa and Bethany, her brows raising.

"We looked around," Bethany said. She poked her fingers together bashfully. "Just . . . maybe not at the things we were supposed to be looking at."

"Did you find anything while we were playing the fool for the crowds?" I asked. No offense to the Vikings, but I wanted to get out of Valhalla as soon as I could.

"I'm pretty sure the sword is hanging over the throne, along with every other damned blade this side of the river Styx," Esther said. "Hiding in plain sight, I suppose. But there's no way of knowing. And too many valkyries around to get a good look."

"You think it might be a fake?" Chesa asked.

"Or not there at all. You saw that wall. There are a lot of swords up there," Esther answered. "That's the first place I want the three of you to look tonight."

"I have questions about that," I said. "Are we really just going to walk in there when everyone is asleep and hope no one wakes up?"

"I promise you, no one is going to wake up. They'll be dead," Esther answered. "The honored dead fight until nightfall, then spend the night dead and rise again in the morning. The valkyries spend the nights scouring the lands for warriors worthy of Valhalla."

"Can't be that many of those on the earth," Chesa said.

"Mostly they troll the voice comms on various *Call of Duty* servers," Esther said. "Point is, they won't be around to get in our way. You'll have free rein of the place. I want you to find that sword and steal it." When Matthew gave her a disapproving look, Esther shrugged. "For safekeeping, of course."

"Of course. And when we have the sword, what are we supposed to do?"

"Hide it? Or find another way out that doesn't involve dying. Look, the valkyries won't be there to bother you, and everyone else will be dead. What could go wrong?"

When someone asks you "What could go wrong?" the answer is always "SO MANY THINGS!" Especially when you're dealing with valkyries, and necromancer swords, and zombie Vikings. But at the moment I didn't have any specific examples, or at least none that Esther would accept as evidence. She wouldn't even leave Matthew behind, just in case things went south and we needed a healer.

"We'll actually need to get him into his domain," she said. "You know. In the extremely unlikely event that something does go wrong, we'll need the healer full of light."

Which of course was correct, but it also left me alone with an unmagical mage and a swordsman who could barely lift his sword. Did I mention that my particular skill was defending other people? Yeah, and my armor was scattered ten ways to Sunday, my shield was tapped out, and I was dressed in a sheet.

Nothing could go wrong with this.

Esther said our good-byes to Runa, then we marched back to the Naglfr. Mr. Valhalla shouted at us to "GET OUT!" and "COME BACK WITH REAL MEN!," which felt great. We took off and, as soon as our escort circled back to the mead hall, Esther dove beneath the clouds and dropped the three of us off at the base of the mountain. We hiked back to the little plateau overlooking the great tree and settled in for the night.

"This is a pretty terrible situation," Gregory said. I was beginning to believe his magic really was connected to his hair care routine, because his locks hung in dreary loops across his forehead, having lost their luster. Somehow that made me feel better. "I can't believe she just left us here."

“We are perfectly safe, once night falls,” Tembo said. “Like Esther said, the dead will die, and the valkyries will leave. We should have the beer hall to ourselves.”

“And what do we do once we find the sword?” Greg asked. “Are we really stealing it?”

“If we can get to it, you’d think the bad guys could as well,” I said. “I like the idea of taking it. At least until this whole thing blows over.”

“That would go badly if we’re caught,” Tembo said.

“You think it’s going to go well if we *don’t* steal the sword and get caught?” I asked. “Way I see it, if we’re going to bring down the wrath of a couple hundred valkyries, we might as well get a magic sword out of it.”

“So we steal the sword, and then what?” Greg asked. “How do we get out of here?”

Silence fell over our little group. I looked to Tembo, hoping he had already worked this out. He had not.

“I might be able to open a portal to my domain,” Tembo said. “If not, then I’m sure Esther will think of something.”

“Or she expects us to get caught after the fact. She just wants us to confirm the sword is safe,” I said, as all hope and joy fled my fragile bosom. “Typical.”

“At least Matthew will be fully charged when we get home,” Greg said. “However we get home.”

I grunted and fell silent. We watched as night slowly fell over Valhalla. The singing from the hall below us slowly died out, until the only sound was the wind brushing through the mountains, and the rustle of golden leaves from the massive tree. After a few moments, the doors to Valhalla opened, and the host of valkyries flooded out in a thunder of wings and laughter. They arced up into the sky, breaking into smaller and smaller groups as they fled toward the horizon, until the air was filled with nothing but stars and the silent, silver face of the moon.

“Okay,” Greg said, standing up from his hiding place and stretching the kinks out of his back. “Let’s get this done.”

We made for a pretty pathetic raiding party. Three men hobbling down the mountainside like lame soldiers coming home to die. Tembo had his magic staff in hand, but instead of using it to cast fireballs or summon protective barriers, he leaned hard against it with each step. Gregory d'Backspasm limped along, doubled over in pain, his face pale and waxy. And as for me, well. I was wearing a sheet.

At least we were armed. Both Greg and I had our swords, though he clutched his zweihander to his chest like it was a baby. I was worried the massive sword would topple him over if he tried to wield it. My shield clattered against my back. I hadn't tried to do any magic with it since the armor competition, but it felt like there was nothing left. At least it was still good metal.

We reached the grassy plain and paused to catch our breath. I had a cramp in my leg that ran all the way up my hip, into my back, and deep into my soul. Greg stared sightlessly at the ground, breathing hard enough to swallow the sky. Tembo . . . just looked old. After a few moments of quiet suffering, we headed inside.

The silence was eerie. The dead bodies were eerier. The fact that I had to deal with all of this while wearing nothing more than a sheet was simply degrading, and not eerie at all. But it didn't make things better.

The flickering of flames and our nervous footsteps were the only sounds. Bodies piled on top of bodies covered the benches and slumped onto the rush-covered floor. At least one deceased reveler had toppled into the fire, and was slowly smoldering. I kicked him out of the flames, wrinkling my nose at the smell of burned meat.

"We should probably leave them where they fall," Greg said. "Don't want the valkyries knowing we were here."

"I'll keep that in mind, next time you're lying facedown in a firepit," I said.

"Stop bickering," Tembo said. "We're here to find the sword."

We wove our way through the makeshift cairns, trying to find our way back to the throne. The hall was a disorienting place, much larger inside than out, and now that it was filled wall to wall with corpses, it was really hard to navigate.

I kept looking at the bodies as we passed. They could have been asleep, except a lot of them still had their eyes open, and none of them were breathing. But I didn't see any signs of violence.

"We still don't have a plan for getting out of here, do we?" Greg asked.

"Let's worry about that after we've found the sword. Speaking of which . . ." Tembo slowed down, ducking behind a mound of glistening muscle and beard. I noticed it was Mr. Valhalla, staring sightlessly at the fire, his hands folded in his lap. Even dead, he was a frightening presence. "Quiet, folks. I think we're almost there."

The area around the throne was clear of bodies. I found that a little strange, considering the absolute litter of deceased man-flesh everywhere else, but maybe there was something special about the three seats that even reincarnated Vikings respected. We walked up to the firepit that lay in front of the thrones and looked up.

"We're supposed to search through all of those? It's going to take days," Greg said. "How do we even know it's here?"

"Because this is where Esther said it would be," I answered. "Besides, this is supposed to be every blade that killed one of these Vikings. At least one of them must have fallen to this total-shriek thing."

"Totenschreck," Tembo grumbled. "And I don't think we're going to have to look too far."

"Why's that?" I asked.

Tembo pointed up at the wall. There, among the hand axes, chipped-stone daggers, Celtic swords, Norman swords, Roman swords, Rus swords, scimitars, arrow points, and at least one bullet hole, was a blank space. Something had been there. The stump-end of one of the piled logs still bore the mark of a thrust blade, and the wood beneath it was stained with blood.

Totenschreck was already gone. We were too late.

CHAPTER TWELVE

I stared at the jagged gap in the wall of swords. Surely Esther would have noticed that earlier? Or Runa? Which meant the thief had taken the sword sometime after the valkyries left for their evening of scouring *Call of Duty* servers for worthy knights. Which meant . . .

"We have to get out of here," I said. "Like, now."

"Not without that sword," Gregory said. "We made a promise to Esther."

"I don't remember making a promise," I said. "I remember getting dumped in Valhalla without my pants, while the girls skipped out. We looked for the sword. It's not here. Time to scram."

"They are still saying 'scram'?" Tembo asked. "Fascinating. I would have thought that phrase had passed into obscurity by now."

"It has," Gregory said. "Sir John is just a nerd."

"Okay, okay, whatever. We're all playing dress-up at the end of the world, but I'm the nerd. Whatever." I rubbed my face, then looked around the throne. "The point is that the sword isn't here. So I think we pivot to the escape plan. What do you say?"

"I say we might have to take a detour in our plan," Tembo said. He was facing away from the wall of swords. "We are not alone."

"Of course we're alone. The Viking-bois are dead and the valkyries are doing a girls-night-out thing. Who else is there?" I asked.

"I was going to ask you the same question." The edgelord from the Ren faire stepped out from behind the slumped bulk of Mr. Valhalla. His armor had gone through an upgrade. Glossy black gauntlets and shoulder guards riveted directly to a Victorian-style leather longcoat, worn over Viking-style leather armor. The visor of his helm was forged to look like a face, impassive and pale, eyes and mouth grotesquely large to allow the wearer to breathe and see. Behind the mask I could see red-rimmed sockets and a mouth clenched in a rictus of pain or rage or both. As he walked, the edgelord limped slightly.

He was carrying Totenschreck. The version he bore in the Mickleville Community Center was just a prop made to look like the monstrosity he now wielded. The scabbard was black leather with silver at locket and chape, and the finial at the tip of the scabbard was a spike that looked like it could put Dracula in the ground. The sword belt hung in loose loops in his other hand. All I could see of the sword itself was the hilt, handle, and pommel, but they looked like weathered ivory. Tembo made a hissing sound at the sight of it. My own reaction was more violent.

"Playtime's over, you creep!" I stepped boldly forward, drawing my sword from the makeshift scabbard at my hip and swinging my shield onto my arm. "I don't know how you got in here, or what you think you're going to do with that sword, but Knight Watch is here! And we're going to stop you!"

"You are?" he asked.

"Yes," I said after a moment's hesitation.

"Oh, well then. I surrender."

"You do?"

"Yes, of course. Knight Watch. A very intimidating prospect. And there are three of you," he said. "The warden, whose magical shield I will certainly never get past. And the mage. Why, I'm surprised my skin isn't already burned to a crisp, with the likes of Tembo on hand. And finally, the knight, with his mighty sword. A pity it couldn't have been Clarence. That would have been some kind of poetic justice." He gestured magnanimously. "Three of you, and only one of me. I am surely defeated. Why resist?"

"Well. Good. We accept your surrender," I said, though I noticed he hadn't really moved.

"Except! Except for one thing. You aren't really the warden right now, are you?" With a song of steel and leather, he drew Totenschreck and pointed it at me, tip unwavering as it drew a line to my heart. The blade was made of some kind of sickly green metal, and glowed with inner fire. "The magic of your shield is used up, isn't it? And I suspect the reason Tembo has not already burned me to cinders is simply that he is out of gas. Aren't you, mage?"

"One thing you haven't counted on," Gregory said. Even though his face was pale and slick with sweat, he spoke with strength. He unlimbered his massive zweihander and brought it to a guard position, stepping forward. "I may not have my magic, but steel is steel, and I'm willing to bet I can still take you in a fair fight."

"A good point," the black-cloaked swordsman said. "But there is something that you have not taken into consideration as well." He brought Totenschreck to the salute position, touching it lightly to the forehead of his gruesome mask. "Some of the souls who died by this steel were Vikings. Dead in battle, and certainly worthy of Valhalla."

He whispered something into the sword. The steel changed, striking a clear note like a tuning fork that washed out across the beer hall. The sound made my skin crawl.

Out in the mounds and piles of dead flesh, there came a chorus of muttering voices. The shadows shifted. I caught sight of fingers twitching, spines straightening, the horrid clatter of teeth snapping convulsively shut. I took a step back, preparing for the rush.

Then Mr. Valhalla groaned and stood up. His eyes were pale white orbs, and a ghostly light wafted from his open mouth. He slumped forward to stand next to Totenschreck's dark wielder.

"Okay," Gregory said. "Now I'm willing to talk about an escape plan."

"Looooooozzzzzersssss," Mr. Valhalla groaned. "Unworthy of Valhalla. BE GONE!"

"Gladly!" I yelped, but he was already bearing down on me. I brought up my shield just as he thumped down at me with one of his meaty fists. The impact threw me flat to the ground. I scrambled back until Tembo pulled me to my feet. My shield lay next to the firepit, well out of reach. I could see my sword, though.

"I know he's a big guy, but that feels a little over the top," I said.

"He is a legend of Valhalla, Sir John," Tembo said. "They are not mere mortal musclemen."

Mr. Valhalla turned and wrenched one of the benches out of the ground. Twelve feet long and hewn from the heartwood of a single tree, the bench must have weighed a thousand pounds. Mr. Vee propped it on one shoulder like he was waiting for his turn at bat.

"Okay, that does seem a bit much," Tembo agreed. "Gregory?"

"Let's go, Captain Testosterone. Let's see you bench press three feet of razor-sharp German steel!" Greg lifted his zweihander over his head and charged, wobbling, forward.

Mr. Valhalla met him with the long edge of the bench, swinging the lumber with both hands. Greg yelped and went flying. He landed on the other side of a pile of still-dead Vikings with a clatter of armor.

The hulking mass of resurrected Viking meat turned back to where Tembo and I stood. He smiled crookedly and hefted the bench once again.

"I like having other people do my fighting for me," the edgelord said. "But you know all about that, don't you, John?"

"I take it you've got nothing in the tank, Tem?" I asked, ignoring the man's taunt. "A portal could come in real handy right about now."

"I'm as cold as a drowned rat," he said.

"That works better with wetness," I said. "But I get the idea. After you!"

Tembo scrambled over the throne and I followed, ducking behind the dais. We were trapped between Mr. Valhalla and the wall of swords. The shadows thrown against the wall told me that our glistening attacker had crossed the firepit, but then he hesitated. Must have been something about the throne itself that gave him pause. I grabbed Tembo by the collar.

"You get to Greg. If he's still alive, then the two of you get outside and go back up that mountain. Hide out until dawn."

"What are you going to do?"

"Maybe earn a place in Valhalla," I said. "Just run when I say run, okay?"

We were interrupted by a titanic roar from the other side of the throne. The back of the tri-seat creaked and then lifted off the ground, revealing Mr. Valhalla, sweating, straining, his face screwed up with the effort of deadlifting the throne.

"Deadlifting," I muttered. "That'll be funny later. Tembo, RUN!"

But of course being a rational human and not an idiot obsessed with slightly funny wordplay, Tembo had already lit out for the hills, his robe flapping like a banner on a rocket ship. Mr. Valhalla and the edgelord watched him vault the stacked bodies, then slowly turned back to look at me.

"I guess that means I go this way," I said, then ran in the other direction.

Mr. Vee dropped the throne with a boom, then loped after me. His feet came down like cannon shots in my wake. Fortunately it seemed to take a lot of energy to move a body that big, and I was motivated by fear. I scrambled around the corner of a row of benches lined with temporary corpses, then rolled between the feet of a couple of them and belly-crawled into the row. By the time I came up, I could hear Mr. Vee already passing me by. Not very clever, the big muscle guys. That's why I wasn't a big muscle guy. Right. That was the reason.

Without a weapon, or a shield, or pants, there was no way I was going to face off with Zombie Valhalla, much less the creepy dude pulling his strings. My best chance was to hide out until the valkyries returned, or hope that Esther could find a way back into the realm. Our plan depended on the fact that we should have been alone to retrieve the Totenschreck. Now that the edgelord had shown up, we were screwed.

Which brought up an interesting question: How did this guy get inside? Did Runa know he was here? Had she cleared the hall so he could grab the sword unopposed? Was that why she had encouraged us to participate in the games, so we'd be drained and have to return to Mundane Actual?

What was going on here?

My thought process was interrupted by a splintering sound ahead of me. A bench-full of slumping Vikings tumbled into the aisle in front of me, and Mr. Vee's ghostly eyes appeared among the shadows. I ducked under another bench, crawling until I reached an extinguished firepit that let me squirm into another row without being seen. My pursuer bellowed his frustration. I went the other direction. The thundering crash of footsteps let me know that Mr. Valhalla was in close pursuit.

I skirted the edge of the fighting pits, trying to stay out of sight as best I could, even though Mr. Valhalla's lumbering pursuit never seemed to vary. I leapt across a firepit whose coals hadn't yet gone cold, then shimmied between two benches before finding myself on the edge of a long row of fighting pits. Most were still occupied, their last combatants lying cold and dead in the sand. I grabbed a discarded sword from one corpse, then unhooked an unattended round shield from a rack before dashing beneath a table littered with cold meat and half-filled flagons of ale.

It amazed me how variable the corpses strewn across the hall were. I would think that if you were preparing to die, and did so every night, you would find a nice place to lie down and expire. To cut down on the backaches, at the very least, if not to avoid burning all night in a firepit, or waking up with a lung full of bloody sand. But the Vikings lay in every possible posture, some with food hanging half out of their mouths, or a sword pressed lovingly into their spleens, or worse. And by the persistent smell of urine and . . . worse . . . it seemed like many of the honored dead hadn't bothered to relieve themselves before death came knocking. It made me shudder.

"Wouldn't want to be their janitor. Or their laundry guy," I said to myself. And that made me think of the feral janitors who haunted the depths of Mundane Actual, excreting vile chemicals to consume bloodstains and other unmentionable acts. "Those two would probably be really comfortable in this place."

Maybe whatever magic brought these idiots back to life also cleaned their underwear. Anything was possible in the magical land of Valhalla.

"He's going to find you!" The voice came from right next to my foot. I jumped, banging my head against the bottom of the table, then came down on something hard and round that immediately started to chew on my kneecap. I screamed and kicked it away, which prompted another round of screaming from whatever I had landed on. I watched as it rolled against a table leg and came to a stop. It was the volleyball.

Volleyball head. Volleyhead? Anyway.

It looked like the head of a Viking warrior, the skin shrunken and stretched tight over its skull. It wore a steel cap crooked across its scalp, covering one sunken eye, while the other contained a wrinkled, blackened eyeball. Its nose was gone, but its mouth hung open, revealing many yellow teeth and a dry, cracked husk of a tongue. The head kept screaming.

"Will you shut up?" I hissed. "There's an undead Viking trying to tear my spine out!"

The head's jaw clapped shut. It rolled that blackened eye around to look at me. I think it winked at me, but it might have just blinked.

"Thank you," I whispered.

"My pleasure," the ball answered.

"Aren't you supposed to be dead?" I asked.

"I am," it said. "Are there a lot of living decapitated heads where you come from?"

"No. But the dead decapitated heads are a lot less talkative."

"Oh! Yes, I suppose they would be," the ball said. Then it stared up at the underside of the table with a distant, contemplative look. "But I'm not really understanding your question, then."

"I mean," I said, "shouldn't you be dead and quiet, like the rest of these folks?"

"Ah, that's the point of it. I see now. No, no, I'm sort of their mascot. A draugr, you understand. The living dead."

"An actual zombie. That's a refreshing change of pace." There was no sound of Mr. Valhalla, or the Totenschreck guy, so I settled onto my haunches. "So is it always like this? Vikings littering the ground like worms after a hard rain?"

"No, no, not at all. They usually sing a little song and then tuck into their grave goods. Bit different tonight," the draugr said. "Not often they forget to put me back on my body. Don't know how I'm supposed to clean everything up like this. Drag myself around on my tongue, I guess. Going to be a hell of a night."

"Wait, so this is different? What happened?"

"Don't know. Everyone just dropped. Floki was carrying me back to my body, but instead he, you know, shat himself and flopped over. I rolled under here. I thought it was going to be kind of dull until you showed up."

"Were the valkyries still here?" I asked.

"Yes, yes, of course. They don't bugger off until after the nightly burials. They seemed quite upset. Said something about that Esther bitch, and went flying. Glad I'm not one of her lot." The head thought for a moment, then squinted at me. "Say, weren't you with them? You're one of those mortal thingies, aren't you?"

"Me? No, no, of course not. I'm . . . just like you."

"You don't smell like me. You smell like fear." The ball grimaced, then started rolling away, using a clever combination of its jaw and forehead. I grabbed for it. "Help! Help! Someone help me!" it shouted.

A shadow fell across the table just as I was coming out from under its protective cover. I looked up, right into Mr. Valhalla's steely eyes.

"Ah. Shoot."

"You are a failure!" Mr. Valhalla screamed.

"Maybe! But at least I know how to wear pants!" I rolled to my feet, bringing up my stolen sword and shield. Unfortunately, my sheet caught on the edge of the table, and tore free from my waist, making my whole "pants" line kind of irrelevant. I blushed furiously.

Mr. Valhalla keeled straight back, landing like a felled tree in the forest. I stared at him for a long moment. He didn't move. I looked down at my nakedness.

"I mean, it's not *that* bad," I said.

"For a mortal," Runa said. She descended from the ceiling on slow, steady wings, flanked on both sides by a dozen valkyries.

"Oh, gods, why does this keep happening to me?" I muttered.

"Because you make poor decisions," Runa said. "Now. You're going to have to answer some questions." She landed hard on the edge of the table, scattering cold turkey and drenching me in warm ale. "Starting with: What have you done with the Totenschreck?"

CHAPTER THIRTEEN

I stumbled onto the moonlit expanse of the grassy field in a daze. Now that night had fully fallen, I noticed that the tree in front of the beer hall glowed with an inner light. Veins of gold and amber shimmered through its bark, and the leaves seemed to pulse in soft waves of crimson radiance. It was by this light that I was able to make out the host of valkyries gathered on the lawn. Their eyes reflected the tree's light, making them look like a pack of wolves, crouching in the shadows.

They weren't alone. The crowd parted, and three figures entered the clearing. Esther looked a little roughed up, and Bethany had a bruise across her cheek and manacles on her wrists. Chesa seemed alright, but there was fear in her eyes. A pair of armored valkyries flanked them, as though standing guard. They wore close-fitting helms that covered their faces, and their plate mail was painted black. Revna stepped forward and shoved Esther and the girls to the ground.

"I take it things didn't go according to plan?" I asked.

"We didn't really have much of a plan in the first place," Esther said. "But what we had kind of fell apart."

"Where's Matthew?"

"Cooling his heels with the Naglfr." Esther craned her neck to look behind me, scanning the crowd. "Tembo? Gregory?"

"They were hiding in the privy," Runa said. She gestured, and four valkyries paraded in, carrying a pair of spits between them. Our mage and our knight hung from the spits like bound pigs, both of them dripping wet. "We hosed them off for you."

"More like they tied us to the Jörmungandr and let us do a couple cycles through the wash," Tembo said. "We're going to need the saint. And some towels."

"Saint never got to his domain," Bethany said. "They've been holding us just the other side of the mountain, waiting for you three to screw up."

"Which brings us to the interesting part of our conversation," Runa said, very loudly, and with special emphasis on the word *interesting*. "You have taken our sword. I want it back. NOW!"

"That wasn't us!" I said. "The edgelord was here! The guy from the Ren faire!"

"We know that isn't true," Runa said. "No one enters Valhalla without my permission. And you are the only mortals to enter these grounds in the last fifty years. So, again, where is my sword?"

"If John says we don't have it, we don't have it," Esther said. "You've searched our ship, our clothes, I'm assuming you've searched John's sheet. Now let us go."

"They might have hidden it somewhere on the grounds," Revna said. "Shall I have them killed until they tell us where it is?"

"If you kill us, how are we supposed to tell you anything?" I asked.

"We have our ways," she answered, stepping forward menacingly.

"That will not be necessary, Revna. If the sword is here, we will find it," Runa said. She gave us one last look, then turned away. "I just want these mortals out of my realm. Expel them."

"Thank the gods," Chesa said. "I never thought I'd be glad to get on that damned toenail ship."

"Oh, no," Runa said, glancing back at us. "You are in clear violation of our agreement. Until this matter is cleared up, we are keeping the boat."

"But then how are we supposed to get back home?" I asked.

I did not want to know.

The words "Rainbow Bridge" imply a certain amount of calm. They imply beauty, and grace, and perhaps trippy visual effects from the 1960s. They do not, in my opinion, imply falling out of the sky at a million miles an hour with nothing between you and the ground but colored light.

My point is that the Bifrost is misnamed. "Screaming Gravity

Chute" is more accurate. "Colorful Terminal Trajectory," perhaps. "Pissing yourself at a hundred miles an hour while riding a slide full of glitter" is a lot closer.

Regardless of the name, we fell screaming from the sky. Esther handled it better than the rest of us, plummeting with her arms folded across her chest and her face set in an impressive scowl. At least they gave me my clothes and weapons back before they tossed us in the gravity cannon. The feral janitors would have been very disappointed if I did all this terror-urinating without a pair of breeches to be cleaned afterward. There was nothing magical about this bridge. Well. There was nothing magical about the first couple hundred miles of howling, madness-inducing, stomach-churning velocity. That last ten feet were technically magic, because just as we were about to splatter into the ground we came to a complete stop, in violation of all the laws of physics and inertia, somehow floating the final bit of our plummet like butterflies. Not that I stopped screaming, mind you. I was locked into the screaming at that point. At least in the darkness you couldn't see the stains.

We landed on the outskirts of a grassy field, somewhere deep in the heart of nowhere. It was hours until morning, and the cold night air burned as I sucked it into my lungs. I lay panting on the ground, trying to recover my composure and failing, all while my heart hammered in my chest like a dwarf angry at his anvil. After a few minutes I realized I was the only one still screaming and shut up. At least the others had the decency to stare up at the sky in wide-eyed horror for a while. Finally, Esther cleared her throat.

"So you really don't have the sword?" she asked.

"My gods, Esther, no! Do you think I'd suffer through all that if I had the sword?" I asked. "I'm not that kind of brave."

"No. I suppose you're not. I was just hoping you were that kind of clever." She stood up and dusted herself off, then snapped her fingers. "On your feet, squad. It's going to be a long walk. We need to get home by first light."

"Walk? We have to walk? Do you even know where we are?" Chesa asked.

"Of course I know where we are," Esther said, pointing. "MA is about ten miles that way. Didn't you see it on the way down?"

"Was it on the inside of my eyelids?" Chesa asked.

"No."

"Then no, I did not see it on the way down."

"How could you tell? Everything's dark. I can barely see my hand in front of my face," I said.

"There are certain beacons set out, in case we have to crash-land the Naglfr," Tembo rumbled. "Though I did not see them. To be fair, I was not looking for them, so much as I was staring at the ground, and our imminent deaths."

"Man, you guys would have hated Normandy. It was that, but with flak, and a hundred-pound ruck on your back." Esther rubbed the small of her back. "At least this time no one's shooting at us. Yet. Let's go!"

Groaning, the rest of the team worked their way to their feet and started after Esther, before we lost her in the darkness.

"Boss," I said, hurrying to catch up with the gray-haired whirlwind. "I think Runa's lying."

"No kidding," Esther said. "This nonsense about us taking the sword and hiding it in Valhalla . . . it's just delusional."

"No, I mean, about more than that." I told her what the volleyball had told me, about the untimely deaths, and the valkyries' sudden flight. "Something happened up there that they weren't expecting. It's too bad you were still in flight. I thought you would have made it back to Mundane Actual by then."

"Wait, it was already dark?" Esther asked. "You didn't go in too early, like an idiot?"

"Sorry to disappoint, boss, but no. We waited just like we were supposed to. Even had time to explore a little bit. But once the edgelord showed up, it was all dodging tables and hiding in the shadows."

"That's . . . interesting." Esther was silent for a dozen vigorous strides, then looked over at me. "They picked us up right away. Those two in the black armor. Swooped out of the clouds and detained us. We thought you'd already been picked up."

"Unless time moves a lot differently on that mountain, we were still hunkered down, waiting for night to fall," I said.

"That means we're dealing with more than a single rogue valkyrie playing muse to a disgruntled outsider," she said. "Chesa, did either of those valkyries look familiar?"

Chesa trotted to match our stride. "The tall-and-quiets?" she asked. "No, why would they?"

"They were in on it. Picked you up before things went bad in Valhalla, then held you until Runa came looking," I said. "So maybe one of them was the same as what we met in Mickleville."

"I don't think so. But hard to say with those helms on," she said.

"So we're maybe looking at three, and if there are three, there'll be more," Esther said. "No time for a leisurely stroll. We need to get home. I want to talk to Clarence."

"What does Clarence have to do with this?" I asked.

"He's the one who killed the bearer of Totenschreck last time around," Esther answered. Then she fell into a steady jog that, while it didn't look fast, quickly left the rest of us in the dust.

Chesa groaned and looked at me. "What did you say to her!"

"Well, it certainly wasn't *Can we please run ten miles in the dark?*," I said. "You can't blame me for this."

"You have no concept of my capacity for blaming you for things, John," Chesa said. Then we all started running, before we lost sight of Esther completely.

The last time I was in Clarence's domain, it was to die. Repeatedly. This was right after I had first joined Knight Watch, while Chesa and I were still in training. Neither of us knew what to expect. What we got was stabbed in the gut each time we screwed up a sword form. But at least we also got to meet a friendly dragon named Kyle.

The entrance to Clarence's domain is in one of the subbasements of Mundane Actual, tucked behind a rather average-looking door. After Clarence retired from the active team, his portal was moved out of the barrel-ceilinged great hall that serves as our central meeting place.

"Try to not get him too worked up," Esther said, handing us each a damp burlap sack. "If he knows there's trouble in the real world, he's going to try to rejoin the team, and frankly our insurance won't cover that."

"We're there to ask Clarence about a magical Nazi zombie sword," I said. "How are we supposed to do that without making it seem like a big deal?"

"Well, of course you'll have to tell Clarence," she said. "It's Kyle I don't want you to upset. What did you think the bags were for?"

"To be honest, I've gotten used to you handing me inexplicably damp packages full of"—I glanced inside the bag—"what appear to be intestines."

"Pig," Esther said. "If he gets curious, just swing them around your head a couple times and give it a throw. And whatever you do, don't get any on you." She shuttled us toward the door. "He sometimes has trouble telling the difference between human in pig blood and just plain old pig. Kyle's more of a bite first, ask questions later type."

"And you're not coming with us?" Chesa asked, holding the dripping mass of her sack at arm's length.

"I need to get down to Reality Control, see if the Actuator can get a fix on what happened to that sword," Esther said. "Don't worry, you'll have plenty of time to catch up with Clarence. Time moves funny down there."

"Tell me about it," Bethany said. "Last time I saw the old guy, he was still talking like bell bottoms were a thing."

"They're not?" Matthew asked, clearly distressed.

"Enough chatter," Esther said. "In you go!" And she pushed us bodily through the portal, barely waiting for my boots to clear the threshold before slamming the door shut.

We were surrounded by darkness. This is always how it is, when entering domains—magical places unique for each member of Knight Watch that supposedly reflect our mythic identities. We went there to recharge our powers after a mission, or to detox following a long exposure to the mundane world. Mine was a cabin in the very dark woods—a warm, cozy place that felt like the home I never knew I missed. Chesa's somehow involved shirtless elf princes and treetop palaces, while Tembo lived on a grass-swept plain, haunted by elephant spirits and the promise of death. Clarence's was a little more typically fantastic. Frankly, he lived in the kind of place I thought I would get, with a majestic castle surrounded by primeval woods and populated by invisible servants. It was also under constant threat of being destroyed by Kyle, the dragon. So there were trade-offs, I suppose.

The darkness passed, and we found ourselves on a forest path.

Every domain had a pathway in, an exit out, and a hearth that served as the center of the mystical world, and this softly lit trail winding its way through an ancient forest was the pathway into Clarence's mythic identity. Our clothes changed slightly as well, bringing them more in line with Clarence's vision of the knightly fantasy. Matthew looked like a slightly drunk monk, tonsure and all, while Tembo squinted out from under a peaked wizard's cap and swooshing blue robes. Gregory and I stayed mostly the same, but Bethany and Chesa transformed into maidens, with velvet overdresses and light-colored tunics. Even as a maiden, Bethany displayed more knives across waist, thigh, and sleeve than an overstocked butcher's block.

"What's the problem with this Kyle person?" Gregory asked. "Is he some kind of cannibal?"

"Kyle's a dragon," I said. "A real sweetie. Nothing to worry about."

"So little to worry about that we've been given pig guts to take care of it."

"Yeah, well. Living the dream."

"This is sort of disappointing," Chesa said, looking down at her dress. "How am I supposed to fight in this?"

"You look nice," I said.

"Now it's downright horrifying," she answered. "I can't go on like this! I'm taking it off."

"Even better," Gregory said with a smile. Chesa punched him, but a great deal lighter than she would have punched me if I said something like that. By the time we got to the edge of the forest, they were joking and laughing and having a grand old time.

The bastards.

Fortunately, I was spared the misery of their conversation by the appearance of Clarence's castle. It was less grand than I remembered, though maybe in retirement Clarence had settled into a smaller space, with fewer crenellations to clean and hallways to dust. Besides, he didn't need the training grounds anymore.

The castle proper sat on a hill at the head of a little valley, flanked by a river on one side and a precipitous cliff on the other. Concentric rings of stone walls led to the top of the hill, where a single tower rose into a sky the color of sapphires. We followed the long trail down to the castle. There was a small village on the banks of the river, but it looked empty and dark, though a few columns of woodsmoke seemed to indicate some form of habitation. We reached the main gate of the castle, a massive twenty-foot-tall double door, bound in iron and thick enough to keep out a dragon. I kept one eye to the skies the whole time, but there was no sign of Clarence's scaly companion.

"So what do we do? Knock?" Gregory asked.

"Worth a try," I said. I pounded on the door with the pommel of my sword, but that only produced a dull thud.

"I could probably scale this," Bethany said.

"Let's not go breaking into someone else's fantasy world," I said. "You never know what you're going to find. I'd rather not stumble across the old guy in the bath."

"Hey," Chesa said. "There's a pull-rope over here."

"Seems pretty obvious," Bethany said. She grabbed the rope and, leaving her feet, gave it a mighty pull.

At first it was just one church bell, ringing in steady rhythm, but then another joined it from the far end of the castle, and then another, and another. Soon the whole castle shook with the sound of hundreds of bells, gonging and tolling, pealing and re-pealing, until the air seemed to vibrate with the sound of their song. We stood at the gate with our hands over our ears until they slowly, one by one, fell silent. My whole skeleton hummed with the aftershock. We waited.

And waited.

For a long time.

"I'm starting to worry," Chesa said.

"This is a little strange," I said too loudly. I had been the last to get my hands over my ears, and the ringing sound in my skull was like a small blacksmith had taken up residence between my ears. "Maybe Bee should go in after all?"

"There you are! I thought I heard someone messing about!" Clarence shouted. He popped over the top of the wall, his head wreathed in a wild mane of white hair. "Whatever are you doing here?"

"Looking for you, Sir Clarence," I said. "We have some questions about an old mission."

"Well, I've certainly got the *old* part covered," he said with a laugh. His face fell as he saw what we were all carrying in our hands. "My gods, what on earth are those?"

I lifted my bag. “We brought Kyle some treats.”

“Well, you better get rid of them. He’s off meat. Got himself a cat, and now we all have to eat vegetables and bits of moss. It’s bloody awful,” Clarence said. “Come on inside! Kyle will be thrilled to see you!”

He disappeared behind the wall. A few minutes later the gate creaked open.

“A dragon who’s gone off meat?” Gregory mused. “What has the world come to?”

“I’m more worried about the cat,” I said, tossing my bag by the side of the road. The others followed suit, and then we went inside.

CHAPTER FOURTEEN

Clarence led us through the courtyard and into the great hall at the foot of the central tower. The space was only dimly lit by smoldering coals in the fireplace at the end of the hall, but as Clarence entered, a series of torches along the walls came to life. A table ran the length of the room, with benches and a set of more comfortable looking chairs nearest the hearth, along with a handful of rugs on the floor and tapestries on the walls. The tapestries appeared to depict scenes from Clarence's days in Knight Watch. At least, that was my assumption. I don't remember a lot of fire-breathing helicopters in the Bayeux Tapestry. There was food on the table, as well, and glasses of wine, enough for all of us. That's how it was last time I was here, as well. Meals appearing in empty rooms whenever they were needed. I didn't even realize I was hungry until the smell of freshly baked bread and thick gravy filled my nose. I made for the table.

That's when I saw that what I had mistaken for coals were actually cinders curling out of the nostrils of Clarence's tame dragon, Kyle.

Kyle lay curled in the fireplace, with his scaly butt sticking out into the room, and his back pressed hard against the mantel. His jaws rested primly on paws the size of heater shields, and with each deep, snoring breath, a plume of flame licked across the stone floor. In the crook of Kyle's neck nestled a white puffball of fur, no bigger than my head, snoring in time with the rise and fall of the dragon's chest.

"Oh, it's a kitty!" Chesa squealed. "I wanna hug it!"

Both Kyle and the puffball snapped their eyes open at Chesa's approach. A long cloud of scalding hot smoke rolled out of Kyle's nostrils, driving Chesa back. Clarence snorted.

"My advice is you let the cat come to you. Or hope it ignores you," he said. "Claws like fish hooks, that one has. I've taken to wearing my chain mail again. Bloody inconvenient."

"Commissar Snowflake loves you, Clarence," Kyle rumbled. "You feed him."

"Yes, well, the commissar has a strange way of showing affection." The old knight sat down in one of the comfortable chairs near the hearth, snatched up a goblet of wine, and leaned back, with his feet on the table. "So. To what do I owe the pleasure of your company?"

"We're having trouble with a Nazi zombie sword," I said, settling into my own chair. The rest of the team took seats. "Esther said you were involved in beating it last time around."

"And which Nazi zombie sword is this?" Clarence asked.

"There was more than one?" I asked. Without thinking, I shoveled some of the stuff on my plate onto a slice of bread and shoved it in my mouth. It was . . . highly textured. And inedible. I opened my mouth and let it dribble back onto the plate. When I looked up, Clarence caught my eye and smiled uncomfortably.

"Mostly moss when I'm not around," he said under his breath. "Can't get the medieval spirits to quite understand the idea behind a vegetarian diet. They try, but . . ." He pushed food-shaped lumps around his plate with disappointment. "They are rarely successful."

"We were talking about Nazi zombie swords," Chesa prompted. "You said there was more than one of them?"

"Sure. They had a whole division dedicated to mythic inquiry. A lot of it fell to Nik's team to handle, but we got the odd resurrected giant or soul-bomb tossed our way. There was a whole operation to bind the ghost of Joan of Arc and crown her Queen of Vichy France. Went about as well as you might expect." He took a long drink of wine, then fished an apple out of the bowl in front of him and peered at it nervously. He took a slow bite, chewing carefully until he was sure it was just an apple. Then he smiled and turned his attention back to us. "So what are we talking about here?"

"The Totenschreck," Tembo said.

"Ah, the valkyries. Always a good time when the valkyries are around. Runa still in charge up there?" he asked. Tembo nodded, and Clarence continued, crunching happily into his apple. "A good one, Runa Hellesdottir. I know she and Esther don't get along, but I wouldn't trade that month in the Hebrides for the world. But the Totenschreck was a nasty business. One of the Kraut scientists found a way to harness the power of Freya's tears, forged it into a blade, and just started wreaking havoc in the Ardennes."

"What exactly does it do? We've seen it in action, or at least a facsimile," Gregory said. "It killed with a touch."

"Worse than that," Clarence said. "I mean, you're right, it doesn't take more than a slice to lay a soldier low. We buried most of a company the first time we met that damnable blade. But the worst part came in the morning." Another bite of the apple, and Clarence stared off into the middle distance, lost in thought. "Those bodies came clawing back up out of their graves, biting and shooting and mean as a hellcat. No offense." This last part was to Commissar Snowflake, who was now watching our conversation with eerie yellow eyes. "Every day we had to kill them again, and every morning they came back. And all the while, the Totenschreck kept adding to their number. Didn't stop until we killed the bearer, and separated the sword from the Tears."

"Why didn't you just burn the bodies? Or put them in steel boxes?" Bethany asked.

"Because this was more than just a cheap zombie movie. These things were mythic. Their actual bodies didn't really matter. Every time they died, their souls went up to Folksvangr to wait. And every morning, the Totenschreck brought them back down. Burning the bodies just meant the Nazis could summon them somewhere else, hundreds, maybe thousands of miles away. Wherever the sword was, that's where they showed up." Clarence threw his apple into the fire, apparently forgetting that Kyle occupied the hearth. The seedy core bounced off Kyle's forehead and tumbled to the ground. Snowflake rose from her nest and went to sniff at the apple, mewing quietly. "They're drawn to it. Like flies to meat."

"You said the souls went to folks winger? I think you mean Valhalla," I said.

"What? No, lad. Folksvangr. The field of the people. Valhalla is only where half the honored dead go. The other half belong to Freya, and end up in Folksvangr. Read a book."

"So killing the guy who carried the sword ended it? The zombies all went back to being dead?" Gregory asked.

"Not at all. We had to hunt them down one at a time and put them back in the grave. And even then, their souls are still up in Folksvangr, waiting to be called again," Clarence said. "If someone manages to reunite the sword and the Tears, all those dead soldiers are going to come roaring back to life. Kill them all you want. They'll be back."

"That sounds bad," I said. "How many do you think it is?"

"Enough to kick off Ragnarok," Tembo said quietly.

"More than enough for that. Valhalla will have to summon their hosts to counter, and Fenrir will come looking for his moon pie." Clarence pushed his food around on his plate one more time, searching fruitlessly for something that could be consumed by the human digestive system, then poured himself another glass of wine. "You said you've encountered a facsimile of the sword, which means someone is training a new bearer. But as long as the real deal is safe in Valhalla, you've nothing to worry about."

"It's not," I said. "Someone got it last night, right in the middle of the Mr. Valhalla competition. Runa blames us."

"Hmm. That sounds like trouble." He drew another apple from the pile and crunched into it loudly. "Next step is to find the Tears. Because if those two get together, you're going to have a lot of dead soldiers coming for you."

"Great. That's just great. Runa says she doesn't know where they are."

"I'll bet she doesn't," he said. "But I do. Or, more accurately, I know someone who does."

"Who?" Chesa asked.

"The last zombie," Clarence said. "Nice guy. You'll like him."

"Wait, some of those things are still wandering around?" Tembo asked. "Esther said that operation was over. You rounded up the last of those guys in the eighties!"

"I made my last kill in 1984, at a roller skating rink in suburban Charlotte," Clarence said. "But there was one left. Clever fellow. Managed to hide for a very long time. Kept moving around so no one would get curious about their ageless neighbor. I just couldn't bring myself to kill him."

"Clarence! He's a zombie!" Bethany said.

"Maybe. But he's also a hell of a gardener. Anyone who can grow roses like that can't be all that dead," Clarence said. "Besides, it sounds like my mercy was providential. If anyone can find the Tears of Freya, it's Percy."

"As in Sir Percival?" Gregory asked.

"As in Percipept Humboldt-Hastings the Fourth," Clarence said, "Apparently it's a family name."

"Family name or no, I can't imagine calling a kid Percipept," Chesa said.

"Not that part. The Fourth," Clarence said. "His dad was named Billy. Actually, Billiam Humboldt-Hastings"—he made a rolling gesture with his hand—"the Fourth."

"So where is he now?" I asked. "Still moving around?"

"No. That was too dangerous. He had to come up with a new identity each time, and the cops were getting curious. Plus he had to start his garden over with every iteration, and that was a bloody tragedy," Clarence said. "I helped him out. Carved off a slice of the old Unreal and gave him some cover. The neighbors don't get curious anymore. As long as he keeps his head down, no one's the wiser."

"But you can get us to him?" I asked.

"Quick as a whistle," he answered, standing up and wiping his hand on the bristling back of Commissar Snowflake. Kyle lifted his head and let out a disapproving snort. "We can walk there from here."

CHAPTER FIFTEEN

Doors out the back of the great hall led to a garden maze that buzzed with swarms of honeybees and the fragrant scent of flowers in full bloom. Pebbled pathways wound between hedgerows that were shaped with laser-sharp precision, leading to a collection of small fountains and statues that peeked between walls of green shrubbery like shy animals. The sky overhead was pearly blue, fading to cobalt in the west. The silver crescent of the moon hung overhead.

"Wasn't it already night back in the castle?" Chesa asked.

"It's always dusk here. Something about the capital 'E' Empire, I think," Clarence said. "Unless it's raining. You can always tell his mood by the rain."

"Prone to depression?" I asked.

"Exactly the opposite. The madman seems happier when it rains. Here we are! Percy!" Clarence stomped toward a bush that was shivering by the edge of the path. His approach startled the bush, which leapt up from its planting and scurried away, like a pheasant flushed from . . . well, itself. "Percy! It's me! Stop being a boob!"

The bush paused in its retreat, though not in its shivering. A thin face emerged from the foliage, itself made up largely of bent twigs and misplaced leaves, with two round eyes as round and as white as the moon. The face blinked at Clarence several times, then revealed itself to be in possession of a smile, though a timid one.

"Clarence!" the face said. "You shouldn't sneak up on a man like that! Still got the nerves from your last visit! Is he . . ." The face, obviously belonging to Percipept Humboldt-Hastings IV, narrowed suddenly, and his eyes darted around our company. "Is *he* here?"

"He's back at the castle," Clarence said soothingly. "I promise, there won't be a repeat of that incident."

"Bloody well hope," Percy said, then emerged from the bush, which proved to be a kind of portable shed made of woven vines, just large enough for a very thin man capable of folding himself into a very small ball, should the need arise. Which was precisely what Percy happened to be. From narrow shoulders to bony chest, and limbs that seemed too thin to support their own weight, Percy was every inch the traditional ghast, except for the fact that he seemed very much alive and willing to smile. He was wearing a tweed body suit with more pockets than the most enthusiastic janitor could imagine, and a pair of rubber galoshes. His hands were caked in mud, which did not prevent him from offering a handshake to Clarence. The knight demured.

"What's with the shack, Percy?" Clarence asked, nodding to the woven shed. "Expecting an air raid?"

"Garden gnomes," Percy answered. "Been lingering ever since that thing with the fountain." He looked us over, nodding to Tembo, squinting at Chesa, smiling brilliantly at me and Greg. "One of the fountains started spouting blood. Damned arterial, it was. Thought it might be a witch thing, but Clarence assured me it was just an aberration. Had gnomes ever since. Nasty buggers."

"Garden gnomes?" Chesa asked. "Fat little fellows with the pointy hats?"

"Aye, the same. Ambushed me in the topiary maze, first time I saw them. Teeth like razor wire, and as crafty as mad foxes." Percy shivered, rubbing his wide hands together. Flakes of dried mud tumbled to the ground. "Been staying in ever since. But the petunias needed replanting, and they weren't going to do it themselves, were they?"

"Well, I assure you, friend. You will be safe from garden gnomes in our company," Gregory said, his tone dismissive. "My sword is guard enough against a fat baby with a novelty spade."

"Garden gnomes are an extrapolation of certain Scottish legends," Tembo said quietly. "Redcaps, their hats stained that way by soaking them in the blood of their victims. If there is an infestation of the creatures, we should seek shelter. They will easily be the match of anything we saw in Valhalla."

"Valhalla?" Percy said. "I *thought* maybe it was happening again.

Bloody headaches, and the smell of blood in my nostrils." He swallowed, a grand gesture that somehow incorporated his entire body. "So is this it, Clarence?"

"You are safe, Percy," Clarence said, patting his friend on the shoulder. "But there are things we must discuss. Your cottage?"

"Right this way," Percy said, abandoning his shed and whatever petunias needed planting, as he led the way. He walked with a long, scissoring gait, hands firmly in his pockets. "Couldn't be a social visit, could it? Couldn't just be dropping by for tea. Has to be bloody Valhalla!"

"So there's no tea?" Clarence asked.

"Of course there's tea!" Percy snapped. "What am I, a barbarian?"

We made our way to a cozy-looking cottage, tucked behind a low wall that contained another garden, this one a little wilder and, somehow, more natural than the well-manicured landscape we had just left behind. The place reminded me of my domain, without all the fear and darkness and dogs the size of office buildings. Percy bustled us inside, then disappeared into the kitchen.

"Are you sure this is wise?" Bethany asked. "Hiding a zombie in your backyard?"

"Hasn't been a problem so far. Occasional gnomes, dryads, the odd revenant. Nothing I can't handle. Though this business with the valkyries—" He fell silent as Percy burst into the room, overburdened with tea cups, kettles, delicate plates of cake and oddly shaped sandwiches, and lace doilies that looked out of place in the hands of the gardener. We sat back in our plush chairs as Percy set out the meal on the coffee table, bustling back and forth as he arranged plates and poured cups of tea. I watched this with growing horror. It seemed possible that my mother, with her commemorative tea sets and tins of butter shortbread, could very well be some kind of British zombie.

"There we are, here we go, that's just right, and one for you. Milk? Sugar?" Percy mumbled as he worked his way around the circle. "The sandwiches are liverwurst and pickle, touch of mayonnaise. The fish sandwiches are over there. The cookies have been basted in linseed oil and licorice. And these . . ." He plucked up a small cake that had been frosted to look like a rose, regarding it curiously. "I can't remember. Rutabaga? Bamboo? I lose track, sometimes."

"I think you're using the wrong words to describe—" I scooped up a sandwich and bit into it. The acidic broth of boiled pickles and overripe cottage cheese bit into my tongue, rushing all the way to my nose before I could spit it out. "Nope. That's precisely what these things are."

"You can take the Brit out of the zombie, but you can never get the zombie out of the Brit," Clarence said, daintily pushing his plate of frog-mash cakes away. "He hasn't eaten anything in a long time. Forgets how it's supposed to go. But the tea is still excellent."

"Yes, yes, the tea is always perfect," Percy said, apparently unfazed at having mistakenly poisoned his guests with pickle sandwiches. He swept the cozy off the kettle. "We will always have tea."

What he had, unfortunately, was a bleached skull, stuffed to the eyeholes with dry leaves and twigs and moss. Percy stared at it for a long heartbeat, then threw the cozy across the room.

"It's the bloody gnomes!" he yelled.

"Maybe we should just get to the matter at hand," Tembo said briskly.

"Probably for the best," Clarence agreed. "Percy, we need to talk to you about something."

"I really don't know how they got into the house," Percy said. He collapsed into one of the free chairs, head in both his hands, staring at the skull. "I have salt on the windows and sprigs of horseradish at the door. Is that right? I can't very well salt the door, can I?"

"Percy, forget about the gnomes for a minute, will you?" Clarence said. "Something has happened. Something very serious." That got Percy's attention, though it seemed a great effort to draw his gaze away from the ruined tea. "This is the rest of Knight Watch. They've just come from Valhalla."

"Yes, I know. I knew you were coming," Percy said. "I could feel it return."

"Return?"

"The sword. Yesterday afternoon. I was out among the lilies, preparing them for winter. It's never really winter here, but still . . ." His voice trailed off. He poked at the skull, then stood up, collecting untouched plates. "Anyway, I felt it come back. First time in years. Decades? How long has it been, Clarence?"

"Decades, at least. Honestly I'm not sure. Time isn't something I keep track of." Clarence slid forward on his seat, the upholstery squeaking under his chain-mail pants. "So you felt the sword return?"

"He couldn't have. It's still in Valhalla. Or at least it was, until this morning," Chesa said.

"How do we know time moves normally here? He could have felt it leaving Valhalla. Or he could have sensed the Totenshrieker trying to break into the Unreal at the Ren-Yay-Ssaince Faire. Either way, we already knew it was back," I said.

"So it's true. I was hoping I was just imagining things." Percy deflated, putting the plates in danger of falling from his hands. Bethany stood and smoothly relieved him of his burden of plate and kettle and skull. He let them go without seeming to realize they were gone. She disappeared into the kitchen. Percy collapsed onto the divan. "So this is it. You've come to put me down."

"No one is here to put you anywhere," Clarence said, quickly put his hand on Gregory, who already had his sword half out of the scabbard. "Just because the sword is back in play doesn't mean you're about to lose your will."

"Perhaps it's better if you did," Percy said miserably. "You have no idea what it's like, the lot of you. Waking up every morning with the memory of last night's death still in your mind. The taste of your last victim still in your mouth. Ready to kill again. Anxious to kill again." He looked up at Clarence with pathetic eyes, his long, thin face drawn sharply downward. "They'll do it again. They'll put me under the leash, me and all the rest of them. And I can't face it."

"That's why we're here, Percy. To prevent that from happening," Clarence said, laying a comforting hand on the thin zombie's shoulder. "But we need your help."

"As we understand this, there are two components to this zombie thing," I said. "The first, the sword, is already in play—"

"'Already in play.'" Bethany snorted. "What are you, Rast, an operator operating operations now? Is this a debrief? Are we gonna go tactical?"

"I do not understand any of these references," Tembo said.

"Just... focus for a second," I said. "The point is that the bad guys already have the sword, and someone to wield it. But without the other bit, that sword is dangerous, just not as dangerous." There was silence, and I turned to Tembo to confirm. "Do I have that right?"

"Yes. The sword can raise the local dead, but without the Tears of Freya, they are limited in what they can do," Tembo answered. "The grand army of the dead raised in the war will remain in Folksvangr, at peace, waiting for Ragnarok."

"At peace, except for you, Percy," Clarence said. "You're the only connection we have to the Tears."

"Then . . . shouldn't I stay here? Where the valkyries can't find me?" Percy asked, shrinking deeper into the divan. "Wouldn't that be best for everyone involved?"

"Listen, Percy, I understand how frightening this is," I said, leaning down in front of him. "But sometimes you have to stand up and be counted. Sometimes you have to—"

"Spare me your pleasantries, Yank," Percy said. "I rode one of Hobart's funnies on Sword Beach under a hail of gunfire. I fought my way through Ouistreham, crawled through the blood of better men than you, killed better men than you. Thought I was going to get through it, and then . . ." He chuckled, a sharp sound, at odds with his mood. "And then a man with a bloody *SWORD* walked out of a shattered patisserie and killed every one of my friends. I put enough lead into him to drown a whale, but he kept coming. Drove that sword right through my heart." He blinked rapidly, though no tears formed in his eyes. "I thought that was it. Thought I was dead. Then I woke up, and that's when the nightmare started. So if you need me to go out there, don't ask me to be brave about it. I've been brave. All courage got me was this half-life, and gnomes in the garden."

We were silent for a long moment. Finally, Clarence cleared his throat and pulled Percy to his feet.

"We wouldn't ask if it wasn't important, Percy. We don't want this to happen to anyone else. And the only way we can do that is with your help."

"Yes, alright, whatever. The petunias will keep. Probably safer out there than it is in here, anyway," Percy said. "At least there aren't any garden gnomes in the real world."

CHAPTER SIXTEEN

We emerged from Clarence's domain just long enough to walk the three flights of stairs to our own domains. None of us had seen the inside of our mythic realms since the incursion at the Mickleville Ren-Yay-Ssaince festival, and I was feeling it. Without some proper domain-time, the members of Knight Watch can't tap into our mythic identities, which means no magic powers, and no interaction with the Unreal world. We could walk past an ice demon with nothing more than a shiver and a cold sweat. We're no better than cosplayers with a very good budget. Unfortunately, time was short, and Esther is a stickler for a schedule. I don't think I was in my domain—that pleasant cabin in a very dark forest I mentioned earlier, but with a magical pot of stew—for more than an hour before she yanked me out and set me on the road to adventure. Again.

"You know, when this whole thing started, I thought being a hero would be a lot more . . . heroic. Derring do and all that," I grumbled as Esther set me down at the banquet table that served as the centerpiece for all our briefings. "Can't we have a decent nap before we charge headlong into certain death?"

"You're not charging headlong into certain death. Probably," Esther said as she walked to the door to Chesa's domain. "At the very worst, you're going to be walking slowly toward certain death."

"What's that supposed to mean?" I asked, as Chesa rose from her domain—literally. Esther opened the door just as a tree limb sprouted from the depths of Chesa's domain, unfurling like a leafy banner into the great hall. The bough split open, revealing Chesa's reclining form, cradled gently in a creche of living oak. The tree, creaking, slowly tilted her upright. She awoke and stepped gingerly to the floor. Its service complete, the bough retreated back into her domain.

"Good morning, everyone!" Chesa said cheerfully. Then she realized Esther and I were the only ones in the room. Her face fell.

"It means we don't have the Naglfr any longer," Esther said, ignoring Chesa's grand entrance. "We'll have to arrange alternative transportation."

"Oh, you mean horsies?" Chesa asked.

"Last time I led a pack of horses down Route 66 it caused a traffic backup that lasted three weeks, and nearly forced the timestream to reverse course. I'm not doing that again," Esther said. "Don't worry about it. I have a plan."

Chesa shrugged and sat down across from me. I have to admit, elf looks good on her. I mean, pretty much anything looks good on her, but elf seemed to particularly suit her. Once again, I found myself regretting breaking it off with Chesa back when we were both just mundane humans in a mundane world. But, as they say, if I couldn't handle her in cosplay, I didn't deserve her in Elfheim.

"Feeling better?" I asked.

"Much, thank you. Do you have any idea what Gregory's domain is like?"

"Probably a lot of damsels in distress," I said, then, much lower. "Especially with that lout prowling the grounds."

"I'll bet it's a grand palace. All chivalry and parties and music," she said. "Did you see your scary dog friend?"

"The World Dog keeps to himself," I said. Chesa took every opportunity to remind me that my domain wasn't exactly the medieval fantasy I had hoped for going in. "What about you? Get any inconvenient splinters?"

Chesa sniffed and looked away. Slowly, the rest of Knight Watch filed into the great hall. Tembo sat at the head of the table with a haunted expression in his eyes, while Saint Matthew slouched in his chair, blissed out and peaceful. When Gregory d'Haute came in, Chesa followed his journey from door to table with keen interest. He flashed her a brilliant smile, then settled into his place.

"So," Gregory said, "what's the plan?"

"The plan is that we get the Tears before the valhellions. That means—"

"Wait, the who?" I interrupted.

"Valhellions," Esther answered. "That's what we're calling them—the valkyries trying to reclaim Totenschreck and empower the Tears of Freya, kicking off Ragnarok. We can't just call them valkyries, for legal reasons, so . . . valhellions."

"Did you come up with that?"

She sniffed and carried on with the briefing.

"We need to get the Tears before the valhellions," she said, glaring at me. "We know that they're in the care of two former valkyries, but other than that, we've got nothing. The only way we can hope to find them is with our friend Percy. I've been talking to him, and he definitely feels drawn to something to our north. We're going to assume it's the Tears. So we're going to saddle up and start in that direction."

"How do we know they're even on this plane of existence?" Bethany asked. "Couldn't these former valkyries be hiding in their own little pocket of the Unreal somewhere?"

"They were forced to give up their powers," Tembo said. "They have no connection to Valhalla, and therefore no way of drawing mythic attention."

"This all happened seventy years ago," I said. "If they've given up their magic powers, won't they be dead by now?"

"Just because they've given up their powers doesn't mean that they're not magical. You can take the girl out of Valhalla, but you can't take the Valhalla out of the girl," Esther answered. "I suspect we're going to find two very brusque Nordic women with funny accents somewhere to our north."

"Thus describing the entirety of Minnesota," I said, settling back into my chair. "This should be a walk in the park. At least it's not winter."

"Yet," Esther said. "Everyone, get your kit together and make your way to Mundane Actual. Clarence and Kyle are coming out of retirement just long enough to secure HQ while the rest of you are in the field. Without the Naglfr we won't be able to get back here quickly at range, and I don't want Percy's gnomes breaching the perimeter."

"There's always Tembo's domain," Chesa said.

"We will not be repeating that exercise," Tembo said gravely.

"Things have changed on the sveldt as a direct result of your... incursion. I cannot take the chance again."

"Right, so, no magical longship, no horses... how are we getting north?" I asked.

"You'll see, Rast," Esther said. "Just be patient."

The good news was that Knight Watch had alternatives to the HMS *Toenail Clippings*. Mundane Actual had drivers in magically inconspicuous cars who could ferry us around, or even enchant those same cars so they could drive themselves. The bad news was that we couldn't get far by those methods, and couldn't be away from our domains for a prolonged road trip. I had never considered just how limited Knight Watch was without the flying ship. Turns out there's a lot of dangerous magic out there, and not all of it occurs within walking distance of Mundane Actual. But apparently there was a solution, and we were on our way to see it.

With Kyle in tow. Kyle, who in Clarence's domain was a majestic dragon of great power and fickle temper, but in the real world... well... in the real world, he was a cross between a cartoon and a puppy. Literally.

Kyle skittered down the hallway, his nails scraping loudly against the tile floor, his wide, purple butt slamming into the walls every time he tried to take a corner too fast. His grape soda–colored scales protected him from the impacts, but left cratered drywall and broken tiles behind. Commissar Snowflake sat impassively on Kyle's head like a puffy round hat with yellow googly eyes.

"Clear the hall! Kyle! Over here, Kyle!" Clarence shouted. "You're going the wrong way! KYLE!"

"Sorry, sorry, sorry, hi! Hi, who are you?" Kyle shoved his head into a room as he passed, drawing a round of shouts and one mad laugh. Kyle's head emerged again, with a HAPPY BIRTHDAY garland around his horns. Snowflake was cleaning one paw, and looked like he didn't have a care in the world. "They were nice."

"Clarence, you need to get him under control," Esther hissed. "Last time he was here we had to rebuild half the hospital wing. Two nurses retired. A third converted to Quakerism, but I think that was just a cover for his nerves."

"I'm doing the best I can," Clarence said.

"You should have just left him behind," Tembo said.

"If I'm not around he gets bored and rearranges the furniture," Clarence said. "And the walls. And parts of the sky. It gets messy." We all winced as Kyle crashed into a wall, sending ceiling tiles raining down. "I think it's the bloody cat that puts him up to it. Vile thing has been trying to knock that castle down since the day he arrived."

Commissar Snowflake turned a yellow eye in Clarence's direction, tail twitching in irritation. The old knight flinched back.

"Alright, alright, everyone calm down," Esther barked. "It's important to stay calm for the next bit. We don't want to scare him off."

"Scare who off, exactly?" I asked.

"You'll see. Right through here." Esther led us up the last flight of stairs and onto the shores of the underground lake that formerly housed the Naglfr. There were underwater passages that led to the lake overhead, which didn't make any sense from a hydrodynamic point of view, but not much about Mundane Actual was actually mundane. There was talk among the team about other things lurking in the depths of the lake, some of which were less than friendly, so as Esther led us down the shore and onto the pier that stretched into the lake, I was beginning to wonder if we were the ones she was trying to not scare off.

"We going to swim north?" Bethany asked.

"Going to be rough going in this armor," Gregory said. "I think I've had enough of drowning for a lifetime."

"Once is usually enough for a lifetime," Bethany said.

"Not to be indelicate, but I do not have the bits that usually float," Percy said. "Fat and blood and all that. I suppose I could walk along the bottom, but—"

"Everybody be quiet!" Esther snapped. She was scanning the surface of the lake. There were always strange currents in the water, but today I felt like they were stranger, or at least more foreboding. "Okay, this is it. Everyone into the water."

"I . . . think I mentioned the problem of armor," Gregory said.

"And there's no way I'm getting my hair wet," Chesa said. "It takes a literal miracle to get it to look like this."

"Stop complaining and get in," Esther said. "No one's going to drown. Probably."

"Listen, I think we need to slow down and talk this through," I said. "Maybe if we knew a little bit more about the plan, we'd be amenable."

"I guarantee you that's not the case," Esther said.

"Then I think you can see why I'm hesitant to—"

"Get in the water, Rast," she said, then grabbed me by the shoulder and hurled me into the lake.

I hit the water with a slap. It was cold, mind-numbingly cold, so cold that I forgot to hold my breath or swim or anything. I emptied my lungs in a single yelp, then started sucking in lake water like a thirsty fish. By the time I remembered I was supposed to be swimming, I had already lost sight of the surface, and my lungs were screaming in pain.

Strong arms surrounded me, pulling me up and cradling me as warm light permeated my skin. We broke the surface of the lake like a pair of corks. Matthew's arms were around me.

"Stop thrashing around, John. You're making this difficult," he said. I tried to calm down, but the cold depths beneath me sent a chill up my spine. Slowly the warmth returned to my skin, and my lungs stopped twitching. "There we go. Just gotta have a little faith." He pulled me upright, and I realized we were standing on the water. "See? No problem."

The rest of the team was standing around us, their feet only sunk a few inches into the water. Chesa peered down at the lake distastefully, while Bethany hopped up and down, experimenting with the surface underfoot. Kyle and Clarence watched from the pier, with Esther between them. Tembo was helping Percy down from the pier. The zombie, dressed in what could only be described as a formal battle cumberbund and spats, did not seem keen on the concept of water. Not at all.

"This isn't so bad," Gregory said. "But I don't see how it's going to get us to where we're going."

"That's being taken care of as we speak," Esther said. "Now, it's important that you pay really close attention to what I'm about to say. Are you listening? All of you? Bethany?"

"Sorry," Beth said. She stopped bouncing. "What were you saying?"

"I just want to be sure that you're all paying really close attention. Look at me," Esther said. I wrinkled my forehead. She didn't seem to be saying anything important, but Esther sure was keen on our attention. In fact, she wasn't really looking at us anymore. Her gaze was fixed over our heads. I glanced at Clarence. The old knight's eyes had gotten big, and he was slowly backing down the pier. Commissar Snowflake, perched safely on Kyle's head, was definitely smiling at us mischievously.

Fear gripped my heart. I turned around just in time to see something break the surface of the water. It was dark and blunt and bigger than anything I'd seen before, big enough to give the World Dog a run for his money. I made some kind of sound, a cross between a shriek and incoherent babbling. Standing next to me with his hands thrust into the pockets of his robe, Matthew glanced at me, his eyebrows up. He turned around to see what I was screaming about.

"Oh, I know this guy," he muttered.

Then the creature's mouth opened, and the lake rushed in, swallowing us whole. I tried to scream, but my voice disappeared into the depths of its throat.

CHAPTER SEVENTEEN

What followed was a great rush of dark, cold water, and the feeling that I was being shoved through a soft tube that was about three sizes too small. Someone kept kicking me in the head, and I wasn't sure if I was going to pass out first from head trauma or suffocation. Finally, my head broke the surface of the water. I sucked in a great, gasping breath. The air smelled like rotten fish and gingivitis, and I immediately started gagging, simultaneously trying to breathe and vomit, vomit and breathe.

It was oppressively dark, and everything was moving. I knelt on a spongy shoreline, water covering my knees and splashing against my wrists. When I tried to crawl forward, the ground spasmed, throwing me onto my face and filling my mouth with an intriguing broth of stomach bile, lake water, and something that could only be described as insufficiently digested fish parts. I leapt to my feet, but that led to me banging into the low ceiling, which, just like everything else here, was slightly warm, soft, and shivering at my touch. I flinched back, only to stumble headlong into Chesa. I knew it was Chesa because of the disgusted sound she made when we touched.

"Oh, God, where the hell are we?" I asked around a mouthful of fishy roux. I spat a few times, rubbed my lips against the raspy chain sleeve of my armor, then tried again. "Is this seriously the belly of a whale?"

"Got it in one." Matthew's voice came from somewhere to my left. "I'm going to try a light. I'm not sure what will happen. Our host might not like getting the way it tickles."

"Forget our host, we might not like what we see," Bethany mumbled. "Maybe the dark is better."

"The dark is definitely not better," I said. Just then, the fish lurched forward, sending us all to the moist ground. A brick of something as soft as cheese and as fragrant as rotting garbage squished between my fingers, working its way into my armor.

With a hiss and a crackle, a spark of light appeared in Matthew's hands. The saint sat huddled near the front of the belly, with Gregory at his side, and Bethany beside him. The three of them looked to have gotten the worst of the drenching. Streamers of seaweed hung from Bethany's hundred knives, and Gregory looked like he had been strained through a film of dripping green muck. Tembo stood hunched on the opposite end of the belly, peering distastefully at the puckered exit. Chesa and I were in the middle, standing in what I now saw was a pile of putrefying fish that had gotten caught in a fold of the creature's stomach lining. Chesa yelped and stepped quickly out of the filth. Unfortunately, she took the last scrap of clean real estate, and I was forced to stay in place.

Only Percy seemed unfazed by our predicament. He sat placidly near the ignominious exit, hands folded comfortably in his lap, waiting for all this to blow over. I envied his calm, if not his complexion.

"So what do we do now? How does this damned thing know where to go?" Chesa asked.

"Matthew's the expert in these matters," Tembo said, his examination of the exit complete. "You say you've had experience with this manner of conveyance?"

"Not personally. Sushi is about as close as I've come," Matthew answered. "But it's a well-documented trick. I think we just have to sit back and let it do its thing." He looked appraisingly around the fish's interior. "I really thought it would be roomier. Not made for high-occupancy travel, I suppose."

"Roomier? I'd settle for cleaner, and less . . ." I gestured hopelessly. "Less the inside of a fish."

"All of our transports have one thing in common," Chesa said. "They smell terrible. I keep hoping we'll hitch a ride on a golden chariot, or fly a Pegasus. But this is ridiculous."

"Look on the bright side," I said. "At least it can't get much worse."

A rush of wind blew through the stomach, closely followed by a wall of frigid water. Those unfortunate enough to be sitting down were immediately submerged, while the rest of us struggled to keep our heads above water. I caught sight of Bethany spinning head over heels in the middle of the room, and grabbed her by the knife strap. Tembo crashed into me, and the three of us joined the currents, slapping against the fleshy walls and bouncing off one another like pinballs. The torrent swirled around us for several seconds, before rushing out the way it had come.

I lay on my back in the same pile of putrefying fish, which had somehow survived the flood unmoved. Bethany squatted beside me. I scrambled to my feet and did a quick head count. Everyone was still here, though in various states of disarray and general poor spirits. But we were no longer alone.

The bilious tsunami had brought with it hundreds and thousands of tiny prawn, each about the size of my little finger. They lay in a thick carpet over everything, chittering anxiously and crunching underfoot anytime one of us moved. The tiny bugs were tangled in our hair, in our clothes, were scrambling into the cracks of my armor . . . everywhere. It was horrific. Just the smell, which had already been awful, was much, much worse.

"You!" Chesa yelled from across the stomach, pointing at me. "Keep your mouth shut! Not one word!"

"But—"

"Silence!"

I held up my hands in surrender. A prawn, slick with whale mucus, crawled up my middle finger and slowly, deliberately, pinched the tip of my finger.

We rested as well as we could on a carpet of dying prawn in the belly of a fish that was somehow magically whisking us northward. I had no idea what waterways we were following, or if we were still inside Mundane Actual, doing short laps around the lake while Esther devised a plan to extract us from our fishy prison. My only indication that this wasn't the case was the fact that every once in a while Percy would sniff the air and announce that we were getting closer. I hoped so. It felt like we were huddled together in a slowly collapsing tent made of damp lunch meat.

Our journey ended abruptly, but no more pleasantly than the rest of our time in the belly of this particular whale. I was just discussing the finer points of getting rotten fish out of your hair with Chesa when the ground beneath our feet lurched, and we were expelled, prawn, bile, and all. I landed with a thump on a pebble beach, the grit and grime forcing its way into my armor and clogging my nose. Dragging myself through cold, shallow water, I crawled until I reached dry land and collapsed. The sounds of misery and struggle surrounded me, not the least of which came from Gregory, who seemed to have brought a good deal of the whale's intestines with him. I lay panting on the shore. When I looked up, it was directly into the barrel of a shotgun.

"Typical," I said, though between the water pouring from my mouth and the reflexive gagging of my throat, I'm not sure it came out clearly. The bearer of the shotgun certainly misinterpreted my statement as a threat, because I heard the clear sound of a shell being cycled, and the barrel pressed closer to my head.

"I know what you're thinking. You're thinking these things don't work on you. That you're special. Well I'm special, too, and so's this gun. Odin blessed, and loaded with the bones of saints who should have known better than to come to Norway. So before you do anything clever, I want you to think about it real careful. Understand?"

I squinted up the length of the barrel. The bearer, a stocky woman in her fifties with a halo of blond-white hair held in place with a cord of braided leather, held the gun unwavering in my face. She was dressed in a faded plaid shirt and workman's slacks, the thighs stained with dirt and grime. Her eyes were pale blue, the color of glacial ice, and just as cold.

"Do you talk, or do you just stare at every beautiful woman you see?" she asked.

"He talks," Chesa said, standing slowly from a pool of muck. "But once he starts, you're going to wish he didn't."

"I don't think that's fair," I said. "I'm a perfectly reasonable conversationalist."

"Perfectly reasonable folks don't use the word 'conversationalist,'" the valkyrie said, because that's obviously what she was. "Now. It ain't everyday that old Jonah comes to visit, and it's less everyday that he brings a pack of heroes in his gullet. So who the Sam Hill are you, and what the Sam Hill are you doing in my lake?"

We had all gotten to our feet by now. Even though there were seven of us, and we were clearly armed, the valkyrie seemed not in the least intimidated.

"That's no way to greet visitors," Tembo said carefully. "We mean you no harm."

"Well, we have this thing called Midwest Nice, so I'll just apologize for the shotgun in advance. But I'm still going to have to ask you to explain yourself." She shrugged. "Sorry."

"Look, lady, there are seven of us and one of you," Gregory said. He hooked his thumbs into his belt. "And even if you're telling the truth about that shotgun—"

"Two," she said.

"Hmm?"

"Two of us. Sorry."

The trees nearby shivered, and a dog the size of a horse poked its head from between the branches. It was some kind of elkhound, with perky ears and a pink tongue, and a face like a fox. It looked at us with friendly eyes.

"Magnus is a good boy," the valkyrie said.

"Yes, yes he is," I said carefully. "A very good boy."

"So, again, who are you, and why are you here?"

"We're friends of Esther MacRae," I said. "She sent us to find you."

"Esther MacRae doesn't have a lot of friends. She has soldiers, and she has enemies." The shotgun swept over us before settling on Percy. The valkyrie's face grew hard. Which was quite a feat, because I thought it was already hard enough to bend steel. Turns out there were hidden depths to this woman's grimness. "And you come here with one of these monsters. You should have left him in the whale."

"Whatever happened to civility?" Percy mused. "Was a time you could count on an offer of biscuits and a decent kettle when you met someone new. Nowadays it's all 'Leave that one in the whale' and 'Who here smells like death?' It's hardly proper."

"Madam, we are here on urgent business," Tembo said, interposing himself between the shotgun and the zombie. "There has been a breach in Valhalla. The Totenschreck has been stolen. We have been sent by Knight Watch to retrieve the Tears of Freya, to ensure their safety."

"Oh have ya now?"

"We have," Gregory said, trying his best hero's smile.

"Well, that's a darn shame, that is. Lillie and I, we got rid of those fool Tears a long time ago. Too much trouble, what with the wolves following us home every night, and the little pixies scaring the guests."

"You . . . got rid of them?" I asked.

"Yeah. Poured 'em down the drain, along with about a gallon of Liquid-Plumr. Good riddance. Too bad you came all this way for nothing." She slung the shotgun over her shoulder, then picked up a fishing pole that had been leaning against a nearby tree. "Well, you've got a heck of a walk ahead of you. Won't do to send you off without some sandwiches. Come on back to the house. We'll fix you right up."

CHAPTER EIGHTEEN

The valkyrie introduced herself as Hildr as she led us to a beat-up white pickup truck that was parked by the side of the road. Magnus pranced by her side, getting smaller and smaller as we walked, so that by the time we reached the truck he wasn't much larger than a very large elkhound.

A yellow-and-blue sticker in the truck's back window declared I BRAKE FOR HYGGE! while another on the back bumper claimed MY OTHER CAR HAS EIGHT LEGS and depicted some kind of horse. I tugged on Tembo's sleeve as we approached the vehicle.

"I thought they were supposed to be incognito," I said. "Those seem a little on point."

"It's Minnesota. That *is* incognito," the mage answered.

"He is correct. All I have to do is maintain a working knowledge of high school hockey and various potato products, and no one suspects a thing," Hildr said. "Which is why I do not like having the lot of you poking around. It will draw attention."

"The real world always makes an excuse for us," I said. "Local Ren Faires. Wandering game nerds. The Unreal finds a way."

"It is not the mundanes who worry me. There are other powers in these woods, older than all of us." Hildr threw her pole and shotgun behind the seat, then jerked a thumb at the bed of the truck. "Hop in. We're going for a ride."

"I don't think I should get in that thing," I said. "Technology tends to break around me. And if you don't have the Tears—"

"You let me worry about the truck. Bessie here has hauled stranger things than you. Go on now. Get up."

Chesa peered distastefully into the bed and sniffed. "Is the passenger seat—" Her line of questioning was interrupted by Magnus, who leapt into the front of the truck, turned around once, then lay down with his massive head resting on the dashboard.

"Pretend it's a chariot," I said, holding out my hand to help her into the bed.

"It most certainly is not a chariot," she said, hopping gracefully into the truck and leaving my hand hanging midair.

We piled into the truck bed and held on for dear life as Hildr the retired valkyrie tore off down the road. Gravel rattled off the rusted-out sidepanels. The ride itself was roughly equivalent to getting kicked in the backside by a metal paddle wielded by an angry and well-muscled god. Magnus hung his head out the window, trailing a long, viscous stream of slobber down the side of the truck. Globules of this would occasionally splatter against the passengers on that side of the vehicle. Including me, of course.

"Why are we doing this?" Bethany shouted over the disturbing rattle and roar of the truck. "If they threw out the Tears—"

"She's lying," Percy said. He was sitting point in the spittle fire zone, and was huddled over, his balding pate gleaming with Magnus-drool. "The Tears are here, somewhere. I can feel them."

"Why would she lie about that?" I asked.

"Wouldn't you?" Matthew asked. "A bunch of yahoos in medieval battle rattle show up on your doorstep, waving around the name of a woman who once betrayed you and asking for the one thing you've given up everything to protect, would you just hand it over? I wouldn't. I'd take them somewhere safe, away from prying eyes, and work them over a little. See who they were actually working for."

"Or just get rid of them," Tembo said. "There's a reason Valhalla did not give the Tears into Knight Watch's possession in the first place."

"So, given that, I'll ask one more time: Why are we doing this?" Bethany squinted into the back of the truck, where Hildr sat comfortably, one hand on the wheel and the other stroking Magnus's back. The shotgun sat casually beside the dog. Hildr's hand was close to the trigger. "The Brit has gotten us this far. Why don't we dodge this old lady and find the Tears ourselves?"

"Because there are two of them," Tembo said. "Two guardians.

Hildr is the first. If we do something to escape her custody, there's no chance we convince the other that we mean no harm. No, we should try to gain her trust, and the trust of her friend."

"By her friend, we're not talking about the dog?" I asked.

"We are not. It's probably this 'Lillie' she mentioned. Though I suspect it would not hurt to gain his trust as well."

"I'm not great with dogs," Chesa said. "Too much . . ." A heavy slug of slobber twisted through the air to land noisily in the middle of her forehead. Chesa's mouth clapped shut, and her eyes burned with hatred. Like, literally burned. The drool started to sizzle.

"One thing at a time. She is taking us to their sanctuary. If the Tears aren't there, they will certainly be nearby. And the closer we can get to them before we set out on our own, the better off we'll be," Tembo said. He settled back against the side of the truck, looking as relaxed as if he were on a pleasure cruise down the Nile. "Patience, friends. Patience."

We zipped through scraggly forests and over slowly rolling hills. I could hear the buzz of hundreds of mosquitoes, and saw the glimmer of standing water flashing between the trees like glimpses of a mirror. It felt like a strange place to hide such a powerful artifact.

"So what do we think this sanctuary is going to look like? What kind of place do two valkyries choose to hide from the Unreal world in? Do they have castles in Minnesota?" I asked.

"Not that I am aware of," Tembo said. "But there *is* an incredibly large mall."

"Let's hope it's not there. We have bad luck with malls," I said. Last year we tracked my friend Eric to a mall that had been turned into a bad version of the Dungeon half of D&D. We had to kill a bunch of trees, and I got the world's worst sunburn. "Isn't there some kind of cheese-castle thing?"

"Wisconsin," Bethany said "Everything in Wisconsin has a cheese version."

"I'm guessing it's a cabin in the woods," Greg said. "The kind of place where you lure children with candy and put them in an oven."

"She does have that 'cabin in the woods' vibe to her," I muttered. "Wherever it is, I'm not too anxious to get there."

It was not a cabin in the woods, or a castle, or even a haunted mall. No, the place Hildr took us was nothing like what I was expecting. The sign at the end of the driveway declared it the Edelweiss House, printed in flowing pinks and greens, with a large stylized snowflake in the background. The house itself stood on a low hill, and looked like three or four Victorian homes that had been thrown into a blender and then dumped, with a handful of clashing colors and cascading shingle roofs, inside a wraparound porch that was larger than most tennis courts. There was a garden that had gone to seed a long time ago, and a handful of gazebos, a fishing pond, and at least three statues that depicted various Norse gods in a questionable degree of undress. Hildr pulled into the long, winding driveway, then slowed to a halt. Those of us in the truck bed tumbled together in a clatter of armor and dog slobber and disgrace. The valkyrie twisted around in her seat and stared at our faces, pressed against the glass of her rear window.

"I don't want you upsetting Lillie. No declarations about the end of the world. No threats of violence, no mention of the war . . . and especially nothing about the Tears. Got it?"

"What are we supposed to do, then?" I asked.

"Sit quietly and have a nice cup of coffee, and maybe some sandwiches." She threw the truck into gear and we lurched forward, sliding unceremoniously to the tailgate, which thankfully held secure.

The ride up the gravel driveway was perhaps the most comically intimate five minutes of my young life. All of us rolling and sliding and gracelessly bumping heads. It felt like there should be violin music going in the background, or perhaps the sounds of Rome burning to the ground. Finally, mercifully, the ride ended. We all stood hastily, tugging mussed armor and misplaced swords into their proper arrangements.

Magnus descended from his perch, barely waiting for the truck to skid to a halt before leaping through the open window and loping up the broad steps to the wraparound porch. Hildr took her time, and offered us no assistance other than a keen eye and a cradled shotgun. Dismounting from a pickup truck in full armor is a lot like getting off a horse, which was something I'd never really gotten the hang of. I ended up scooting down the side of the truck, taking a good deal of paint with me as my chain-mail britches scoured the side. That drew an angry look from the valkyrie, but I couldn't bring myself to care. Heartless bitch deserved it, the way she was holding that shotgun pointed in the general direction of my crotch.

The front door of the porch swung open and a large woman strode out, wiping her hands on a faded yellow kitchen apron that she wore over weathered overalls and a crisp white button-down shirt. A wispy gray halo of hair framed her head. It was difficult to nail down her age. Wrinkles around her eyes and the color of her hair placed her in her seventies, but her hands and shoulders belonged to a much younger person. She folded thick arms across her chest and made a dissatisfied sound.

"I thought you were fishing, Hildr," the woman said. Her voice had the stiff formality of a schoolmarm. "These do not look like fish."

"No, Lillie, they aren't. But they came out of a fish. So maybe we can make an exception."

"And what am I supposed to fry for dinner, hmm?" Lillie asked.

"The skinny one might do," Hildr said. I looked back at her, startled.

"He is nothing but bone and cartilage," she said, then drew in a long, sharp breath. "They stink of make believe. How did they find us?"

"That would be my fault, mum. I can sense . . . well, I think you know what I can sense," Percy said, stepping forward. Both valkyries glared at him as though he had just stepped, gleaming and naked, out of their mother's birthday cake. Percy cleared his throat awkwardly.

"Yes, I suppose we do," Lillie finally said. "Well, you had better bring them inside while we figure out what to do with you. We are expecting guests shortly, and it wouldn't do to have to explain the stains on the porch."

The big lady turned and went back inside. Hildr snorted at our horrified expressions. She clapped me on the shoulder.

"Don't worry. She's only joking." Hildr clomped up the stairs, knocking her muddy boots on each step to clean them off. "The guests aren't getting here until tonight. We will have plenty of time to clean up any stains."

"Do we really want to go in there?" I asked. "I don't feel super welcome."

"You've been to Valhalla. You know what kind of things valkyries find funny," Matthew said. "We'll be fine."

"If I remember correctly, the kind of things valkyries find funny include drowning me with a bear, disrobing John with a cloud of spears, and playing volleyball with a skull," Gregory said.

"Talking skull," I corrected. "Well, screaming skull."

"Have a spine, Rast," Chesa said. She walked up the stairs and onto the porch. "What's the worst that could happen?"

"Isn't that my line?" I mumbled.

"There was talk of a fish fry," Percy said uncomfortably.

"You don't like fried fish?" Matthew asked.

"I don't like *being* fried," Percy said. But after an awkward silence, we followed Chesa into the motley-colored house.

CHAPTER NINETEEN

The interior of Edelweiss House was just as mismatched and random as the outside. The foyer contained no fewer than three staircases of different designs that led in different directions. There was a grand Victorian flight of carved wood, adorned with carved fruits and nesting birds and a suspicious-looking snake that ascended to a landing that overlooked the entrance hall, along with a more utilitarian craftsman-style staircase that descended into the bowels of the house, adorned with stained glass insets. The third staircase was a simple wrought-iron spiral that rose to a single door in the wall, about six feet up, roped off with a sign that read NO TRESPASSING ON PAIN OF A STERN APOLOGY. The rest of the room was a mishmash of styles, with glossy white subway tile fading into peeling velvet wallpaper that surrounded rustic wood paneling. Even the furniture looked like it was the result of a time travel accident, thrown together from every stratum of the timeline.

"Who decorated this place? Dr. Rubik?" I asked.

"I recognize that as a cultural reference, but am not familiar with the context," Tembo said. "Was Dr. Rubik a madman?"

"Pretty much," I said. "This place looks like a puzzle someone started to put together and then gave up halfway through."

"Do I come into your house and make fun of your furnishings?" Hildr asked. She motioned to a door that opened beneath the sweeping arc of the Victorian staircase. "Go on through to the kitchen. Lillie will find something for you to eat, and we can talk. I need to put the dogs away before the next round of guests arrive."

"You know, on a scale of one to impossible to count, I did not expect to find a pair of valkyries hiding in a bed and breakfast in rural Minnesota," I said as I made my way to the door. "It almost feels too obvious."

"As Esther said, 'You can take the girl out of Valhalla, but you can't take the Valhalla out of the girl,'" Tembo said. "It is in their nature to provide hospitality."

"By hospitality, you mean scouring the corpses of a battlefield, taking the worthy to a beer hall in the clouds, and then keeping them drunk until the apocalypse?"

"Drunk and fighting," Tembo said. "That counts as hospitality in some places."

The tiny door beneath the stairs led to a long, dark hallway, its ceiling a low archway that branched off to half a dozen cubbies and coat closets before terminating in the kitchen. A black-iron wood stove radiated forge-like heat in an otherwise modern kitchen. Lillie paid us no mind as we filed in, and it wasn't long before the space was crowded. I started to sweat through my hauberk. Lillie continued to ignore us.

"Is there something we can do to help?" I asked.

"Sit," she said sternly. When none of us moved, she took me by the shoulders and marched me to a small linoleum table in the corner with a plastic-coated bench that squeaked as she slid me down its length. The rest of Knight Watch followed my involuntary example. There wasn't enough space for all of us, but Lillie somehow made it work. When we were seated, the older valkyrie bustled back to the stove and busied herself with a dizzying array of kettles, pans, and a battle-scarred cleaver that looked like it could cut the head off a giant with a single blow. It made me wonder what was boiling in that pot on the stove.

"I don't understand what's happening here," I said after a few awkward moments of sitting, squished too close together, while the former valkyrie made us lunch. "Shouldn't we be tearing this place apart, looking for the Tears?"

"You want to keep your voice down, Rast?" Chesa hissed. "We're here as allies, not as an invading army! We're supposed to be the heroes."

"I mean, sure, the heroes. But Hildr said they dumped them, and we know that's a lie because Percy here can still smell them. So it's not like they're being straight with us!"

"You are very bad at whispering," Lillie said, looming over us. She leaned past me and distributed a round of soup served in cheap plastic bowls. The soup was the color of dishwater, and contained pearly white chunks of meat that could have been anything. "And Hildr is very bad at lying. Obviously we have not thrown out the Tears. That would be foolish."

"Why did she lie?" Chesa asked. Bethany huddled next to her, pushing her spoon around her soup bowl and grimacing. I looked down at my bowl. The bowl looked back. At least half a dozen eyes, some as large as a dime, stared at me with glassy apathy. I swallowed the bile that was rushing up my throat.

"Because you are either from Esther, or you are from Runa. And in either case, you are not to be trusted." She went back to the stove, collected her cleaver, then returned to the table and stood there with the knife in hand, fists pressed firmly against her hips. "But you seem like nice people, and I don't think we want to have to kill you just yet. Why are you not eating?"

"Besides the constant threats of murder, you mean . . . ?" I muttered to myself.

"What is this, exactly?" Bethany asked.

"Fish soup. Walleye."

"I don't think you're supposed to include the eyes," Bethany said.

"Are you sure?" Lillie asked. "It's in the name."

"Positive."

"Hmm. That may explain many things," Lillie said. "Well, eat around them. I won't throw away good fish just because it's a little heavy on the eyes."

"Can we get back to the question of whether or not you'll have to kill us just yet?" I asked. "That feels important."

"Personally, I have nothing against either of them," Lillie said. "Esther can be a little harsh, and sometimes forgets that most people still have their souls, but she's a good fighter. I would do battle at her side. And Runa . . . well, Runa isn't exactly a born leader, but she means well."

"Why are you talking to them?" Hildr asked as she bustled into the room. She was wearing a Kevlar vest with arm guards, the surface of which was dented and torn. "Have they not eaten the eyes yet?"

"They saw the eyes, and will not eat. And even if they hadn't, you have now told them about the eyes," Lillie said with an eyeroll. "I'm sorry. It is a trick the trolls taught us. Getting people to eat eyes lets you see inside them, if you do it right."

"You probably overcooked them, anyway," Hildr said, tearing the Velcro sleeves off the vest and tossing them on the table. They were slick with dog slobber. "So what do we do now?"

"Maybe we just have a civilized conversation?" Tembo asked. "You are correct, we are with Knight Watch, sent here by Esther MacRae to retrieve the Tears of Freya. But I do not think that makes us particularly untrustworthy."

"Hel's tits, it doesn't," Hildr spat. "She already tried to steal them once back in Mexico."

"That was Mississippi. In Mexico, it was Runa, and then the Russians." Lillie sighed and folded her arms, nearly taking off Gregory's head with that cleaver. "We thought we had finally escaped their notice."

"I'm sorry, but that seems unlikely," Tembo said. "I have been with Knight Watch for a very long time, and we have never attempted to retrieve this item. We aren't a very large organization, madam."

"This might have been before Knight Watch officially formed. When did you say she came after you?" Bethany asked.

"Shortly after the war. All of this, shortly after the war. We had just been given the assignment, and all the involved interests made a play for the Tears. Including your captain," Hildr said. "We had just surrendered our powers and were not yet comfortable with the mundane world. I think they thought we would be easy marks."

"They thought wrong," Lillie said with an affectionate smile, then turned her attention to us. "We moved around a lot after this. But when no one came after many, many years, we thought the pressure might be off. That's when we bought this place. I thought we would be able to settle down, maybe even retire. I am not the young girl I once was. Nor are you, Hildr."

"I'm young enough to kick these children to the curb, with or without our powers."

"We aren't here to take the Tears by force," Chesa said. "But things in Valhalla have changed. We need your help, and we need the Tears."

"Things are always changing in Valhalla," Hildr said with a dismissive snort. "How are they so much worse now?"

So we told them. We described the attack at the convention

center, then again in Valhalla, and the theft of the Totenschreck. And finally we told them how Runa had expelled us from Valhalla and taken the Naglfr from us. Hildr snorted.

"Losing that ship is something of a blessing. We were always trying to pawn that horrible thing off on enthusiastic heroes and greedy mortals. Runa probably gave it to Esther out of spite. But the rest . . ." Her voice trailed off. "What do you think, Lillie?"

The older valkyrie didn't answer. She was busy drying dishes by the old farm sink, her hands red and chapped from the hot water. Her mouth was pressed into a tight line. When she answered, her voice was as stern as iron.

"Lillie?" Hildr prompted.

"I am thinking, woman!" Lillie snapped. "I am thinking, and washing dishes, and trying to keep this house together. The sheets in the Folksvangr suite need to be changed, and the bathrooms cleaned, and I still haven't gotten the garden weeded. And now this! This, of all things, at all times." She threw her dishrag into the soap water and rubbed the corner of her eye with the back of her hand. "It's just bloody bad timing."

"There is no good time for things like this," Tembo said quietly. "As with most disasters. They are disastrous."

"We were safe here. We were comfortable. And we're not hurting anyone," Lillie said. "Why did you have to come here? We've hidden for decades. We could have hidden for decades more."

"We found you," I said. "And if we can do it, it stands to reason that the valhellions could find you as well."

"That's terrible logic," Hildr said sharply. "And an even worse name. Valhellions. Odin's foul breath, that's got Esther all over it."

"She has a point," Percy said. "You only found them because you had me, and it's safe to assume there aren't many people like me left, if any at all."

"But there might be a few left. We don't know how many of the sword's victims survived the war, or where they may be hiding," I said. Percy shrugged and went back to his soup, which he seemed determined to eat at least a little bit of, if only to be polite. I turned my attention to the pair of retired valkyries. "You must have some idea of who in Valhalla would be looking for the Tears, and who would be willing and able to steal the sword in the first place."

Hildr and Lillie exchanged meaningful looks. Lillie, muttering, went back to her dishes. Hildr cleared her throat meaningfully.

"We are not comfortable discussing this in the present company," she said.

"Present company? What's that supposed to . . ." I followed her piercing stare to Percy, who was chewing experimentally on a mouthful of eyes. "Oh. I get it. Ranks of the dead, and all that."

Percy looked up when he realized the general silence that had fallen over our company. He glanced from me, to Hildr, to the rest of the team. Then he slowly opened his mouth and let the eyes, unchewed, fall back into their soup.

"Am I imposing?" he asked politely.

"This man fought under Freya's banner in the war. He bears the mark of Totenschreck, and will always be beholden to its will," Hildr said. "Now that the sword once again strides the stage of history, you must know that he cannot be trusted." Hildr slammed her fist down on the crowded kitchen table, upsetting several bowls and spraying eyeball soup across the party. "He is an abomination!"

There followed a long and awkward silence. Percy cleared his throat, very neatly folded his napkin, and stood up.

"I see that I am not welcome here. That's fine. I believe I saw a garden on my way in. Perhaps the flowers will be more welcoming."

He marched out with a stiff lip and stiffer back, though it was clear he was hurt. Hildr watched him go, waiting until he was outside before she turned back to us with a sniff. "Well, now that that's settled . . . What?"

We stared daggers at the old valkyrie. Tembo sat back, his arms folded, while Chesa and I glowered at her like disapproving housewives.

"That was very rude," Chesa chided. "He's a pleasant if odd old man, just trying to do what's right."

"He's a damned draugr, bound to the will of a cursed sword, wielded by a madman," Lillie said without turning around. "Be happy he is in the garden, and not burning on a pyre. For now."

"You're going to get some pretty bad reviews with that kind of hospitality," I said. "Guests don't like seeing human bonfires out their window."

"Don't be ridiculous. We would do it in the basement, by the altar," Lillie said. "You can never be too careful with the draugr."

"Well, now that you've been rude to our friend and tried to serve us eyeballs, do you think you could tell us where the Tears are?" Bethany asked. "Or at least who might be trying to steal them?"

Lillie shrugged majestically, drawing a resigned sigh from Hildr. But she answered.

"There have always been factions within the valkyries. Runa's rebellion during the war made her a lot of enemies . . . enemies who ended up dead once Esther MacRae got involved," Hildr said. "That's why we were cut off from Valhalla. Not even Runa Hellesdottir could be trusted with Freya's Tears."

"So what makes the two of you so special? Why did they trust you, of all the valkyries?" Bethany asked.

"Because we were the ones who tried to stop Freya in the first place, when the war first started. Some of us tried to stop the forging of the sword you call Totenschreck. Freya found out, and sent her lieutenant to hunt us down," Lillie said. "Hildr and I were the only ones to survive. Freya stripped us of our wings as punishment, and sent us to Earth, to die with the rest of the mortals in the middle of a war. We barely escaped with our lives."

"That sounds awful," Chesa said.

"It was. And worse? The valkyrie they sent to hunt us down, the sister who killed our friends and returned the sword to Freya?" Hildr put a gnarled hand on Lillie's shoulder, as though to hold her friend up. "Her name was Runa. Runa Hellesdottir. The new queen of Valhalla."

CHAPTER TWENTY

Stunned silence settled over the kitchen. The only sound was Lillie, working furiously at cleaning the stains off a jam jar.

"Wait. So the woman in charge of protecting the sword also gave it to Freya in the first place?" I asked. "Explains why she was a bit dodgy back there."

"How many people know this?" Tembo asked. "Esther and I have discussed the end of the war many times. She has never mentioned Runa's role beyond her betrayal of the valkyries, and the signing of the peace."

"That's because Runa has tried to bury her past, just as she buried my friends," Hildr said. "Not even Esther knows of her role in the forging of Totenschreck. I would not be surprised if she already knows who is doing all this. In fact—"

"There is a man in the garden," Lillie said, quite suddenly. She was standing straight as an arrow, the jar forgotten in her hands.

"Of course there is a man in the garden. It is that zombie man, the Brit," Hildr reminded her.

"No. A different man. He looks very . . . dramatic," Lillie answered. "Like a dirge in the shape of a man."

Knight Watch stood as one. Tembo rushed to the window, with Bethany at his side and Gregory close behind. They crowded Lillie out of the way.

"It's him," Tembo confirmed. "How did he find us?"

"You probably led him here. You or that damned draugr," Hildr said as she swept the shotgun off its stand. The old valkyrie cracked the breach, checked the load, then snapped it shut again. "I'll see the bastard off."

"Let the heroes do their jobs," I said, stepping forward. With a shrug I slipped my shield off my back. It crawled down my arm on leather legs that spun around my wrist, securing it in place. "If he gets past us you can fill him full of buckshot."

"Magic shield, eh? Never thought much of magic shields," Hildr said. "You can only protect yourself for so long before you must strike. I prefer a good sword."

"The lady knows what she's talking about," Gregory said with a smile. He whipped the zweihander from his back, the silver blade slithering like a razor sharp snake in the kitchen's harsh light. "Let's get out there and cut this moron down to size."

"Patience. There's no way he's alone out there," Tembo said, flicking the kitchen curtains aside to get a better view of the garden.

"He looks pretty alone to me," Bethany answered. "In that kind of performative loneliness sort of way."

I shouldered my way to the front of the small mob that was crowded around Lillie's kitchen window. The view was entirely rural, except for the looming profile of a swordsman standing in the middle of the garden path. He wore the same black, hooded cloak that I had first seen at the Mickleville Convention Center, but now it seemed to fit him better. A glimmer of steel around his eyes revealed that the cheap Halloween mask had been upgraded again, and I could see more traditional armor plating at knee and elbow. He could be wearing full plate under that cloak. With sword out to one side, and his off hand held waist high with palm facing the sky, it looked like he was posing for us, waiting to be seen.

"However he got here, however he found us, this has gone on long enough," I said. "Chesa, you and Tem stay close to the house. Give us whatever support you can without getting too close. Remember what that sword did at the convention. One cut and you're down." I drew my sword and tested the fit of the shield against my shoulder. A few pulls on the cords wrapped around my hand and the shield grew into a full bulwark, tall enough to protect me from head to toe. "Greg, you and I are going to go out there and see what this guy's got. Bethany, see if you can get behind him without being seen."

"My kind of plan," Gregory said. "Give me one good swing at him and he'll be totenSHRIEKing, heh."

"And who made you team lead?" Bethany asked.

"He made himself lead," Tembo said. "We have you, warden. Be careful."

"If mind-numbing fear is careful, then careful is my middle name. You guys ready?"

"Sure, whatever." Bethany flipped up the hood of her cloak and disappeared into a cloud of swirling shadow. Tembo gave a stiff nod.

"There an upper window I can shoot from?" Chesa asked as she strung her bow. Lillie nodded and led Chesa out of the kitchen.

"Are we going to wait for her to get in place?" Gregory asked.

"I don't think we have that kind of time," I said. "Tembo can provide air support until Chesa finds her spot. And I'm pretty sure Bee's already out there. Right, Bee?" There was no answer, and she hates being called Bee, so Bethany was definitely already in the garden somewhere. "Let's get moving."

We came out of the kitchen door and spread out, with the saint, Tembo, and Hildr guarding the house while Greg and I made straight for the black-clad swordsman. Low clouds swirled overhead, and the wind was picking up. My steel boots sank into the thick mud of the garden path. There was no sign of Bethany, or Percy, or anyone else. Just the swordsman and the storm overhead. The man tilted his head in our direction, almost in greeting. The blade was a peculiar black merging into deep green, without any sort of reflection on its surface. Silver-sick mist wafted off its trailing edge.

"I'm sorry if I'm disturbing your vacation," the edgelord said. His voice scraped through the air like quiet thunder, a lot different from the earlier squeaky indignation. With one gloved hand he drew back his hood. The skull mask was now a full skeletal helm, with only his mouth uncovered. Bright blue eyes stared at us from the skull's empty sockets. "But you have taken something of mine, and I want it back."

"Then you should have brought help," I said. "Cuz we're ready for you this time!"

"Do I look like a fool?" Edgelord asked.

"You look like a prop from a heavy metal album cover shoot," I answered. "The kind of guy who had one good song but never realized everyone was making fun of him the whole time."

"One good song? Well, then you're going to love the sequel," he said.

"Maybe we shouldn't be talking? Maybe we should skip directly to kicking his ass?" Greg asked. "I've heard enough of his preening."

"John! John, you idiot!" Chesa yelled from overhead. I craned my neck around until I found her, balanced on the edge of the porch roof. Lillie watched from an open window behind Chesa. My ex pointed to the sky. "Air support!"

Black wings circled in the clouds. A bolt of lightning flashed across the sky, and the rolling thunder that followed sounded a lot like war horns.

"Stay tight," I snapped at Gregory, then charged forward.

The edgelord didn't move until I was close. The tower configuration of my shield didn't really lend itself to charging heroically through a domestic garden; the bottom edge kept snagging on the grasping branches of a row of barberry bushes, and every third step the top of the shield would bang against my forehead. But that guy's sword was deadly, and I wanted every inch of steel between me and its cursed edge as I could manage. Even so, he nearly took me off guard once I got to him. His first strike swept at my front leg, forcing me to ground the shield. I tried to poke at the dark knight with my sword, but he battered the blow aside and followed up with a series of quick downward swings that rang off the top edge of the shield like a tolling bell.

"Give us some space, Rast," Gregory snapped as he came around me. "Just make sure he doesn't get to the ladies."

"Greg, wait!" I shouted, but the handsome knight was already on the attack.

"I like the enthusiasm," the edgelord said with a smile. "But you should listen to your cowardly friend."

"Glory is for the strong!" was Gregory's only answer, as it usually was, in all things. Typical.

Greg's sword was impressive, just like the rest of him. He wielded a zweihander, or two-hander, of specific German stock. The blade was nearly four feet long, made of a length of wavy metal that was designed to hook enemy blades and leave gruesome wounds in its wake. He kept it in constant motion, a whirring disc of deadly steel that snipped a scattering of branches from the cursed barberry and pushed the man back. The black-clad swordsman tried to parry Gregory's assault, but there was so much weight and speed behind that blade that it was impossible.

Impossible, but also unnecessary.

"Back, you pathetic sop! Away from this sunlit land!" Gregory advanced in a series of shuffling steps, cutting off the edgelord's retreat and driving him toward a thicket. "You will taste my steel! I shall—UNGH!"

The zweihander lost momentum and speared into the muddy earth as it slipped from Gregory's hands. His opponent stood nearly still, arm extended, the tip of his sword barely nicking the inside of Gregory's bicep. A thin trickle of blood leaked down the blade, before soaking into the unnatural green steel like rain into thirsty soil.

"A palpable touch," the edgelord said with a growl in his voice. "A very palpable touch."

"But my . . . my . . ." Greg's voice faltered and his skin turned gray. Then he collapsed to the ground in a clatter of honor and pride.

"You bastard!" Bethany screamed as she burst out of the thicket, behind the dark knight's looming form. Much closer and he would have been a dead man, but it took her a handful of steps to close the distance, and the swordsman didn't have to worry about the strength of his blows. She ran straight at him, glowing daggers overhead, her face twisted in fury.

The edgelord twisted around just in time, bringing his sword up to bat away Bethany's first blade, then driving the pommel into the wrist of her second attack. That dagger went flying, but she was already counter-swinging with the first, and it was only luck and armor that kept the man moving. I was trying to close the distance between us, but Gregory had pushed the swordsman well back, and I had to get around his limp body. Just as I reached them, the edgelord caught Bethany's dagger with the guard of his sword, twisted, then levered the blade's tip down and into Bee's shoulder. She sucked in a sharp breath, then stepped backward, her retreat covered by a wake of shadows. I thought she was going to escape, but just then she collapsed against a tree, one hand pressed against her shoulder.

"Damn it," she muttered, pulling her hand away from the wound. Her palm was slick with blood. "I always knew it would be a goth."

The color drained from her face and she tumbled forward. The edgelord turned to face me.

"Alright, little man," he said. "Now it's your turn."

CHAPTER TWENTY-ONE

The black-clad Viking stalked toward me, the Totenschreck held out to one side like a flag in the wind, his other hand hooked casually in his belt buckle. I took an uncertain step backward and nearly tripped over Gregory's unconscious (and still magnificent) body.

"I have been looking forward to a proper introduction, John Rast. Ever since you and your girlfriend—"

"I'm not his girlfriend!" Chesa yelled from the rooftop, then sent a volley of arrows down on the edgelord's head. He sidestepped them nimbly and continued his droning diatribe.

"Ever since you slighted me at that pathetic convention, I have savored the thought of putting you in your place," he said. I fell back a little farther, then stopped when my tower shield scraped against the line of barberries that flanked the path. "What was it you called me? A lonely man-child?"

"I think it was 'pathetic man-child,' actually," I said. "Though I would like to update that to lonely, pathetic, overdressed man-child coward . . . bastard . . . idiot."

"Really? I thought you said I was so brave, facing you and your friends alone." He gestured to Greg and Bethany, and then the sky overhead. I glanced up and saw a slight of dark valkyries streaking out of the clouds in tight formation. The man's laugh rolled like thunder. "Who is alone now, Sir John?"

"Are you going to keep asking rhetorical questions all day?" I asked. "Or are we going to fight?"

"Oh, I don't think it will be much of a fight," he said. "But if you insist."

He lunged forward, striking my shield halfheartedly before taking a swing at my leg. Expecting this, I was already shifting my weight to my back leg and parrying the blow, but then he drove his shoulder into my shield. I stumbled back, arms flailing as I tried to regain my balance. That left me open for another strike. I watched the blade come in, my mind slowing to a crawl as it got closer, but at the last second he turned the sword and struck me with the flat, right in the belly. The edgelord sighed dramatically, as edgelords are wont to do.

"Aren't you supposed to be the shield guy? The tank?" He took another couple experimental swings at my shield. "I thought at least the tank would be an interesting grind. Are you holding back, or something? Waiting for the appropriate dramatic climax?"

"I am not," I said. The base of my tower shield dragged through the mud as I pulled back. He continued raining steel down on the bulwark, forcing it to ground every few inches. I swore and called for air support. "Chesa! What the hell are you doing back there?"

"Get back, you bitch!" Chesa shouted. I twisted around to see if I was the bitch in question, but no, Chesa had been forced to abandon bow and arrow and had switched to her dual crescent blades. One of the dark valkyries had landed on the porch roof, and was stalking toward her with spear and shield, while two more flew in lazy circles overhead.

"No help there," I muttered. Just then, the edgelord kicked my shield, nearly toppling me. I tried to riposte, but was answered by a flurry of slick-green steel thrusts that whistled inches above my head. *One touch and I'm done*, I thought. *Gotta be careful.*

"Are you going to come out from behind that thing?" he asked.

"Don't have a good reason to," I answered.

"Fine, fine," he said, exasperated. "Hardly heroic, but what was I expecting?"

The green blade of the Totenschreck appeared beside my elbow, waving around like a magic wand. It brushed my tricep, and I felt a shiver of magical energy pass through my skin. There was no strength in the attack, but there didn't have to be. He just needed to cut me, and that blade was razor sharp. This was some bullshit, let me tell you. All that time spent training with Clarence to break my Ren faire habits, and now...

Now I was playing for points again. Of course.

I took three quick steps back, tossing my shield to the side and activating its transformational powers. The broad face of the tower shield scissored closed, folding like an origami flower into the blunt wedge of a heater. Leather enarme straps slithered tight, bringing the shield against my knuckles. Holding a shield like this is a real fight was a great way to get your wrist broken, but there was no power to the attacks, just speed and that deadly cut.

"Trying something new, eh?" the edgelord asked. "Something you learned from one of your masters?"

"Something I learned on a suburban soccer field, actually, facing dickheads like you," I said. "You've screwed up. You're about to fight the reigning county champion of full-contact sword and board. Would've gone to state, too, if this whole hero thing didn't come up."

"Oh, so you're a nerd?" he asked with a sneer.

"Buddy, I'm a super-nerd!" I shouted, then moved forward, sword hidden behind the shield, poised to strike.

This took the skull-faced warrior off guard. He poked experimentally at the shield, then took a slash at my leading foot. I slammed my shield into his face, then followed that up with a hard block on his wrist with the edge of the heater. He swore and pulled back, but only far enough to reset his guard.

"Okay, so the nerd has some skills," he said. "You'll make a good addition to my zombie army."

"Going to have to disappoint you on that one," I said.

"We shall see, little man. We shall see."

He came at me again. His movements were awkward and almost casual, but he didn't have to move too much to threaten me. That sword was deadly. But he rarely moved more than his sword arm, slashing back and forth like a weed wacker, just as content to strike my shield. He treated the sword like a garden hose. Swing enough, and eventually something will land.

Again, in a real fight that was a terrible strategy. But given how dangerous the slick-green edge of the Totenschreck could be, I had to take it seriously. I spent a lot of time shifting my shield back and forth, only risking a hilt block when I was sure I could keep any counterstrike away from my body. My shield wrist started getting tired from swinging the steel back and forth. Whenever I tried to counterattack, he just fell back, covering his retreat with a whirlwind of green steel that I didn't dare charge through. I had to think of something before he wore me out.

Watching his movements, I started to see a pattern in his attacks. He wasn't used to armor, and he'd never fought with a shield or the risk of grievous bodily injury. Not that different from me when I first joined Knight Watch, fresh off the Ren faire circuit and convinced I was God's gift to swordplay. Clarence had stabbed, sliced, hacked, chopped, skewered, and disemboweled that delusion out of me. Confidence is great, but it'll get you killed once folks start swinging around three feet of sharp steel.

"What's the matter, super-nerd? Cat got your secret powers?"

"Just doing some math in my head," I answered. His third swing kept overreaching. I held my breath as he came in, once, twice, then he drew back for the big hit.

I shifted my shield enough to give him a look at my shoulder. He took the bait, letting me bat his strike aside and go in with the shield. The way he held the blade and his body made it clear that he wasn't used to being on the defensive, especially not while wearing restrictive metal armor. He tried to dodge out of the path of my blade, but ended up dancing like a puppet whose strings were tangled. As he started to fall backward, I kicked at his sword, making satisfying contact with the thick heel of my boot. Totenschreck went flying.

"No! You bastard!" the edgelord shrieked. Then he hit the ground with a thump. To his credit, he scrambled to his feet faster than I could take advantage, but with his creepy Nazi toy lying in a bush, there wasn't much he could do to hurt me. I smiled and lowered my shield.

"That's what happens when you talk too much," I said. "If you'd just focused on—"

He was still wearing metal gauntlets, I still had a nose and a smart mouth. He punched me with all his emo strength, which was more than enough to send me reeling. I spat blood out of my mouth and blinked tears out of my eyes. My vision cleared just in time to see him scoop up the Totenschreck and scamper into the woods surrounding Edelweiss House.

"I'm going to have to start wearing that damn helm again," I mumbled, then started after my quarry. Just in time to hear a heavy crash behind me, followed by a chorus of screaming.

The dark valkyries had descended. There were two sizable holes in the B&B's shingle roof, one on the upper level, and another close to the kitchen. Guests were boiling out of the various exits and streaming from the open windows on the first floor. I spotted Chesa hopping from the porch roof down into the hedgerows below, closely followed by a spear-wielding valkyrie. A flash of light turned the interior of the kitchen into a blast furnace. Seconds later Hildr and Matthew hustled out of the conflagration with Tembo's limp form strung between them. They dumped the unconscious mage onto the ground. Matthew went to one knee at Tembo's side and started glowing like a firecracker. The valkyrie grabbed a rusty shovel that was leaning beside the back door and plunged back into the rapidly spreading fire.

I looked up the hill to where the edgelord was disappearing into the surrounding woods, then reluctantly raced through the garden to help my friends. And maybe to keep the Tears out of the hands of those valkyries.

Another blast shook the house, this one more mundane but no less devastating. The few unopened windows blew out, spraying fleeing guests and the remaining members of Knight Watch with broken glass. Chesa and her valhellion opponent were fighting their way through the shrubs, the valkyrie using her spear like a quarterstaff to bully Chesa away from the porch. I reached them just as the valkyrie went on the offensive, stabbing out with her spear in a flurry of blows that threatened to puncture Chesa's swirling defense. I tackled Chesa, sliding through the rough gravel of the garden path like a homebase runner, shield deployed overhead. The spearpoint rattled off the face of my shield, dimpling the steel.

As soon as we stopped sliding, Chesa pushed me away and rolled to her feet. The valkyrie smirked and swept away, circling the house with long, lazy flaps of her wings.

"That was hardly necessary, John," she said, straightening the steel-reinforced furl of her skirts and adjusting her hair. "I had things well in order."

"Sorry, got carried away with the heroism," I said, getting to my feet. "You looked like you could use a hand."

"That was a lot more than a hand. That was a full body," she said as she picked gravel out of her bracers. "Where are the others? Did you get the goth-creeper?"

"They're down. Saint's going to have to manage them. Speaking of which . . ."

Our attention went to Tembo and Saint Matthew. The lanky mage was breathing, but his eyes were squeezed shut in pain, and dark blood soaked his robes from hips to hands. Matthew's diamond-bright skin flashed. We went to his side.

"There's a lot of damage," Matthew said. "They kill in weird ways, those girls. We need to get him back to Mundane Actual."

"Not just him," I said, gesturing up the garden path. "Bee and Greg are up there. Maybe dead. Tatertots got 'em."

"I don't have a lot of juice left," Matthew said, "but I think Tem can wait. Up the path, you say? Is it safe?"

"Not at all. Our creepy friend is still up there, somewhere."

"I'll go with you," Chesa said. "John, you stay here and hit anything that comes out that door."

"What's going on in there?" I asked, peering into the flames.

"Valkyries came through the roof. Went straight to the basement stairs. Lillie went after them with that shotgun, just as Tembo tried to blast them with a fireball. She shot him and ran."

"Lillie shot him?!" I shouted. "I thought this was the work of those valkyries."

"Yeah, well, we may have fewer allies here than we thought," Matthew said. "Come on, Ches. Let's see what we can do about our dead friends."

He and Chesa went up the path. I turned back to the burning house. A section of roof collapsed, sending a plume of sparks towering into the air. The interior was blazing and bright, and the heat pressing down on my face made it clear the last thing I should do was go inside.

With a last look at the garden path, I kicked open the door, held my shield over my head, and ran into the flames.

CHAPTER TWENTY-TWO

Burning cinders bounced off the face of my shield, heating the metal and stinging my arm beneath. Curls of thick smoke wafted through the ruined kitchen. Abandoned bowls of eyeball soup boiled on the table, while sheets of flame flickered across the ceiling like sulphurous weather.

"Hildr! Lillie!" I shouted, then collapsed into a coughing fit and scalding hot air filled my mouth and lungs. I spat ashes and peered into the smokey haze.

The kitchen was a disaster. Pillars of flame swirled in the hallway that led to the rest of the building, but it felt unlikely that the valkyries would have hidden their prize among the guests. Besides, the hole in the ceiling lay directly over a set of stairs leading, presumably, to some kind of basement. I vaulted the burning remnants of a boot rack and made my way down the stairs.

It was like descending into some kind of mildew-based underworld. A flickering tube of fluorescent light provided thin illumination to an otherwise dark room. The basement was cluttered from wall to wall with all manner of debris, from stacked shoeboxes to dozens of coiled garden hoses, and something that looked suspiciously like an erotic statue of Thor. Narrow pathways led between the stacks, occasionally interrupted by collapsed walls of newspapers and toppled storage bins. A rusted out washer and dryer rattled nervously at the base of the stairs. Moss-stained cinder-block walls stretched into the darkness. Along the far wall, partially obscured by intervening terrain, stood a phalanx of freezers, humming placidly to themselves.

"Well this is definitely act one of a horror movie," I muttered to myself. "Hero descends into the underworld to confront Mr. Preppy Cannibal, only to be slain, flayed, roasted, and served with a side of couscous and a snifter of bourbon."

Something shifted in the back of the room. An avalanche of moldy paperbacks slid into the nearest walkway. I caught a glimpse of a shadow lurching deeper into the darkness. I crept to the bottom of the stairs and set foot on the concrete floor, shield held nervously in front of me, sword at my side. A cascade of cinders followed me into the dimly lit basement, swirling like fireflies. A few landed on the discarded paperbacks with a hiss.

"Hello? Who's down here? Lillie?" I called out. No one answered, but I could hear a low moaning, and the drip of viscous liquid. Swallowing, I stepped over the now-smouldering paperbacks and started toward the back corner.

"I know we got off on the wrong foot, but I really think we're working toward the same goal." The path narrowed, half walls of mold-spotted hatboxes crowding me to the shoulders. I had to pull my shield flat to my chest, sword behind me, as I edged sideways toward the shadows. Upstairs, something collapsed directly overhead. The floorboards flexed and groaned, and cinders crawled between the planks like termites. "We need to get out of here before this place burns to the ground. And if we can take the Tears with us, all the better. Maybe—"

Something shattered to my right, followed by a quick tattoo of breaking glass and what sounded like an avalanche of bricks sliding to the floor. I ducked, but nothing came my way. The basement was starting to fill with smoke. I didn't have a lot of time left, and whatever was lurking in the shadows clearly didn't want to talk about it. I came around the corner.

An armored valkyrie perched over the open lid of a chest freezer, black, glossy wings pulled tight to her body. A pile of broken casserole dishes lay at her feet, their contents glistening icily in the harsh light of the fluorescent bulbs overhead. Bricks of casserole, frozen meat, gritty Jell-O, and a variety of unidentifiable foodstuffs lay naked on the floor. A cube of something brown and slick shrugged free of its tin foil cover and spun toward me, stopping only when it ran into my foot.

"Can you believe they eat these things, John? Tatertots in cream cheese? This has been in here for three years," the valkyrie said, holding up a casserole dish. "To think they gave up the pleasures of Valhalla for . . . for . . ." She gestured helplessly at the contents of the freezer. "For whatever the hell this is."

"I'm sorry, have we met?" I asked. The valkyrie turned sharply in my direction, using her wings to propel her body in a tight spiral. She lifted a spear from its resting place on a pile of carpet scraps. For a brief second I thought I recognized her, a glimpse of familiarity from my brief stay in Valhalla, but the feeling passed as she lowered the spear and pointed it at my midsection.

"You are quite famous, John Rast. The boy who killed a dragon by accident, and then nearly helped his friend destroy Knight Watch. We've heard all about you," she said, stalking toward me. I backed up, setting my shield, though there wasn't enough room for a proper guard stance. At least she couldn't fly in this cramped room. But that spear was a lot longer than my reach, and there was no way I was going to be able to dodge her thrusts.

"Well, it's nice to have fans," I said. "But can I ask what the hell you're doing? Why are you trying to end the world, anyway? What's the damn point?"

"Ragnarok is not the end of the world," she said. "Merely the merciful death of this horrible existence, and the start of a new, golden age, full of—"

"Full of bullshit and light, I get it," I said. "But I think I'd rather stick with the world I know, thanks."

I kicked the glistening meat-thing at my feet toward her. It came down right beneath her advancing boot, slipping mercilessly out from under her. She yodeled in surprise, wings flapping in a desperate bid for balance, battering down towers of boxes and carpet and mold. I lowered my shield and charged, bowling into the flailing valkyrie and sending us both slipping and sliding across the basement floor.

We slammed into a standing freezer, bouncing it off the wall and sending it wobbling back and forth. Unseen bulk shifted inside, and the whole freezer tipped forward, straight at us. I jumped to my feet and sprang backward. The valkyrie scrambled in the other direction, disappearing behind a stack of newspapers before the falling freezer came down with a crash. The lights cut out in a shower of sparks and fluorescent brilliance, then darkness fell across the basement.

Slowly, I got to my feet, careful to make as little noise as possible. The only light came from the narrow, cobweb-choked windows at ceiling height, and the throbbing red glow coming from the staircase. The crackle and roar of the inferno overhead filled the room. I crept forward, sword and shield close to my chest to keep them from dragging on the surrounding detritus. My boots came down on broken dishware and the slippery corpses of shattered casseroles, each step crunching and squelching. There was no noise from the valkyrie, which meant she was either staying still, was unconscious, or had some way of moving that I couldn't hear.

I reached the fallen freezer and paused, listening carefully. In the dim light I was able to make out a body splayed out on the ground, near the top of the freezer but tucked into a small clearing in the piles of junk. Peering more closely, I could make out Lillie's pale face, marred by a trickle of blood. If I had come down a different aisle, I might have stepped on her before reaching the valkyrie.

Vaulting the freezer, I knelt beside Lillie and pressed two fingers into her neck in search of a pulse. Unfortunately, I was still wearing my gauntlets, so all I managed to do was crush her windpipe, but at least it forced her to cough. Her eyes fluttered open.

"Tears . . . the Tears," she whispered, one hand pawing at the air. "Don't let her get them."

"I'm doing what I can, Lil. But you need to tell me where they are first," I said.

"Tots . . ." she answered, then her voice faded and her eyes closed.

"Yes, yes, the tots-in-shrieker, I know all about that bastard," I said, frustrated that the old valkyrie hadn't given me more to work with. Then I remembered something the dark valkyrie had said, and I froze. "Tatertots in sour cream. Who *would* eat that?"

I fumbled my way back to the chest freezer. In the dim light, I was able to make out a glimmer of illumination from the icy depths of the freezer. Something glowed inside. Sheathing my blade and shouldering my shield, I rummaged through the frozen wreckage of leftovers. Packages of deer meat wrapped in butcher paper, frost-rimed casseroles, and a collection of unidentifiable sauces in ziplock bags filled the bottom of the freezer. I tossed them aside, looking for the source of the dim glow.

I found it nestled between a container of clearly spoiled reindeer meat and a block of chili that had escaped its container and was slowly dissolving into soup. A tan casserole dish printed with cornflower blue petals and covered with a tight lid of tin foil. Printed on the foil in marker were the words *Freya's Tears. Do not microwave.*

I ripped off the lid and stared in disbelief at a crust of tatertots held together with melted cheese. Using my rapidly numbing fingers (metal gloves do not go well with freezers), I scraped aside the tots. Beneath shimmered a layer of a metallic silver substance that jiggled like pudding and glowed with a blue-ish light.

"I'll take those." The voice came from behind me, and was immediately followed by a spear point that skittered off my shield and buried into the gap between my backplate and the stiff belt that held my chausses in place. Pain burst through my hip, and I spun around, struggling to draw my sword as the casserole slipped from my fingers. I got around just in time to meet the butt of the valkyrie's spear with my chin. Stars filled my vision, and when I could see again, I was curled up on the floor with empty hands and a skull that felt like a church bell on New Year's Day.

The valkyrie stared down at the Tears, her face limned by the light coming from the casserole. She smiled, then tucked the casserole against her chest and unfurled her wings.

"Chalk one up for the bad guys," she said, then launched at the ceiling. The smoldering wood planks burst aside, her shoulders punching a hole directly through the floor above, disappearing into the swirling maelstrom of the fire consuming the house overhead. I heard two more massive crashes, and then the ceiling of the basement started to collapse around me.

I struggled to my feet and crawled to Lillie. She was still breathing, if barely. I hefted her over my shoulder and limped through the stacks of burning paper and smoking boxes. By the time I reached the stairs, the air was black with smoke, and the heat of the fire pressed against me like a hammer blow. The wooden staircase groaned and buckled underfoot, but I pushed forward, emerging in the remnants of the kitchen. I stumbled forward in a dreamlike state, my mind empty of everything but the next step, the next obstacle, the door that I could barely make out through the flames. By the time I reached the kitchen door, there was nothing left of it by charred wood and shattered glass.

I crashed through it like a cannonball, fell to my knees, and collapsed.

As was often the case when I passed out, especially in battle, I awoke to the placid face of Saint Matthew staring down at me. He had a curious expression on his face, almost like he was surprised to see my eyes open. The saint squeezed my cheeks and tapped my forehead, then shrugged dramatically.

"Well, at least you stayed around," he said. "I was starting to think they were trying to avoid me. I've got enough issues without corpses ghosting me."

"Ha," I said, which was an abortive attempt at a laugh, halted halfway through by sharp pain in my lungs. "Corpses. Ghosting."

"Hmm? Oh, yeah. I meant that literally," Matthew said as he stood. "You've got new lungs. Sucked down enough smoke to give you permanent scarring. Had to cut them out and start over."

"Cut them out?" I sat up and peered down at my chest. My breastplate and gambeson were peeled away, and the pale, sickly skin of my chest was slick with sweat. But there was no sign of lung removal. "What are you talking about?"

"Your lungs. We had to cut them out. valkyries were pretty useful for that, to be honest." He wiped his hands on a bloody cloth, then tossed it into a pile of many, many equally bloody clothes. "Don't worry about it. You're as good as new."

I lay back and ran a hand over my chest. I felt normal enough, though my lungs did feel a little . . . tight? Just the kind of thing that happens in Knight Watch. I sat up again.

"Wait. What did you mean about corpses avoiding you?" I asked.

"Bee and the new guy. Soon as I tried to heal them, they both sank into the ground. Disappeared. Tembo's still here, but he didn't die, so . . ." He shrugged again. "Must have something to do with the sword."

"The Totenschreck has claimed them," Lillie said. The old valkyrie was sitting on a barrel next to the ruins of her house, holding a damp cloth to her head. "They are lost to you now. Mourn them, and move on."

"That's not how Knight Watch works, lady," I said. I worked my way to my feet and started to tie my gambeson shut. My armor lay in pieces all around me, and my sword and shield hung from an apple tree at the foot of the garden path. There were handfuls of feathers scattered about, as though they had been tucked into my armor. I ignored them for now. "We're going to find this tater-tot-shrieker, and we're going to get our friends back."

"Then you will die," she answered. "May you find your way to Valhalla."

"Not really my scene," I said. "Where are the others? Tembo and Chesa and Hildr?"

"We had to hide Tembo from the fire department," Matthew said. "Chesa had to distract them while we were finishing with you. But now that you're up and about, we should get out of here. As for Hildr . . ." He looked awkwardly at Lillie.

"My companion is dead," Lillie said quietly. "And there is no Valhalla for us."

"Shit, I'm . . . I'm sorry," I said. "I thought you guys were, you know . . . immortal or something."

"I appreciate your sympathy, but it is unnecessary. Hildr lived well, and she died just as well. I will mourn her, and then I will continue. Though without the Tears to protect, I don't know what I'll do with my life." She pulled the cloth away from her head, blinked down at the blood spot on the clean white linen, then folded it neatly and put it into the pocket of her apron. "Perhaps I could see the fjords again. Minnesota is nice, but it is not home."

As if on cue, Chesa appeared from around the burned-out husk of the house. She was cradling her bow on her shoulder and, other than a few nicks and cuts, looked none the worse for wear. Her battle-dress was stained with soot, and she walked like someone who had just had the worst customer service in her life.

"Those guys ask a lot of questions," she said, then looked at me. "Good. You're not dead."

"That's the nicest thing you've said to me in a long time," I said with a smile.

"Don't get excited. I barely mean it." She turned to Matthew. "No luck on the missing bodies?"

"They're gone. Lillie insists the valhellions have them."

"Then that's where we're going," she said. "Back to MA, then the express to Valhalla."

"They will not be in Valhalla," Lillie said. "Those taken by Freya go to Folksvangr."

"Different beer hall?" I asked.

"Different beer hall," she confirmed. "And you will need to get the key from Runa Hellesdottir. There is no other way."

"Well, that still has us going to Valhalla," I said, gathering my weapons. "Lillie, do you need anything else from us?"

"I need you to get your life-destroying asses out of my garden, before I throw them out." She stood stiffly, then started up the garden path. "I must bury my sister, and I wish to do that in private. Thank you."

We watched her disappear into the garden, shifting nervously on our feet until we were alone. I turned to Matthew.

"I don't feel like we did a lot of good here," I said.

"Destroyed their lives, burned down their house, lost two members of the team, badly disabled a third, and lost the world-ending magic device we came to find?" he asked. "Nah. We did great."

"What's with all these feathers?" I asked. Chesa had a cluster of them in her hair, and now that I looked around I could see dozens of feathers floating in the breeze. I nabbed one and peered at it. "Looks kind of like down."

"I think they're turkey," Matthew said. "Who knew that valkyries had turkey in them?"

"Anyone who's had to deal with valkyries," I said. I shoved a couple into the pouch at my belt, just in case they turned out to be useful later on.

"Hey, where's Percy?" Chesa asked. We looked among ourselves.

"I haven't seen hide nor hair of the man," I said.

"Me neither. Disappeared just before the valhellions arrived. Think he was in on it?" Chesa asked.

"Don't know. But if you can't trust an English gardening zombie, who can you trust?" Matthew asked. "Come on, we've got to find a telephone. Preferably a really old one that can get through our bubble of magical interference. If we can get a hold of MA, they can probably arrange a ride for us."

CHAPTER TWENTY-THREE

There are good and bad things about being a magical hero stuck in the real world. The good thing is that we're immune to modern threats—no guns, no radar guns, no radio. The bad thing is . . . we're immune to modern conveniences as well. No phones, no cars, no microwave ovens. Appliances break around us. Cars usually stall out when we try to ride them. None of us have tried to get on an airplane, for pretty obvious reasons. I've completely forgotten how the Internet works, though I do remember there being trolls online, so maybe we have some kind of back door? I don't miss it.

That's why we have Mundane Actual. They deal with all the dull, modern, technological aspects of running a worldwide magical strike force. We're usually able to get around by arcane means, either the Naglfr or various magical portals, leylines, shadow roads, or more obscure methods. MA itself has a fleet of augmented vehicles that are marginally magical, normal enough to not draw attention on the road, fey enough to keep running when Chesa or I sit in the back seat.

This is how we ended up in the bed of a ramshackle pickup truck with no engine, no seats, and apparently no suspension. Chesa, Matthew, and I huddled on the runners, while Tembo lay in the middle of the bed, resting on a mattress of hay. Tem looked rough, and spent most of the trip muttering feverishly and trying to pull away the bandages that Matthew had strapped across his chest. It was grim. Which is why we really hoped the truck could go faster. Unfortunately, fast was not in the cards. A team of tired horses dragged the vehicle along the side of the road at a breakneck shamble, urged on by a member of MA who sat on top of the cab. His name was Jeff. His uniform hung loosely over thin shoulders and thinner arms, and the collar of his coat nearly covered his head. Most MA operatives looked like they could bench-press a small bus, and usually carried enough firepower to face off against a small country. Not Jeff. Jeff had a flintlock strapped to his thigh, a tricorn hat pressed tight to his forehead, and a pinched look in his eyes. Jeff was not terribly talkative. After a great deal of prying and the sort of incessant rambling that she specialized at, Chesa got him to engage.

"Can't you go any faster? This isn't much better than walking," Chesa said.

"Then walk," Jeff said.

"But, I mean, at this rate we won't get back to HQ before the end of the world," she answered.

"Well, that would certainly solve most of my problems," Jeff said. "Don't have to clock in if the world ends."

"But you'll be dead."

"Mm-hmm."

"Everyone would be dead."

Jeff answered with a long and protracted sigh, then settled deeper into his coat. We exchanged a look. Chesa was about to speak again, but Matthew held up a hand.

"The sooner we're home, the sooner you can get back to . . . whatever you would rather be doing. Did Esther give specific instructions on when and how we should be getting back to HQ?" he asked.

"There's a shadow road about five minutes away," Jeff said. "Ten minutes, if you keep talking. Horses don't like talking."

"Not just the horses, I imagine," I muttered. Jeff apparently heard me, because he gave the reins a little tug and slowed us even more.

The shadow gate, when we finally arrived, was a simple stone fence in a cornfield in the middle of nowhere. Jeff drove the horse-truck straight through the field, battering stalks of corn aside with the slow persistence of a glacier. The fence formed a circle about twenty feet in diameter, with a rickety iron gate on the near side. Inside the fence, the ground was gray and silty, like the surface of the moon. Jeff dropped us off and then trundled away, much faster than he had ever gone while we were with him.

"So, do you know how to operate this thing?" Chesa asked as she peered uncertainly at the fence. "Are there runes or something? A necessary sacrifice?"

"If I understand correctly, we just walk through the gate, our minds firmly fixed on our destination," Matthew answered. "But to be honest, this kind of thing is Tembo's territory."

"Well, Tem's not answering questions at the moment," I said. "Let's just walk through. We all know what HQ looks like."

"But do we need to focus on HQ in general? Or the shadow gate at HQ?" Chesa asked. "Because I have no idea what that looks like."

"We're overthinking this," I said. "Through the gate! Matthew, grab Tem's feet. We can carry him through."

"Maybe I should go through first?" Chesa asked. "In case it's dangerous?"

"Overthinking!" I declared once again. Then, with Tembo's shoulders supported by my shield, and his feet in Matthew's hands, we sidestepped through the gate.

Nothing happened. Chesa stood outside the circle, staring at us in disappointment.

"Maybe there are words," she said. "Have you tried saying magical words?"

"I don't know any magic words!" I shouted. "I just want to go hom—"

Everything happened.

I've mentioned falling before. In fact, sometimes I think there's too much falling in my life. I need to work on that. But at that moment, the only proper description was *falling*. Through the world. Without the world getting out of the way. Thick gravel slid past my head and forced its way into my armor, while more substantial rocks battered my legs and feet. I curled into a ball, but that just sped my descent without lessening the impact of my passage. I passed through an underground river thick with silt and strange grasping creatures, then there was a flash of heat and steam. For a brief moment I thought I was about to be flash-fried at the center of the earth, but just then I popped out into open air. I fell about eight feet and landed with a thud on a shelf of hard material. I lay in a fetal position for three long, shuddering breaths before I moved at all.

A shell of slimy grit cracked and fell away from my eyes. I coughed, and a stream of gray water splashed out onto the floor. I stood slowly, armor grinding as an avalanche of gravel slithered free and rattled into a pile at my feet. My shield had fallen out of my hands, but lay in a mound of rubble nearby, half-buried in grime and dirt. Tembo was gone. Matthew was gone. Presumably Chesa was still standing in a field somewhere, staring at an empty spot on the ground. But I wasn't dead. So I had that going for me.

I looked around. I was in the strangest place; there was a pair of stuffed chairs arranged in front of a raging fireplace, and a table that looked like it had been used for sword practice by an enthusiastic berserker, and a pair of doors... Wait a second. Shield over the hearth, the smell of stew in the air, the general patter of rain on the window, the sound of someone softly humming and clattering around the kitchen...

I was in my own sitting room. In my domain. And there was someone in the kitchen.

Drawing my sword, I crept across the room to the narrow door that led to the kitchen. My sneakiness was hampered by the crunch of gravel underfoot, and the fact that I was wearing steel full plate mixed with a three bags of landscape pebbles, and also I'm not very sneaky in the best of circumstances, nevermind when I just fell through half the world and my own roof after nearly dying in a fire. But I got to the door, and the sound of gentle humming did not abate, so I steeled myself for battle and then kicked open the door and charged forward.

Percival the wayward garden zombie stood at the sink, cheerfully washing a bowl. When I came through the door he shrieked, then dropped the bowl and grabbed the ladle out of the pot of stew simmering away on the stove. We yelled at each other in bestial tones for a few heartbeats, then scorching hot soup drooled down the handle of the ladle and poured over Percy's pale white hand.

"God's grocery list, that's hot!" he screamed, throwing the ladle into the sink and shaking his hand like a party favor. "You scared the ichor out of me, Rast!"

"You! You abandoned us, you two-timing, weasley little runt! I ought to run you through and see what comes out of that cold heart of yours!"

"It would be blood," he said. "Kind of old blood, and yes, cold as tar, but still my blood and I'm kind of attached to it. Plus then I'd go to that damned field and they would have their hooks in me again."

"Where did you go? How did you get here?" I shouted. Then, because two questions are never enough, "Are you on their side?"

"The valkyries? Gods, no. I just . . ." He looked exasperated, then stopped rubbing his hand and picked up the ladle to wash it. "I was out in the garden, and I could feel them pressing in. Feel them getting closer. And the last thing . . ." He took a moment to collect himself before continuing. "I'm not going to let them take me again. I don't care what it costs, and I'm sorry if I let you down, but the last thing I'm going to do is stick around and fall under their sway again. For any reason."

I lowered the tip of my sword. He looked miserable, even a little pathetic, but he certainly didn't look threatening. Still, I had a mighty fury in my heart.

"You very much did let us down, Percy. Greg and Bee are gone now, their bodies swallowed whole by the ground, and Hildr's dead. All that, plus we lost the Tears. So I'm sorry, but sorry isn't going to cut it."

"I understand," he said, tossing the rag he'd been using to clean the ladle onto the counter, his shoulders slumping. "I'll go. The garden gnomes have probably run rampant in my absence."

"Like hell you'll go. I don't even understand how you got here in the first place! This is my domain, Percy! It's supposed to be a secure place, a place that no one else can get to! In fact, the last time something got in here, it was to try to kill me! So I'm going to need—"

There was a sharp knock on the door. Percival and I both froze. He raised one bushy, zombified eyebrow.

"For a place no one else can get to, it's getting kind of crowded in here," he said.

"Stay here," I ordered. "Don't move."

The knock came again, commanding and clear. I dug my shield out of its pile of rubble, slipping it over my forearm as I approached the door. The window shutters were closed, so I couldn't see outside, but I knew that beyond that door was an entire magical domain of murderous monsters, hungry hobgoblins, and a dog the size of three school buses. But none of those things had ever knocked on the door. Carefully, I slid back the bolt and eased the thick wooden door open an inch.

A battering ram wrapped in floral print shot past me, spraying rain water and indignation across the room. It bowled me aside, not stopping until it reached the center of the room, and the piles of gravel that my recent transportation had deposited on the floor.

"Land of Goshen, John! How long were you going to keep us waiting in that rain! It's hardly civilized." My mother stood in the center of the room, her dress spotted with rain, face creased with disappointment. She looked around, her steely gaze eventually settling on the gravel underfoot. "And it's a complete mess, of course. Can't leave you alone for a week without the place falling into the Middle Ages, can I? And such dreary furniture. This place needs a woman's touch, it does."

"Mom . . . how did you . . . how are you . . . ?" I swallowed and tried again. "How did you get here?"

"You paying to heat the outside?" Dad asked as he trundled past me. He walked straight to the largest of the stuffed chairs and, with a great deal of complaining and oofing and general drama, settled into the cushions.

"How did we get here?" Mom asked. She had somehow found a broom and apron, and was already herding the rubble into a tidy pile. "We drove, obviously. Have you forgotten about cars?" She looked up at me, then made a *tsk*ing sound at the sword in my hand. "Gracious, John. It's no wonder no one comes to visit, if you're answering the door in costume. I thought this move would be good for you. Might straighten you out."

"I don't understand . . ." I said. "Anything that is happening. At all."

"Well, close the door before the horses get out. You don't actually have a horse in here, do you? It smells like you might."

Dumbfounded, but trained from youth to simply do what my mother said, especially when it came to opening and closing doors, I turned and put my hand on the bolt. That's when I froze in place.

Beyond the doorstep was a nicely manicured lawn, and a concrete sidewalk, and a road lined with majestic oaks and midrange cars and at least one person walking a dog that was *not* the size of three school buses. None of this was the realm of nightmare that was supposed to be outside my door. Everything here was perfectly . . . mundane.

It was terrifying.

CHAPTER TWENTY-FOUR

"No, no, no, no, NO!" I yelled as I rushed out my front door and into the manicured hellscape of suburbia. The man with the dog drew up short and stared at me. My ash-and-gravel-smeared plate armor, dented shield, and vintage longsword were a touch out of place, but I didn't care. The dog started to wag his tail. His owner, less outgoing or perhaps more concerned for his safety, began to back slowly down the street. A minivan full of kids rolled past, mother-driver yelling cheerfully into her cellphone while the passenger gawked at Mr. Medieval. I went to my knees.

"NOOOOOOOOOOOOO!!!!!"

"John Malcolm Rast! You get inside this house this instant!" My mother was on the stoop, hands to hips.

Still under the influence of motherly instruction, I stood and trudged back into the house. I was encouraged to see that my house, at least, had not changed significantly. The outside was still a rough-hewn log cottage built into the side of a hill that rose incongruently out of the suburban landscape like a little pocket of Hobbiton in Highland Park. Mom grabbed me by the shoulder and dragged me the last ten feet, slamming the door behind me.

"What is wrong with you? Do you know what the neighbors will say, if you keep acting like that?" She pushed me down into the chair next to Dad. I squirmed around my sheathed sword and the uncomfortable burden of my shield. "Now stay here. I'll be back with sandwiches in a jiffy."

"Roast beef," Dad said. He had produced a remote from somewhere and was patiently clicking it at the fireplace. "TV's broken."

"TV is a fireplace," I said. Then I heard the door to the kitchen swing shut, and I realized Mom was about to meet a zombie. I jumped to my feet. "Wait!"

I rushed into the kitchen and directly into my mother. She was standing just inside the kitchen door, hands to her mouth, with a horrified expression on her face. I pushed her aside and stood between her and the zombie.

Except there wasn't a zombie. The kitchen was empty. The pot of stew boiled happily on the woodstove, the dishes lay in the sink with the cauldron of rainwater next to it. Everything looked normal. Percy must have fled when he saw my mom, though where he could have gone was a mystery. I turned to my mom.

"I can explain—"

"Can you? Can you explain why my son, who was raised in a good and decent household, doesn't even have a microwave? Or a refrigerator?" She shouldered her way past me and went to the sink. "OR RUNNING WATER! Do you have any idea how embarrassing this is for me?"

"Oh. It's the kitchen that horrifies you. Right." I looked around the room, trying to see it through her eyes. The lack of appliances had never bothered me, simply because the house spirits that made the soup and kept the bread fresh also refilled the water bucket and—until Percy showed up—cleaned the dishes. I had a cupboard and some dishes. What more did I need?

Lots, apparently. Mom was listing a litany of absences, from can openers to mixing bowls, and she kept repeating the bit about a microwave. Fortunately, she hadn't figured out the lack of electricity. Or, you know, conventional bathroom facilities. I suddenly realized I needed to get these people out of here before Dad had to "live through Pompeii," which was the cute little term he had for his afternoon bowel movement.

"This is all part of the Ren faire thing, Mom," I said, moving her firmly out of the kitchen. "I'm trying to be a knight. Kinda."

"Knights had castles, John. They had servants. You have . . ." She gestured helplessly at the piles of gravel and my father, still futilely trying to change the channel on the fireplace. "You have whatever this is."

"A home," I said. She sighed heavily, then went to the table and moved the chairs around. She was fussing. "Mom, what's bothering you?"

"Nothing, it's just... we never see you. After that storm..." One of my very first adventures involved a storm harpy trying to kill me, and resulted in a tornado going through my parents' house. "We had to move in with your aunt, and you just... disappeared. We see Eric sometimes, and Chesa, but you—"

"Wait, you see Eric and Chesa?"

"Around town, sure. Shopping. But you never visit, you never call, and the last time we tried to visit you, the address you gave us led to a dead-end road in the middle of a forest." She wouldn't look up at me, just busied herself with the chairs that she had already moved three times. "It feels like you're avoiding us."

How do you say *I'm not avoiding you, I'm avoiding the modern world, because that's how my magic powers work* without sounding like a madman? I don't think you can. Or at least, I don't think I can, because when I tried it came out like this:

"Yes, I'm avoiding you."

"Oh. Well, then." She pushed the chair violently into the table. "Come on, Frank. We're not wanted here."

"That's not what I meant! I mean, it is, but—"

"No, no, you don't have to explain it. You've got important KNIGHT things to do. Maybe if you could find a damsel to save, I wouldn't have to worry so much about you getting sepsis from your own kitchen sink!" She stormed to the door. "Frank!"

"I think Vesuvius is—"

"No! Mom, we can talk about this later. I promise to come visit more, but right now it's probably best if we just leave things alone."

"I agree. Besides, we have a ten-minute walk ahead of us," she said. "The stupid car broke down on the way over."

Father, grumbling, made his way to the door. Mom exited the house with a flounce and waited on the sidewalk. As he passed, Dad thumped the remote into my grasp.

"You're going to need to get this thing looked at. Probably the batteries. Or the cable. Squirrels sometimes chew the cable," he said.

"I'm pretty sure you brought this with you," I said, trying to force the remote back into his hands. But he was already gone, rolling side to side as he and Mother made their way down the sidewalk. With a sigh, I wrapped the remote in a towel and hid it under some bushes at the end of my driveway to keep it from infecting the domain any more than it already had. Mom and Dad had already disappeared down the street.

"I'm going to have to fix that before this is all over," I said. "Can't have them showing up randomly. As for this . . ." I looked around the suburban neighborhood. "This is going to take a conversation with Esther, I think. If I can just find a way back to HQ from here."

The good news was that HQ came to me. The bad news was that they brought friends. Lots of friends.

The sound of a helicopter reached me while I was still sitting on my front stoop, glaring at the neighbors and wondering how I was going to re-establish my domain's connection to the mythic world. I didn't think much of it at first. After all, if there were minivans and leashed dogs, why wouldn't there be helicopters? Then it started getting closer, and closer, and louder, and lower. The sirens started shortly after.

"Well, this has got to be for me," I said, getting stiffly to my feet. "Waving a sword around in the street will get you some attention. Though I really just expected a letter from the homeowners association, or maybe a stern cancellation online." I drew my sword and laid it carefully on the sidewalk, next to my shield. "Really wish I'd thought to get out of the armor first. Ah well. At least I won't have to worry about getting shivved."

A caravan of black vans came squealing around the corner, sirens blaring and headlights blinking in a seizure-inducing sequence. They didn't look like cop vehicles, though, more like high-end delivery vans, or maybe the kind of monstrosity a family of eighteen might take on vacation. Kind of like the *Death Star*, only square. Three of them screeched to a halt in front of my house, while a fourth barreled up the driveway and plowed into my yard. Just then, the aforementioned helicopter roared over my roof, flattening the surrounding trees. The chopper appeared to be some kind of gunship, with a bulbous nose and enough gun emplacements to shred a column of tanks, much less one hero in full plate. I shielded my eyes from the downdraft and peered up at the helicopter, half expecting a shower of incendiary rounds at any moment.

Not that it would matter. I was magically bulletproof, just like the rest of Knight Watch. Unless this whole thing with my domain meant that I had lost that power. In which case . . .

I slowly raised my hands over my head and tried to smile.

The sliding door of the van that had parked itself in my lawn slid open, and a particularly disheveled Esther MacRae sprang out. She marched up to me and slapped a clipboard into my chest.

"Do you have any idea the ruckus you're causing, Rast?" she shouted.

I looked up at the helicopter with its slowly rotating assault cannons, and the battalion of combat vans arranged haphazardly in my street.

"Me? The ruckus *I'm* causing?" I asked. "Are you serious?"

"In the Unreal!" she amended. "The Anomaly Actuator is glowing it's so hot. I have MA teams deploying to half a dozen sites across the country, and most of the team is MIA. You're the first one back, and you decide to go for a stroll in your old neighborhood, like some kind of TOURIST!" She slapped the clipboard into my chest again. I reluctantly took it. "I want a report, and I want it yesterday!"

"The report is simple. This isn't my old neighborhood, it's my domain. Do you really think I grew up in a cottage built into a hill? Hell, Esther, you've seen my old house. It's still a ruin. Chesa, Matthew, and I used a shadow road, and somehow I came directly to my domain. Only it isn't where it's supposed to be, is it?" I slapped the clipboard back at her, which earned me a stern look, but I didn't care. There was too much going on to worry about hurting the old lady's feelings. "I don't know what's going on, but the valhellions have the Tears, Greg and Bee are probably dead, Tembo's badly hurt, and I have no idea where Chesa and the saint have gotten to, so we don't really have time for paperwork."

"There's always time for paperwork," she said, though the anger was gone from her work. She squinted up at the rough-hewn walls of the cottage, then around at the brick-fronted, aluminum-sided monstrosities on either side. "I guess this is a little unusual, isn't it? Guess we better figure out where the other three are and get you all back to HQ. We can figure out what to do from there."

"What about Greg and Bee?" I asked.

"You think this group is the original team? You think I haven't been through fifty iterations of sorcerors, archers, knights, and thieves?" she asked. Esther turned around and waved off the helicopter. Both it and the armada of vans extricated themselves from the neighborhood, disappearing as quickly as they'd arrived, leaving us alone with the single van that sat in the middle of my lawn. She turned to me and sighed. "Heroes die, John. Better you get used to that sooner rather than later."

"That's hardly encouraging."

"Yeah. Wait until you see the paperwork for *that*." She turned back to the van, motioning for me to follow.

CHAPTER TWENTY-FIVE

Chesa was stuck up a tree at the edge of the city park. We found her by following a trail of dumbstruck elves, faeries, and woodland sprites who were wandering the streets like small-town tourists on Ambien. She was sitting in a treehouse that had been painted to look like a faery castle, complete with cardboard tube towers and a drawbridge painted in glitter gel. When we drove up, she glared at me.

"I'm assuming this is somehow your fault, Rast," she said as Esther and I disembarked.

"To be honest, I don't think it is. This time," Esther said. "All of the domains are in limbo at the moment, and I've got half a dozen lesser anomalies that will need to be rounded up before they make the evening news. No time to waste, Chesa. You need to come down."

"I . . . can't," she said.

"Because?"

"Because I look ridiculous." Chesa had been addressing us through the plastic-framed window of her princess castle, and I realized there was something slightly wrong with her face. Or more precisely, she looked human for the first time since we had joined Knight Watch. The slight glow to her eyes, the supernatural beauty, even the runic markings on her cheeks . . . everything that marked her as Chesa Lazaro, elven princess, rather than Chesa Lazaro, my ex-girlfriend, was gone.

"It can't be that bad, Ches. We still need to find Matthew and Tembo," I called up. "We've all seen you without your makeup on."

"It's a lot worse than that," she said. But after a long second and a meaningful glare from Esther, Chesa lowered the glitter-drawbridge and dropped a rope ladder.

Even before we joined Knight Watch, Chesa looked like a cosplayer who spent more time and money on her costume than most brides did on their wedding dress. Her elven princess uniform was always on point, always perfect, always a dream away from being absolutely real. So when she crossed over into the Unreal, it wasn't much of a leap for Chesa to start looking like an actual elf. She had been like that for so long that I had forgotten she was still just a girl under all that glamor.

That's what bothered her. That she looked normal. Like any other twentysomething on her way to a night out with her friends, as long as her friends didn't mind the cloak and high leather boots, or the bow strapped to her back. She looked like the girl I had first met years ago. No less lovely than the elven princess.

"What are you staring at?" she growled at me.

"A bit of history," I said. She brushed past me and tumbled into the back seat of the tactical van, taking up the rest of the bench with her bow and quiver. I squeezed into the middle bucket seat, sword and shield and greaves and pauldrons clanking awkwardly against the seat belt. Esther got in up front and gave the driver the go signal. We roared off down the road.

"So if this isn't Rast's fault, what exactly is going on?" Chesa asked.

"It looks like our connection to the Unreal has been partially severed. This means a half dozen lesser realms, from personal domains to some of the more complicated demesnes of our allied anomalies, have settled back into the mundane world," Esther said. We took a corner particularly hard, and I had to grab at the ceiling to keep from sliding onto the floor. Chesa snorted in my general direction. "In most cases that just means a collection of misplaced mythologies wandering through the real world. MA can handle those, as long as they don't get hostile. The Anomaly Actuator gave us a fix on the three of you. But there are a lot of implications."

"Not the least of which is that our domains are exposed," I said. "My parents showed up at my cabin. Percy, too."

"Percy the Zombie?" Chesa asked. "How'd he get there?"

"I don't know, and neither did he. And then when my parents arrived he just . . . disappeared."

"He's been hiding out in Clarence's domain for so long, there's no telling what sort of connection he has to the Unreal. Was he able to help you find the Tears?" Esther asked.

I rolled my eyes and told the story: how we found the Tears and then lost them, how Percy disappeared slightly before the attack, how we lost Gregory and Bee. She already had some of this from our initial report when we requested transport back to HQ, but Esther still had questions. Was Percy in on it? (Maybe?) Did we recognize the valkyries from our time in Valhalla? (Not really, no.) Should we trust Runa Hellesdottir? (You're asking the wrong guy.) And so forth, and so on, until she fell into a contemplative silence that only broke as we approached the site where Matthew was supposed to be.

"This is getting complicated," she said.

"You think? We've lost more than half the team, our domains are shot, and the end of the world seems to be just around the corner," I said. "Any idea what's causing this?"

"I'm guessing something has happened to Valhalla. Knight Watch's position in the Unreal is at least partially based on an agreement with Runa after the war. She helped us establish our domains, and we helped her secure the peace. We've never been friends, but we've certainly been allies." Esther settled back in her chair, her eyes taking on a far away look. "We're going to have to pay her another visit."

"How are we supposed to do that?" I asked. "We've got no way of getting there without the HMS *Hangnail*. And I doubt that whale of yours knows how to fly."

"That's something you haven't quite understood, Rast," she said. "Every bit of the Unreal also has a mundane address. Your friend Kracek the dragon was just as much an investment banker as he was a scaled wyrm. Same with your domain. Like it or not, your dream cabin also exists on a quiet suburban street. The real world does its best to maintain the balance."

"Which means Valhalla isn't a beer hall up in the clouds?" Chesa asked. "It's down here?"

"It is both a beer hall in the clouds as well as... well, you'll see soon enough," Esther said with a smirk. "Unreal and Mundane mingle together, and Unreal things impact the real world. Which is why our job is so important. Can't let the mundanes know what's going on, and can't let the myths take advantage of their powers."

"Huh," I said, thinking back to my various encounters with the Unreal. "So where's Saint Matthew's domain? If I live in suburbia, and Chesa hides out in a park"—that earned me a solid punch in the shoulder, which didn't matter because I was still in armor—"where does a saint take a break?"

"A church, you'd think," Chesa said.

"And you'd be wrong," Esther said, just as the tactical van screeched to a halt.

Chesa might have been wrong, but she wasn't far wrong. We had pulled up in front of a small industrial building on the murky border between the suburbs and the city proper. Warehouses and barbed wire fences stretched in both directions, but this small building had a garden beside its cracked concrete parking lot, and a stone archway in front of the door that looked like it belonged in an English garden. A chipped wooden sign over the door read ST. MATTHEW'S REFUGE and depicted two angels lifting a miserable-looking figure up into the heavens. A small group of unkempt men milled around in front of the door, smoking aggressively and casting furtive looks in our direction.

"He's a little on point with that sign," I said. Esther kicked open her door and hopped out. I looked at the unwashed masses swirling between us and the door. "Hey, do you think it's safe out there? Those guys look a little rough."

"Classic suburban insecurity," Esther said, then marched toward the building. I hurriedly got out of the van and started to follow her. Chesa grabbed my shoulder.

"I'm . . . gonna stay here," she said. "With the car. To make sure it's safe."

"Sure," I said. "Whatever."

It didn't take me long to figure out this was a homeless shelter. The men, once I got closer, didn't seem that dangerous. If anything, they looked curious, even nervous. I suppose they didn't get many visits from men in armor. They gave us a wide berth, then closed in behind us and followed us to the doors. But they didn't come inside, just stared through the filmy glass windows on the doors.

"So a homeless shelter?" I asked. "Was he a priest, or a parishioner?"

"Matthew was a man who wanted to do as much as he could with his life. To do the greatest good for his community. In his case, that meant Knight Watch." She checked in at a small window, probably happy to fill out even that minimum of paperwork, then led me through a winding maze of hallways and heavy wooden doors. "And he does a lot of good for these people. They probably don't even know how much good. Most of the time you guys are chilling in your domain, he's here, doing the work."

"Huh. He always seemed kind of like a stoner to me."

"High on joy," she answered. "Joy and the angels."

We found Matthew in the kitchen, preparing some kind of thick stew. The smell of it hit me right in the stomach, and I was reminded that I hadn't really had a chance to recuperate in my domain, or eat any of the marvelous soup that was eternally bubbling there. Matthew was completely in his element. His usual jeans and white blazer were covered in a stained gray apron, and he worked with the dedication of a zealot. The sheen of sweat on his brow could have been glowing, in the right light, if you squinted. At his side worked two slight, older women, their soft gray hair and heavily wrinkled faces as placid as a child's doll. They moved with unnatural grace, but were also a little disconcerting to look at, as though they weren't attached to the ground.

When we walked in, Matthew barely glanced at us before going back to his work.

"I was hoping I'd have a little longer before you guys showed up," he said. "Big crowd tonight."

"The girls can take care of it," Esther said.

"Yeah, I know. But I like to help when I can."

"No good helping here if the world ends," I said.

"The world is always ending," Matthew answered. But he set aside his spoon and balled up the apron, tossing them on the stainless steel counter. "Might be the last time I get to do this."

"Might be," Esther agreed. "But let's see what we can do about making sure you come back here in one piece. Do you have any idea where Tembo is?"

"In the back. He's banged up pretty bad, and I'm not getting enough juice out of this place to do the miracle thing." He glanced at Esther. "It's pretty bad out there, isn't it?"

"Yeah, it's pretty bad. I'll get a van to come by and move him to HQ. Mundane Actual can take care of him from here. But we're going after Valhalla, and we're going to need our priest."

"Yeah, I know," he said. "I know."

Matthew exchanged a quick word with the ladies, then followed us back to the van. The crowd at the door knew him, and he knew them. He stopped to talk to each man, asking a question or telling a joke, until the unruly mob that had made me nervous coming in was transformed into a crowd of smiling, laughing men. We ended up having to drag Matthew away.

"What was that all about?" Chesa asked as we got into the van.

"Just doing what I can to help out," Matthew said. "So, what's the plan? We're really going back to—"

"Valhalla," Esther said.

"And how do we get there without—"

"You'll see," Esther said.

CHAPTER TWENTY-SIX

Valhalla, it turned out, was a banquet hall in a strip mall in the shadow of the interstate. The parking lot was a cracked expanse of asphalt, with faded lines and an outcropping of shoulder-high weeds that had broken through the blacktop. The stucco walls had been painted a fading pink that was streaked with grime and bird shit and despair. A giant neon sign hung crooked over the front door. It read MEADHALL DISTINCTIVE BANQUETS, but the first *E* had gone out, leaving "Madhall" blinking down at us as we approached. We tumbled out of the van and stared up at the billboard on the roof. A whole murder of crows nested between the letters. A tattered banner hung over the entrance. HAPPY BIRTHDAY, IAN! YOU'RE A BIG BOY NOW!

"This is not what I was expecting," I said.

"It's seen better days," Esther answered. "Eighties and nineties, this was a great place for a party. Now they rent it out to any wandering convention or corporate meeting they can lure through those doors."

"Oh, how the mighty have fallen," Chesa mumbled. "Serves 'em right. Bunch of stuffy warrior babes. Look at me, so fancy, I have *wings*..."

"Let's keep the condescending talk to ourselves, shall we?" Esther said. "At least in front of the crows. You never know who's looking through their eyes."

With an uncomfortable look up at the murder, we walked through the wide glass doors and into a realm of chaos.

The room was much larger on the inside than outside, which was pretty typical for anything with a trace of the Unreal about it. Gaudy, industrial-grade carpet dazzled the eyes, even through decades of traffic patterns and gravy stains (maybe a little blood, too), matched by wallpaper that looked like something M. C. Escher would have drawn, if Escher had been a frustrated commercial artist with a seashell fetish and an endless supply of glitter. Cheap faux-golden chandeliers hung from the water-stained ceiling. Half the bulbs were out, and those that were still lit cast an unsteady fluorescent glow that cut through my eyes and straight into my soul. The air smelled like spilled beer, burned meatballs that had been sitting in a chafing dish for too long, and congealed fat, soaked into the fabric of the chairs. Dozens of tables, covered with fireproof white linen and set with plastic utensils, spread unevenly across the floor. There was no sign of a living soul.

The dead, though, were everywhere. Stacked like cordwood, splayed across the parquet dance floor, propped against the buffet tables... dozens of dead bodies. Hundreds. They were dressed in a variety of formal wear, from corduroy leisure suits to neon cumberbunds, tuxedos lined with flannel, and sequin evening dresses that would have dazzled the sun if they hadn't been covered in a thin layer of their owner's blood.

And every dead eye, every slack face, every deceased visage was turned to face us. Like they were watching, and waiting.

"This is more like it," I said. "Peak Valhalla. I would expect nothing less. When do you think they'll be serving dessert?"

"Stuff it, Rast. Something's wrong." Esther marched between the tables, stepping over bodies and around puddles of blood. "It's the middle of the day. These corpses should be drunk on cheap beer and halfway through the buffet by now, not lying in state."

"I'd hardly call this lying in state," I said. "Unless the state in question is Disarray."

"Isn't there supposed to be a volleyball court?" Chesa asked. "With... shirtless Vikings? Playing volleyball?"

"Keep it in your pants, Lazaro," Esther snapped. "Everyone, look around for the valkyries. Something weird is going on here, and I'm willing to bet it has something to do with our domains."

Grumbling, we set about the task of searching the bodies for their winged companions. It was joyless work, especially since most of the dead seemed very comfortable in their repose, and didn't want to budge. I began wondering if I would find Solveig among them. I recognized a few of the bodies, but for the most part the charnel carpet contained a steady supply of athletic men and women suffering from grievous and obviously fatal wounds.

We found the valkyries in the kitchen. Or, technically, *the* valkyrie. The rest were dead. Lined up along the back wall of the kitchen, dressed in an odd mix of ballroom wear and combat gear, they looked like the lineup of a beauty contest with a trial by combat that had gone terribly wrong.

Runa Hellesdottir lay on the dull brown tiled floor, hands tented over the hilt of the dagger that had been thrust into her heart. There was surprisingly little blood. She was dressed in a high-waisted all-black tuxedo with a silver hatchet dangling from the hip. Revna, the raven-winged valkyrie who had escorted us to the throne on our earlier visit, knelt at her side. Revna's eyes were rimmed with red, and tears stained her cheeks. A brace of spears lay discarded nearby. She made no notice of our entrance.

"What happened?" Esther asked. "Who did this?"

"This is your fault, you know," Revna said. "Whenever Esther bloody MacRae shows up, it's valkyrie blood, and valkyrie tears."

"You know we had nothing to do with this," Esther said. She knelt by Runa's side, checking the fallen valkyrie's throat and wrist. "Why is there so little blood?"

"She was already dead. The mortal you led to this place, the wielder of Totenschreck, struck her down. The dagger was to send a message." Revna pulled Runa's hand from Esther's grasp, then set it gingerly back on the hilt. "We are not safe. Even in our own hall. Even from our own sisters."

"Who did this?" Esther asked again.

"I don't know," Revna said after a long pause. "This is how I found her."

"Then how do you know it was the Totenpops?" I asked.

"I saw them leaving in your damned boat," she said. "The whole host of them. They killed their way through the blessed dead, killed Runa, and then fled like the cowards they are. I tried to catch up, but they were too fast."

"And where were you when all this was going down?" Chesa asked. "Of all the valkyries, only you were absent?"

"I was . . ." Her hesitation was as thick as wine in a poet's blood. "I was on a mission."

"Right," I said. "What kind of mission? Looking for an excuse to be somewhere else while your friends stole the *Hangnail*?"

Revna stood and drew one of the discarded spears, setting the tip against my throat faster than I could blink. She stared at me with impassive eyes.

"I did not kill my friend. I do not kill those I love." She pressed the spear firmly into my skin. "I do not love you."

"Yeah, yeah, I get that. Not a very lovable guy." I swallowed and immediately regretted the decision, as the spear drew blood. "Just, you know, curious."

"I have already lost three members of my team, Revna. If I'm going to solve this problem, I'm going to need you to not kill any of the remaining," Esther said. "Even John."

"Even John," I repeated.

Revna snorted, then whipped the spear away. I rubbed my neck and took a step back, nearly tripping over the dead Runa. Fortunately, Revna was looking elsewhere.

"I was following you and your ridiculous whale," she said. "One of your companions burned as bright as a bonfire in the Unreal. The British one. Once I locked on to him, it was like following a burning cart down a hillside in the middle of the night."

"Why were you following us?" Esther demanded. "You already kicked us out of Valhalla. What more could we do?"

"Apparently, a great deal. Runa didn't trust you. She thought you might go for the Tears. I've spoken with Lillie. I guess Runa wasn't far wrong, was she?"

"So either the valhellions followed Percy, or they followed you. Either way, we led them straight to the Tears," Chesa said quietly.

"What have I been saying? All of this is your fault."

"Well, whatever you believe, all we're trying to do is stop the end of the world," Esther said. "But this certainly explains a lot. Knight Watch's compact is with Runa. If she's dead, even the half-death of the Totenschreck, it will severely inhibit our ability to access the Unreal. Revna, we'll need to swear a new compact with you. Without our domains—"

"I will do no such thing," the valkyrie said. "Your bumbling and interference have brought this about. Knight Watch has always overstepped its bounds. Now you are grounded. Good."

"Who else is going to help you?" Esther asked, gesturing to the line of dead valkyries at the back of the room. "Unless I miss my guess, our fascist friend nicked the whole lot with his cursed blade before scampering off. If they do come back in the morning, and there's no guarantee that they will, it's going to be on the wrong team."

"I will manage. These are my sisters. I will be able to convince them—"

"No, you idiot, you won't be able to *convince* them of anything," Esther snapped. "You were at Dunkirk. You know what they're going to become. Best you'll be able to do is keep them from eating you raw, and that's only if you can run fast enough."

"We have other allies. I will call upon the Jotun, or the aelves. You are not the only power in heaven, Esther MacRae!"

"By the time you rouse them, and convince them this isn't some elaborate trick to steal their memories or some such nonsense, it'll be too late. You said they fled in the Naglfr? You know where they're going, Revna. You know what this means!"

"Where are they going?" Chesa asked.

"Folksvangr," Revna said reluctantly. "The field of the people. The place where Freya's portion of the dead wait for the end of the world."

"So, like Valhalla!" Chesa said. She bit her lip and leaned forward. "Is there . . . volleyball?"

"Wait a second," I said. "If you came straight from Lillie to here, how did the valhellions have time to kill Runa and the other valkyries, not to mention the host of blessed bloody dead, before you arrived? We used a shadow gate and barely had time to clear our heads before we came here."

"It could have been a second team," Esther said. "One to retrieve the Tears, another to strike at Valhalla."

"No. Tatertots was in both places. And I'm guessing it takes more than a heartbeat to storm a place like Valhalla, even if you're ready for it. You saw what this place looked like when we left? Runa had the girls packing for bear," I said. "Something about this is bugging me."

"What does it matter?" Revna asked. "They are in Folksvangr by now. Without Naglfr, you will not be able to reach it."

"Sure we can," Chesa said. "We got *here*, didn't we?"

"Folksvangr is different," Esther said. "After the war it was cut off from the mundane, to keep someone from accidentally stumbling through the veil. It's one of the few places that is entirely magical. You would need a magical vessel to reach it."

"Something like the *Hangnail,*" I said.

"Yes," Revna confirmed.

"Then why the hell did you let them take it from us?" I asked Esther. "We could have kept it safe."

"I thought it might be safer in Valhalla," she said. "I guess I was wrong."

"So, you see, it is hopeless," Revna said. "In the morning they will raise the army of dead soldiers contained in Folksvangr, and they will kick off Ragnarok. The Gjallarhorn will blow, Hrym will descend from his mountain with his shield, the world tree and the serpent will shake the heavens, and mighty Fenrir will break free from his bonds and consume the moon. Then the world will die in ash and flame."

"Fenrir, you say?" I asked.

"Yes. The mighty wolf, bound only by the trickery of the gods. He is destined to consume the moon, kill Odin, and then—"

"I have an idea," I interrupted. "But we're going to need to find some bacon."

"Bacon? Rast, I know you get hungry a lot, but third breakfast is going to have to wait until after the end of the world," Chesa said.

"It's not for me," I said. "It's for the dog."

CHAPTER TWENTY-SEVEN

The contract had a lot of subclauses, glowing runes, and at least three different kinds of ink. Some of the words squirmed on the page even as Esther put her name on the dotted line. I did not feel good about this.

"Shouldn't we at least read it first?" I asked.

"You know a lot about interdimensional contractual law?" Esther finished signing. "No, of course you don't. In fact, the person who knows the most about these kinds of contracts was Kracek the Destroyer, but we can't consult him because . . ."

"Because I killed him, yeah. But he really was an asshole."

"An asshole, yes, but the best damned draconic lawyer in the seven realms. Bit of a good golfer, too." Esther put down the pen and gestured to Revna. "I assume you're screwing us over somehow?"

"That is for me to know, and for you to find out," Revna said. "At the least opportune moment, I imagine. Unfortunately I cannot return the Naglfr to your service, as it has been stolen. And until the matter of the Totenschreck is managed, I can't even return all of your domains to full and working order."

"That's fine. We only need mine," I said.

"Hang on, that's hardly fair. I can't walk around looking like . . . like . . ." Chesa gestured to her jeans and comic book T-shirt. "Like a human!"

"Not to elf-shame you, but we're all humans here," I said. Revna cleared her throat. "Most of us. Point is, you'll be able to get by on residual glamor until we can straighten out the realms. For now, we just need to ramp up my domain. I can get us to Folks Fanger."

"You don't even know where it is," Chesa said.

"If John believes he can get the team where it needs to go, then I'm willing to believe him," Esther said. "With just the three of you—"

"You're not coming with us?" I asked.

"No, dear child, I am not. I need to work with Revna on establishing the links to the rest of your domains. If we can get them up and running, you'll start recharging immediately. That's more important than anything my old bones could contribute."

"So . . . just the three of us. Huh." I looked from Chesa to Matthew. "You guys ready to go?"

"Reborn ready," Matthew said. "Let's light this candle."

"Do we really have to go through your domain?" Chesa asked. "I'm a little nervous finding out what my ex-boyfriend's mythic ideal is like. Can't you just go there, get whatever you need, and bring it back here?"

"What, you're expecting legions of waifus or something?" I asked. "Don't worry, it's nothing that pathetic. We're going to be leaving directly from there to Ragnarok."

"You mean Folksvangr," Esther said. "Right?"

"Whatever," I said with a shrug. "So, what, you're going to open a portal or something?"

"Something like that," Revna said. "You have everything you need?"

I lifted the grease-spotted pillowcase with a smile.

"Then let us begin," Revna said. "Security! Get these buffoons out of here."

"Security?"

The floor rumbled and shifted under our feet. The tables slid like cannons on the deck of a storm-tossed ship. Two shapes rose from the ground, with rough-hewn rock faces and skin as rough as sandpaper, and eyes that glowed like magma. Revna gestured to the three of us.

"They've overstayed their welcome. Send them home."

"Esther!" I shouted as the stone elementals loomed toward us.

"There are only two ways out of Valhalla," Esther said. "Walk out the way you came, or get thrown out. And the way you came leads back to a suburban parking lot, so . . ."

"Try to land on something soft!" Revna called, as the elementals picked the three of us up, each with one giant hand. They waddled toward the front of the ballroom and, with a slow windup, tossed us through the front window.

The second the glass shattered around my shoulders, the world changed around us. The dim light of the parking lot was replaced by smothering night. A crystal-bright moon shone overhead. Below us was an expanse of forest that stretched to the horizon. We were hundreds of feet in the air, but I could just make out a pinprick of light, nestled in a clearing far below.

Home. Now all we had to do was fall the hundreds of feet between here and there.

"You're not going to like this part!" I shouted to Chesa and Matthew. They probably couldn't hear me, though, on account of their own screams of terror. I crossed my arms and plummeted to earth, the cold wind whipping past my face. I sighed. "Ah, it's good to be home."

My domain is all about fear. I should have mentioned that to Chesa and Matthew before we did this, but that would have spoiled some of the effect. Plus if they knew that, they might have anticipated something even more horrific than falling to their death, and I didn't want to see whatever spirits ran the domain taking their fears and running with it. So instead of being chased by flying knives, or eaten by giants, or whatever it was that Chesa and Matthew would have thought up, we simply fell to our deaths.

Not actually. We fell for a long time, screaming the whole way, but when we hit the ground we bounced a couple times. Kind of like a trampoline, only it was the earth itself. I'd done this a dozen times, and was getting used to it. Chesa had been through this once, though that was before she had her own domain. For Matthew, this was a first.

"You should have warned us!" the priest yelled once we'd come to a halt. "I assumed she'd thrown us straight to Hel. Good God, that was terrifying!"

"Yeah, that's kind of the point. Fear, and overcoming fear. Though how you overcome the fear of falling when you're actually falling . . . Yeah, I'm not sure about that." I led us up the gentle hill to my cabin. It was the same as I'd left it, only no longer on a quiet street. Thin smoke rose from the mossy chimney, and the flames of the hearth flickered against the thick, wavy glass of the front window. "Anyway, we're here. Everything seems to be in order."

"This is your mythic domain? This is the best you could come up with?" Chesa asked. "You could create anything, and you settled on a cabin in a creepy forest?"

"We're not all elven princesses," Matthew said. He wiped the sweat from his face and looked around the clearing. "I like it, John. Humble."

"That's what I was going for. Humble." I eased the front door open and, sword and shield in hand, peered into the front room. Seeing Chesa give me a weird look, I tried to explain. "Last time I was here, Percy was hiding in the kitchen. I don't know what he has to do with all this, but I'd rather not stumble onto any more zombies."

"Great domain, John. You're not even safe here," she said as she brushed past. "Is there at least a bathroom?"

"You don't want to know about the bathroom," I said. "Should have gone before we left."

"Anything can be a bathroom if you try hard enough," Matthew said. He sat down in front of the fireplace, hands steepled in his lap. "I smell soup!"

"Yeah, a pot of eternal stew in the kitchen. It may not be a treehouse castle, or the brilliance of a chorus of angels, but it's still tasty."

"Sure sounds good," Matthew said.

"It is." I stuck my nose into the kitchen, saw nothing of interest, then started toward the hallway that led to the bedrooms. Matthew cleared his throat. When I looked back, he blinked at me expectantly. "Would you like some stew?"

"I mean, if you're offering."

"I wasn't," I said. His mien remained unchanged, so after a long second I sighed and headed back to the kitchen. "Just keep an eye on this hallway. Should be empty, but you never know."

"Loving this place more and more by the second," Chesa said. She perched uncomfortably against one of the chairs, legs crossed daintily. "Do we really have time for stew?"

"Apparently," I said.

When I ducked into the kitchen, I ran directly into a cleaver the size of my head, held precariously close to the parts of my head that were most incompatible with cleavers. I yelped and scrambled to bring my sword around. The sound of my scream brought Matthew and Chesa running, and startled my assailant just enough to cause him to drop the cleaver.

Percy backpedaled into the stove, upsetting the pot of soup and burning himself on the hot metal. He joined his scream to my own, accompanied by the sound of several gallons of scalding hot stew spilling out across the kitchen floor. Chesa and Matthew burst into the room, weapons drawn.

"Percy, damn it! What are you doing here? *How* are you doing here, for that matter?" I shook the now-soaked leg of my greaves, slopping bits of stew around the room. "I looked in here not ten seconds ago, and the room was empty!"

"I . . . I'm not sure, Sir John," the terrified zombie said. "All I know is that I wasn't here, and then I was, and I heard sounds in the antechamber. I took up the first weapon I could find, and that's when you burst in like some kind of barbarian."

"I'm not the one sneaking around other people's houses and threatening them with kitchen implements!" I shouted. "If anything, *you're* the barbarian!"

"I don't even know where 'here' is," Percy said miserably. "All I can remember is being in the garden, and then the storm started, and then I was here, and then I wasn't, and now I am again . . ." He rubbed a khaki arm across his face, rubbing away thick, silty zombie tears. "All I want to do is go back to my garden, and my flowers, and those stupid gnomes!"

"That's all I want, too, Percy! For you to go back to—"

"Alright, alright, that's enough of that." Matthew imposed himself between us, putting a hand on Percy's quivering shoulder. "The guy's been through enough. We drop into his world out of nowhere, drag him on a quest he didn't choose, and now the ancient Nazi sword that controls his soul is back and digging at his mind. You can understand that, right, John?"

"Everything except the sword bit," I said. But seeing the way Percy responded to Matthew, I immediately felt bad about yelling. Hardly my fault. He's the one who appeared out of nowhere.

"So what do we think is going on here?" Chesa asked. "How does this guy just keep popping up?"

"Definitely something to do with the sword. Revna said she was able to track him to the Tears, and he disappeared around the same time we all lost a firm grip on our domains. He's probably flickering between the Unreal and the mundane." Matthew scraped a little stew out of the toppled pot and pushed it into Percy's hands. "It's okay, buddy. You're not going to have to go on any more adventures today."

"The hell he isn't," I said. "If there's any chance he can help us with the Tears, we have to bring him along."

"I don't know what help I could be," he said.

"You were in the army, right?" I rummaged through the umbrella rack next to the door. It contained all the various murdering paraphernalia I had looted from the monsters in my domain. I came up with a warhammer with a long iron spike at the end, and handed it to Percy. "This is like a rifle, only you have to swing it to shoot someone, and they have to be right next to you."

"I know how a hammer works," he said gruffly.

"What if the Totenschreck can still control him?" Chesa asked. "What if he falls under the control of the valhellions, and tries to kill us?"

"Well . . ." I said, looking nervously from her to the recently armed zombie. "Well, we just won't let that happen."

"Sure we won't," Chesa said. She looked around the kitchen, seemingly half expecting the cabinets to come alive and try to eat her. "Shouldn't we get going? You said you have something in here that can help us reach Folksvangr?"

"Not in here," I said. "Out in the forest."

"So what are we looking for? And why is it in the forest?" Matthew asked.

"A dog. And because that's where he lives."

"How is a dog supposed to help us?" Chesa asked.

"Not *a* dog. *All* of the dogs," I said, leading them outside. "Oh, almost forgot." I ducked back inside and opened a cabinet beside the door. There, behind a silk curtain, was my spare helm. I tucked it under my arm and looked around. Then, closing my front door and hoping the house was still intact when I came back, I led them into the forest.

CHAPTER TWENTY-EIGHT

We marched into the forest single file, with me at the front, Chesa and then Matthew behind me, and the hesitant Percy bringing up the rear. Thick grown trees quickly swallowed the light from the cabin, and the canopy overhead drowned out the moon's silver glow, leaving us in murky darkness. Matthew summoned a ball of burning amber that was just enough light to make walking treacherous instead of impossible, while leaving the surrounding shadows appropriately malevolent.

"I still can't believe you chose this as your domain," Chesa said. Something rustled in the branches overhead, and she spun to face it, bow pulled taut. When nothing appeared, she slowly lowered the bow but kept her eyes in that direction. "This place is damned creepy."

"I'll admit, it isn't exactly what I would have chosen. I fancied Clarence's domain, to be honest. More of a castles and servants kind of guy. But the creepy forest chose me, so here we are."

"There are worse options," Matthew said. "Bee lives in a sewer."

"A sewer? I mean, I know she's not the kind of girl to go in for dresses and formal dances and all that, but . . . a sewer?" Chesa shook her head, finally taking her eyes off the offending branch. "That just seems like performative—"

No sooner had Chesa turned away from the branch than it transformed into a snake as thick as her waist and as long as a city bus. It struck, black scales glistening in the meager light of Matthew's globe, its eyes the color of nuclear waste, with daggerlike fangs that dripped poison. I barely saw it and could only throw up my shield.

The snake's head banged into my shield like a battering ram, knocking me into Chesa and sending the both of us flying. I rolled over her, slashing blindly with my sword as I came around, just catching the tip of the snake's nose with the blade. The beast snapped back into the tree, then slithered to the ground, coiling for another strike. It moved like liquid lightning, silent and quick. Chesa rolled to her feet and loosed a pair of arrows. The bolts bounced harmlessly off black scales, but it was enough to draw the creature's attention. Hissing like a zeppelin going down in flames, the snake slithered toward Chesa, its gaping jaws weaving back and forth just over our heads.

Before the beast could strike, I leapt forward and thrust my shield into its mouth. Translucent fangs clamped down on the heater, nearly reaching my forearm. Viscous poison dripped onto my arm, sizzling as it splashed across the metal of my vambrace. Pulling the straps of my enarme, I expanded the shield's face, growing from heater to tower in the blink of an eye, cranking the snake's mouth open. I heard the hinge of its jaw strain, and the hissing grew violent. It shook me back and forth, whipping my legs in the air, but I clutched the sturdy support of the enarme like a lifeline, refusing to be thrown off. Swinging around the anchor of my shield, I planted one foot in the hinge of the snake's mouth. The beast's throat convulsed as it tried to swallow me. I slipped free, dangling from the shield like a fish on a hook, but quickly regained my footing against the snake's neck. Unfortunately I was now upside down, and staring at the pale gray underbelly of the monstrous snake.

"That'll do," I muttered, and swung hard at the base of its jaw. The steel of my blade cut into the softer scales around its mouth. Slick black blood washed down my arm, but I pressed an armored boot into the wound and shoved the sword in deeper. Something popped, and the lower half of the snake's mouth flopped open like a broken shutter.

I fell hard to the ground. The impact knocked the air from my lungs, but I quickly rolled into a crouch. The snake's body whipped overhead, spraying blood and poison around the narrow forest trail, and its mouth gaped open, all throat and fangs. It slammed down on me, either maddened with pain or determined to crush the life out of me in its final moments. I met it with the tip of my sword, held in both hands, and braced against my shield like a ram on the prow of a ship. The force of the blow flattened me, but then I was wrapped in darkness and numb silence. Slowly, I stood.

The dead snake rolled off me like a carpet, my sword lodged in its brain pan. I planted my foot in the soft meat of the roof of its mouth and pulled the sword free, then shook it clean. I was covered head to toe in black blood and boiling poison, but the beast was dead.

"Good God, John! Are you alright?" Chesa asked. She cowered behind a tree, with Percy peering out over her shoulder. Matthew stood up from behind a stump, blinking numbly at the dead snake.

"Sure. Perfectly fine. This happens all the time." I smeared some blood off my chest, then stared distastefully at my fingers. There was an odd taste in my mouth, a cross between tar and bad fish. I spat. "You were saying something about a sewer?"

"Have you considered cutting down the trees?" Matthew asked.

"Oh, man, no! They would *not* like that," I said with a laugh. "Come on, there's a clean pool about forty yards that way. Rarely has anything in it. And you can watch my armor while I clean off."

"That thing could have killed you," Chesa said.

"I feel like that was the plan, yeah. It's why I carry a sword." I shook again. The blood fell off me in quickly congealing lumps, but something hot and uncomfortable rose in my blood. Stars twinkled in my vision."You know what? Never mind about the pool. This stuff seems to be coming off on its own. And the last time I tried to take a bath out here, the pool turned out to be an elemental. All a big misunderstanding, but I wouldn't want to go through that again. We still need to find that dog."

"Wouldn't it be safer in the cabin? We could just set out some food for this . . . dog? Or something?" Chesa asked.

"Much safer. But I don't have that much food, and besides, we don't really have that much time," I said. I took a step forward, nearly collapsed, and covered by leaning against the snake's head. "End of the world? Remember?"

Chesa crept from her shelter, with Percy still clinging to her like a cloak. She prodded the dead snake with her foot.

"This place sucks," she said.

"It's not so bad, once you get used to it," I answered. My vision swam with shadows. "Hey, Saint. Could you do something about this poison? Pretty sure I got some in my mouth."

Matthew lit up, quite literally, and a wave of warm light passed through my flesh. The burning feeling in my lungs disappeared, replaced with a gentle glow, like the first hit of a good whiskey in your blood. I sighed.

"Much better."

"Are we going to get attacked by giant snakes all that frequently?" Chesa asked. "Because if so, I really think I should wait back in the cabin."

"Won't be a snake next time. Chitinous bear, maybe. Or a murder of vampiric crows. The forest gets pretty creative with what it throws at me," I said. "You should have seen the baby-headed centipedes. Oh, I have never wished for a flamethrower more than—"

A heavy thud passed through the earth, then another. Each loping stride shook the trees and sent us scrambling for support. Chesa's eyes got wide. Matthew snuffed out his light, plunging us once again into absolute darkness.

"That's no good, Saint," I said. "He has the scent."

"Who has the scent?" Chesa yelped.

On a ridgeline overlooking our little patch of forest, the trees shivered and parted. Two pointed ears loomed over the treeline, each the size of a galleon's sail, followed by a giant head. Eyes as big as wading pools caught the moon's pale light. We could just barely make out the glistening fangs and hear the rough, rasping sound of its breath. The ground shook again, and the beast loped closer.

The World Dog.

"There's a good boy," I whispered, and set my shield firmly in the ground.

"This is your plan? This . . . this . . . monster?" Chesa asked. She swung her quiver from her shoulder and nocked three arrows, for all the good that would do her. "What are we supposed to do, play with it?"

"He tends to break his toys," I said. "Let me do the talking, okay?"

"What is that thing?" Matthew whispered as it loomed closer. The creature's head split, and an avalanche of bumbling, squirming, furry shapes tumbled into the forest. Its one giant head became two, and then a dozen, each the size of a car. As it grew smaller, the beast disappeared beneath the treeline, though the drumbeat of its footsteps swelled into a symphony of rumbling beats, growing closer and closer.

"Every dog in the world," I said, and then the forest around us lit up with hooded eyes and slavering jaws. The arched backs of hounds appeared briefly between the trees, joined by impossibly large Dobermans and feral wolf-beasts, straight from some primeval nightmare. Shadows circled our tiny light, an endless parade of jaws and claws and muscular, furry shoulders, a noose that grew tighter with each heartbeat. Chesa whimpered and pressed close to my side. The four of us went back to back, weapons out, Matthew's amber light barely reaching the trees nearby.

"Are they just going to watch us?" Matthew whispered.

"They're stalking. Hunting," I responded. "Waiting until we let our guard down. Then—"

Foliage shuddered nearby, and all four of us whirled in that direction. A pair of eyes, knee-high and glowing with green malevolence, appeared among the leaves. I steeled myself, ready to strike or run, though there was nowhere to flee from the herd of circling hounds. I had faced this beast before, and only survived at its mercy. My plan, half formed, started to look even more desperate. The bush shivered again, and my heart leapt into my throat as the leaves parted and a creature stalked into view.

It was the world's largest Bichon Frise. A snow-white crown of fluffy hair, groomed into a perfect globe, framed bright eyes and tiny mouth. It trotted into view, small pink tongue lolling out to one side. It looked at us one by one, then sat daintily in the middle of the path.

"We smell bacon," it said, and a chorus of anxious yelps filled the air.

"Right! Bacon!" I answered. When no one else moved, I turned around. "Who has the bacon?"

"Oh, right," Matthew said. He produced the greasy pillowcase from under his robes and tossed it on the ground. An avalanche of bacon slithered out.

The Bichon Frise changed. A dozen shapes darted out of the shadows, melting into the dog's fluffy body, altering it. Jaws grew, fur warped, shoulders bent and swelled and rippled with killing power. Still transforming, it leapt on the bacon and hoovered it up, pillowcase and all. The second the bacon was gone, the changed beast—half dog, half wolf, one hundred percent nightmare fuel—sat primly at my feet and licked its jaws hungrily.

"More bacon?" it asked.

"Not at the moment," I said, sheathing my sword and reaching toward it. "But I can get more. I just have a request."

A low rumble rose up from the shadows, and the dog-thing snarled at my outstretched hand.

"We don't do tricks," it growled.

"Not a trick, just... uh... an audience. There's one of you we need to talk to."

"We are all one, and one in all. Speak to me, and you speak to—"

"Fenrir," I said.

The dog leapt up and backed away, the hackles on its back standing straight as spears. The air hummed with a chorus of growling, yipping dogs.

"The exile," it said. "The world-breaker, the bad boy."

"More bacon?" I asked. The dog paused.

"You do not know what you ask," it said. "He cannot be trusted. He seeks to catch the ball-which-can-not-be-returned."

"Yes, but... bacon?"

The dog's nose twitched. It stretched closer to my hand, cold nose bumping against the steel fingers of my glove.

"If we do this, you will bring more bacon?"

"Yes. So much bacon. More than you can—"

"Three plus three bacon, and the bone of a giant's leg," it said. "Also, we would like a ball to play with."

"A... ball?" I asked. "Three plus three..."

"Dog's can't count," Matthew said. "Or at least not very high. He just means a lot of bacon."

"Yes, okay, a lot of bacon. And some kind of ball. The bone..." A ripple of growls from the forest. "Alright! The bone of a giant's leg. I'm sure Esther has one of those lying around somewhere. Just take us to Fenrir."

The dog hesitated. Barking from the forest that sounded like a conversation, and then the creature nodded once, sharply.

"Very well," it said. "But do not break this word-oath, human. For if you do, we will break through your door, and we will use the bathroom. Everywhere!"

"Okay, okay, jeez," I said. "Let's not get crazy."

Apparently satisfied, the dog disappeared into the forest. It paused at the edge of our light source, waiting for us to follow. Matthew gave me a look.

"Fenrir? What have you got planned, John?"

"I'm going to end the world before those bastards can do it," I said.

"Of course you are," Chesa said. "Brilliant. Beat the villains to the punch."

"Trust me," I said.

"No," Chesa answered. But when I chased after the World Dog, she followed.

CHAPTER TWENTY-NINE

The path to Fenrir's den was like something out of a dream. A bad dream. The kind of dream where you wake up in a cold sweat and fall out of bed trying to reach the lightswitch, but then you laugh it off and pretend like you weren't really scared until you have to walk to the bathroom and you end up turning on every light in the house and sitting in your shower with a skillet waiting for the sun to rise.

So a nightmare, I guess.

Mists clung to the path as it rose out of the forest. The terrain grew rocky, providing less and less soil for the undergrowth, and soon we were surrounded by jagged slate canyons and hardy scrub brush. Water trickled down mossy embankments, turning the footing slippery and the air damp. Overhead, the silver moon peered down on us.

Despite the lack of forest, there was the persistent feeling that we were being watched. Deep shadows filled the dozen dead end canyons that we passed. The rocks themselves seemed to leer at us as we passed. We crept up the pass, constantly bumping into one another and jumping every time something creaked or clattered or chuckled.

The feral Bichon Frise led the way, prancing with those short, quick steps typical of dogs that were too small to be fast, no matter how they moved their legs. It left the rest of its global pack behind. As we rose out of the forest and into this strange, rocky cleft, I had the feeling that we were leaving my domain and entering someplace ancient.

Finally, the Bichon stopped and edged to the side of the path. It looked back at us expectantly.

“The bacon?” it asked.

“Well, we don’t have it with us right now, obviously,” I said. “Don’t worry, you’ll get your bacon.”

“Could you go get it and come back? I’m just not sure that you’re going to make it out of here, is all.”

“I’m loving this plan more and more,” Chesa said.

“We’re coming back,” I answered. “And when we do, you’ll get your bacon, and your ball.”

“And the leg bone of a giant,” the bison said.

“Yes, yes.” I marched past the dog. Beyond him the canyon opened up into a quarry. The path descended rapidly and precariously into the sea of mists that boiled up from the floor of the quarry. I hesitated, then looked back. “Is there anything we should know before we go in there?”

“Fenrir is large, and dangerous, and will likely kill you,” the Bichon said. It whined nervously. “Perhaps one of you could go back for the bacon while the others are slaughtered?”

“I volunteer!” Percy snapped. He had already taken three steps back the way we’d come before Matthew could grab his shoulder.

“We all go in together,” the saint said. “There are too few of us, and little magic to go around. John’s the only one who’s spent time in his domain.”

“I am feeling pretty mundane here,” Chesa said. “Are we sure about this? If we could get Revna to power up the other domains, we might have a better chance.”

“No time. You saw what happened to Valhalla. I suspect they knocked us out so we wouldn’t be able to interfere with whatever comes next. They expect us to take the time to power up,” I said. “Which means we need to get in there before they do . . . whatever it is they intend to do.”

“Good enough for me,” Matthew said. “Just don’t expect much healing.”

“Don’t get hurt. Got it,” I said. “Let’s get this over with.”

The mists rapidly enfolded us in their damp grasp, and the world closed around us. Between the unstable footing and the cloying mists, I was soon forced to put all my effort into not tumbling to my death. Chesa crowded close behind me, bumping into me each time I slowed to test the next step. I could hear Matthew and Percy chatting nervously, and the dripping of water, and my own hammering heart. I lost track of how far we descended. Slowly, another sound crept into my awareness. It was a soft roar, like a distant airplane passing overhead, except it came every few seconds from somewhere down below. The mists stirred in rhythm with the sound. I stopped and looked up.

"Breathing," I said. Chesa yelped softly, and Matthew and Percy fell silent.

We continued on. Eventually, we came to the floor of the quarry, and the mists cleared a bit. There was a stagnant pool the color of moss, and a great expanse of flat, slick slate. Broken chains the size of my waist lay scattered about, slowly rusting into gritty sand that stained the stone the red of dried blood. The far side of the quarry was overgrown with thick, curling vines the color of pewter.

There was no sign of the famous wolf. The breathing continued, echoing off the walls of the quarry, making it impossible to tell which direction it was coming from.

"Well, this is hardly encouraging," Matthew said. "Do you think it's a metaphor? Like... *we're* the scary wolf that's going to end the world?"

"That doesn't seem right. But nothing about this seems right," I said. Walking across the floor of the quarry, I could feel the beast's breath swirling around me. The air smelled like old blood and fresh meat. The farther I got from the path out, the less I liked this place. "Should we go back? Try to get clearer direction from that little runt?"

"There must be a den," Chesa said. "Maybe behind this wall of vines? John, you and Percy go that way, Matthew and I will look over here."

"'Split up the party,' they said. 'It'll be fine,' they said." But I took Percy and headed in the indicated direction. At least it was warmer over here. The tangled wall radiated heat, as though a vein of magma ran through it. I peered at the vines. They were the strangest growth I had ever seen—thick and glossy, with curls that were caked with dirt and tangled with other growths. I was pretty sure I could climb them fairly easily. "At least if we get cut off from the path, we'll have a way out."

"Pardon?" Percy said. "You said something about a way out?"

"Nothing. Just try to find—"

The breathing sound intensified. There was one long, loud inhalation. Beside me, the wall swelled. I froze in place.

"Oh dear," Percy said, very quietly.

The exhalation came and blew a sour wind across my face. The mists disappeared, and I realized I was standing toe to snout with a giant wolf. It was curled in on itself, paws tucked under its chest, with its tail lying flat on the ground. The top of its head was pressed hard against one wall of the quarry, and a small flap of pink tongue stuck out between its teeth. The vine-covered wall was its rib cage, fur matted and tangled with dirt. One cataract-filmed eye flicked open and stared at me.

"What do you want, mortal? Come to mock the great Fenrir?" Its voice echoed in my brain like a church bell, loud and gravelly and more than a little bored. "Or do you wish to try your hand at slaying me? I have a nice collection of bones, but I could always use another skull for my den."

"John, I think we found . . . Oh." Chesa came running up, skidding to a halt as she saw the giant wolf's head. "Um. A den. Full of bones. But, uh . . . nevermind."

"Three heroes. No, wait . . ." A long inhalation through the cracked black expanse of his snout. "Four mortal souls. How quaint. Usually they come alone. More glory that way."

"We're not here for glory," I said.

"That's good. None of your predecessors found it, either." Fenrir's massive eye closed. "But if you're not here to fight, then I have no use for you. Best be gone before I get hungry. Or bored."

And then he promptly went back to sleep. His breathing settled, his body relaxed, and moments after his eye closed the giant wolf was twitching.

"I don't want to know what sort of dreams a dog this size has," I said. "He doesn't seem very interested in helping, does he?"

"Been here a long time," Matthew said, strolling up from out of the mists. "Not good for a dog to be cooped up like this. Fellow like that needs exercise. A good walk. A job to do."

"He has a job. He needs to take us to Folksvangr," I said. Gingerly, I prodded the hairy toe of his front paw. When that didn't get any kind of response, I gave it a kick. "Hey! Fenrir! Fame-wolf! World-ender!" Nothing. "Bad boy!"

"Well, there's no need to be nasty," Fenrir rumbled. "If you want me to kill you, all you have to do is ask. Who's first? The crunchy one with the shield? The girl? How about . . ." He raised his head and waved it over us, nose twitching, until he stopped over Matthew. "That one smells like the gods. He'll do."

"Wait, wait, wait!" I shouted, putting my crunchy self between Matthew and the wolf. "We're not here to fight you, or get eaten by you, or anything remotely like that."

"Then why are you here?"

"To free you."

Fenrir's eyes narrowed, and his brow furrowed.

"Free me?"

"Yes."

"Do you know what is prophesied to happen when I slip my bonds?"

"Something about eating the moon?"

"Something about . . ." He snorted and settled his head back on his paws. "I will fly to the heavens and kill the gods for what they've done to me. For imprisoning me in this place, for tricking me, for taking my freedom from me! I will end the world, mortal, and the seas shall quake and the mountains tumble!" His eyes started to slide shut, only to stop while a fraction of his golden irises still peeked out. "And yes, I'm going to take a nip at the moon on my way by. It's been up there all this time, taunting me with its roundness. I just want to give it a good chase. Maybe shake it in my jaws for a while."

"What is it with dogs and tennis balls?" Chesa muttered. "Look, if we free you, can you take us to Folksvangr?"

"Folksvangr? Why would you want to go there? Dreary place, everyone napping all the time, hardly any bloodshed. Now, Valhalla!" His attention stirred, and he peered up at the sky with a dreamlike look on his face. "I've heard great things about Valhalla. Walls made of meat. Great flagons, also made of meat, brimming with blood, just lying around. And meat-people you can chase around, and catch, and shake for awhile and then they get up again for more chasing. Ah, it sounds so marvelous."

"I think we just call those people," I said. "Not meat-people."

"Whatever. Either way, it doesn't matter. If I haven't been able to break free for all these three plus three ages, how are you supposed to release me from my bondage?"

"I don't even understand what's holding you here," Matthew said. "All I see are these broken chains."

"The first two tricks of the gods," Fenrir said. "Dishonest bastards. But no chain can hold me, no rope bind me. No, I am held by a much greater power." The wolf slid to one side, revealing the nape of its neck. There, a pink ribbon, no wider than my little finger, lay tangled in the beast's fur. I snorted.

"That? That's what's holding you here? What's the matter, worried about ruining the silk?" I stepped forward, drawing the razor-sharp steel of my sword. "You may be a big damned doggie, but us meat-people have this thing called tools."

I slipped my sword beneath the ribbon and cut with a grand flourish. My blade rasped against the ribbon, pulling it taut. But nothing happened. No cutting. I blinked in surprise.

"Big bad meat-person has tools, does he?" Fenrir asked. He smiled, showing off row after row of enormous teeth. "If something as flimsy as that blade and your arm could cut that ribbon, don't you think I would be free by now?"

"There has to be a latch or something," Chesa said. "He gets free in the prophecies, doesn't he? There has to be a way."

"Trust me when I say this," Fenrir growled. "Prophecies have a way of being tricky to interpret."

"Well, we're going to interpret this one right now. Everyone up." I sheathed my sword and hitched my shield onto my back, then gathered a huge handful of matted fur into my fingers and hauled myself onto the side of the giant wolf. "Look for a knot, or a buckle, or even a bell. There has to be something."

"That sounds incredibly dangerous," Percy said.

"You'd rather stay down there next to his mouth, for when he gets bored of talking and decides he's hungry enough to eat a dead man?" Chesa asked. She vaulted up Fenrir's paw, landing in a crouch on the knobbled ridge of his spine. Fenrir twitched and snorted, but didn't shake her off.

"I see your point," Percy said. With Matthew's help, he scrambled up onto the wolf. Soon, all four of us were pulling at his fur and running our hands down the length of pink ribbon, looking for a flaw or break in its design.

"This is hopeless," Fenrir said. "That is Gleipnir. Fashioned by the dwarves of six impossible things; the breath of a fish, the spittle of bird, the sound of a cat's footstep, the beard of a woman—"

"Dwarves haven't met my aunt Elda," I muttered.

"—the roots of a mountain, the sinews of—"

"I found it," Chesa said. She pulled a length of ribbon free of the wolf's fur. There, as tight as a sailor and as small as a mouse's burp, was a knot.

"Did they use the opposable digits of a wolf?" I asked. "Because meat-person has one trick you might not have thought of."

With a pluck and a pull, the knot came undone. The ribbon fluttered to the ground.

Fenrir's eyes shot open. He leapt to his feet, craned his head to the sky, and let loose an earth-shattering howl.

"Everyone hang on!" I shouted.

"I'm coming for you, bitch!" Fenrir howled, and leapt straight at the moon.

CHAPTER THIRTY

We left the forest behind in a heartbeat. Wind tore at my face, whipping Fenrir's fur like iron wires against my skin. Percy's screams cut through the sky. For once, I wasn't screaming at all. Screaming would have taken my attention away from hanging on for dear life. My arms burned with the effort, and Fenrir's matted fur started to slowly slip through my fingers.

"Hey, fame wolf!" I shouted. "Come on, big boy. We talked about going to Folksvangr, remember?"

"Have you seen the size of this ball? It's getting bigger!" the hound answered. "Man, I'm going to bite the living HEL out of this thing!"

"Fenrir! Fen! I don't think you can bite the moon!"

"I think maybe he can," Chesa said. She had crawled up close to me, her wrists wrapped in the stiff fur of Fenrir's hackles. "John, what happens to us when he leaves the atmosphere?"

"That's a science question. This isn't a science situation," I said. "For all we know he's going to bump into the Viking ideal of the moon, swallow it whole, and then get bored and put us down."

"It's getting pretty cold," she said. And she was right. I risked losing my lunch and leaned out to look around. The earth spread out beneath us like a carpet, bending slightly at the horizons. I thought I could see a glimmer of sunlight to the east, and the sky was definitely brighter in that direction. I took a deep breath. My lungs clawed at my throat for more oxygen.

"Maybe it's a metaphor," Matthew said cheerfully. "Like, maybe *we're* the moon that—"

"It's not a metaphor!" Chesa and I shouted in unison. I wiggled my way up the beast's neck, until I reached the tufted crevice of his ear.

"Fenrir, you have to put us down! If you take us to the moon, it'll kill us!"

"Sounds like a meat-person problem," he said.

"We freed you, and this is the thanks we get?" Chesa yelled.

"I will remember your names fondly, and see that your glory is added to the Edda," the wolf answered. After a long pause, he added. "What were your names again?"

"I'm Saint Matthew, and this is Percival—"

"Just take us to Folksvangr like you promised, and then you can chase the moon to your heart's content," I urged. "We need to stop the end of the world!"

"You're . . . aware that the end of the world is kind of my thing?" he asked.

"Well, yes, but not this specific end. Or I guess it's the same ending, but not . . ." I took a deep breath and found that I couldn't get enough air into my lungs. I started to get dizzy. Chesa grabbed my shoulder and shoved me against the wolf's neck.

"Listen up, you bastard!" she snapped. "We released you, now take us to Folksvangr!"

"But . . ."

"Now! Bad boy! Down!"

Fenrir's hackles raised, and a low rumbling shook his ribs. I began to worry that we were about to be shaken off, but after giving the moon one last, longing look, he turned and slowly descended through the clouds. Eventually I lost sight of the moon, and the air grew warm, and my lungs stopped screaming bloody murder at me. And that's when we arrived in the mythical Folksvangr.

There wasn't much to recommend the place. On our initial descent, I thought Fenrir had lost his way, and was simply dropping us off at the first field he came across. A cloud-wreathed hillock framed by exposed granite cliffs, with a tumble of broken stones scattered across its crown made up the majority of the terrain. But as we drew closer I saw that the grass field was littered with bodies, laid in stately lines. Wind blew the grasses back and forth, covering up most of the corpses, so it was difficult to get any kind of count. But there must have been hundreds, if not thousands, laid to rest across that hill.

Fenrir landed hard at the base of the hill. I slithered gratefully to the ground, followed by the others. The giant wolf swung its head in our direction.

"Happy?" he asked.

"This is the place? You're not just ditching us?" I asked.

"This is Folksvangr, the realm of Freya's dead. Abandoned since her misdeeds of the last war, or so I've heard." His attention focused on Percy, and he snorted. "Though you will know more of that than I, draugr. Be careful, mortals. Those who come here do not leave."

Then he leapt in the air, flying straight at the moon, his enormous bulk getting rapidly smaller and smaller until he disappeared against the moon's silver face. The trail of the Milky Way blotted out most of the sky, turning the purple night into a veil of diamonds.

"Well, there goes our ride," Matthew said.

"We'll find a way back, if we're lucky enough to need one," I said. "Now, what's next?"

"What's next? I thought you were the one with the plan!" Chesa said.

"Sure, I am. And my plan got us here. But I was expecting there to be a bunch of rebellious valkyries, and the creepy dude with the death sword. Not an empty field."

"An empty field full of corpses," Matthew said. "Doesn't really look like Valhalla, does it? More like the battle of the Somme."

I turned my attention to the nearby dead. Matthew was right. In Valhalla we were met by Viking warriors, bare chested and armored, dressed in leathers, with steel blades and ash-hafted spears. But the corpses lined up around us were much more modern, if no less dead. Bloodstained khaki uniforms framed surprisingly young faces, hands folded peacefully over oiled rifles or clutching bayonets. Flat-brimmed steel helmets lay jauntily over shattered skulls. They wore the kind of boots punk bands used to wear, spattered with mud so thick it was impossible to tell what color they had once been.

"Sword Beach, actually," Percy said. "We came in with the Free French, made it nearly to Caen before the counterattack. We were expecting Panzers, you know, so when this ridiculous Jerry in a cape came marching down the middle of the street with a sword in his hand, well... we had a bit of a laugh." He smiled at the memory. "Duff thought it would be funny if we challenged him to a duel, but the sarge just wanted us to shoot him. Neither worked. Took everything we could dish out and kept on coming. He cut straight through us. I remember wondering what they were going to tell the generals."

"These are your men?" I asked.

"Not my unit, no. These are Suffolk boys, from the 8th. I was with the 185. But they didn't get to go home to their mothers, either, so I guess we're more alike than most." Percy rubbed his eyes, then looked out across the field. "They're all here. Germans, Yanks, a pack of Finns they used to test out the sword. The whole damned army of the dead. Every soul that bastard killed and raised again."

"How many do you think it is?" I asked quietly. This place had a serene quality to it, almost like a graveyard, without the burying. It felt weird to talk too loudly.

"Thirteen hundred and thirty-seven," Percy said. "Well, thirty-six, I suppose. Present company excluded. Built up a little at a time. A patrol here, a brigade there, cut off and cut down. They could have turned the whole invasion back, if Esther and her people hadn't intervened."

"We can't fight back thirteen hundred zombies, John," Chesa said. "Especially since you're the only one with any magical power. I'm a pretty good shot with this bow, and I imagine Matthew can cludge a couple over the head with that staff, but other than that we're feeling pretty underpowered."

"We'll be fine," I said, not feeling fine at all. Chesa had a point. She and Matthew probably only had a glimmer of power remaining, and I had only passed through my domain on my way to Fenrir's den. Whatever we had in our tanks, it probably wasn't enough to go up against a cadre of valkyries and their pet necromancer. But what other choice did we have?

"That's the spirit, John. Can do! Team spirit!" Matthew strolled between the bodies. "And these guys don't look so tough. I could probably take most of them in a fistfight."

"Even if that were true, these men are more than they appear," Percy said. "The power of the Totenschreck gives them inhuman strength and durability. They could crush your skull with one hand." To demonstrate, he picked up a discarded rifle and broke it in half. His hands turned the color of grape jelly. "It damages our bodies, but we heal. And nothing hurts anymore. Not really."

"Looks like you've been holding out on us, Perce," I said. "We could have used that superhero energy back at the B&B."

"It is not in my nature to be violent. I just want to go back to my garden."

"Yeah, well, we don't always get what we want. So, not only are we facing thirteen hundred and thirty-six soldiers, each one is a slightly moldy Superman. Swell."

"Thirty-eight," Chesa called.

"Hmm? I think I did that math correctly. Unless Percy has his count wrong?"

"No. But there have been some additions," Chesa said.

She was standing off to one side of the hill, pretty far down the hill. The grasses there were higher and less beaten down, with few bodies to separate them. The nearby forest was overgrown, almost too thick to walk through. I trotted down to see what she was looking at.

Greg and Bethany lay in perfect state, hands folded over their weapons of choice. They looked like statues in a mausoleum, except for the bloodless wounds at neck and heart. Their skin was pale, their eyes closed. Matthew went to one knee and started mumbling something in Latin.

"Them too, huh?" I said quietly. "I suppose we should have expected it." I looked up to where Percy watched at a slight distance. "What does this mean for us? You seem pretty together. Are we going to be able to talk to them? Get them to fight for us?"

"No," Percy said sadly, shaking his head. "When the Totenschreck calls, it wipes clean all memory, all thought. They will be entirely under the sword's thrall."

"So what happened to you? How come you're all . . . gardens and tea and nonsense?"

"Clarence broke the first sword. It took a long time for me to remember what I had been. The other memories remained, of course. Everything I did under the sword's influence." He smiled weakly. "They will not be your friends if they awaken."

"Fine, fine. Matthew, see if you can do anything for them. Maybe we tie them down or something," I said.

"I've got this," Chesa said. She produced a ribbon of thin pink material from under her sweatshirt.

"Gleipnir? You stole the ribbon used to bind the world wolf?" I asked.

"It's a nice pink," she said. "And Fenrir clearly didn't want it anymore."

"Whatever. Tie them up. Hopefully its magic works as well on zombies as it does on wolves." I scanned the woods and rocky field while Chesa bent to her task. Matthew came to stand next to me. "So what do you think happens now? Why aren't they here yet?"

"Perhaps you were right. Perhaps they weren't ready to end the world, and we beat them to the punch."

"If we hide among the bodies, maybe we can get the drop on them," I said. "I just don't understand why they're waiting."

"Beats me," Matthew said. "Don't know much about this place. Maybe it's difficult for valkyries to come here or something."

"In the old times, they served both Valhalla and Folksvangr," Percy said. "A true valkyrie would have no trouble finding their way to this place."

"Hmm. Well, then I'm not sure what's going on. But at least we'll be able to get the drop on them," I said. "They have no way of knowing we're here."

"Well..." Matthew shielded his eyes, peering skyward. "I think *that's* probably going to get their attention."

Impossibly, Fenrir appeared on the horizon, so large that he dwarfed the sky. The great wolf bounded across the Milky Way and pounced on the moon, shaking it like a rag doll before throwing it. The moon... somehow... bounced across the starry expanse and rolled over the horizon. The sun popped up from the treeline, instantly turning the world into day. Fenrir barked enthusiastically and loped after the moon.

No sooner had night passed and day risen than the sky split along the seams. A longship tore through the fabric of the air, appearing from nowhere, traveling fast. It was gray, and shaggy, and crowded with black-armored valkyries. They spotted us as soon as they came through. Several leapt from the boat, pinwheeling in our direction, while the Naglfr continued on to the crown of the hill.

On the prow on the ship, sickly green blade held high, stood the edgelord. He stared down at me. Even at this distance, I could see the wicked smile on his face.

All around us, the dead began to stir.

CHAPTER THIRTY-ONE

"Keep moving!" I shouted over the sounds of battle. Matthew and I fought shoulder to shoulder, battering our way through the ranks of the undead. Chesa followed in our wake. Her arrows had little effect on the tough flesh of the zombies, but each shot landed in an eye, or a throat, or through the skull of an attacker. Even zombies fall to that kind of precision. "The only way this works is if we stay ahead of them."

"Not so sure about this, Rast," Matthew said. He was fighting with his improvised staff, cracking skulls and blessing the fallen. "Where are we even going?"

"And do we have a plan once we get there?" Chesa followed up.

"That circle of stones at the top of the hill looks like a ritual site to me," I said, nodding at the broken ring of menhirs crowning the grassy knoll. "The *Hangnail* touched down right in the middle. I figure that whatever they're doing there, we want to stop them."

"I mean, they've already animated the army of the dead. What more can they do?" Matthew asked. A zombie in the tweedy tan and tanner of the BEF—British Expeditionary Force—grabbed at the saint's shoulder and tried to pull him down. I slipped behind Matthew's back, lay my blade against the undead creature's elbow, then sliced clean through flesh and bone. Gargling, it fell back, staring at its new stump in shock.

"These things are barely fighting back," I said. "Think of the stories Percy told us. Organized units of the dead. Ambushes." Another zombie grabbed at my legs, but I was able to kick it down and keep going. "This is a mere fragment of their power. They're not even using their guns."

"Feels like they're fighting just fine to me," Chesa said. She was struggling to keep up with us. Every step we took, the zombie horde collapsed behind us like water in the wake of a boat. She had to keep moving to avoid being overrun, but aiming and shooting took time. There were a dozen long scratches on her arms and face, and at least one tear in the shoulder of her sweatshirt that looked like it had been done with blunt teeth.

"It's going to get worse," I said. "We're almost there. Maybe save your arrows for the creep in the skull helmet, or those valhellions circling overhead."

The valkyries in question had me nervous. They had yet to strike, despite having ample opportunity to drop down. Instead they flew in slow, lazy circles around the battlefield. I counted three, but there had been a dozen more on the *Hangnail*, and who knew how many in the clouds above, waiting in reserve. If we could barely hold back the zombies, what chance did we have against their winged masters?

"So our plan is to keep fighting against impossible odds, keep pressing into the endless mob of soldier zombies, and keep moving, no matter what? Kill everything, or die heroically?" Chesa shouted. "Do I have that right?"

"Yeah," I said. "That's the plan."

A German soldier in gray fatigues shambled out of the horde. He swung a dented submachine gun off his shoulder and pointed it in our direction. I had a moment of existential dread. Being a member of Knight Watch is supposed to protect you from modern weapons, in the same way the various mythic creatures we battle are immune to bullets and taxes. But a gun carried by a zombie? Does that count as magical? Or just really unsettling?

The point was moot. The SMG let out a loud, solitary click. The zombie shook the gun, then threw it to the ground and drew a knife.

"Okay, knives I understand. Knives I can deal with," I said. "I think I have the reach advantage, big guy."

What I had forgotten were Percy's warnings about the nature of these zombies. Their strength and durability. Their smarts. The soldier lumbered up the hill toward me. When it got close enough, I swung hard at its head, thinking to end this quick so I could get at the edgelord.

The zombie caught my sword in one hand, twisting as the blade cut through his palm and stuck into the tiny bones of his wrist. While I tried to wrestle my weapon free, he drove his knife into my shield, puncturing the face just above my fist, then slammed into me with his shoulder. I went flying, leaving sword and shield in the creature's grasp.

Digging a rut in the grassy hill, I came to a stop ten feet away, with my feet in the air and a healthy supply of sod down the back of my cuisse. Pants. My steel pants. I rolled clumsily to my feet, drawing my mercy dagger. The long, thin blade of the dagger wouldn't do much to the zombie's dead flesh, but I had to try something.

The zombie tossed my shield to the side and marched toward me. Levering the blade back and forth, he worked my sword free, giving it a practice swing as he approached.

"*Willkommen in der Armee der Toten*," he said. His voice was thick and slurred and in German, but I assumed he was being a smart-ass. I backed up.

"No, you're fat," I said. His head tilted to the side but he kept coming. "Probably all the tatertots you ate. Chunky boy."

"*Kartoffel Toten. Ja.*" He raised the sword overhead. "All zee dead potato heads."

He swung too hard, and I dodged to the side, watching him bury the sword in the ground. He was holding it with his one good hand and, despite his strength, could not maintain the grip. I plunged my dagger into the side of his throat, which drew a fountain of clay-thick blood and a disappointed grunt from the zombie. Then he grabbed me and lifted me effortlessly off the ground.

"You put! My boyfriend! Down!" Chesa shouted. With each exclamation, an arrow went into the zombie's face. He swatted at them like flies, blinking uncomfortably around the shaft of an arrow embedded in his nasal cavity and through his cheek. He dropped me and shambled in Chesa's direction.

"I had no idea you cared!" I said as I scooped up my shield and banged it, two-fisted, into the back of the zombie's head. His skull came loose, and he stumbled forward, falling flat in front of Chesa. She jammed the heel of her boot against his neck and put one more arrow through the back of his head. The squirming stopped.

"Ex-boyfriend," she clarified, glaring at me.

"I wasn't really expecting a romantic reunion in the middle of a zombie battle," I said, trotting back to pick up my sword. "Though that would be pretty on point for us."

Chesa didn't answer, which was fine, because we were being overrun with zombies. Matthew was drawing lines in the grass with his staff that glowed whenever the undead tried to cross them, but he couldn't close the circle because they kept lurching around the sides before he could reach them. It meant he looked like the first dancer in a dangerous conga line, backpedaling away from the rest of the party.

That's when the valkyries circling overhead decided to join the fray. The three of them landed in a triangle around us, scattering a few of their shambling brethren and throwing up a wall of blowing grass and scattered debris. I was still blinking the dust out of my eyes when the one closest to me attacked.

She was kind of short for a valkyrie, but thickly muscled and quick with her spear. She held it in both hands, moving the petal-leaf tip smoothly, first striking at my head then quickly switching to my exposed leg when I lifted my shield. The spear danced off the thick armor of my greaves, but the impact sent me stumbling backward. As I reset, she chuckled.

"This is what passes for a hero these days?" she said. Her voice had a hollow resonance to it. Her helmet was closed, so I could see nothing of her face, but she sounded familiar. I ran through the valkyries I had met. Most were lying unconscious back at the Madhall. She struck again, this time catching the gap between my chest and shoulder plates. The spear dug into the chain mail. I heard rings pop and felt hot blood run down my bicep. The pain came a second later. She laughed again. "It's no wonder Valhalla has grown stagnant and weak."

"I'm still in training," I said. "The onboarding process is kind of a bitch."

"At least you're clever. I do enjoy killing clever boys."

Just then, Chesa cried out in pain. I glanced around in time to see her collapse backward, tripped by the spear of the valkyrie she was facing. I was about to go to her aid when my valkyrie pressed her attack. She was overconfident, but I was distracted. The first spear thrust drove my shield down, the second reached my chest and slid back toward my already injured shoulder. I twisted away, but that left my right side exposed with only the sword to defend. The valkyrie swept the butt of her spear toward my leg. I parried and tried to recover my guard position, but the valkyrie kicked at my thigh and followed it up with a quick strike to my neck. The haft of her spear crashed into my chin, snapping my head to the side and dealing a glancing blow to the soft flesh of my throat. Choking, I stumbled backward, barely catching myself before going ass over teakettle into the grass.

"We need a new plan, Rast," Chesa growled. She was on the ground next to me. She had lost her bow, and was drawing her crescent blades. If Chesa was going to the knives, we were in some trouble. Matthew, to his credit, was holding his own. The priest could swing a staff, it turned out.

"Gotta save the magic for the edgelord," I gasped. "Keep fighting."

"Idiot," Chesa said, but her heart wasn't really in it. We pulled each other up, then turned back-to-back, facing our opponents.

"Brave idiots, clever idiots, heroic idiots," the valkyrie said. "In the end, dead idiots."

"Sometimes it takes a healthy dose of stupid to be a hero," I shouted. "Chesa, with me!"

"Yuck, teamwork," she said, but followed me into the fight.

The stout valkyrie was surprised by our sudden charge. She tried to disengage, flapping her wings desperately, but I came in low and Chesa went high. The edge of my shield slammed into Stout's kneecaps, and Chesa leapt over my back, scything her way through those wings like they were wheat. Stout screamed in pain and frustration, then went down.

Unengaged, the valkyrie that had been kicking Chesa's ass rushed us, but only came far enough to cover her fallen sister. Then she motioned to the third valkyrie and yelled.

"Veldi, I think we're done here!" she called.

"Yes, okay. This one is getting tired anyway." The one fighting Matthew disengaged in a flutter of wings. She tilted her head in Stout's direction. "Why is she lying down, Leddi?"

"The mortals overwhelmed her," Leddi answered. With one last thrust of her spear to drive us back, Leddi took to the air.

"Typical," Veldi said. Together she and Leddi swooped down, forcing us to the ground as they swept overhead. They landed just long enough to grab the fallen valkyrie by the arms and hoist her into the air. She looked different. Her wings hung in tatters, and her black armor had lost its otherworld shine. As they flew off, a plume of feathers trailed in their wake. They made their way to the crown of the hill, struggling with their fallen companion's weight suspended between them.

"Well, I'll be damned," Chesa said. "That actually worked."

"I'm just as shocked as you are," I said. "Doesn't seem like they're used to fighting in groups."

"Too much dueling in Valhalla, I guess," Chesa said. "Matthew, you okay?"

"Doing great. Had her right where I wanted her," he said, rubbing his jaw. There were bruises all up and down his face, but the glow in his eyes was a little more than divine. "That chick really packed a punch."

With the valkyries gone, the surrounding mob of zombies seemed to lose interest in us, and went back to shuffling back and forth and groaning pitiably. I was glad for the reprieve. Matthew had just enough Brilliance to bind our wounds and wick the fatigue out of our bones. While he was doing that, I stared at the spot where the valkyrie had fallen. Something about it bothered me.

Kneeling in the beaten grass, I pulled up a fistful of feathers. They looked like . . . chicken? And they'd been daubed with black paint.

"What do you guys think this is about?" I asked, holding up the feathers. Chesa squinted at them and shrugged.

"She got hit pretty hard. Lost a little plumage, I guess."

"No, you don't understand. These don't look particularly . . . mythic. Do they?"

Matthew got closer and plucked one of the feathers from my hand. He ran it under his nose, then sneezed.

"Goose," he said. "And maybe tar, or just cheap paint. That doesn't make any sense."

"None of this makes any sense," I said. "Valkyries trying to end the world, a field full of zombies that can't seem to be arsed to attack us, and now goose feathers. There were turkey feathers at the B&B, too."

"In your armor, yeah. And lying around the outside of the house," Chesa said. "What do you think it means?"

"Some kind of costume, maybe? But those wings looked real

enough while they were flying away," I said. "There was something about her armor, too. Lost a lot of its shine when she went down."

"You know what it reminds me of?" Chesa asked. She kicked at the ground where the valkyrie had fallen, finally coming up with a bit of armor that must have fallen off. It was leather, and old, the clasp rusty and worn. "The skeletons at the convention center."

I had to go way back to remember those. After we'd driven off the edgelord and his winged girlfriend, the skeletons that he had summoned had all collapsed into cheap plastic bones and Halloween masks. The convention-goers he had zombified all turned back, as though nothing had happened.

"You think someone is dressing up as valkyries and trying to make it real through sheer willpower?" I asked.

"Willpower and whatever magic they're able to squeeze out of that sword," she said. "But who the hell would do that?"

"Who cares about Valhalla enough to try to end the world to fix it?" Matthew mused.

I looked up at the crown of the hill. The HMS *Hangnail* was parked haphazardly between two monolithic stones, but I could see a circle of winged figures, with the edgelord in the center. The sound of chanting rolled down the hill. The air was filled with supernatural power, the kind of power that could really screw with the world.

"I think I know," I said. "And if I'm right, we need to get up that hill before they finish whatever the hell they're doing."

"What? Why?" Chesa asked.

"Because they're not trying to end this world," I shouted as I took off through the mob of listless zombies. "They're trying to start a new one!"

CHAPTER THIRTY-TWO

Chesa caught up with me after a dozen strides. She ran easily alongside me. I mean, I was in full armor, with shield and sword, while she was in jeans and a T-shirt. But still, it was a little embarrassing.

"What the hell do you mean, John?" she shouted over the sound of my laborious breathing and the rattle of my armor.

"What's the first thing we did when we joined Knight Watch?"

"Failed our roll to Disbelieve."

"Besides that." I shouldered aside a German soldier whose face was torn off at the jaw. "To establish our powers, and ensure our place in the Unreal. Think trees."

"Our domains?" she asked.

"Our domains. And if these aren't valkyries, but a bunch of wannabe grimdark cosplayers trying to carve out their own place in the Unreal . . ." I let the implication hang.

"They'll need to establish a domain. You think that's why they took ours down?"

"I think that's something to do with it, but—" I took a gasping breath, then spat to the side. "Look, can we talk about this later? After the running?"

"Sure thing," she said. "I'll see you at the top!"

She took off, long legs eating up the hill in bounding strides. I groaned and stumbled to a stop. My lungs were on fire, and my heart felt like it was going to punch its way straight out of my chest.

"Don't make me do the celerity trick again, John," Matthew said as he trotted past. "You don't want that kind of sunburn, do you?"

The celerity trick was when he made me superfast to kill some tree-monsters a few months back. Thing was, the air didn't get out of the way fast enough, and I ended up with a sunburn an inch deep and super-superbright. I groaned again at the memory, but rumbled up the hill after Chesa and the saint.

"Bloody cloth-wearers," I mumbled to myself. "Always prancing around without a care in the world."

As we approached the crown of the hill, the circle of valhellions broke and strolled in our direction. They formed a loose line between us and the edgelord. There was a clear area around the top of the hill, kind of like a tree line except... with zombies. Shortly after we cleared the zombie-line, I stumbled to a halt. The others were waiting.

We formed a semicircle, facing off with the valkyries. I stood at the center, with Chesa to my right and Matthew hanging back a little. The saint's glowing skin turned the grass a brilliant shade of emerald. Our two groups stood warily, measuring each other. I saw the two thin valkyries we had just faced, Veldi and Leddi, along with two others, one with soft tan skin and distinctly Asian features, while the other wore her copper hair short, and had so many freckles along her cheeks and exposed arms that she could have been orange. The stout valkyrie stood at their center, apparently recovered from our attack. Her wings were gone, though, and instead of a spear she carried two light hand-axes. She grinned cheerfully as we gathered ourselves.

"They sure look like valkyries to me," Chesa said, eyeing the skirmish line of winged warriors. "Are you sure about this, John?"

"No. But it's a good theory," I said. "And let's be honest. Either I'm right, and they're nothing more than a bunch of punks trying to trick their way into the Unreal, or they're actual valkyries who have gone completely rogue and need to be put down. Either way, we're the ones who are going to stop them."

"You are going to *try* to stop us," Stout said. "And we are going to try to kill you. What happens, only the gods truly know."

"Not a fan of destiny, personally!" I shouted across the gap between us. "I'd rather make my own fate."

"It doesn't matter what you believe. All that matters is how you fight, and how you die," Stout answered. She raised her axes in grim invitation. "So let us see, John Rast. Show us that you are worthy of the new Valhalla!"

"She's baiting us," Matthew whispered.

"And I'm taking it," I said, then rushed forward.

The four flanking valkyries lowered their spears like a Greek phalanx, broad tips pointed at my chest. Engaging the magic of my shield, I folded the buckler out into a Roman scutum, tall and cylindrical. The spears slid off the convex front of the shield, and then I was past the pointy bits and running by their ashen hafts. I heard Stout shout an order, and the spears dropped into the grass. The sound of swords sliding from scabbards filled the air.

Having broken their spear line, I snapped the enarme straps of the shield, transforming the shield all the way down into a buckler, not much larger than my fist. The valkyries stood right in front of me, swords and round shields in hand, ready to butcher me. I shouted, punched at the shield of the copper-haired valkyrie, then spun around to meet Veldi's attack with the hilt of my sword. Another sword banged off my shoulder, pushing me off-balance. I met another shield with my face, but got my own shield up in time to deflect the follow-up slice that would have cut my skull in half.

Two on one is tough. Five on one is impossible. Fortunately, I wasn't alone.

A hail of arrows from my right turned the ground into a bristling thicket of fletching, thudding into valkyrie shields and finding at least one target in Leddi's thick valkyrie thigh. She screamed in pain, then snapped the shaft of the arrow with her sword and charged at Chesa. There was a brief exchange of arrows and insults as Chesa fell back, but finally my ex had to drop her bow and draw the twin crescent blades. All I could hear was a symphony of steel and ladylike grunting. Chesa could handle herself. I had other concerns.

Veldi and the copper valkyrie ran at me, shields up and swords over their heads. The viking sword is incredibly sharp, designed to chop through thick leather, flesh, and bone without breaking stride. Even the ring mail that the hosts of Valhalla wore couldn't stand up to it. But magically forged steel plate was another matter. I met Veldi's attack with my shield, but let Copper get past my defenses. Eager, she struck down hard on my shoulder, expecting to slice clean through to my lungs. The steel face of my pauldron turned the blade aside, dimpling with the force of the blow but holding solid. Her arm slipped over mine as she overreached, falling forward until her armpit was flat against my elbow.

"Sorry, lady," I said, then twisted away from her, bringing my sword through the meat of her underarm. I felt the blade slice through tricep and pectoral. Her arm flopped limp, and her screams reached the sky. I kicked her aside and turned my attention to Veldi.

"The mortal has some bite," Veldi said. "This is good. I was starting to worry that—"

I punched her with the rim of my shield, blocked her swing with my sword, twisted both blades over my head, and then stabbed down. The tip of my blade caught her in the shoulder, severing ring mail and cracking her shoulder open. She screamed and backpedaled, sword arm hanging limp at her side.

"Too much talking," I said.

"This is as far as you go, John Rast," Stout said, stepping between me and the retreating Veldi. "You've had a good run. But I have already taken your measure." She fell into a fighting stance. "This strand of fate is already cut."

"You're saying that I'm a frayed knot?" I asked. "See. Afraid not? It's good, right?"

"You are funny, John. And cute. But that is not going to save your life."

"Have we . . . have we met?" I asked. I looked from her to the other valkyrie. Neither looked familiar. "I feel like I would remember."

Stout and Tan stalked toward me, spreading out as they got close. I started to fall back, but then realized I would be exposing Matthew, who wasn't wasn't much use in this kind of fight. But if I stayed where I was, the two valkyries would flank me. As good as my armor was, getting stabbed in the back would definitely put a crimp in my plans for staying alive. Triggering the magic in my shield one more time, I expanded the buckler into a kite, giving me some protection for my legs while maximizing maneuverability. I couldn't just stand here. I had to go on the offensive.

Tan was closer, so I lunged in her direction. Apparently expecting this, she fell back, and I was barely able to spin around and meet Stout's attack. She spun both axes at me, coming down on my shield in a quick succession of blows that shivered the bones in my shield-arm, the impact traveling through my shoulder into my lungs. I blindly stabbed out with my sword, contacting something hard and impervious. Just then, Tan slammed her shield into my backside. I went to my knees, flailing to one side as I tried to drive Tan back with my sword while still holding off Stout and her flying axes of doom. A solid blow skittered off my helm. Blood filled my mouth, and the sound of funeral bells echoed through my skull. Blindly, I kicked at a pair of muscular legs, then scooted backward. Twin shadows loomed over me.

"You've been a good hero, John. But not good enough," Stout said.

An arrow sprouted from Stout's shoulder, then another from her forearm. She and Tan whirled to face Chesa, bringing up their shields just in time to catch three more rapidly fired shots. I breathed a sigh of relief. Chesa stood twenty yards away, one foot braced on the unconscious form of Leddi, shooting as fast as she could put arrow to string and draw.

"I'm getting tired of her interruptions. Take care of her, will you?" Stout growled. "See that the elf whelp doesn't get the better of you. I can take care of this one."

"See that you do," Tan answered. Then, huddling behind her shield, she hurried toward Chesa.

"Stand up, Rast. We aren't done just yet."

"You know, it bothers me that you and the creepy grimdark dude all seem to know my name, but I have to call you Shorty," I said, scrambling to my feet.

"My name doesn't matter to you. The skalds will know it, once the new Valhalla has been established, and my reign begins."

"So that's what this is all about? You don't like bowing to Runa?" We both knew I was stalling for time, but she didn't seem to care. I glanced over her shoulder at the edgelord. He was performing some kind of ritual with the potato sword. The air around him crackled with dark lightning, and fog wafted out of the ground. She followed my eyes and laughed.

"It's not the bowing that gets to me. It's the drinking. And the dancing. And the endless games of volleyball."

"Hrapp?" I asked. "No, that can't be right. He didn't have a body. Revna? Did you betray your sister?"

"Enough talking. It's time for you to die. I promise I will be nice, once we raise you from the dead to serve in our infinite army," she snapped. "I've always liked the idea of a perfectly compliant servant."

She came at me fast, but without the other valkyries to worry about, I felt more confident about my ability to hold her off. She was good with the axes, spinning them around, banging into my shield or taking swings at my exposed legs, arm, and head. I did a lot of circling around, adjusting my shield from kite to tower to heater depending on her attack. At first she fought with reckless glee, but as my defenses held she grew more desperate, less precise. One ax missed, sliding off my shield and into the churned sod of the hillside. She released it, but before she could draw another from her belt, I rushed forward, pinning her remaining weapon between my shield and her chest. She swore in Old Norse, something about testicles and frostbite, then dropped her ax and grabbed the edge of my shield, yanked it to the ground, and pulled me with it. I saw her other arm come free, stubby dagger in hand and pointed at the thin slit in my helmet. I did the only thing that I could: I dropped my shield, but not before willing it into a new shape.

The bottom rim of the shield hit the ground just as the heater transformed into a giant's tower shield. It wasn't a very useful configuration for me, considering the steel face of the shield was twelve feet tall, and weighed about as much as a Mack truck loaded with gravel. But it was great for catching confident valkyries off guard. The top of the shield shot up like a magical beanstalk. It clipped Stout right in the wrist. I heard bones crack and saw the dagger tumble from her fingers before the shield rose up between us, a sudden wall of steel and wood. I fell on my butt and sat there for a minute, listening to Stout moan on the other side of the shield, which had dug itself a rut in the ground and seemed to be a now-permanent wall.

"See, that's what happens when you forget who you're fighting," I said, standing off and dusting my hands. "Magic shields aren't as flashy as fireballs, or as sexy as a glowing sword, but they get the job done." I strolled around the edge of the shield-wall, sword in hand, ready to finish the job. "All but the killing part. And I think—Solveig?"

There, at the base of my giant shield, in a pile of painted feathers and cradling a broken wrist against her chest, was Solveig the

Bashful. Her valkyrie disguise had come apart around her. She stared up at me with tears in her eyes.

"Why couldn't you have left us alone?" she whispered. "Who are we hurting? A few valkyries? Some mortals? Who cares?"

"I care," I said. "I'm one of those mortals."

"You would have been happy dead," she said. "We would have made a marvelous couple, in my new Valhalla."

"If I'm following your plan correctly, I would have been a zombie, and the world I knew would have been a smoldering ruin. Or, at least, the magical parts of it would have been." Regretfully, I raised my sword. Her eyes didn't flinch.

"It doesn't matter. You're already too late."

I paused, puzzled, then heard the crack of thunder and the rumble of an earthquake. I looked over at the edgelord and his weird sword. He stood at the crown of the hill, which was wreathed in rapidly swirling smoke. Shadows moved in the mists. I glimpsed a door in the darkness, and a path leading up to it. The bastard was forming his domain while Chesa and I talked shit with these fake valkyries.

"Well, ain't that a bitch," I muttered.

"It gets worse," Solveig said, then stabbed me in the stomach with the dagger in her good hand.

The chain-mail skirt between my breastplate and greaves turned the worst of the blow, but it was still enough to knock the wind out of me, and put me on my knees. I grabbed at the wound with both hands, convinced I was going to look down to see my guts spilling onto the grass. But other than a sharp pain and Solveig's abandoned dagger (how many blades did that girl carry?) there was no blood leaking between the links of my chain mail.

I looked up just in time to see Solveig run past Matthew, slipping through the ranks of the dead, her hand clutched tight to her belly.

CHAPTER THIRTY-THREE

"Chesa! Gonna need you to finish up over there!" I shouted. "We've got bigger problems."

"I am doing!" Smash! Clatter! "The best!" Rolling grunt. Clashing steel! "That I can!"

"Well, do better!" I faced off with the line of zombie soldiers. They stood in uneasy formation, a hodgepodge of weapons in hand, from Mausers to Garands to MG42s slung over slumped shoulders and PIATs held in bony hands like cricket bats. They watched us with sunken eyes.

"Why aren't they attacking?" Matthew asked. He stood over the fallen body of the valkyrie I had cut nearly in half, his hands bloody, but his attention was fully on the undead horde that surrounded us.

"It's like they don't want to come any closer to the top of the hill," I said. I glanced down at the dead valkyrie. "Learn anything from our fallen friend?"

"Death due to massive blood loss. Nicked a lung, too. She probably drowned in her own heart blood," he said. "Kind of horrible."

"No, I mean . . . did you learn anything about who they are? The other one was posing as a valkyrie in Valhalla."

"Oh. Yeah, that makes sense." He pushed her over onto her back. I recognized the woman from the audience of the Armor Competition. Just another face in the crowd. Now she stared sightlessly at the sky. "I think they're all Vikings."

"Explains how they got into Valhalla without Runa knowing about it. And how they took the valkyries by surprise at the Madhall." I twisted my sword nervously in my hand. The zombies just stared at us. "I don't think they're coming for us."

There was a strangled yell from the direction of Chesa's fight, and the third valkyrie limped into the air, one wing trailing blood. Chesa was on the ground, but as soon as the valkyrie got some altitude, Chesa crawled to where her bow had fallen and drew it. Three quick arrows and the valkyrie fell, disappearing among the ranks of restless dead. I ran to her side, with Matthew close behind.

"Thanks for the help," she said with a grimace as I went to a knee beside her. I slammed open my visor and looked her over. Her comic book T-shirt was soaked in blood, and a deep gash ran from her hip all the way across her belly.

"Hey, you usually yell at me if I try to lend a hand," I said.

"Because you usually just make things worse," she said. A cough brought blood to her lips. "Ah, this is bad."

"You guys just gonna sit there holding hands, or do you want me to heal her?" Matthew asked.

"Sure, right, of course," I said, standing rapidly to get out of the saint's way.

Matthew did a quick examination, pulling the shirt back to stare at the wound. I turned away, partly to give Chesa some privacy, and partly because I hated seeing her hurt like this. Plus there were zombies to monitor. They still weren't getting any closer. I almost wished they'd make their charge and get it over with. The suspense was killing me.

"Decision time," Matthew said. "I didn't get a lot of time in my domain. This is going to take the rest of my light. She'll be in fighting shape, but I'll be useless to you. Or I can do just enough healing to keep her alive and hold the reserve for when you get mauled."

"Maybe I don't get mauled?" I asked.

"Let's be realistic here, John."

"Okay, okay. I think I'd rather have her up and fighting," I said. *And as far away from dead as you can manage*, I thought but didn't bother saying. "No amount of healing will get me through this many zombies."

"No amount of fighting is going to get you through them, either," Chesa said weakly. "I can stay out of the way. Better keep some Brilliance for when you do something stupid."

I looked her over. I'd never seen Chesa looking so bad. There was a thick lump in my throat. I shook my head. "No. Get her on her feet. I'm not taking the chance."

"You're the boss," Matthew said. He pressed his palms flat into Chesa's belly, then turned the color of the sun. I shielded my eyes until the Brilliance passed. Even the zombies murmured and turned aside. When I looked again, Chesa was as right as rain.

Matthew stood up, clapping his hands together.

"Right, that's the last of my light. I can hang back and provide—" All of a sudden he looked over my shoulder and shouted, "Whoa! Not the face!"

Saint Matthew disappeared in a flash of light, almost like a door opened in the air and someone pushed him through. And from over my shoulder, so close that I felt the wind through my open visor, came a soccer ball. It passed through the place Matthew's head had been a second earlier, then bounced across the field before rolling to a stop at the feet of one of the zombies. The undead soldier looked down at it numbly, then gave it a lurching kick that passed it to another nearby zombie. Within moments there was a clear space and an impromptu game of soccer, without sides or goals or much organization.

"What the hell just happened?" Chesa asked, staring at the empty air where Matthew had been.

"I have no idea. Less than no idea." I looked over my shoulder where the ball had come from, but I couldn't see anything more unusual than an army of zombies. "That was just strange."

"It's like he ran out of magic and fell through the world," Chesa said. "If Valhalla is a strip mall banquet hall, this place might be a soccer field somewhere. Maybe that's where Matthew went."

"I guess. Hope he's alright."

Chesa stood up, running a hand across her stomach. "He did a great job with this, at least. That really hurt."

"You feeling okay?" I asked.

"Yeah. I'll be fine." She stretched her shoulders, then kicked the bow up into her hand and started collecting the quiver of arrows that lay scattered all around her. "I've still got a little magic juice left, but not a lot. How about you?"

I tested my shield, switching it from heater to kite with the flick of a wrist. It happened effortlessly. "I'm still pretty well stocked," I said. "You think we're going to disappear when we run out of magic?"

"Could be. Quick way out of trouble, I suppose."

"Yeah, but we wouldn't have a way of getting back here," I said. "Maybe that's why the zombies aren't getting any closer. Whatever magic is animating them might not be strong enough yet to sustain them up here. Proximity to the altar or something?"

"Your guess is as good as mine," Chesa said.

"Either way, it's probably best to hang on to whatever magic we have," I said. "We can get by on skill alone."

"Well, I can. You? Not so sure," she said. With her quiver reset and her bow in hand, she turned to where the edgelord was still performing his magic trick. "Let's hope they stay away long enough for us to stop this nerd."

The soccer ball bounced out of the mob and landed against my foot. The zombies shuffled closer, dozens of them staring longingly at the ball. I sighed, then kicked it back to them. The game resumed with enthusiasm.

"This has gotten weird," Chesa said.

"Yeah. But that's all the proof I need that they'll leave us alone." I slammed my visor down and marched up the hill. "Let's beat the shit out of this edgelord."

The top of the hill looked like it had been cut off with a giant Sawzall, forming a flat circle about thirty yards in diameter that was ringed with standing stones, most of which had long ago settled into the sod, leaning lazily together like drunk college students. The surface of the circle was made of loose gravel the color of gravestones. The edgelord stood in the middle of the circle with his back toward us, arms raised to the sky. The Totenschreck had been thrust into the ground at his feet. Tendrils of smoke corkscrewed out of the ground to surround the bearer and sword, and a low cloud hung overhead, spinning slowly. A sharp wind blew across the hill, pulling at my tabard and turning Chesa's hair into a maelstrom of dark locks.

"Let's finish this quick." She tucked her hair behind her ear and drew an arrow to her cheek.

"There's no way you make that shot in this wind," I said.

"There's no way *you* make this shot," she answered. "I'm special."

Whispering into the arrow, Chesa exhaled a breath of glowing light that twisted into the shaft, then released the bowstring. The arrow danced gracefully through the wind, arcing slowly toward its target with all the inevitability of elven magic.

A bolt of green lightning crackled out of the Totenschreck, striking the arrow and splitting it down the shaft. Splinters flew across the skull-faced warrior's back. He glanced back at us over his shoulder, then stepped to the side, putting the sword between us.

"I thought I was finished with the pair of you," he growled. "You're like stink on warm fish. You end up having to burn down the fish shed, and then the whole village stinks for a while."

"That's . . . evocative," I said. "But you're not getting rid of us, no matter how many fish sheds you burn to the ground."

"Can you not see the futility of your efforts? If all the valkyries in Valhalla could not stand against me, who do you think you are to oppose me?"

"I'm the guy who killed a dragon in single combat, stopped an evil wizard with a machine gun, and sleeps comfortably in the middle of a forest of monsters," I said. "Hell, I rode Fenrir to heaven, slew your precious guardians, and now I'm going to knock your silly skull-helmet off your head and put you back in your place."

"Back in my place? That is how you boast?" The edgelord thumped his chest, throwing his shoulders back and thrusting his chin at the sky. "Child, I will wear your entrails as a belt, and your skin as boots. I will pick my teeth with your bones. I will wipe my ass with your scalp and use your skull as a piss pot."

"You *do* need to work on your threats," Chesa said to me. "Not that I'm encouraging you to go full pisspot. You're just sometimes too polite."

"You wanna give this a try?" I asked.

"I like to keep my arguments short," she said, then drew three shots in rapid succession and let them fly. Lightning struck down each arrow, spraying splinters all over the enemy.

"Will you stop doing that?" he complained, wiping broken arrows off his chest. "This matter will be settled with steel, or it won't be settled at all."

"How does he keep doing that?" she muttered.

"Rules of the realm, maybe? This place is becoming his domain. If his mythic ideal is dying in glorious battle, I doubt taking an arrow in the eye will be part of that."

Still mumbling to herself, Chesa tossed the bow to the ground and dropped her quiver, then drew the twin crescent blades. He nodded approval.

"Very good. But as much as I would like to tarry in this place, I am called to someplace better. A new heaven, for a new god." He grasped the handle of the Totenschreck. Sickly green static danced between his hand and the hilt, crackling over his bracers as he took the blade. A shock of electricity rolled across the hill, washing over us harmlessly.

The spot where the sword had been yawned open. A pillar of stone rose out of the ground, twisting open like a flower to sprout a staircase. It rose into the cloud overhead, its top disappearing in the swirling storm. The edgelord put one foot on the first step, then saluted us.

"One more thing before I go," he said. "There's someone I want you to meet."

About ten feet in front of us, the gravel started to shake and rattle. Two mounds formed among the stones, quickly pushing up like stony fountains. A hand erupted from one of the eruptions, pale and dusty, followed by an arm, a shoulder, a body. The second mound followed suit, producing a more petite form, delicate compared to the first. Though I would never call her delicate to her face.

Sir Gregory d'Hotpants was clearly a zombie. His face hung slack, and his shoulders were twisted under the shiny steel of his pauldrons. The armor of his left leg was crooked, the foot on that side pointing in the wrong direction. Bethany stood next to him, her typically wry smile even more wry (wryer?), and her clawed hands grasped bony daggers close to her chest. A thin pink ribbon hung loosely around their shoulders, waists, and one leg each, running between them half a dozen times.

"Have fun killing your friends," the edgelord said, then ascended the stairs.

CHAPTER THIRTY-FOUR

Zombie Gregory groaned quietly. Even in death, his oiled curls shone glamorously in the sun's steady light. This was offset by the sickly green tint of his flesh, and the way his skeleton didn't seem to be fully attached to his muscles. Pale bone protruded from his fingertips, and every time he moved, his whole body twitched spasmodically. I sheathed my sword, then held up my free hand and waved it in his face.

"Hey, buddy," I said soothingly. "How ya feeling? Feel like taking a nap, maybe?"

"Hhhhhiiiiiiiii." His voice sounded like an engine that hadn't been oiled since the Paleozoic period. His breath was of a similar vintage. I gagged and stepped back. "Buuuhhhdddiieeeeeeee."

"Buddy, right. Remember that we're buddies?" I glanced from Gregory over to Bee. Our young assassin wasn't moving all that much. Her shadow-woven cloak was fringed with mildew, and a thin milky glaze hung over her eyes. Bethany had always been quiet, but this was unnerving. "Bethany, you remember we're friends, don't you?"

There was a rattle of steel. When I looked back, Gregory had unlimbered the massive zweihander sword from his back, and was staring at it with curious detachment. I took another step back, resting my hand on my sheathed sword. I didn't want to provoke a confrontation if I didn't have to, and I wasn't sure how much of Greg and Bee were still in these bodies. If they had the same amount of agency as Percy apparently did, then it wouldn't do to start cutting them when a little talking might do the trick.

"You probably don't need that, Sir Greg," I said. "You can just put that away and—" I jumped back as he gave it a practice swing. Behind me, I heard the creak of Chesa's bow. She had Bee's attention. The assassin was staring (almost literal) daggers over my shoulder in Chesa's direction. "I'm trying to de-escalate here, Ches. Maybe hold back on filling them full of iron?"

"And I'm trying to not get killed," she answered. "So until they prove—"

Bethany let out a snarling roar and leapt toward Chesa. There was some magic in her movement, her body flickering into shadow as she jumped, bone-white daggers drawn back to strike. She got about four feet before the thin pink ribbon tying her to Gregory snapped tight. Her snarl turned into choked frustration as her feet flew out from under her. Gregory twisted in her direction, stumbling a few steps but staying upright as Bee smacked into the ground. She was on her feet in a flash, straining against the tether, slowly dragging Greg forward.

"Chesa! You're making this worse!"

Two arrows sang through the air, the first skimming off Bethany's leg, the second snagging her cloak and pinning it to the ground. That first arrow ricocheted into Gregory's chest, startling him. He roared his displeasure and charged.

"Damn it!" I intercepted Gregory, taking the full brunt of his charge on my shield, sending us both stumbling away. Bethany turned her attention to me, slashing mindlessly at me with her daggers. They bounced off the steel plate of my thigh, then traveled up hip and into my ribs. There was a brief moment when I felt the blade press against the chain-mail seam between hip and belly, but Bethany continued up my side rather than plunging the dagger home.

I battered her aside with my shield and fell back. Chesa was already on the retreat, dancing backward while drawing and firing her bow with enviable grace. Arrows stitched the ground around Bethany, slowing her attack and occasionally striking a glancing blow to limb or shoulder. At least Chesa hadn't gone full murder hobo on our wayward team members just yet.

As for Gregory, once the cobwebs had cleared and his attention was drawn, he *had* decided to go full murderous sword fight. He came at me like a maniac, swinging that sword with all his strength.

The zweihander is a ridiculous weapon, nearly five feet long with a wave-pattern blade designed to trap blades and leave gruesome wounds. It always struck me as funny to watch Greg wrestle that much steel around the battlefield. I no longer found it funny. The blade whistled through the air, steel in constant motion as Gregory advanced. It was so well balanced that he could change direction with a shift of his shoulders, even altering his attack into a thrust or counterswing. I kept my shield in heater form just so I could see where the strike was coming from. The blade cut hunks off my shield, and I kept having to tap into my magical reserves to reconstitute the steel and bolster my defense.

The only thing saving me was Bethany and her single-minded fury at Chesa and her buzzing arrows. Bee kept pulling Gregory off-balance, sending his sword thudding into the gravel and shedding sparks, or yanking him back just as he charged at me. Eventually, Gregory gave a furious roar and swiped at the ribbon.

Whatever those Nordic dwarves used to make that ribbon, it was truly miraculous stuff. The zweihander's razor-sharp edge tangled in the thin pink loops, jerking Bethany back. When Gregory tried to slice the ribbon, he only managed to tighten the bond between himself and Bethany. She turned on him and yelled in Undead. He yelled back.

In the brief break this gave me, I signaled to Chesa.

"This might be our only chance. Keep her attention while I work on Greg. If we can get them—" I wasn't able to finish my thought, because some random loop of the ribbon slipped free, and the two zombies stumbled away from each other. Immediately, Gregory turned and rushed me. I barely got my shield up in time, and had to bash a pommel-strike aside with the forte of my blade, twisting my wrist awkwardly.

Fortunately, Chesa didn't need further instruction. She wheeled around the perimeter of the gravel circle, putting arrows into Bethany's cloak and at her feet. Bee gave Gregory one last miserable glare, then pranced off after Ches. The length of ribbon between them was troublingly lax. I suppose it had to be long enough to bind Fenrir, but that wasn't doing much to keep Gregory off me.

The big knight lurched closer, thrusting experimentally with the blade. I caught the attack with my sword, then punched his blade away with my shield and rushed closer. The zweihander rattled along the face of my shield, traveling down to the point of the heater, almost low enough to slip free and strike my legs. I countered with my sword, but that left me with nothing to strike with as I got closer. I tried to force him back with my shield, but Gregory was a big guy, combined with whatever strength undeath gave him, making him impossible to shift. He simply laid the pommel of his sword into the middle of my shield and thrust, sending me flying backward. Gregory followed up with a transition strike, striking down from an overhead position. The blow rattled my bones and drove me to one knee.

Fortunately, that was as far as Gregory could press. Straining against the ribbon, he waved his blade over my head, growling in frustration. I scrambled backward, resuming my guard and glaring at him. I spared a glance in Chesa's direction.

She and Bethany were well engaged. Chesa danced at the edge of Bee's reach, firing arrows and falling back, tricking the young assassin into pulling on Gregory at critical moments. Her shots were no longer aimed at the ground, or Bee's extremities. Chesa shot with desperation, but Bethany deflected each shot with those bone-shard daggers. A few arrows got through her defenses, but Bethany ignored them, even though they stuck out of her leg, chest, and shoulder.

Our eyes met. Chesa was on the verge of panic.

"John?" she shouted. "We need to do something, and fast. I'm running low on arrows."

"I didn't think you could run out of arrows."

"Usually not, but—" Her mouth clapped shut as Bethany jumped at her. Bee had lured her too close, and Chesa had to somersault onto one of the standing stones, balancing precariously before leaping to a nearby broken stub of granite and then rolling to the ground. She somehow fired mid-leap, but Bethany swatted it into the sod. As she fell back, Chesa called back to me. "Usually a magic thing. But I'm low on the juice."

"Do what you have to do to keep her busy, Ches!" I shouted. "If both these bastards come at me, I'm finished."

"That's the point. If I run out of magic and drop back into the mundane world like the saint . . ." She let the implication hang. That would leave me alone on the hill with Bee and Gregory, all while that creepy bastard did whatever he was doing up that pillar.

My eyes went to the pillar. It was maybe four feet in diameter and looked as solid as Esther's impatience. An idea formed in my head.

"Right. New plan." I nodded to the pillar. "Let's knot 'em up."

Chesa glanced at the pillar, then nodded confidently. Hopefully we were on the same page for once.

Gregory came at me again, sword over his head, the tip pointed menacingly at my face. As he thrust I caught it on the shield, but he switched to a slice at my leg that required some fancy magic on my part. I folded the shield out into a tower, slamming the bottom rim down on his striking sword. That drove the blade into the gravel, pulling Gregory along with it. Ecstatic, I swung hard for his hip, forgetting that I wasn't trying to kill my old teammate. My blade bit deeply into his exposed chain mail, breaking links and drawing tar-thick blood. Gregory howled, but I was already running toward the pillar.

This brought me closer to Bethany, which wasn't a problem as long as she didn't notice. I ran at her with my sword overhead. There's no way to be stealthy in plate armor, and Bethany spun around long before I reached her. Still on plan, because as she rolled out of the way, Chesa was able to cross toward Gregory.

He met this new threat with a clumsy swing that earned him three arrows in the chest. None of them did more than dimple the steel plate of his armor, but that was enough to stun him. I scooped up the length of ribbon that hung between them and crossed to the pillar. Chesa grabbed her own length of ribbon and went in the opposite direction.

Bethany was the first to figure out what we were about. Knots were always her thing, and she knew when the noose was closing. She went after Chesa, but that just crossed her line close to Gregory's, and soon they were drawing tighter together. I got the ribbon around the pillar just in time for Chesa to cinch her strand to an arrow and fire it into the surrounding zombie crowd. The arrow thumped into a Russian officer with exposed teeth and eyes like burnt matchsticks. He went down, and the line went taut.

Gregory finally caught on. He ran toward me, but he was already caught. I gave my length a pull, dragging it around the pillar like a pulley. He came to a halt, his boots sinking into the gravel as he was dragged toward the pillar. Bethany let out a series of furious snarling threats, cutting at the loops of ribbon that were sinking into her skin, but with each lurching step she came closer and closer to the pillar. Chesa wrapped her arms around the taut line that ran between pillar and downed Russian and pulled, dragging at it like a lonely tug of war. Gregory gave up on reaching me, and turned his attention to slicing through the ribbon. But each time he looped a section around his blade, or slashed at a length of pink material, all he did was tighten the bonds.

With a final titanic effort, Chesa and I closed the knot. Gregory slammed against the pillar, arms pinned to his chest, sword akimbo in his hands, covered in cheerful loops of ribbon. Bethany was down on both knees, one leg pulled against her chest, a section of ribbon in her mouth as she chewed at it fruitlessly.

Chesa dropped her line and ran to me.

"Can you hold that?" she asked.

"Forever? No. We'll need something to keep it in place. Do you think—" I fell forward on one knee as Gregory renewed his efforts at escape. I straightened, desperate to hold the pair in place.

"I've got it," Chesa said.

"Look, I'm all about that liberation, but if I can't hold them in place, there's no way you can do it."

"No, not like that. One last bit of magic," she said, drawing an acorn from the pocket of her jeans. "Let's hope it works here. Hold the loop open, like you're trying to catch something."

I did as she said, spreading the two strands in my hands like a basket. She tossed the acorn onto the ground in the middle. No sooner had the acorn hit the gravel than it sprouted into a mighty oak. I was thrown to the ground by the force of its growth, losing my grip on the ribbon. The sound of groaning wood and rustling leaves filled the air, and when I opened my eyes the sun had been blocked by a large, leafy canopy. A spiderweb of pink ribbons ran from the trunk to the stone pillar at the center of the hill. Greg and Bethany were trapped, bound tightly to the staircase by the tree's verdant anchor.

"Well, that was a hell of a trick," I said, slowly standing up and dusting the grit from my legs. "Do you think it'll hold for long? I don't want to leave them here forever, you know, what with the army of zombies . . . Chesa?" I circled the tree a couple times, but there was no sign of the elven princess. "Well, I suppose that answers that question. Hopefully you and Matthew are someplace safe."

"Mr. Sir Rast!" The voice came from the zombie horde. I turned just in time to see Percy fighting his way through the impromptu soccer match that had consumed the shambling mob. He stepped over the fallen Russian and stared up at the tree for a long moment, then remembered his urgency. "Sir Rast, your friends are gone! They sank into the earth. I tried to grab them, but . . ." I pointed to the pillar, and the two former members of Knight Watch trying to bite their way free of their bonds. "Well. Glad to see that's in order."

"Yeah, me, too. Think you can stay here and watch them? Make sure they don't get away again?" I asked.

"Of course, sir. Where are you going?"

"Not really sure. Guess I'll just have to find out," I said.

I climbed the stairs up into the storm, squinting against the wind and sudden rain that struck me about ten feet off the ground. The clouds closed around me, and the gusting wind took my breath. Soon all I could see was each step before me, and all I could hear was the rain on my helmet and the hammering of my heart.

CHAPTER THIRTY-FIVE

The clouds parted, and the world turned dark. The filtered sunlight of Folksvangr gave way to inky blackness. The only light was red, like the distant eruption of volcanoes. I set foot on rocky ground. The screams of tortured souls filled my head.

I stood on a stony precipice overlooking a plain of broken souls. Black, amorphous shapes fought across the field below me, their bodies made of the stuff of shadows, only their eyes and mouths distinct, and then only because they glowed with a red inner light that matched the sulphurous explosions that lined the horizon. Storm clouds churned overhead, giving voice to low, growling thunder, their depths punctured by bright lightning and brighter flames. The battle below was carried out in absolute silence. The screams I heard seemed to come from all around me, as though the rocks themselves suffered underfoot. The precipice on which I stood led down onto the plain below. Other bluffs dotted the horizon, their surfaces scarred by lightning and the twisted forms of dead trees.

"What the hell is this place?" I wondered aloud.

"An appropriate turn of phrase." A shadow detached itself from the trail, strolling to the very edge of the precipice. It faced away from me, arms comfortably crossed at its waist. The edgelord, carrying what appeared to be a skull in his hands. "This, my friend, is the death I was promised. The death of glory, and the afterlife to go with it. An endless battle, in preparation for the war to come. All of it a lie." He turned in my direction and lifted the skull mask, as though to offer it. I recognized him.

"Aelwulf?" I asked. "But that . . . you were honored among the valkyrie. You seemed happy!"

"I did not want happiness," he spat. "The fat, lazy joy of that place was an abomination to the name Valhalla. I wanted the glory I was promised!"

"This?" I asked, throwing my arm out over the hellscape stretched below. "This miserable place? You would trade eternal life at a party for this?"

"You wouldn't understand. Weak, soft-willed men like you, happy to drink beer and burp and . . ." His frustration became too much. He slammed the helm back down on his head and drew the Totenschreck. "Solveig saw a better way, when she learned of your pathetic domains, and the history of the Totenschreck. I was only too happy to follow. She hoped to convert you. A pity you didn't die at her hand." He raised the sickly green blade, its length squirming with unfettered energy. "You will find my offer much less pleasant, and impossible to deny."

"We'll see about that," I said. "I've faced everything you threw at me, and I'm still standing. This domain of yours is just a figment, or I wouldn't even be able to enter against your will. That sword is the only power you have, and it's a borrowed power. You're nothing without it!"

"I'm enough to destroy you!" Aelwulf shouted. He came at me with the sword in both hands, slicing down, but then pivoted the blade to slice at my side. Steel rasped against chain, and I scampered back. That blade was deadly, but it appeared my armor was enough to keep me safe. Aelwulf growled in frustration, but kept swinging, dropping the forte of his blade against the rim of my shield, then trying to swing the tip down, looking for some break in my armor. All he had to do was scratch me, and this was over. Desperately, I chopped at his ankle. It was enough to drive him back, if only for a moment.

"This is hopeless, Rast. I have died the death of steel a thousand times, fought against warriors of legend, even tried my hand against the gods." He stalked toward me, blade loose at his side. "Do you think you are more dangerous than any of them? Because I think you are just a little boy who is in over his head."

"I've been to Valhalla. I've seen what passes for fighting there," I said. "You want me to get a volleyball so we can settle this like real Vikings?"

Aelwulf roared in outrage. He slammed my shield hard with his pommel, once, twice, a third time that forced me back. I tried to strike back, sliding my shield to the side and stabbing out with my sword. Derisively, he slapped my sword aside with Totenschreck's ornate hilt, striking me so hard in the wrist that my blade went flying. With his backswing he took a swipe at my head, ringing my helm like a bell. I stumbled back, then turned to run. Aelwulf's laughter followed me as I scrambled through the rocky path.

"What did I say, Sir Rast? You are outmatched. Overpowered. A pathetic excuse for a hero," Aelwulf called after me. "Have the courage to die like a warrior. Perhaps I will find a place for you in my new Valhalla."

"Solveig made a similar offer," I said. "Still not very tempting."

"Then why are you running? Do you think I will tire? Or that your friends may arrive to save you?"

"Pretty sure that's not going to happen," I mumbled to myself as I turned a corner on the trail. The geography here resembled a small river canyon, with dozens of narrow passages between steep, rocky walls snaking away from the precipice. I lost sight of the plain and its warring shadows, though the sound of screams and rumbling thunder followed me. I took one turn, then another, trying to stay out of Aelwulf's view. I ducked behind a low stack of flat boulders and drew my dagger. Trying to control my breathing and slow my hammering heart, I sat and waited for Aelwulf.

"Hiding will do you no good," he called a few moments later. He was far away, his voice echoing among the stones. Several moments later he spoke again. "This is my domain, Sir Rast. There is nowhere for you to run. No escape. Only death."

That only confirmed that his domain was barely formed, and lacked the power of a true domain. It took a great deal of magical energy to form a domain. Even with the Totenschreck, Aelwulf must be testing the limits of his power.

Now if I could just poke some holes in his world, maybe the whole thing would come crashing down.

Metal scraped against stone nearby. I sank deeper into my nook and held my breath. The light here was dim and the shadows thick, so it wasn't that difficult to stay hidden. At the same time, I didn't see Aelwulf until he was on top of me.

He loomed around the corner, Totenschreck held up to provide some light from the putrescent glow emanating from its blade. I almost yelped in surprise, but then he walked right past me, eyes scanning the path ahead. I waited until he was a few yards down the way before I launched myself at him.

Jumping at someone while wearing plate armor has one big disadvantage, and one big advantage. Disadvantage, there's no way to do it quietly. Advantage, once you're flying through the air you're pretty much an unstoppable battering ram of steel and chain.

Aelwulf spun around to face me. He tried to sidestep, but the lane here was too narrow, and the sides of the trail were littered with loose rocks. His shoulder banged into the wall just as I ran into him, shield first. We went down in a clatter of steel and stone. The Totenschreck slid along the top of my shield, passing over my head and harmlessly bouncing off the wall. As we rolled along the rocky ground, I brought my dagger up and slid it across the front plate of his armor, blindly trying to find the seam between chest and arm. Aelwulf hammered on the top of my helm with the pommel of his sword, driving the metal cap down my forehead and twisting the visor out of position, obscuring my vision. Just as I thought I'd found a place for my dagger to go, he drove his right knee into my rib cage. The dagger almost slipped from my fingers, and the force of the blow rolled me onto my side.

Quickly, Aelwulf shoved me onto my back and pried my shield away from his face. His right foot went down on the wrist of my shield arm as he sat on my thighs, pinning me in place. I tried to roll out of it, but I couldn't do it without ripping my arm out of its socket.

"Can we talk about this?" I gasped. "Look, I'm not a big fan of volleyball, either. Maybe we could get together and produce a better talent competition. Something with class! I could—"

"This is how you end, John Rast: sweating and begging for your life." He reversed his grip on the Totenschreck and lifted it over his head, preparing to drive it through my throat. "Perhaps the valkyries will get you, but I don't think there are many of them left, and they can't reach you here anyway."

Wriggling my hips, I kneed Aelwulf in the back. It didn't have the kind of force I was hoping for, and did little more than upset his balance. He regained it, stretching his right leg and grinding down on my wrist with his boot. I screamed in pain, sure that my hand was broken, but when I looked over I saw that he had overextended his foot. The gap between greave and cuisses lay open, exposing the inside of his knee.

I drove the narrow blade of my mercy dagger hard into the chain mail. It punched through the mail and flesh, skidding off the bone. Aelwulf screamed and fell backward, crushing my legs. I kicked him off and rolled clumsily to my feet, leaping as he swung at my heels. When I turned around I saw him pluck out the dagger and throw it to the side, then slowly drag himself to one leg. Damned Vikings were tough, especially those who had died a thousand deaths and so forth.

"You're going to pay for that, Rast," he swore. "Death is too much glory for you. I'm going to pare you down, fingerbone by rib cage, keeping you alive and screaming, until there's nothing left but—"

"Yeah, yeah, guts for entrails, I get it," I said, then ran back the way we'd come. Aelwulf's lurching footsteps followed, laced through with some very creative and vile threats regarding my digestive system.

My sword was right where I'd left it. Aelwulf didn't think enough of me to kick my blade into the pit of warring shadows, or pick it up and stick it in his belt. That was fine by me. I didn't mind being underestimated. After all, I wasn't the one stabbed in the kneecap, was I? I picked up the sword, then adjusted my helm. The visor was hopelessly broken, so I twisted it off and tossed it aside, then looked around for a suitably heroic place for my last stand. The terrain was choked with small passages and steep cliffs, but about ten yards down the trail I found an open bluff surrounded on three sides by sheer dropoffs down to the plain of endless war. It seemed like as good a place to die as any.

Aelwulf limped out of the shadows. Blood soaked his right leg from knee to heel, and before he saw me he was using the Totenschreck to support himself. Hardly a glorious purpose for a magical sword. As soon as he laid eyes on me, though, he brought the sword to his hip and tried to disguise the limp with swagger.

"You have chosen the place of your death? Good. In honor of the blood you have drawn, I will erect a cairn at this spot once I am done with flaying your legs and feeding them to you."

"My mother always said I wouldn't amount to a hill of beans," I said. "Well, look who's piling stones now, Mom! Ha! Showed you!"

"You have a strange sense of humor. You might have made a good Viking, if not for your cowardice and misplaced entitlement."

"Cowardice? What the hell do you mean by that? I've chased you all the way to hell, and I'm going to drag you back to the real world if it's the last thing I do."

"It will be," he said casually. "You want to show your courage? Take off that girlish armor. It's not fitting for a man to be so precious with his skin."

"This coming from a man wielding a magic sword that kills with the slightest cut," I said, shaking my head. "I'll stick with my steel, thanks."

"Very well." He reached the clearing and looked out over the warring shadows down below. "Look at them, John. Don't they look happy?"

"They do not," I said. "Are you done with your break time, old man? Can we start fighting, or do you need a nap?"

"The dead never sleep," he said. "As you are about to find out."

Our swords met in a crash of steel and necrotic magic, spitting sparks like fireworks. Below us, the silent dead fought on.

CHAPTER THIRTY-SIX

The thing about a longsword is that it's long. I know that's obvious, but I can't emphasize it enough. The longsword replaced the shield in traditional fighting around the fourteenth century. That feels counterintuitive—you would think that having a shield would always be an advantage—but the fact is that the longsword's superior reach coupled with the fighting style that developed around the double-handed grip made the shield obsolete. The only way I was able to defeat Gregory and his zweihander was with Chesa's help, and the intervention of a magical pink ribbon. But now I was alone with Aelwulf and the Totenschreck, and all he had to do was draw blood to win this fight.

Our blades crossed, steel dragging along steel until we met at the hilt. He forced me back, twisting my arm away from my torso with the full weight of his body. I punched at his arm with my shield, but he just growled and pressed harder. Finally I spun in the direction he was pushing, risking a counterswing just long enough to get my shield between us. His strike came in low, denting the armor over my shin. I swore and scuttled back. That was going to leave a bruise.

I didn't have time to think about that, though. He struck again and again, each time pushing me back with the weight of his blows and his superior reach. I began to despair. This wasn't the kind of fight I was supposed to be in. As a warden, I was meant to protect the softer members of the team while Tembo, Gregory, and Bethany went on the offense. I could probably stay alive until I dropped from exhaustion, but I wasn't going to be able to break Aelwulf's defenses on my own.

Another exchange of steel and we both fell back. Aelwulf grinned at me.

"Ah, there it is," he said. "Despair. I can see it in your eyes. You have taken my measure, and discovered that you are outclassed. There is no shame in that. You are a mere child. I have been a warrior for a thousand years, and will be for a thousand more."

"Honestly, I'm worried that you're going to hurt yourself. You're limping around like an old man. You want to take another break?"

"Perhaps after you are dead, and my valkyries have returned to care for me," he said.

"I don't think they're coming back. The zombies probably ate one, I cut another in half, one of them got crushed . . . I think you're left with Solveig the Bashful." I started circling to my left, away from the precipice. Aelwulf followed my movement carefully, keeping the weight off his right leg. "And the last I saw of her she was running for the hills. Literally, I think."

"Solveig will be back. She always comes back," he said.

"Maybe not this time. Maybe she got tired of being bossed around by a guy with his face cut in half." I slid faster. Aelwulf struggled to keep up. "There's been a lot of women's liberation stuff going on in the last thousand years. You might want to keep up."

Just then, the old Viking's injured leg got hung up on an uneven lip in the stone clearing. Hardly an inch of elevation, but Aelwulf was dragging that leg around like a sack of potatoes. He caught himself quickly enough, but I was already on the move.

I crashed into him with my shield, catching his sword with the boss of my shield and shoving him backward. He stumbled, struggling to stay upright with half a leg, swinging wildly with the sword, more to keep his balance than to hit me. I chopped down on his wrist, then deflected his instinctive pommel strike with my shield. Rather than falling back, I circled quickly to his right, forcing him to pivot on his injured leg.

"Stand still, you bastard," he spat.

"Sounds like a bad idea." I struck again, but this time he fell back rather than let me get close. I smiled. "Who's running now?"

"You are incredibly annoying," he said. "Worse than Loki. Do you have troll blood in your veins?"

"No, I never could get the hang of Reddit." I backed away a little, dancing to my right, slowly herding Aelwulf toward the precipice. When he was close enough, I quickly strafed left. Scowling, he let Totenschreck's shimmering tip touch the ground. I thought I was finally wearing him out, but then he said something in a broken tongue.

The ground shifted under my feet. Something pinched my ankle, and then I felt the sharp probing of fingers against the chain mail at my calf. I looked down in horror. Skeletal arms reached out of the earth and crawled up my right leg. I tried to shake them off, but they held me firmly in place. I kicked at them with my other boot, cracking bone and turning the hand into dust. Once I was free, I quickly scooted back.

"Who's running now?" Aelwulf asked, his voice mocking. He sauntered forward. "It's no use, Rast. The dead are everywhere."

To demonstrate, he swirled his blade overhead, speaking again in that halting, broken voice. The whole bluff shook, and skeletal forms unfolded from the shadows, rising from the stone like stop-motion trees, reaching for me. Bony fingers grabbed at the edge of my shield, my wrist, encircled my arm, seized my knee, pulled at me. I screamed and struck out desperately.

Smashing my shield into the nearest leering face, I hacked at the dozen or so arms that were grabbing at me. Bones scattered like dice. But for every skeleton I knocked down, two more rose up, and then three more. The horde pressed in on me.

"You see? This is hopeless. I don't even need my sword to destroy you." Aelwulf came closer and closer, his skeleton army leaving a space around him. He held Totenschreck overhead. A tornado of green light swirled around the blade.

And then I saw it.

Over Aelwulf's shoulder, the sky parted and light shone through. Fluorescent light. Three long bars of flickering, bright fluorescent light, as mundane as a ham sandwich. Whatever magic the sword contained, Aelwulf was burning through it like a torch through butter. His domain, barely formed and still unstable, was collapsing back into the real world.

All I had to do was push it over the edge. And hope my own magic lasted long enough to survive.

"One thing I know about skeleton hordes!" I shouted as he stalked closer. “You can break all the bones you want, they’ll just make more. Only way to win—KILL THE GUY WITH THE CREEPY HAT!”

Aelwulf seemed taken aback by this. I planted my shield and, with a complicated series of gestures, activated the bulwark’s ultimate form. This was the kind of thing I could only do once, and I felt the power needed to fuel it leave my body with a snap. The shield came free from my arm, hovering just over my shoulder before separating into a half dozen smaller shields, each the size of a notebook. It was a real loaves-and-fishes moment, with more shield than I started with. My little armada of flying shields zipped around me, blocking attacks and shattering skulls.

Taking my sword in both hands, I charged forward, screaming. The shield-fleet kept most of the skeletons away, but I still had to smash my way through a trove of weather-beaten bones, skulls, rib cages, and spinal columns that snapped under the steel of my blade. Aelwulf watched my progress with amusement at first, then concern. Shouting in his broken tongue, he drove Totenschreck into the ground. The stone split beneath the glimmering blade, and a crevasse opened, cutting the plateau in half. Green light poured out of the hellish depth, and out scrambled hundreds of skeletal warriors. Their eyes glowed and their bones creaked, and the air filled with the smell of decay and ancient tombs.

They came at me in a wave. The flitting helix of my shields strained under the onslaught, and my swordwork shifted to defense, as I plugged the gaps between the hovering panels with my blade. And still they came. My forward movement stalled out. I could feel the Totenschreck’s power overwhelming me. I looked up at the sky in desperation. The clouds thinned, but the real world was no brighter, no closer.

One of the buzzing panels of my shield crumpled to the ground. Another, trying to protect me from a lumbering skeleton, flattened itself against the creature’s skull and disappeared. Three simply winked out of existence, their magic spent. *My* magic spent. But the horde thinned. I reached out my left hand and summoned the shield. The orbiting panels collapsed against my fist, reforming into a Viking round shield. Appropriate.

I sliced through the remaining skeletons, whirling my shield back and forth, putting my sword into rib cages and my boot through bony legs. Aelwulf watched me with increasing trepidation. He drew more power, made manifest in a final row of diaphanous skeletons still dressed in the misty cloaks of their living souls. It wasn't enough to stop me. I smashed through them and struck at Aelwulf. He caught my blow with Totenschreck's hilt, ending his channeled spell. The last few skeletons tumbled to the ground, piles of bones now that their animating magic had fled.

"Very well," he growled. "We will do this the old-fashioned way."

"No," I said. "I don't think we will."

The swirling clouds of greenish light that had been emanating from Totenschreck collapsed in a storm of light and shadow. They brought the rest of the domain with them, drawn in by the emptiness of the sword's magic, the void left by all the power Aelwulf had just expended. Like Chesa, and Matthew before her, Aelwulf had used all the magic that was keeping him grounded in the Unreal. The domain collapsed.

"What the HEL is going on?" he shouted. And then a door of light appeared and swallowed him whole. He vanished like fog at sun's first light.

I took a shaky breath and tried to gather my thoughts. I had done it! I had knocked him out of his realm. Now he was somewhere in the mundane world. It was time to hunt him down like the dog he was. On my turf. On my terms.

"Let's see what kind of place dreams that it's an undying hellscape, filled with souls of the undying, trapped in eternal war," I said, then drew in the last reserves of my mythic power and released it. I became mundane, and fell out of the Unreal.

My feet came down hard on cheap tile flooring. Harsh fluorescent light filled a hallway that stretched in both directions. The air smelled like industrial-strength disinfectant, body odor, even more body spray, mildew, and desperation. A long line of lockers ran the length of one wall. The other was covered by a glass case, filled with trophies. My eyes locked onto a sign over the case, draped in crimson and gold banners.

HACK PLAIN HIGH SCHOOL, HOME OF YOUR FIGHTING VIKINGS! it read, and below it was the most culturally inappropriate cartoon of two Vikings punching each other in the guts. Someone had drawn in unrealistic genitals, using a ballpoint pen and a shockingly optimistic imagination. I nodded to myself.

"High school," I looked around. The hallway was silent, though in the far distance I thought I could hear cheering, and someone yelling over a loudspeaker. "Seems about right. Now, where did that bastard get to?"

Somewhere down the hallway, something crashed through glass, followed by a string of angry swearing that could only have been Nordic in their syllable choice. I turned and ran in that direction.

CHAPTER THIRTY-SEVEN

My footsteps rang through the eerily halls of Hack Plain High. I passed a dozen closed doors, more lockers, and a trophy case that had been smashed open and pilfered of its many golden cups. There was a smear of blood on the jagged glass of the broken display. A trail of blood drops led down the hall. I followed them at a slow trot, sword and shield in hand, fully aware of how ridiculous I must look. Hopefully, I wouldn't run into a security guard, or Cerberus, or anything in between.

The trail led through a science classroom and then directly through the windows that overlooked the athletic fields below. There was a Viking-shaped hole in the glass. Outside, night had fallen, but an array of metal-halide lights turned the field into day. There was a soccer game going on, and bracketing bleachers filled with students and parents cheered the participants forward in their endeavours. There was no sign of Aelwulf or the Viking dead.

"Cool," I mumbled. "Just a bunch of normal people who aren't going to be freaked out by a couple guys with swords wandering the field." I started clearing the broken glass from the window frame with my sword, then stepped gingerly through, hopping into the low shrubs that surrounded the school. "Let's try to not get shot, shall we, Rast?"

Sheathing my sword and slinging my shield over my shoulder as I approached the crowds, I looked around for any sign of Aelwulf. The trail of blood was gone, but there was also a distinct lack of tall, fully armed and armored warriors. Other than me, of course. I tried to look natural as I made my way across the asphalt track that ringed the field. Hopefully the mundane world would work its magic and make me look normal. Or as normal as I could be, given the circumstances.

As I walked, I peeled off my helm and tossed it to the side. I had a good-sized cut where Aelwulf had dinged me across my forehead, but the blood seemed to have dried, and other than a dull ache behind my eyes, there seemed to be no harm. Hopefully I'd look a little less alarming without the helm.

I still got a lot of curious looks from the attendees. Most of them were wearing some kind of school spirit gear, in the same crimson and gold I had seen inside, often with the cartoonish Viking emblazoned on their shirts. Apparently his name was Oofsen, and he spent his entire life punching things in the belly, or being punched in the same way.

"Hey, it's their mascot!" some kid yelled at me as I walked past his little clique of friends. The rest of the crowd turned and looked at me. "Boo! Boo the Knights! Boo!"

"What are you . . . ?" I looked around, then saw a giant white school bus parked nearby. It was painted yellow, and had a giant blue helmet on the front. The side read NOUGHTON KNIGHTS, written in an appropriately scrolly font. I sighed. "Oh, you have to be kidding me."

"I heard there was a knight over here, marauding our villages!" A life-sized Oofsen pushed his way through the crowd, plush hands and oversized head in full effect. "Well, you've come to the wrong village, buddy!"

"Look, I don't want anything to do with—OOF!" I said, as Oofsen laid a solid right into my temple. I felt the scab break, and a fresh gout of blood poured down the side of my face. Oofsen cackled and rather cartoonishly wound up to hit me again.

"Aelwulf, is that you?" I asked. The mascot swung again, padded fists banging off my armor to little effect. The crowd cheered him on. It wouldn't surprise me if reality had somehow bent the bearer of the Totenschreck into this ridiculous caricature, but I didn't want to hit him back until I was sure. This guy didn't have a sword, but he sure was enthusiastic with those punches. "Listen, Aelwulf, if that's you, we need to—"

"Oofsen goes OOF!" the mascot shouted, then kicked me in the (well-armored) groin. The crowd went wild.

I decked him with the steel knuckles of my gauntlet, going through six inches of collapsible fleece headpiece before connecting with a human skull. The mascot reeled, arms cartwheeling as he fell back into the supporting arms of the crowd. They pushed him up onto his feet, but the guy inside the suit wasn't interested in fighting any longer. Instead, he was pushing his cartoon hands through the Viking's mouth, trying to get at his real human face.

"Hey, I think he actually punched Oofsen!" someone in the crowd shouted. "Not cool, man! What's wrong with you?"

"So many things," Chesa said, appearing from the crowd. She seemed to have ditched her bow and blades, and didn't look terribly out of place in her comic book T-shirt. She clapped her hands on my shoulders and dragged me back. "Come on, John. Time to stop beating up the high school kids."

"I thought it was our guy. You know the weird things that the mundane world does to protect itself." They had gotten the kid's head off. I'd given him a bloody nose, and maybe broken some small cartilage bits. Hopefully he still had all his teeth. But the crowd was looking pretty angry. I looked back at Chesa. "How'd you get here?"

"Fell out of the sky, like any other normal person," she said quietly. "Fortunately, no one saw me. Matt's over by the concession stands, watching our stuff. Can't go around armed. People notice."

"Aelwulf's here, somewhere. He was the edgelord. We both came through the school," I said. "I think he's carrying some trophies."

"One thing at a time. Need to get you out of that armor before someone calls the police," she said. We reached the concession stands and went around back. Matthew sat on a small pile of items that had been covered by a tarp. He was wearing his shades. I was going to point out that that was at least as weird as me going around in armor, but then he stood and pulled back the tarp.

"Your elven armor! And bow! And Matthew's vestments!" I said.

"And all of Bee's stuff, and Gregory's as well," Chesa pointed out. "When we fell out of the sky, it came with us. So hopefully Greg and Bee aren't naked and tied together up there somewhere."

"Hopefully they are! I don't know which of them would be more pissed about that."

"Point is, we've got our stuff. But can we walk around dressed like Ren faire rejects?"

"Why not?" I asked. "Aelwulf's certainly not going to hide his sword in the woods."

"We're fully in the mundane now, man," Matthew said. "No magic powers. Someone calls the cops and we're done for."

"Have you tried to reach Mundane Actual?" I asked. "They usually run interference on this kind of thing."

"Put a call into Rodriguez twenty minutes ago. But it's going to be a while before she and the rest of the team are here. In the meantime, we're on our own." Chesa motioned to the pile of armor. "Get to it, John. Strip."

"You seriously want me to take off my armor?"

"Until you look a little normal. Then we spread out and find this Viking guy."

"No chance. You guys might look out of place in your silver leaves and vestments, but I fit right in. Some idiot has already mistaken me for the other team's mascot," I said. "There's no way I'm going out there unarmed."

"Not completely unarmed. You can probably keep your dagger."

"Aelwulf tossed it away."

"Well, then you'll have your charm, wit, and personality," Matthew said.

"Meaning he'd be completely unarmed," Chesa answered with a sigh. "Fine. Keep your armor. Just tell us what you know."

So I did, talking about the false domain, and how I tricked Aelwulf into expending his magic to the point that the whole domain collapsed.

"So if Aelwulf doesn't have any more magic than us, it's just a matter of cornering him and holding him in place until Mundane Actual shows up," I said. "Shouldn't be that difficult. Have you seen any sign of him?"

"Nope, but things have been strange. Ten minutes ago this was a game between the Vikings and the Cougars," Matthew said. "All of a sudden it's the Knights, and all the banners changed, and we knew something weird was going on."

"Really? That seems like a pretty big change for reality to make," I said.

"Not so much. It takes a lot more mojo to make a dragon look like a tax attorney, or a storm harpy to pass for an isolated tornado."

Both of these things had happened to me. Violently. Matthew continued. “The newspapers will write all this off as a typo, or a prank, or something equally mundane.”

“Unless we go around pushing credibility,” Chesa said. “We don’t want a full-blown anomaly on our hands, especially with half the team MIA and our magic reserves tapped. So try to keep a low profile.”

“Low profile is my middle name. Right up there with stealthy,” I said. Armor notwithstanding.

“So do we stick together, or do we split up to find Aelwulf?” Matthew asked. “I don’t like the idea of coming across him alone, but we can’t let him get away, either.”

“We stay together. If he’s not taking precautions, a guy named Aelwulf from the 1400s should be easy enough to find in this crowd,” I said. “By body odor alone.”

The others took what weapons we could easily conceal, Chesa hoisting a pair of cheer batons, Matthew rummaging a shovel from a shed. I draped some yellow-and-gold crepe paper around my shield. Then we said a prayer that no one would find the rest of our stash, and came out from behind the concession stand. We made our way through the crowd to the bleachers, then started down the length of the field. We were on the Vikings sidelines, still getting odd looks and the occasional nudge, but most folks seemed focused on the game.

“So what do you think happens if he gets away? He’s just as mundane as us, right?” Chesa asked.

“I guess? Except he’s an undead Viking who’s spent the last six centuries partying in Valhalla and generally preparing for the apocalypse. Fits the description of half the guys on my high school football team,” I said. “Well, except the undead part. Isn’t he supposed to drop dead at nightfall?”

“Killing Runa ended that, just like it cut us off from our domains,” Matthew answered. “He’s running on his own power now.”

“And that power has run out,” I said. “I figure if he gets away he’ll just try to blend in long enough to find a way back into the Unreal. We’ll have to monitor Ren faires, CrossFit competitions, cosplay conventions . . .”

“Or we could just run over there and knock him out,” Chesa said, pointing across the field.

Out of the milling mass of opposing fans flew a cardboard-clad knight in dull pewter armor. He landed in the midst of a knot of players, sending them and the ball flying. The crowd peeled back, and Aelwulf strode onto the pitch.

He was naked. Like, absolutely naked, and long cuts across his chest and shoulders leaked bloody over his massive chest and abs. He carried Totenschreck over one shoulder, and held a burlap sack in his other hand, a bottle tucked under his elbow. He threw the sack onto the ground. Out tumbled dozens of cheap trophies, their paint chipped and tin cups dented. Then he raised the bottle and took a long swig from it. From here, it looked like a plastic two liter of something bright and orange.

"I am Aelwulf, Terror of the Dead, and slayer of gods!" he shouted. "Bring me your champions, that I might tear them limb from limb, and claim their glory for my own!"

The crowds screamed. The people fled. Numbly, I unlimbered my sword and shield and started running in Aelwulf's direction. Chesa and Matthew flanked me.

"They're going to chalk this one up to a junkie," I said. "Until I kill him with this sword. That's going to take some explaining."

"Not as much as that, I think," Matthew said. He pointed at the sky.

The moon was full. It disappeared in a series of bites, each one accompanied by a loud, thundering chomp. The shadow of a giant wolf passed over the stars, and Fenrir's cruel howl echoed across the field.

The absent moon left a hole in the sky. Black as pitch, the hole yawned wider, until I thought I could see flames in the darkness. And then the armies of the dead spilled out, tumbling out of the sky like a hard sleet. Pale white bodies clad in tattered uniforms hurled through the air, shattering when they hit the ground. To the horror of the onlookers, the zombies slowly stood, bodies reforming around broken bones and smashed faces. The crowds, moments ago watching a simple soccer game, suddenly found themselves on a nightmarish field of living death. Madness reigned.

"Okay, yeah. That's going to take some pretty clever copyediting," I said.

"John! I'm so glad to see you!" Aelwulf bellowed, then he ran to meet me in the center of the field.

CHAPTER THIRTY-EIGHT

Bodies crashed into the turf all around me, spraying me with sod and splintered bone. They slowly reformed, shattered ribs jigsawing back together, wasted faces leering as their spines straightened, arms outstretched to drag me to hell. I ran through them, pile-driving my way forward with the shield while swinging my sword at any that got too close. Chesa was a whirling storm of tasseled strikes and high kicks. She severed a soldier's skull from its body with one of her batons, then crescent-kicked it across the field.

"Matthew, keep up!" she shouted as she stomped down on a skeleton as it reformed. "They only form once. All you have to do is break them."

"Yeah, yeah," Matthew said. He was jogging slowly behind us, shovel loosely in both hands. A skeleton rose up right behind him. The saint drove the rusty blade of the shovel through the neck of the creature, then drew back and sliced clean through its thighs. "All this running nonsense has me tuckered out. Can't we wait for him to come to us?"

"This is hero stuff, Matthew," I said. "You don't stand around and wait when you're doing hero stuff."

"Maybe you don't. I do. I do that all the time."

"Healers," Chesa said with a roll of her eyes. She hurled one of her batons through the air, puncturing a skull and pinning a gray-uniformed soldier to the ground. The creature twitched as it struggled to stand. Chesa somersaulted over the fallen zombie, grabbing the baton as she passed, and smashed down on two more revenants that were harassing a group of soccer players near the middle of the pitch.

"Keep at it, you two!" I shouted, passing Chesa. "All we have to do is hold them off. Their magic will wear off eventually!"

"This is a full incursion, Rast!" Matthew swept his shovel into the foot of a soldier whose uniform was so tattered that it could have been from any country in any war. The creature lurched, grabbed Matthew's shoulder, and tried to rip his arm off. The saint drove the haft of the shovel hard into the zombie's rib cage. Bones broke like kindling. "A self-sustaining anomaly! We're going to have to contain it before it spills into reality and does some real damage!"

"Glad I didn't get rid of my armor," I muttered. An old man in a gray-and-black dress uniform seized on my leg, gnawing toothlessly on my boot. I kicked him in the face, then tried to transform my shield into a tower, so I could smash his neck. Nothing happened. I stared at the heater for a long second before my mind wrapped around the problem. "Right, no more magic," I said, then plunged my very ordinary sword into the old man's chest. "Not a lot of glory in this, is there?"

"I will offer you glory!" Aelwulf shouted as he bounded closer. There was a mad glint in his eye. "These halls are rich with gold and mead! I could plunder them for a thousand years and not have my fill!"

"Mead?" I asked, glancing at the bottle in his hands. "That's just orange soda. Have you never had sugar before?"

"I understand the source of your power, John Rast!" He took another swig of soda, then tossed the bottle aside. Sticky orange liquid leaked down his beard, mingling with the blood on his chest. "Now it is mine, and soon I will wash it away with the blood of my enemies!"

"At least you're consistent," I said, then braced myself for impact.

If this was what sugar did to the Viking's system, I would hate to see him on caffeine. He stood three feet away from me, legs spread wide, hammering down at my shield with the Totenschreck. Each blow drove me back. My head rang like a bell, and my bones screamed in protest. He was vulnerable, but such was the fury of his attack that I couldn't slip past to land a deciding blow. The mad Viking cut deep grooves in my shield, and sliced thick notches from the rim. Robbed of its magic, the shield could do nothing but splinter further apart with each hammering strike.

Chesa blurred past me, vaulting over Aelwulf's barrage and landing behind him. The Viking's face remained locked in its mad rictus, but he spun, swinging at Chesa before turning back to me. Sensing an opportunity, I pressed the attack. Aelwulf held his sword loosely in one hand, spinning back and forth to engage us both. But that sort of fighting is only for the mad and Hollywood, and we were able to land a couple blows on his arms, and Chesa got a firm shot on his knee, the same one I'd stabbed. Aelwulf swore, but didn't relent.

"Give it up, man," I said. "You're in a hopeless situation."

"There is always hope," he answered without letting up.

I didn't understand. Aelwulf had been a consummate fighter up to this point. Maybe the orange drink really had screwed him up. Or maybe—

I looked up just in time to see Chesa's eyes go wide. She was looking over my shoulder in absolute terror.

Dropping to one knee, I spun around and raised my shield. All I saw was a shadow and teeth the size of the sky, then something heavy and fast rammed into me. I rolled over, wincing as sharp pain burned through my forearm. Strong paws clawed at my thighs, claws scraping loudly against the steel, and heavy, musky breath washed over my face. Fenrir's jaws clapped shut inches from my face, once, twice, a third time. I was on my back, the fame wolf standing on my shield, straining to reach my throat. I put both hands against my shield and pushed, slamming the top rim into Fenrir's throat, forcing his jaws shut and his muscular neck back. With a firm kick I unseated the wolf, rolling away as he scrambled back to his feet. By the time I was upright, Fenrir and Aelwulf stood side by side, glaring at us. Fenrir was no longer the size of the sky, or even a very large car, or a small horse. But he was still a big dog. His hackles rose, and he growled menacingly. My sword lay discarded between us.

"Dude, I freed you!" I shouted.

"I meant to thank you for that," Aelwulf said. "I had not figured out how to release the fame wolf. And what's Ragnarok without Fenrir, hmm?"

"But . . . but he helped us reach you."

"Fame wolf don't care," Fenrir growled. "Fame wolf just here for the fight."

"Yes, he can be . . . indiscriminately destructive," Aelwulf said. He ran a loving hand down Fenrir's hackles. The wolf pawed at the ground. "Just what the prophets ordered."

"John, are you okay?" Chesa circled around to my side. I was bleeding from my shield arm, but the armor had saved me from anything more serious.

"Sure, I'm great. How are you?"

"Feeling a little outnumbered," she said.

A meaty bell rang out over the soccer field. I turned around to see Matthew busily thumping skulls and shoveling throats. He wiped a spray of blood off his face, then shouldered the shovel and strolled over.

"I think we're about to sort that out," he said. "Notwithstanding the hundreds of zombies, of course."

"It will take more than a gravedigging priest and an acrobatic girl to best us," Aelwulf said confidently. He raised Totenschreck and yelled, "I command the armies of the dead!"

The surrounding zombies turned curiously toward Aelwulf. A British paratrooper, still dragging the severed harness of his chute, looked him up and down, then shrugged.

"Get buggered," he said, then trundled off.

Aelwulf stared at the zombie with indignation.

"Fine! I didn't need an army of the dead anyway! Whatever!" he shouted.

"Ah, but you see, you *do* need an army of the dead," I said. "Because our reinforcements just arrived."

Blue lights flickered across the parking lot. A series of black tactical vans, sirens roaring, tore across the lot and bumped onto the soccer field. Gabrielle Rodriguez jumped out of the lead van and started directing Mundane Actual agents to form a cordon. I gave her a friendly wave, which she probably didn't see and certainly didn't ignore because she had better things to do with her time. I cleared my throat and reached down to pick up my sword, then turned my attention back to Aelwulf and Fenrir.

"No running now, big guy," I said. "So why not give yourself up peacefully and everything can go back to normal."

"Do I look like the kind of coward that runs away?" Aelwulf asked. To underscore the point, Fenrir bared his teeth and crept closer.

"I suppose not," I said. "Well. Let's get this over with."

Fenrir leapt across the distance between us in a single bound. I took the brunt of the charge on my shield, but then Aelwulf lunged into the gap and I had to swiftly pivot to meet his attack. Catching Totenschreck's green blade with the hilt of my sword, I pushed his swing wide and stepped close. Aelwulf responded by hammering his pommel into my wrist, but the long skirt of my gauntlets protected me from the worst of the strike. I got my shield into his shoulder and pushed him back. As he stumbled away, I drew my sword along the underside of his left arm, cutting deeply into the meat of his triceps. He grunted in pain, then punched me hard in the jaw and fell back.

"You fight better than I expected," he said as he limped back.

"Regional runner-up, three years running," I said.

"Do you get to drink from the skulls of your defeated foes?"

"Uh, no. But there's a ribbon."

"Ribbons," Aelwulf spat. "They are for girls."

"And for binding the world's largest wolf," I said. "Speaking of which, where is—"

Fenrir's jaws clamped around my ankle, and I felt steel wrinkle like tissue under his teeth. I banged down hard on the wolf's back with my shield, trying to connect with his neck, all while parrying Aelwulf's blade.

"Chesa!" I screamed. "Little help?"

"Doing what I can," she answered. Her lithe form slipped past me to strike at Fenrir, beating a tattoo across his back with her batons. Fenrir released me just long enough to drive Chesa back with a series of quick, snapping bites, then he took her batons in his jaws and snapped them in half. Chesa fell back, hands curled into fists, a furious but helpless look on her face.

"You may find better use of this, sister." Revna swooped down out of the sky, black wings fluttering as she pulled up short over our battle. She tossed a spear into the ground beside Chesa. She turned to the Viking and nodded. "Aelwulf. I never did like the way you smiled."

"None of this would have happened if you'd just done your job, valkyrie," Aelwulf said with a sneer. "You and Runa were always too content with the way things were, instead of the way they should have been."

"And you're a whiny man-child, upset that he doesn't get to be the hero in every story ever written," Revna said. "You have destroyed enough things. It's time to go home."

"We are *making* our own home!" Solveig appeared out of the mob of zombies, still wearing the remnants of her valkyrie disguise. She took two long steps, then hurled a spear into Revna's wing.

The valkyrie screamed and pinwheeled to the ground. Fenrir leapt at her, but Chesa stood between them, spear at the ready. Matthew hurried to her side.

"Right, so . . . I think we have you outnumbered now. Unless you have—" I looked over my shoulder at Aelwulf. Or, at least, at where Aelwulf had been standing a moment ago. He was hobbling hell for high water through the mob of zombies, cloak fluttering behind him. "Huh. I guess he *is* the type to run."

"He's making for the woods," Chesa said. "I don't think MA has that closed off. Don't let him get away!"

"But what about . . . ?" I motioned to Solveig and Fenrir.

"We have this. Go!"

"Sure," I mumbled. "Send the tank into the woods alone. No problem."

"What was that?"

"Nothing!" I called over my shoulder and I rumbled across the field. The zombies were ignoring me, and Aelwulf, and everything else. Mostly they just stood around chatting. A couple were continuing their soccer game. A bunch of the British soldiers had queued up in front of the concession stand, despite the fact that the attendant had long since fled. I shook my head. "Not the army of the dead I was expecting."

Then I was in the woods, chasing Aelwulf's fleeing shadow.

CHAPTER THIRTY-NINE

We made a desperate, ridiculous pair. Aelwulf hobbled through the forest ahead of me, left arm hanging blood-streaked at his side, limping from the dagger I'd put into his knee. I was in hardly better shape. Every time I put my foot down, my ankle screamed in agony. I strongly suspected that I was only still upright because of the stiff support of my sabatons, and the fact that I was too angry to quit.

There was something fae about the woods, too. When I first emerged from Hack Valley High School, I remembered the surrounding trees as sparse, barely hanging on to their leaves. But not ten paces into the forest and I was engulfed by trees with trunks as wide around as my mom's car, and the air was alive with lightning bugs and other, more mischievous lights that hovered and spun overhead.

"You're not going to get away, Aelwulf!" I shouted. "We have this place surrounded. You've either got to deal with me, or with Mundane Actual. And those guys don't mess around."

"If that's true, why are you still chasing me?" he asked, twisting around to watch my hobbled pursuit. "Eh? You look like you could use a break, Rast. Why don't you find a nice log and fall off it?"

"No, I'm fine," I said, though I wasn't. "You're the one leaking more blood than a vampire movie."

"I've had worse."

"In Valhalla, maybe. This isn't Valhalla. You die here, and it's over."

"Everything ends." He turned back around and picked up the pace, jerking back and forth as he limped away. "Even these miserable conversations."

"I'm an excellent conversationalist!" I called after him. The Viking answered with a rude gesture, then disappeared behind a tree. I hurried to catch up with him. In the distance, the sirens from the MA tactical vans grew silent, to be replaced by the ratchet of crickets and the hooting of owls.

I was starting to regret my earlier statements about hero business. This was quickly turning into too much running, and not enough heroing. At least I was running toward danger, rather than away from it, as had been my wont for so much of my life. I considered that an improvement. Perhaps not the kind of improvement you put on a plaque and hung on your wall, but still. A step in the right direction. Well. A limp in the right direction.

Just as I came around the tree, I heard a twig snap to my right. I barely turned in that direction before Aelwulf erupted from a stand of bushes and rammed into me with his shoulder. I flinched back just enough to make it a glancing blow, but as he barreled past me, the big Viking took a swing at my jaw with his elbow. My mouth clapped shut, sending stars spinning through my vision and filling my mouth with blood.

Aelwulf screamed in fury as he stomped to a halt, then spun and slammed his sword straight at my skull. I barely got my shield up in time, but he followed that up with another swing at my leg, then a third at my suddenly exposed midsection. This assault forced me back, wincing in pain each time my weight came down on my left ankle. My head was swimming in shock. Tingling numbness stretched down my arm, and my vision narrowed into a roaring black tunnel, with Aelwulf at the bright spot in the middle, trying to kill me. Fatigue sapped my every movement, while the Viking seemed tireless, furious, and unstoppable.

I went on the defensive. If I held sword and shield close together, supporting one with the other, I could just hold off Aelwulf's assault. Each blow he landed rattled my bones. I spat blood and bore down. There was no way he was going to beat me. I wasn't going to let him. But my mind was reeling and my body failing. I had to figure a way around this, no matter the cost.

There was a moment's reprieve. Aelwulf retreated, his chest heaving. Blood dripped like a leaky faucet from his wounded arm. If I was tired, he must be completely drained. But thousands of years of practice fighting and dying gave him a clear edge in our little competition. How could I get around that? What was he doing wrong that I could exploit? Listening? Was that it?

"How'd a hack like you get into Valhalla in the first place?" I asked through gritted teeth. "I mean, I get Mr. Valhalla and Solveig. They're tough bastards. But you're just a loser with a magic sword."

"Ah, very clever, Sir Rast. I know how your type works. Anger the opponent, in the hope that they'll make a mistake." He shook his head in amusement. "But that is not how Vikings work. Anger makes us stronger."

"So you're not going to fall for that?"

"Not unless you want me to hit you harder?"

"I think I'll pass," I said. "But I meant what I said about your stupid magic sword. Only reason you beat Gregory and Bee was because you cheated. You were fighting for the touch. I used to do that, before Knight Watch. Before I learned how to fight for real."

"Vikings never fight for the touch," he said.

"Yeah, well, just calling it like I see it."

"I'll show you fighting for the touch, you bastard." He tightened his grip on Totenschreck's complicated hilt, then came at me hard. "I'll touch your damned heart!"

He approached sword first, slicing a long gutter down the face of my shield before reversing and cutting upward. Each of his blows was with the edge of the blade, and suddenly I saw his mistake, and my chance. It's a little difficult to analyze in the middle of a sword fight, but the simplest explanation is that he was fighting with the longsword the same way he fought with a Viking blade, which were shorter and lighter and designed for chopping. Ironically, the typical Viking sword was designed to be used with a round shield, and was optimized for chopping through ring mail or leather, and thought nothing of cutting clean through a leg bone. But steel plate was another matter.

The longsword, on the other hand, was a thrusting weapon. Its narrow point and wide ricosso were ideal for finding the chinks in heavy plate armor. It could slice, as Aelwulf was handily demonstrating, but it usually wasn't suited to the task. Meant to be held two-handed, while Aelwulf was forced to swing with one hand due to his injury. And the manner of his attack, focused on slicing limbs and crushing skulls, instead of poking its way into the joints of my armor or seeking out the seams between plates. Everything about his attack was wrong. Still deadly, but wrong.

"What's the matter, Rast? Forgotten how to swing a sword?" he asked, taunting. "I'm perfectly happy breaking this shield if you'd like. What will you do then?"

"I don't know. Die, I guess?"

"As you wish." He made a quick pass, two feinting strikes on my shield and then a blow meant to cut off my injured foot. Fortunately, I didn't have any weight on it, so could move it quickly out of the way. The Totenschreck's green blade sliced through the gnarled roots of the earth, sending a clod of dirt flying.

The strength of his blow overextended him, though. The weight of the sword carried his arm clear across his body, only stopping when it reached his opposite shoulder. I slid forward and poked at his bicep, drawing a pinprick of blood before he dragged the sword back. I caught the blow with my shield, but the force of that swing nearly tore my arm from my socket. He laughed.

"Not much longer, Rast. I have the reach, and the experience, and the strength." He shuffled back, leering at me.

"Then why are you screwing around? Come, kill me, if you have it in you. Kill me, old man. Before the valkyries show up and drag you back to hell where you belong!"

He answered with an overhand chop that shattered my shield down the middle. The two halves hung on my arm like missized bracelets. I clenched my fist and secured the half closest to my hand, letting the rest fall to the ground, holding it like a long, thin buckler. Aelwulf tried to cut me in half, but I clipped the edge of his sword with the lower half of my poor shield. The blade stuck in the wood, twisting my wrist until I could hear the joint pop. Sharp pain blossomed down my arm as Aelwulf tried to jerk the weapon free. I took the chance to punch him once with the hilt of my sword, catching him in the shoulder and leaving a long, fresh cut from collarbone to ear.

Finally, he worked the sword free and kicked me back. I fell onto my butt and tried to scramble away, but he was on me, fast and angry.

"You are a sorry excuse for a hero, Rast!" he shouted, chopping down at my head. "And I'm going to make sure your name is forgotten, and that no one remembers your deeds! You will die alone, and frightened!"

I deflected the first blow with what remained of my shield, but the second turned the buckler into splinters in my hand. I got to one knee and leaned toward him, throwing my sword overhead, tip near my shoulder, flat of the blade resting against the crown of my head. He struck with fury, and it was all I could do to fend him off. Still, my blade reverberated against my scalp, dragging the edge across my face. Hot blood spilled down my forehead from fresh cuts at brow, nose, and chin. Aelwulf reared back to strike again. I stared up at him, helpless.

When the blow came, it was straight at my eyes. I wasn't going to be able to stop it, not with my sword, not even with my shield, if it hadn't already been destroyed. I didn't need to.

Sometimes part of being a hero is sacrifice. Sometimes it's the only part that matters.

Sliding forward, I let my sword drop, rotating it so the point was up. Aelwulf's blow skidded off my skull, took my ear, then buried itself in my left shoulder. Bones cracked. Steel bent. Flesh tore, and blood flowed. But none of those things were fatal. My counterstrike, however, was as deadly as old age, and as fast as lightning.

The dull gray steel of my sword entered just beneath his rib cage and traveled up, through lungs, through heart, into his throat and skull. His eyes went wide and he opened his mouth to scream, but nothing came out but blood and a dying whimper. Letting go of the sword, I collapsed backward. Totenschreck wrenched free of my shoulder.

Aelwulf took a step back before collapsing. With my one good arm, I dragged myself to his side. He stared at me with wide eyes, gurgling quietly in his heart blood.

"I am not alone," I whispered. "I fight, and die, and overcome bastards like you, with my friends."

"John!" Chesa's furious voice reached me. I closed my eyes and slumped against the dying Viking. "Matt, over here! John, are you alright?"

I was. For once. I passed out just as soft hands turned me over.

Valhalla was waiting.

CHAPTER FORTY

The next day, a newspaper headline declared FREAK LUNAR ECLIPSE COMPLETELY EXPLAINED BY SCIENTISTS and, on the next page, MASS DRUG EVENT RUINS SOCCER GAME. The reporters made reference to hooligans fighting on the pitch, and a brief description of Aelwulf's sugar-induced rampage, but chalked it up to tampered hot dogs from a childish prank. I folded the paper and set it on the bed.

"So that's it?" I asked. "The end of the world averted, and they blame it on hot dogs."

"Hot dogs are a good excuse," Esther said. "No one really understands what's in them. So how are you feeling?"

"Like someone buried a sword in my shoulder." I eased my way back onto the bed, closing my eyes as pain racked my body. I was in the medical wing of Mundane Actual, between the real world and the magical. This area was kind of a containment area, to ensure no trace of the mundane got into our domains. The team's doctors had done what they could with my shoulder and the bite on my ankle, along with the dozen other small cuts and bruises I had picked up over the last week, but there was only so much they could do. I had to wait until the mundane had dissipated before I could get back to the magical world, and get some real healing.

At least the real world had good drugs.

"How long until I can get back to my domain?" I asked.

"Not yet. Soon," Esther said. "That was a significant incursion, and you spent a lot of it in the mundane. We have to ease you back into the Unreal, or that dog of yours is going to get loose. And no one wants to clean up after that."

"Yeah, I guess." I pushed the newspaper away. "Doesn't a newspaper count as a modern convenience? Isn't it corrupting me further just sitting there?"

"Not really," she said. "No more newspapers in the real world. I could have brought you a scroll, or had a bard sing you the news, but the printed word is mostly harmless."

"Well, the sooner I'm back in the cabin, the better. How's everyone else?"

"Chesa and Matthew are fine. She was scared to death when she found you. Nearly tore Rodriguez's arm off dragging her to your body." Esther chuckled. "Tembo healed up just in time to help round up the last of those zombies. I couldn't bring myself to killing all those zombies. I know a lot of those folks." She sighed and sat back, hands folded on her knee. "I think we're just going to leave them where they are. Keep them supplied with soccer balls and books and whatever else they need."

"They seemed harmless enough, once Aelwulf lost control of the Totenschreck."

"They're just people, after all. And Bethany and Greg aren't really talking about what happened. We figure the less said, the better, though Chesa keeps leaving pink bows in places they'll find. Gonna have to step on that, eventually."

"I'd rather not get involved. But I'm glad everyone else is doing alright." I closed my eyes and stretched. "Too bad Solveig got away."

"Yeah. She and that wolf took off like heat lightning. Chesa had to choose between following her and saving your life."

"Well, I guess I'm glad she made the right choice. Just wish we'd gotten our hands on Bashful." I put my arm over my eyes. The lights in here were relentless. "Can I get a little rest?"

"Actually, no. I woke you up because we need you for something."

"For what?"

"A closing ceremony of sorts. The valkyries want words with you," she said, standing up. "So get some pants on. We've got enough drugs in you."

"I don't like the sound of that," I said.

"It'll be fine. They don't have a lot of bite left. Not after what happened." She started to leave, but paused in the doorway. "They owe you one."

I waited until she was gone before I tried to get up. My gambeson and leggings were waiting, along with my sword. The shield, magic or not, was still lying in splinters on a soccer field somewhere in the real world.

"They owe me a lot more than that," I said as I started to get dressed.

The trip on the Naglfr was less terrible than usual. I don't know if my travels in the whale or down the rainbow bridge had softened my attitude, but the HMS *Hangnail* seemed positively luxurious. I almost couldn't smell the foot odor of thousands of dead Vikings. Almost.

The whole team was there. Bee and Greg sat on opposite sides of the boat, never making eye contact. Tembo was on one side of me, and Matthew the other, while Chesa sat beside me, fussing with my cloak or asking if I was comfortable every time I shifted. Esther watched us with barely disguised amusement.

Valhalla was much changed. The pennants and music declaring MR. VALHALLA were gone, along with all the sounds of merrymaking and war. We settled down right in front of the main door. A figure leaned beside the door, arms crossed. It was Lillie, still in her overalls with a meshback trucker hat pulled close to her eyes. Her ever-present shotgun leaned next to her. As we disembarked, she turned and shouted inside. A short time later, Revna and Inge came out. I barely recognized them. Their wings were gone, and instead of leather armor and steel, they wore mundane clothes.

Wincing, I limped across the field alongside Esther, to stand in front of them. The rest of the team hung back.

"What the hell happened to you guys?" I asked.

"Ragnarok," Revna said. "For us, at least, it was the end of the world." She motioned to the beer hall behind her. "Our loyal dead are gone, and the ranks of the valkyries have thinned to nothing. We are all that remains."

"Wow. That sucks. So you're just . . . shutting down?"

"Not exactly. There will still be worthy dead, and some portion of them must come here. But not until we have valkyries to ferry them across the veil." She motioned to Lillie, then Inge. "The three of us can't do that on our own. So we are going to be recruiting, searching the world for women worthy of bearing the shield and standing guard against the end of the world."

The *real* end of the world, I took that to mean.

"You looking for suggestions? My mom can pack a hell of a wallop, but I'm not sure she would put up with the kind of shenanigans you guys get up to." I jerked my thumb over my shoulder. "Chesa, maybe? She seemed to enjoy herself here."

"Knight Watch is off-limits," Esther said.

"Of course. You have your duty, and we have ours," Revna said. "Like it or not, we must close Valhalla for a time. But before we go, I think we owe you something."

"Is it a hug?"

"It is not," Revna said firmly. "Inge?"

The other valkyrie sighed. "You're sure about this?"

"He sacrificed much protecting us," Revna said. "Do it."

Inge pulled her mirror shades off, then lowered the visor on her helm. Wings sprouted from her back, and she launched into the air, flying straight at the sun. I followed her path until I couldn't bear staring at the light any longer. Suddenly, there was a dimming of the sun's brilliance. A shadow moved across the sun's surface, and it got unnaturally cold.

"This feels ominous," Chesa said.

"Quiet," Esther whispered.

A moment later, Inge returned, carrying a round shield. Its face was glossy and black, with clasps of dark iron, and a leather strap for a handle. She held it gingerly, as though it might bite her.

"This is Svalinn, the shield that hides the sun, and protects the earth from its flames," Revna said, taking the shield from Inge. She pressed it against her forehead, then lifted it up and presented it to me. "It is yours, if you wish to bear it."

"I . . . I don't . . ." Esther kicked me in the shin, and I stumbled forward. "I would be honored."

The three valkyries nodded as I accepted the shield from Revna. Its surface was cold to the touch. It was as light as a breath, but felt harder than steel.

"Thanks," I said. "I'll wield it with pride."

"I trust you will," Revna said. "Now, if you'll pardon us, we have valkyries to find."

There was a rumble of diesel and the screeching of gears. Lillie's old pickup rolled around the corner, no driver, but a curious look on its headlights. It lumbered to a stop in front of Lillie and Inge. With a final look back at Valhalla, they got in the cab. Revna closed the beer hall's massive doors, then hung a sign across it and hopped into the bed of the pickup. The throne was back there, and she lounged on it like a queen.

"Good luck," Esther called.

"We don't need luck, Captain," Revna said. "Keep the world safe while we're gone."

"We'll do our best."

"Well. That will have to do."

The pickup roared to life and pulled away. We watched as it rumbled down the hill, until it disappeared into the clouds. The sound of its engine lasted for a long time after that, until finally that, too, faded. I looked toward the sign on the door.

CLOSED FOR RENOVATIONS.
PLEASE TRY AGAIN LATER.
OR GO TO HELL.
WE DON'T CARE.

"Such friendly people," I said.

"They'll be back," Esther answered. "Come on. We need to get you home. That shield will meld into your old one, eventually, but you'll need practice. And I need a drink."

"Not mead," Chesa said.

"Not mead," I confirmed. "Maybe orange soda."

"No sugar for you. Not if you want to get back to your domain anytime soon."

We loaded back into the HMS *Hangnail*. I looked back to Valhalla. The silent hall was creepy, especially knowing that it was full of dead Vikings. I wondered where Solveig had gotten to, and whether I would see her again. I was still thinking about this when the clouds closed around us, and we fell back down into the real world.